Jilly Cooper comes from Yorkshire but now lives in Gloucestershire with her family and an assortment of dogs and cats. Her journalism was a feature for many years of the *Sunday Times* and she has made many television appearances. She has written six romances: *Emily*, *Bella*, *Harriet*, *Octavia*, *Prudence* and *Imogen*. Her novels, *Riders*, *Rivals*, *Polo*, *The Man Who Made Husbands Jealous* and *Appassionata* and *Score!* are also published by Corgi and were all Number One bestsellers.

D1280839

www.**booksattransworld**.co.uk

EMILY
&
BELLA

Jilly Cooper

CORGI BOOKS

EMILY & BELLA
A CORGI BOOK : 0 552 14695 1

PRINTING HISTORY
This Corgi collection first published 1999
Copyright © Jilly Cooper 1999

including

EMILY
Originally published in Great Britain by Arlington Books Ltd
Copyright © Jilly Cooper 1975

BELLA
Originally published in Great Britain by Arlington Books Ltd
Copyright © Jilly Cooper 1976

3 5 7 9 10 8 6 4

Set in 11/12pt Sabon by
Kestrel Data, Exeter, Devon.

Corgi Books are published by Transworld Publishers,
61–63 Uxbridge Road, London W5 5SA,
a division of The Random House Group Ltd,
in Australia by Random House Australia (Pty) Ltd,
20 Alfred Street, Milsons Point, Sydney, NSW 2061, Australia,
in New Zealand by Random House New Zealand Ltd,
18 Poland Road, Glenfield, Auckland 10, New Zealand
and in South Africa by Random House (Pty) Ltd,
Endulini, 5a Jubilee Road, Parktown 2193, South Africa.

Printed and bound in Great Britain by
Cox & Wyman Ltd, Reading, Berkshire.

EMILY

Jilly Cooper

CORGI BOOKS

To Claire with love

Author's Note

The idea for *Emily* first came to me in 1969. I wrote it as a long short story called *Circles*, and it appeared in serial form in *19*. I took the story and completely re-wrote it, and the result is *Emily*.

EMILY

1

If Nina hadn't bugged me, I'd never have gone to Annie Richmond's party.

'Cedric is beginning to take you for granted,' she said, hurling clothes into a weekend case.

'Cedric,' I said crossly, 'is getting his career together. As soon as he's adopted as a candidate, we'll get married.'

'Because it's better for candidates to have wives,' said Nina. 'He shouldn't leave you alone so much. Your first weekend back from holiday, looking a million and a half dollars – anyone else wouldn't be able to keep his hands off you – but old Seedcake just swans off to another political rally.'

'I'm very happy about my relationship with Cedric. And that's mine,' I snapped, removing a yellow shirt she was surreptitiously packing in one corner of her case. 'Cedric keeps me on the straight and narrow,' I went on.

'He's turned you into a bore,' said Nina. 'You used to be lovely company when you were playing fast and loose with half of London.'

'I want a sense of purpose in my life,' I protested. 'I don't want to die in Chelsea with my knickers down.'

Nina went to the mirror and started slapping Man-tan all over her face.

'Where are you off to?' I said.

'Home. I don't want my mother fussing about me looking washed out – and tomorrow I'm going out with an amazingly dishy new man. Now aren't you jealous?'

'No,' I lied. 'You just give up certain things when you're engaged.'

'Like fun. Just because Seedcake's put a ring on your finger, he thinks he's entitled to neglect you all the time. I think you ought to go to Annie Richmond's orgy; she's got this fantastically good-looking cousin coming. If he gave you a whirl, you'd soon forget about Seedcake.'

'Don't call him that,' I stormed. 'Anyway, I've nothing in common with Annie Richmond's friends any more.'

Nina laughed meaningfully. 'You mean Cedric hasn't. She reminds him of your past and that come-hither look your eyes had once. You're scared of going because you think you might fancy someone. If you were really hooked on Seedcake, you wouldn't be frightened to go.'

I felt depressed after she'd gone. I'd done all the boring things like washing my hair, shaving my legs and doing my nails yesterday, in the hope that I might see Cedric tonight. After a few minutes moping I settled down to half-heartedly cleaning the flat, then washing the suntan-oil out of a few shirts.

I looked at Cedric's photograph beside my bed, thought how good-looking he was, then I read a book on Conservative policy. It was incredibly boring and nearly sent me to sleep. Cedric telephoned – as he said he would – on the dot of ten o'clock.

'How heavenly to hear you, darling,' I said, overwhelmed with love. 'How are you?'

'Oh, full of beans,' he said in his hooray, political voice, which meant there were people in the room. As he told me what a success the meeting had been and how well his speech had gone, I examined the diamond and sapphire ring he'd given me.

Finally he said, 'What are you going to do with yourself all weekend?'

'Annie Richmond's throwing an orgy,' I said lightly. 'As you're not here, I was thinking of going.'

Cedric laughed heartily and disbelievingly. 'I thought you'd grown out of that sort of party,' he said. 'I must go darling. I'll ring you on Monday and we'll have dinner. Take care of yourself; and remember, no orgies. They're bad for my reputation.'

I put the telephone down feeling extremely irritated. What was the point of spending ten days alone in the South of France – Cedric naturally couldn't get away – boring myself silly getting a suntan for his sake, when he wasn't around to appreciate it?

I looked out at the September evening – the dusk with its suggestion of autumn and nights drawing in and another year passing, shot waves of repressed lust through me. I thought of sex and sin and all the men in the world I'd never have the chance to get my hands on now.

It was such a long, long time since I'd been to a good party. Cedric thought all my friends so

13

frivolous and idiotic, he'd scared them away.

I looked at his photograph again – short, fair hair, clear, blue eyes, a determined chin.

'Life is earnest, life is real,' I said to myself firmly. 'Cedric would hate me to go to Annie Richmond's orgy, so I won't go.'

An hour later, feeling horribly guilty, I crept up the stairs to Annie Richmond's flat, having heard the roar of the party all the way down the street. Annie opened the door.

'Emily,' she cried joyfully, giving me a huge hug. 'I never dreamed you'd come.'

She was wearing a dress so cut out there was hardly any of it left. I was wearing a backless black dress, pretty low at the front and welded together with safety pins, as usual, which I'd never dared show Cedric. I'd put on weight since I last wore it and was falling out all over the place. I just hoped I looked a bit like Sophia Loren.

Annie looked at me with approval. 'Stripped for action, that's more like the old Emily,' she said, handing me a glass.

'I've only just popped in for a quick drink,' I said. 'Cedric's away.'

'I know,' she smiled knowingly. 'There's lots of talent in there, so go in and forage for yourself.'

The next room was impossibly, clamorously full of good-looking people trying to shout each other down. I felt very nervous, so I drank my disgusting drink straight down, and quickly had another. I didn't know a soul, but then Annie turned over her friends so fast.

A handsome Australian in a red shirt came over and started to chat me up. His eyes smouldered under bushy black eyebrows.

I knew that look of old: I feel I know every inch of you already, so let's get on with it – it stated unequivocally.

'Bloody awful row,' he said. 'Pity I can't lip-read.' He gazed at my mouth and then at my black dress, which was descending fast. Any minute I'd be topless. I heaved it up. 'Leave it,' he said. 'I'm enjoying the view.'

He was clearly a superstud, and would have whipped me down the passage and under Annie's duvet in two seconds flat. But I wanted to stay upright, not flat. Suppressing the waves of lust that were sweeping over me, I started to shout at him about Cedric and his political career. He can't have heard much of what I was saying, but seemed to get the message and drifted off.

I was then collared by an ancient or more an elderly Wren, a model with long red hair and skinny white hands, who went on and on about her split ends.

Suddenly there was a commotion by the door.

'But Annie,' said a man's voice, 'I thought I was coming to an orgy. Where are the wall-to-wall couples? The lovely girls in tiger skins?'

Split Ends caught her breath. I, like everyone else, turned around. My jaw clanged – for standing in the doorway was one of the most sensationally attractive men I had ever seen. He was tall, with broadish shoulders, long black hair, restless dark eyes with a wicked gleam in them, and an arrogant sulky mouth. He oozed sexuality. He looked round the room, as cool and haughty as a prince, yet he had an explosive quality – I've come out of the jungle and no-one's going to tame me, he seemed to say. Every woman in the room was going mad with

15

desire; me included. The only problem was a very beautiful dark girl dressed in what looked like a bikini entirely made of flowers, who was hanging possessively on his arm.

'You promised me an orgy, Annie,' he said, coldly. 'All I can see here is a deb's tea-party.'

Annie Richmond took him and the dark girl by the arm and hustled them towards the bar.

'It'll start warming up soon,' I could hear her saying. 'There's a lot of fun people coming later.'

I noticed she gave him a whole bottle of whisky to himself, while the rest of us had to make do with the revolting cough mixture.

Gradually the conversation started to soar and dip again. 'Who's that?' everyone was asking.

I turned to Split Ends. 'Who's that?' I said.

She looked at me incredulously. 'You mean to say you don't know?'

A stockbroker with a pink face whose eyes were about level with my cleavage, came past and filled up our glasses.

'That's Rory Balniel,' he said. 'He's a bit of a menace.'

'He's Annie's cousin,' said Split Ends, watering at the mouth, 'and quite the most evil man in London.'

'In what way?' I asked.

'Oh, getting drunk and breaking people's hearts deliberately. Everything you can think of, and a lot more besides.'

'He looks like the leader of a Cossack horde,' I said. 'What nationality is he?'

'Scottish, with foreign, I think French, on one side. His family own masses of land in the Highlands, but all the money's tied up in trusts, and he

16

can't get his hands on it. He's been sent down from everywhere imaginable. He hit London about a month ago. I don't think he's been sober since.'

'He's a bit of a menace,' repeated the stockbroker, looking longingly at my cleavage.

'He's supposed to be a very good painter,' said Split Ends.

'The only thing he's been painting recently is the town red,' said the stockbroker.

'He treats women appallingly,' said Split Ends.

'Has he treated you appallingly?' I asked.

'Not yet,' she said with a sigh, 'but I'm working on it.'

I looked around again. Rory Balniel was leaning against the mantelpiece. Two girls who looked as though the head groom had been polishing and curry-combing them for weeks, so sleek and patently glossy were they, were vying for his attention.

He filled up their glasses from the whisky bottle, then suddenly, he lifted his head, yawned slightly and looked in my direction. I shot him a glance I hadn't used in months. One of pure naked come-hithering sex. It didn't work. He looked away without interest.

'Hard luck,' said Split Ends, avidly drinking in this classic case of indifference at first sight. 'You're obviously not his type.'

'He's probably queer,' I said crossly. 'Most Don Juans are latent homosexuals anyway.'

Split Ends looked at me pityingly, then grabbed a plate of food from a nearby table.

'I'm going to offer him a stuffed date,' she said with a giggle, and wheeled across the room towards him.

17

I turned my back and talked to the stockbroker. It was a calculated gesture. If anything was likely to turn Rory Balniel on, it was my back – brown, smooth and bare from the nape of my neck almost to the base of my spinal column, unmarred by any bikini marks.

I imagined his dark, restless eyes ranging over me and thinking, 'That's the sort of girl who sunbathes without a bikini top. Mettlesome, ready for anything, even being treated appallingly by Rory Balniel.'

But when I looked around, he was talking to Split Ends, and was still hemmed in by the masses.

Sexless beast, I decided; or perhaps it's my sex appeal that's slipping.

Cedric was right. These people were frivolous and uninteresting. The evening wore on. People were dancing in the next room, drinking a lot and necking a little. No-one was actually orgying. I kept making up my mind to go home, but some instinctive lack of self-preservation made me stay. I felt jolted, uneasy and horribly aware of Rory Balniel. There was an unconscious glitter about him, a sinister stillness that set him apart from everyone else. One had to admit his force.

Split Ends and the girl he'd arrived with, who I discovered was called Tiffany (I bet she made it up), were still trying to engage his attention. He was laughing a lot at their jokes, but a little late on cue. As he filled his glass, his hand was quite steady. Only the glint in his eyes betrayed how much he'd drunk.

Annie Richmond went up to him and removed the bottle of whisky, 'Rory, love, I don't mean to nag.'

'Women always say that when they're about to nag,' he said, taking the whisky back from her.

People were really getting uncorked now. Couples had disappeared into other rooms, a beautiful African girl was dancing by herself. A fat man was telling filthy stories to an ugly American girl who had passed out on the floor. The Australian in the red shirt, who had chatted me up earlier, turned out to be Split Ends' boyfriend. He was not pleased at her paying so much attention to Rory Balniel and came strutting into the room wearing a Mickey Mouse mask, expecting everyone to laugh.

'Where did you get that mask?' said Rory Balniel.

'Annie gave it to me.'

'You should wear it all the time. Every day. Always. To the office. It suits you. Gives your face a distinction it didn't have before.'

'Don't be stupid,' said the Australian furiously, wrenching off the mask. He nearly tripped over the ugly American girl who was now snoring on the floor.

'Jesus Christ, why doesn't somebody move her?'

'She's quite happy,' said Rory Balniel. 'I expect she needs sleep. Anyway, she gives the room a lived-in feeling.'

'Someone might tread on her face,' said the Australian, lugging her out of the way.

'Good thing, too. It could only improve things,' said Rory Balniel. He was trying to balance a glass on one of his fingers, managing to look like a Siamese cat. Inevitably, the glass crashed to the floor.

Split Ends and Tiffany howled with laughter. A blonde, attracted by the tinkle of broken glass, came over and joined the group.

'I hear you paint,' she said, 'I'd love to sit for you some time.'

Rory Balniel looked her over. 'But would you lie for me later, darling? That's the point.'

He started to undo the buttons of Split Ends' dress.

'I say,' said the pink-faced stockbroker. 'You can't do that here. Unfair to Annie. Know what I mean?'

'No,' said Rory Balniel unpleasantly.

He had now undone all Split Ends' buttons to reveal a very dirty bra.

'Don't,' she said crossly, trying to do them up again.

His dark face set into a mask of malice. 'If you throw yourself open to the public, sweetheart, you must expect people to want to see over you.'

Split Ends flounced off.

'Good riddance,' said the blonde, snuggling up to him.

'She's a silly cow,' he said unemotionally, draining his drink.

'What did you say?' said the Australian, who was still smarting under the crack about the Mickey Mouse mask. 'Are you referring to my girlfriend?'

'I was referring to the silly cow,' said Rory. 'And if she's your girlfriend, she's even stupider than she looks. And don't come on all macho with me, you bloody colonial, or I'll kick you back down under, where you belong.' Picking up a wine bottle, he deliberately cracked it on the edge of the mantelpiece and brandished the jagged end in the Australian's face.

The Australian clenched his fists. 'I'll call the police,' he said, half-heartedly.

'*What* are you going to call the police?' said Rory Balniel.

He picked up another glass from the mantelpiece, and smashed it on the floor.

The Australian puffed out his cheeks, and then beat a hasty retreat.

The two girls roared with laughter again, enjoying themselves hugely. Then they looked around for the next distraction.

He's absolutely poisonous, I decided. How does anyone put up with him?

Picking his way disapprovingly over the broken pieces of glass, the little stockbroker came over and asked me to dance.

'I told you he was a menace, did I not?' he asked in an undertone.

He then proceeded to make the most ferocious passes at me on the dance floor. I can never understand why little men are so lecherous. I suppose it's more concentrated. Fortunately, one of my safety pins gave way and plunged into him, which cooled his ardour a bit. But two seconds later he was back on the attack.

A quarter of an hour later, black and blue and as mad as a wet cat, I returned to collect my bag. I was really leaving this time. I found Rory Balniel was sitting on the sofa – Tiffany and the blonde on either side of him. Both girls were holding hands with each other across him, but were so tight, neither of them realized it.

'Rory, darling,' whispered the blonde.

'Rory, angel,' murmured Tiffany.

It looked so ridiculous I burst out laughing. He looked up and started to laugh too.

'I think they're made for each other,' he said. And extracting himself, got up and came over.

I leaned against the wall, partly because I was slewed, partly because my legs wouldn't hold me up. The impact of this man, close up, was absolutely faint-making.

'Hullo,' he said.

'Hullo,' I said. I've always been a wizard at repartee.

He looked me over consideringly as if I was a colour chart and he was selecting a shade.

'The drink has run out,' he said, taking a final slug of whisky from the bottle.

He had very white, even teeth, but his fingers were quite heavily stained with nicotine.

'What did you say your name was?' he said. His voice had lost its earlier bitchy ring – it was soft and husky now.

'I didn't,' I said, 'but since you ask, it's Emily.'

'Emily – pretty name, old-fashioned name. Are you an old-fashioned girl?'

'Depends what you mean by old-fashioned – prunes and prisms Victorian or Nell Gwyn?'

He took my hand.

He's drunk, I said to myself firmly, trying not to faint with excitement.

'You're like a little Renoir,' he said.

'Are those the outsize ones, all grapes and rippling with flesh?' I said.

'No, that's Rubens. Renoirs are soft and blonde and blue-eyed, with pink flesh tones. It's funny,' he added, shooting me an Exocet look, 'you're not my

22

type at all, but you excite the hell out of me.'

I looked down, and to my horror, saw that my fingers were coiling around his, and watched my only unbitten nail gouging into the centre of his palm.

Then suddenly I felt his fingers on my engagement ring.

I tried to jerk my hand away, but he held on to it, and examined the ring carefully.

'Who gave that to you?' he said.

'Cedric,' I said. 'My – er – fiancé. It's a terrible word, isn't it?' I gave a miserable, insincere little giggle.

'It's a terrible ring, too,' he said.

'It cost a lot of money,' I said defensively.

'Why isn't he here?'

I explained about Cedric being in Norfolk and furthering his political career.

'How long have you been engaged?'

'Nearly eighteen months.'

The smile Rory Balniel gave me wasn't at all pleasant. 'Does he make love on all four channels?' he said.

I tried, but failed, to look affronted. 'He doesn't make love to me much at all,' I muttered.

Rory Balniel was swinging the empty whisky bottle between finger and thumb.

'He doesn't care about you at all, does he?'

'Cedric and I have a good thing going.'

'If you're mad about a girl, you don't let her out of your sight.'

Instinctively my eyes slid to Tiffany, who was now sleeping peacefully, her head on the blonde girl's shoulder.

'I'm not exactly mad about her,' he said.

'She's stunning looking,' I said, wistfully.

He shrugged his shoulders.

'Rolls-Royce body maybe, but a Purley mind.'

I giggled again. Suddenly he bent his head and kissed my bare shoulder. I could feel the ripples of excitement all the way down to my toes. Any moment my dress, safety pins and all, was going to burst into flames. I could have died with excitement.

I took a deep breath. 'I've got a bottle of whisky at home,' I said.

'Well, let's go then,' he said.

2

I wasn't proud of my behaviour. I knew I was treating Cedric abominably, but then I'd never before in my life encountered such a personification of temptation as Rory Balniel. And, like Oscar Wilde, I've always been able to resist anything except temptation.

We wandered along the King's Road, trying to find a taxi, and giggling a great deal as we tried out all the baths sitting outside the bath shop. Then we passed an art gallery. Rory peered moodily through the window at the paintings.

'Look at that crap,' he said. 'There but for the gracelessness of God go I, the greatest genius of the twentieth century – which reminds me, I've got to see a man about my painting at eleven tomorrow. You'd better set your alarm clock when we get home.'

Presumptuous, I thought. Does he think I'll succumb so easily?

Rory suddenly saw a taxi and flagged it down. We kissed all the way home.

God – I was enjoying myself. I'd never felt a millionth of that raging, abandoned glory, the whole time I'd known Cedric. As the taxi chugged

along, and the orange numbers on the meter
rocketed relentlessly upwards, so did my temperature. Rory had such a marvellously lean, broad-
shouldered body. It must have been something to
do with both being an artist and having Gallic
blood, but he was certainly an artist at French
kissing.

All the same, somewhere inside me, an insistent
voice was warning me to call a halt. I was back-
sliding at the speed of light, doing all the things I'd
done before I'd met Cedric, giving in too quickly,
losing too quickly and feeling just as insecure and
unhappy as I'd been in the past. I'll say goodbye to
him firmly at the door, I told myself. Then when
we got to the door I thought: I'll just give him a
very quick drink to be sociable and then out he
goes.

No sooner had we entered the flat and I'd given
him some whisky, than I rushed off to the bathroom, cleaned my teeth and emptied half a bottle
of Nina's scent over myself. I then went and removed the Georgette Heyer novel from my bedside
table and replaced it with a couple of intellectual
French novels.

I went into the drawing room.

'Where did you learn to pour drinks like this
one?' he asked.

'I once worked in a bar,' I replied.

'This is a septuple,' said Rory, draining the glass.

'I'm seeing septuple,' I said. 'After all the booze
I've shipped, I can see at least seven of you at the
moment. A magnificent seven, admittedly.'

'Then we can have a gang-bang,' said Rory with
a whoop. 'Annie's orgy is going to materialize after
all.'

Primly, I sat down on the sofa. He sat beside me.

'Well? Orgy on?' he asked, staring at me, but making no move.

I hunted around nervously for something to say.

'Keep still,' he said. 'You've got something in your hair.'

I never knew if I had or I hadn't. But he removed whatever it was and then, unsmilingly, he came closer and kissed me.

After a while, I had a pang of conscience and tried to push him away. 'I'll make some coffee,' I muttered. 'Really, I am engaged to Cedric and he wouldn't approve at all.'

'Shut up,' he said gently. Very slowly, he undid all the safety pins holding my dress together – first the one joining the bodice and shoulder-strap, then the little gold pin just below the zip top, and finally the two securing my strapless bra.

Naked to the waist now, I still couldn't move.

'Little Renoir,' he said softly.

Stop! I said to myself, but I couldn't move.

It was morning when I woke. I hadn't closed the curtains properly, so the sun seared straight into my eyes like a laser beam. Even more searing was Cedric's smile – his photograph stared right at me. Frantic with thirst, I reached for the glass by the bed, gulped at it, and nearly threw up. It was whisky.

Inching my hand to the right, I practically went through the ceiling as I encountered a body. Cedric's. I gave a groan. Cedric was in Norfolk, rallying the faithful. The unfaithful was lying in my bed. I drew back the covers to look at the man beside me. One glance told me I had impeccable taste when I was drunk. And total lack of judgement too, by allowing myself to get laid on the first date.

Slowly piecing the evening together, I looked at the clock. Half past ten. I was supposed to wake him up to see a man about some paintings. I got up and washed. My face looked all blotchy, like garlic sausage, so I slapped on some casual-looking make-up. Then I threw a handful of Alka-Seltzers into a glass of water, waited until the froth subsided, drank it down and went back to bed.

I think Rory was still drunk when I woke him up. He got up, drew the curtains, and then groped for a cigarette.

'What happened last night?'

'Oh, Rory,' I wailed. 'Don't you remember anything?'

'Well, I remember spending a rain-soaked childhood among the sheep in Scotland, and being sacked from Harrow and being sent down from Oxford. I remember coming to London to sell some paintings. After that I think the drink took over. Then there seems to have been a lot of parties.'

'We were at Annie Richmond's party,' I said.

'So we were.'

'And we both had quite a bit to drink and then we came back here.'

'Well, well, well,' he said, getting into the crumpled bed. 'And did we?'

'Oh, God! Can't you remember that?'

'Was I . . . er . . . did I perform adequately?' He didn't seem embarrassed, only curious.

'You were absolutely sensational, that's what makes it so awful,' I said and, rolling over, I buried my face in the pillow and burst into tears.

He stroked my hair, but I went on sobbing. 'I'm

28

not usually like this. I don't just pick up men at parties and leap into bed with them on the first night. At least, not recently,' I wailed. 'And you'd better step on it, you've got to see that man about your paintings at eleven o'clock.'

'So I have.' Slowly he clambered out of bed and started to get dressed. I was shot through with misery, but I tried to make a joke of the situation.

'Don't think I've enjoyed meeting you, because I haven't,' I said with a deliberate sniff.

He laughed, and when he had dressed and cut himself shaving on Nina's pink plastic razor, he came back into the bedroom and said, 'You'll remember exactly what happened last night, won't you? When I write my memoirs, I'll need to pick your brains.'

I pulled a pillow over my head. 'There aren't any to pick,' I groaned.

'See you,' he said. Then he was gone.

I went through every kind of hell wondering if he'd come back. I castigated myself for the insanity of going to Annie Richmond's party, for letting Rory make love to me – which, despite his not remembering anything about it, had been an utterly intoxicating experience which would spoil me for Cedric for evermore.

The telephone rang three times, each time for Nina, and each time the caller got his head bitten off for not being Rory. At four o'clock, realizing he wasn't coming back, I got up, had a bath, cried for an hour and then poured myself a large whisky. Really, I was acquiring a lot of bad habits. I'd be eating between meals soon!

At six o'clock the doorbell rang. Keep calm, I

told myself. Play it cool. It's bound to be the milkman, or some Salvation Army lady after loot.

But it was Rory, swaying in the doorway and looking green. 'I've just been sick in a dustbin,' he said.

I laughed, trying to keep the joy out of my face. 'Come in,' I said.

He headed straight for the whisky. 'May I have a drink?' he said. 'My hang-over ought to go down in medical history. Childbirth has nothing on it.'

He had the most awful shakes.

'There's a reason for all this drinking,' he went on. 'But at the moment, I'm glad to say, I can't remember what it is. I really oughtn't to have come back – I'm afraid I've run out of money.'

'I've always wanted to keep a man,' I said. 'Stick with me, baby, and you'll be up to your ears in race-horses.'

'It's not as bad as that. I got on well at the Art Gallery.'

'Did he like your paintings?' I said.

He nodded. 'He's going to give me an exhibition in the spring.'

'But that's wonderful,' I said. 'You'll be famous.'

'I know.' He peered in the mirror, pushing a lock of black hair out of his eyes. 'I don't think it suits me. I feel terrible.'

'You ought to eat something,' I said.

'You're admirable. I wish I had a mother that fussed over me like that.'

In fact he was very ill all night and most of the next day; delirious and with a raging temperature, pouring with sweat, clinging to me, muttering incoherently and shaking like a puppy. On Sunday night, however, he felt better. Suddenly, picking up Cedric's photograph, he threw it out of the window.

'That wasn't very friendly,' I said, listening to the tinkle of broken glass.

'When's he coming back?'

'Tomorrow. Cedric's very good to me. He keeps me on the rails. Before I met him, it was one layabout after another.'

The restless dark eyes travelled over me. 'That's because you're a giver, Emily, and you hate hurting people. You slept with all those men because you couldn't say no rather than because you wanted to say yes.'

'Oh, not always. Anyway, there weren't that many of them – in single figures, that is.'

'If I rang you up and asked you out,' he went on, undeterred, 'even if you didn't fancy me, you'd say yes because you couldn't bear to upset me. Then you'd send me a cable at the last moment, or get one of your mates to ring up and say you were dying of food poisoning.'

'How do you know?' I said sulkily.

'I know,' he said, and pulled me into his arms. The waves of lust were rippling all over me again.

'You're ill,' I protested.

'Not that ill,' he said.

'I like sleeping with you,' he said, a couple of hours later. 'Let's get married.'

I looked at him incredulously, reeling from the shock.

'You'd better send Cedric a telegram immediately,' he said. 'I don't want him hanging around being a bloody nuisance to us.'

'Did you say you wanted to marry me?' I

whispered. 'You can't want to marry me. I mean, what about all those girls after you? You could marry anyone. Why me?'

'I'm kinky that way,' he said. 'I'll try anything once.'

'But where will we live?' I said, bewildered.

'In Scotland. I've got a place up there. I'm much nicer in Scotland, London does frightful things to me – and I'm due to inherit a bit of money shortly, so we won't starve.'

'But . . . but . . .' I stammered. I really wanted him to take me in his arms and say he loved me to distraction, but then the telephone rang.

Rory picked it up. 'Hullo, who's that? Oh, Cedric.' A slightly malicious gleam came into his eyes. 'We haven't met. My name's Balniel, Rory Balniel. How was the political rally? Oh, well that's splendid. You deserve some compensation because I'm afraid Emily has just agreed to marry me – and she'll be dispensing with your disservices from now on.'

'Oh, no,' I protested. 'Poor Cedric.'

I could hear him spluttering away on the other end of the telephone.

'Well I'm afraid you've lost your deposit on this one,' said Rory, and put down the receiver.

'Cedric will be very, very angry,' I said in awe.

3

Cedric wasn't the only one who was angry. Annie Richmond was livid, too.

'You can't marry Rory, he's never been faithful to anyone for more than five minutes. He's immoral and dreadfully spoilt. He even used to cheat at conkers when he was a little boy!'

Nina was even more discouraging. Genuine concern for me combined – when she'd actually met Rory in the flesh – with overwhelming envy.

'I know he's lovely to look at, but he's an absolute devil. You're batting out of your league. Cedric was far more suitable.'

'It was you in the first place,' I said crossly, 'who was so against Cedric, and hustled me off to Annie Richmond's party.'

'I never dreamed you'd go to these extremes. Where are you going to live?'

'In the Highlands, on an island. It sounds too romantic for words.'

Nina sighed. 'It is not romantic living on an island. What will you do, except talk to sheep and go mad while he slaps paint on canvases all day? You won't hold him in a million years. You'll be thoroughly miserable, and then come and snivel all over me. The only thing a whirlwind courtship does is blow dust in everyone's eyes.'

I didn't care. I was hanging from chandeliers, swinging round lamp-posts. I was so deranged with love I didn't know what to do with myself. I felt I was drowning and I didn't want anyone to save me.

Another aspect that delighted me was the being married part of the whole thing. I'd never been cut out for a career and the thought that I could chuck in my nine-to-five job and spend the rest of my life looking after Rory filled me with joy. I had fantasies of greeting him at the door, after a hard day at his studio, a beautiful child hanging on each hand.

Three days later, Rory and I were married at Chelsea Register Office. I had been to see the Reniors at the Tate, and wore a Laura Ashley dress and a black breton on the back of my head. Even Nina admitted I looked good.

Rory was waiting when we arrived, smoking and gazing moodily at the road. It was the first time I'd seen him in a suit – pale grey velvet with a black shirt.

'Isn't he the most beautiful thing you've ever seen!' I said rapturously.

'Yes,' said Nina. 'It isn't too late to change your mind.'

He smiled when he saw us, then his narrowed eyes fixed coldly on my hat. Tearing it from my head, he threw it on the ground and kicked it into the Kings Road, where a milk van ran over it.

'Don't you ever dare wear a hat again,' he said, ruffling my hair.

Then he took my hand and led me into the Register Office.

Afterwards we had a party and drank champagne, and flew to Paris for our honeymoon. When we arrived at our hotel – which was pretty, with shutters, vines and pink geraniums, overlooking the Seine – Rory ordered more champagne.

He was in a strange, wild mood. I wondered how much he'd drunk before he got to the Register Office. I very much wanted him to pounce on me and ravish me at once. I suddenly felt apprehensive, lost and very much alone.

I went off and had a bath. Isn't that what all brides do? All my things were new – sponge bag, flannel, talcum powder, toothbrush. Even my name was new – Emily Balniel.

I said it over and over to myself as I lay in the bath, with the water not too hot so I wouldn't emerge like a lobster.

I rubbed scented bath oil into every inch of my body and put on a new white negligée, fantastically expensive and pretty and virginal. I went into the bedroom, and waited for Rory's gasp of approval. It never came. He was on the telephone, his face ashen.

'Hullo,' he was saying. 'Hullo, yes, it's me all right. I know it's been a long time. Where am I? In Paris, at the Reconnaissance. Do you remember the Reconnaissance, darling? I just wanted to tell you that I got married this afternoon, so that makes us level again, doesn't it?' And, with a ghastly expression of triumph on his face, he dropped the telephone back in its cradle.

'Who were you ringing?' I asked.

He looked at me for a minute as though I were a stranger. There was the same sinister stillness, the lurking danger that I'd been so aware of the first night I met him.

'Who was it?' I asked again.

'Mind your own business,' he snarled. 'Just because I've married you, it doesn't give you the right to question all my movements.'

I felt as though he'd hit me. For a minute we stared at each other, bristling with hostility. Then he pulled himself together, apologized for jumping down my throat – and began to kiss me almost frenziedly.

When I woke up, in the middle of the night, I found him standing by the window, smoking a cigarette. He had his back to me but there was something infinitely despairing about the hunched set of his shoulders.

With a sick feeling of fear, I wondered why he had felt it necessary to ring up a woman on the first night of his honeymoon, and taunt her with the fact that he'd just got married.

Marriage, as I discovered on my honeymoon, may be a bed of roses, but there are plenty of thorns lying around.

Not that I found myself loving Rory any the less; rather the reverse, but he was not easy to live with. To begin with, I never knew what mood he was going to be in. There were the prolonged black glooms, followed by sudden firework bursts of affection, followed by an abstracted fit when he would sit for hours watching the sun on the plane trees outside our window. There were also the sudden, uncontrollable rages – in a smart French restaurant he had picked up a dish of potato purée, and hurled it at a passing fly!

I also had to get used to everyone looking at Rory rather than at me; and that was another thing about marriage. I couldn't spend hours tarting myself up to compete with all those svelte French women. If Rory suddenly decided he wanted to go out, it was straight out of bed, into the shower and 'what the hell do you want to bother with make-up for?'

I found being with him day in, day out, slightly claustrophobic. There wasn't a moment to shave my armpits or touch up the roots of my hair. He did quite a lot of work. I was longing for him to sketch me, and kept sweeping my hair back for him to admire the beauty of my bone structure, but he was far more interested in drawing old men and women with wrinkled faces in cafés. The drawings were amazingly good.

4

We were sitting in bed one afternoon after one of those heavy French lunches, when suddenly there was a pounding on the door.

'Who the hell's that?' I asked.

'A chambermaid gone berserk and unable to contain herself,' said Rory, and shouted something very impolite in French.

The pounding went on.

'Perhaps it's the flics,' said Rory, getting out of bed and putting on his trousers. Through a haze of alcohol, I looked at his tousled black hair and broad brown shoulders.

Swearing, he unlocked the door. A beautiful woman stood there.

'Chéri,' she cried ecstatically. 'Bébé, I knew you were 'ere. The man on the desk was so discreet. He refuse to admit it.' And flinging her arms round Rory's neck, she kissed him on both cheeks.

'I think you are ver' unkind,' she went on reproachfully in a strong French accent, 'sloping off and getting married without a word to anyone. I mean, think of the wedding presents you missed.'

Rory looked half exasperated, half amused.

'I'm afraid this is my mother,' he said.

'Oh gosh,' I squeaked. 'How fright . . . I mean, how lovely. How do you do?'

It was a fine way to meet one's mother-in-law for the first time; sitting up in bed, wearing nothing but a crumpled sheet and a bright smile.

'This is Emily,' said Rory.

Rory's mother rushed across the room and hugged me.

'But you are so pretty,' she said. 'This pleases me very much. I keep telling Rory to find a nice wife and settle down. I know you will make 'im 'appy, and he will start behaving beautifully.'

'I'll try,' I faltered.

She was stunning looking – lush, opulent, exotic, with huge dark blue eyes, hair dyed the most terrific shade of strawberry blonde, the most marvellous legs and lots of jewellery. It was easy to see from where Rory got his traffic-stopping looks.

One of her eyelids was made up with brilliant violet eyeshadow, the other smeared with emerald green.

'I have just been to Dior for a fitting. I tried out their new make-up, it's a very pretty shade of green, no?'

'Where's Buster?' asked Rory.

'Coming later,' she said. 'He's having a drink with some friends.'

'He's lying,' said Rory. 'He couldn't possibly have a friend.'

Rory's mother giggled. 'Now, chéri, you must not be naughty. Buster is my second 'usband,' she explained to me. 'Rory's father, Hector, was my first.

'When I marry Buster, Rory say to me, "You're

39

getting better at choosing husbands, maman, but not much." '

Rory's mother suddenly gave a shriek. 'Ah! *Mon Dieu*, I remember the taxi is still waiting downstairs. We 'ave run out of money. We knew you would have some, Rory, you're so rich now. Could you ring down and get the manager to pay the taxi?'

Rory looked at her with intense irritation, then he laughed, picked up the telephone and gabbled away in French.

'Ask 'im to send up some champagne,' said Rory's mother. 'At least two bottles, I want to drink my new daughter-in-law's health. You must call me Coco,' she said.

I caught Rory's eye and tried not to giggle. Everything was getting out of hand.

Later, when the champagne arrived, Rory said, 'Why have you run out of money? Pa didn't leave you badly off.'

'Of course he didn't, darling, it was just that we had to have central heating for the castle, or we'd have frozen to death.'

'And a sauna bath, and a flagellation room?' said Rory.

'Of course, darling, Buster 'as been used to the best, and he's been shooting four or five times a week and that all adds up. Everything's in such a muddle, we can't decide whether we want to spend the winter in Irasa.' She turned to me. 'I hope you're going to like our island, chéri, those Highland winters can be very terrible, and it's so boring seeing the same old people all the time, and all those sheep. That's what Buster's seeing his friend about.'

'What?' said Rory.

'Buying this aeroplane. He thinks he can get it cheap. Then we can all escape to London, or Paris, or the Riviera when we feel like it.'

Rory raised his eyes to heaven.

'He does need it, darling,' said Coco, almost pleadingly.

'Who told you we were here?'

'Marina did. She telephoned me in Cannes to tell me the news.'

'The bitch,' said Rory.

'Who's Marina?' I asked.

'Marina Maclean,' said Coco. 'At least, she was. Now she's Marina Buchanan. She's just married Hamish Buchanan, who's very rich and more than twice her age. She lives on the island too. I saw her just before we left, Rory. She didn't look very happy. Sort of feverish; she's spending a fortune on clothes and jewellery.'

'That's what comes of trying to marry one's grandfather,' said Rory unemotionally.

'Hamish looks terrible too,' said Coco. 'He's suddenly gone all hip, growing his hair, not eating meat, and dancing in the modern way – trying to keep up with Marina, I suppose. He looks twenty years older. Oh well, it's no use wasting sympathy on Marina. She's made her bed.'

'And now she's about to lie in someone else's,' said Rory.

'Oh, look, here comes Buster.'

'I should like to get dressed,' I said plaintively.

'Oh, nobody dresses for Buster,' said Rory.

Buster Macpherson, when he arrived, turned out to be the kind of man my mother would have gone mad for. He had well-brushed blond hair and blue

41

eyes that let out a perpetual sparkle. He looked like the hero in a boy's comic. He showed a lot of film-star teeth.

He was absolutely not my type. He had none of Rory's explosive feline grace, but he obviously exerted considerable fascination over Coco who, although she didn't look a day over thirty-five, must have been nearing fifty, and a good ten years older than Buster.

'Congratulations, you chaps,' said Buster. He peered through the gloom at me under my sheet.

'May I kiss the bride?' he asked.

'No,' said Rory. 'You'd better watch Buster, he's going through the change of life.'

Buster shot him an unfriendly look, helped himself to a large glass of champagne and sat down.

'Ah, honeymoons, honeymoons,' he said, shaking his head.

'Did you buy that aeroplane?' asked Rory.

'I think so,' said Buster.

Coco gave a crow of delight.

'Where are you going to land it?' asked Rory. 'In the High Street?'

'No,' said Coco. 'We've got a little runway on the island now. I knew I had something to tell you, darling, Finn Maclean is back.'

Rory's eyes narrowed.

'The hell he is. What's he poking his nose into now?'

'He's thrown up his smart Harley Street practice and come back to Irasa as Medical Officer overseeing all the islands,' said Buster. 'He's persuaded the Scottish Medical Board to build him a cottage hospital in the old church hall and buy him an aeroplane so he can hop from island to island.'

'Our own flying doctor,' said Rory. 'Why the hell has he come back?'

'I think he wanted to get out of London,' said Buster. 'His marriage broke up.'

'Not surprised,' said Rory. 'No woman in her right senses could stand him.'

'Finn Maclean is Marina's elder brother,' Coco explained to me. 'Rory and he don't get on, you understand. He never got on with Rory's father either – he kept complaining about the poorness of the tenants.'

'He's an arrogant sod,' said Rory. 'You won't like him.'

'I rather like him,' mused Coco. 'He does not have the bedroom manner, but he is all man.'

Life on Irasa, I decided, certainly wasn't going to be dull. The unpredictable Marina running rings round her ancient husband; Rory feuding with Finn Maclean, who was 'all man'; plus Buster and Coco, a knockabout comedy act in themselves.

'This is a nice hotel,' said Coco meditatively, trying on some of my scent. 'Can you get Buster and me a room here, Rory?'

'No I can't,' said Rory. 'I happen to be on my honeymoon, and I'd like to get on with it without your assistance.'

5

After a fortnight, Rory started getting restless and decided to return to England. We stopped in London and booked in at the Ritz. I must say I did enjoy being rich – it was such bliss not having to look at the prices on the menu.

We were in the middle of dinner, I lingering over a crêpe suzette because it was so delicious and Rory halfway through his second bottle of wine, gazing moodily out at Green Park, where the yellow leaves whirled and eddied away from the wet black branches of the plane trees.

Suddenly he summoned a waiter:

'I want my bill,' he said, adding to me, 'finish up that revolting pudding, we're going home tonight.'

'But we're booked in here,' I protested.

'Doesn't matter. If we hurry, we can catch the sleeper.'

'But it's Friday night,' I said, 'we'll never get a bed.'

'Want to bet?' said Rory.

We tore across London in a taxi, fortunately the streets were deserted, and reached Euston station just five minutes before the train was due to pull out.

'You'll never get on,' said the man at the booking office, 'it's fully booked.'

'What did I tell you,' I grumbled. 'We'll have to sleep in a cattle truck.'

'Stop whining,' said Rory. His eyes roved round the station. Suddenly they lit on one of those motorized trolleys that carry parcels round stations and are always running one over on the platform. It was coming towards us. Stepping forward, Rory flagged it down.

The driver was so surprised he screeched to a halt and watched in amazement as Rory piled our suitcases on.

'What the bleeding hell do you think you're doing, mate?' he said.

'Drive us up Platform 5 to the first-class sleeper for Glasgow,' said Rory.

'You want me to do what?' asked the driver.

'Go on,' said Rory icily, 'we'll miss the train if you don't hurry.'

He climbed on and pulled me up beside him.

'We can't,' I whispered in horror, 'we'll get arrested.'

'Shut up,' snarled Rory. 'Go on,' he added to the driver, 'we haven't got all bloody day.'

There was something about Rory's manner, a combination of arrogance and an expectation that everyone was going to do exactly what he wanted, that made it almost impossible to oppose him. Grumbling that he'd get the sack for this, the driver set off.

'Can't you go any faster?' asked Rory coldly.

The driver eyed the fiver in Rory's hand.

'You won't get a penny of this,' said Rory, 'unless we catch that train.'

We gathered speed and amazingly stormed through the barrier unopposed and up the platform. Train doors were being slammed as we reached the sleeper.

'Put the luggage on the train,' said Rory to the driver, and strolled over to the attendant who was giving his lists a last-minute check.

I edged away, terrified there was going to be a scene.

'I'm afraid we're booked solid, sir,' I heard the attendant say.

'Didn't the Ritz ring through?' said Rory, his voice taking on that carrying, bitchy, upper-class ring.

'Afraid not, sir,' said the attendant.

'Bloody disgrace. Can't rely on anyone these days. Expect your side slipped up, one of your staff must have forgotten to pass on the message.'

The attendant quailed before Rory's steely gaze. He took off his peak cap and scratched his head.

'Well, what are you going to do about it?' said Rory. 'I'm on my way back from my honeymoon, my wife is quite exhausted. We booked a sleeper and now you're trying to tell me you've given it away.'

As the attendant looked in my direction, I edged further away, trying to merge into a slot machine.

'I really don't know what to say, sir.'

'If you value your job,' said Rory, 'you'd better do something about it.'

Two minutes later an enraged middle-aged couple in pyjamas were being shunted into a carriage down the train.

'I'm awfully sorry, sir,' the attendant was saying.

'You might have thanked him,' I said, sitting down on the bed, and admiring the splendour of our first-class compartment.

'One doesn't thank peasants,' said Rory, pulling off his tie.

6

We drove towards the ferry which was to carry us to Irasa. I glanced at Rory hunched over the wheel, demons at his back, the beautiful face sullen with bad temper. His black mood had been coming on for several hours now.

At last we reached the ferry. Under a grey and black sky a mountainous sea came hurtling towards us, thundering, moaning and screaming, and dirty with flying foam.

'Hello, Mr Balniel,' said the man on the gate. 'I wish you'd brought some better weather. It's been raining six weeks in Irasa, even the seagulls are wearing sou'westers.'

On the boat the sky darkened noticeably, the temperature dropped and the gulls were blown sideways like pieces of rag in the wind.

I'm not sure Scotland's quite me, I later thought disloyally, as we bumped along one-track roads with occasional glimpses of sulky-looking sea.

On our left a huge forbidding castle lowered out of the mist.

'Nice little weekend cottage,' I said.

'That's where Buster and Coco live,' said Rory. 'This is us.'

*　　*　　*

I suppose it had once been a rather large lodge to the castle – a grey stone two-storey house, hung with creeper, surrounded by a wild, forsaken garden.

I started to quote Swinburne, but Rory shot me such a look.

I shut up.

I decided not to make any flash remarks, either, about being carried over the threshold. Rory was extraordinarily tense, as though he was expecting something horrible.

He certainly got it. I've never seen such shambles inside a house; broken bottles, knocked-down lamps and tables, glasses strewn all over the floor, dust everywhere, thick cobwebs. The bedrooms looked as though someone had used them as ash-trays, the fridge like a primeval forest, and someone had written 'Goodbye forever' in lipstick on the mirror.

The house consisted of a huge studio, a drawing-room almost entirely lined with books, two bed-rooms upstairs, a kitchen and a bathroom; all were in absolute chaos.

'Oh God,' said Rory. 'I left a message with my mother to get someone to clean the place up.'

'It's all right,' I said faintly, 'it'll only take a few hundred years to put to rights.'

'I'm not having you whisking around like Snow White,' snapped Rory. 'We'll sleep at the castle tonight. I'll get someone to come in tomorrow.'

I looked out of the bedroom window. The view was sensational. The house grew out of a two hundred and fifty foot cliff which dropped straight down to the sea.

'I hope we don't fall out too often,' I joked weakly, then I saw a cellophane packet of flowers on the bed. 'Oh look,' I said, 'someone remembered us.' Then I shivered with horror as I realized it was a funeral wreath of lilies. Inside the envelope, on a black-edged card, was written 'Welcome home, darlings'. 'How beastly,' I said in a trembling voice. 'Who could have done that?'

Rory picked up the card. 'Some joker who's got it in for me.'

'But that's horrible.'

'And quite unimportant,' he said, tearing up the card. He opened the window and threw the wreath out, so it spun round and round and crashed on the rocks below.

Startled I looked into his face, which glowed suddenly with some malice I couldn't place.

'Come here,' he said softly.

He pulled me against him, pushing my head down on his shoulder, one hand tracing my arm, the other moving over my body. Then he smiled and closed his long fingers round my wrist where the pulse pounded.

'Poor little baby,' he whispered. He could always do this to me. 'Let's go next door,' and he pulled me into the dusty spare room with the huge window on to the road and began to kiss me.

'Shouldn't we draw the curtains?' I muttered. 'They can see us from the road.'

'So what?' he murmured.

Suddenly I heard a scrunch of wheels on the road outside. Swinging round I saw a blue Porsche flash by. In the driving seat was a red-headed girl who gazed in at us, a mixture of despair and hatred in her huge, haunted eyes.

*   *   *

I enjoyed staying at the castle, living in baronial comfort, and making the acquaintance of Rory's black labrador Walter Scott, who had been living with Buster's gamekeeper while he had been away. He was a charming dog, sleek, amiable, incurably greedy and not as well trained as Rory would have liked.

After a few days we went back to live in Rory's house (very pretty it looked, after it had been cleaned up) and began marriage proper.

I didn't find it easy. I was determined to be one of those wonderful little homemakers putting feminine touches everywhere but, as Rory remarked, the only feminine touches I added were dripping pants and stockings, and mascara on his towel.

I tried to cook, too. I once cooked moussaka, and we didn't eat until one o'clock in the morning. But Rory, who was used to Coco's French expertise, was not impressed.

I also took hours over the washing. There weren't any launderettes in Irasa, and then it lay around for days in pillowcases waiting to be ironed; and Rory never seemed to have clean underpants when he needed them.

After a couple of weeks he said, quite gently, 'With all the cobwebs, we seem to have formed a spider sanctuary here. You're obviously not into housework, so I've hired a char, four days a week, and she can iron my shirts too.'

I felt humiliated but enormously relieved.

The char, Mrs Mackie, turned out to be a mixed blessing. She was wonderful at cleaning, but a terrible gossip, and obviously irritated Rory out of his mind. As soon as she arrived he used to disappear into the mountains to paint, and she and I sat round drinking cider and talking.

'I've got a wicked bad leg,' she said one morning. 'I shall have to go and see Dr Maclean.'

'Finn Maclean?' I said.

She nodded.

'What's his sister Marina like?'

'She's no right in the head, although I shouldn't say it. The old Macleans never had any money. Dr Maclean, her father, was a gud doctor, but he dinna know about saving. Marina married this old man for his riches, and it's dancing him into his grave she is. Perhaps now young Dr Maclean's come back he'll keep her in order.'

'Why's he come back when he was doing so well in London?'

She shrugged. 'Irasa has an enchantment. They all come back in the end.'

7

Irasa – Island of the Blessed, or of the Cursed. I could understand why none of them could escape its spell, and why only here could Rory find the real inspiration for his painting.

The countryside took your breath away; it was as though the autumn was pulling out all the stops before succumbing to the harshness of the Highland winter. Bracken singed the entire hillsides the colour of a red setter, the turning horse chestnuts blazed yellow, the acacias pale acid green.

With Rory painting all day, Walter Scott and I had plenty of time to wander about and explore. The island was fringed with wooded points like a starfish. Out of the ten or so big houses, on one point lived Rory and me, on another Buster and Coco, on another Finn Maclean and on yet another Marina and Hamish. The islanders' white cottages were dotted between.

One afternoon in late October, I walked down to Penlorren, the island's tiny capital.

Penlorren was a strange sleepy little town, exquisitely pretty, like a northern St Tropez. Wooded hills ringed the bay, but the main street was an arc of coloured houses, dark green, pink, white and duck-egg blue. In the boats the fishermen were sorting their slippery silver catch into boxes.

As I walked about I was aware of being watched. Suddenly I looked round and there was the blue Porsche parked by the side of the road: the same red-headed girl was watching me with great undefended eyes. I smiled at her, but she started up the car and stormed down the main street, scattering villagers.

'Who's that?' I asked a nearby fisherman, and somehow knew he was going to answer, 'Marina Maclean.'

I'd forgotten to get any potatoes and I went back to the main store. Three old biddies were having a yap, they didn't hear me come in.

'Did you see Rory Balniel's wee bride?' said one.

'Pur lassie, so bonny,' said the second. 'She might as well have married the divil.'

'There'll be trouble ahead,' said the third. 'Now young Dr Maclean's back again.'

Then they suddenly saw me, coughed, and started taking a great deal of interest in a sack of turnips.

8

The feeling of unease I'd had since the first night of my honeymoon grew stronger. Another fortnight passed. I had to stop fooling myself that our marriage was going well.

I was so besotted with Rory I wanted to touch him all the time; not just bed touching, but holding hands and lying tucked into his back at night like two spoons in a silver box. But Rory seemed to have no desire to come near me, except when he made love to me, which was getting less and less often.

I tried to kid myself he was worrying about work. I knew about geniuses, secretive, more temperamental, of finer grain than ordinary mortals, and more easily upset. I tried to talk to him about painting, but he said I didn't understand what he was doing and, anyway, talking about it ruined it.

I was in the kitchen one morning. I had learned to be quiet when work was going badly, the clatter of a pan could drive him mad. He wandered in yawning, rubbing a hand through his hair, looking so handsome with his sleepy, sulky face, I felt my stomach tighten.

'Do you want some coffee?'

'Yes, please.'

Feeling more like a normal wife, I went into the kitchen, started percolating coffee, and sighed inwardly for the days when Nina and I had lived on Nescafé. I thought of the beautiful, haunted girl in the blue Porsche.

'I keep seeing Marina Buchanan,' I said.

Rory looked at me. 'So?'

'Not to speak to,' I stammered. 'She's terribly beautiful. Shall we ask them to dinner?'

'I'm sure they'd enjoy your cooking.'

I bit my lip. I didn't want a row.

'I'm sorry about my cooking. I am trying.'

'Sure you are, extremely trying.'

'Rory, please, what's the matter? What have I done? You haven't laid a finger on me for at least four days.'

'You can count up to five? That is encouraging,' said Rory acidly.

'Most newly weds are at it all the time,' I said.

'We might be, if you were less unimaginative in bed. I'm surprised all your exes didn't expect something a bit more exciting.'

I jumped back as though he'd hit me. Sometimes there was a destructive force about Rory.

'God, you bastard,' I whispered. 'If you were a bit more encouraging, I might be less unimaginative. And if I'm no good in bed, why the hell didn't you say so in the beginning?'

'I was probably too drunk to notice,' he said.

'I hate you!' I screamed.

I stormed out of the room, rushed upstairs and threw myself on the bed, bursting into tears. Five minutes later I heard a door slam and his car driving off down the road.

I cried for hours. 'He's only doing it to hurt me,' I kept saying, trying to reassure myself. I got up, washed my face and wondered what to do next.

I thumbed through a magazine. You could have pulled corks with the models' hair. I liked music but you couldn't listen to records all day. I supposed I could put on a deeply felt hat and go for a walk.

I sat up, dismayed: I realized I was bored. No-one was more aware than I that boredom was a mark of inadequacy. People with inner resources didn't get bored. No; as Rory had discovered, I'd got hidden shallows. I went to the fridge and ate half a tin of potato salad.

There was a knock on the door. Delighted, I leapt to my feet and rushed to open it. There stood Marina Buchanan, quivering with nerves as if even now she might turn and run. She was lovely, if haunted, in a red coat and long black boots, her shining Titian hair blowing in the wind like a shampoo commercial. Her mouth was large and drooping, her face deathly pale, and there were huge blue shadows underneath her extraordinary eyes. I understood everything my mother had told me about Garbo. I wished I hadn't eaten that potato salad.

'Hello,' she said. 'I'm Marina Buchanan.'

'I know,' I said, 'I'm Emily Balniel.'

'I know,' she said, 'Coco sent me a postcard suggesting we should get together.'

'Oh, how lovely,' I said. 'Come in and have some coffee or something.'

'How nice it looks,' she said, gazing in admiration at the drawing-room.

'Let's have a drink, not coffee,' I said. 'I know

one shouldn't at this hour of the morning, but it's such a celebration having someone to talk to.'

We had the most tremendous gossip. She didn't seem haunted any more, just slightly malicious and very funny. She adored Coco, she said, but couldn't stand Buster. She wasn't very complimentary about her husband either.

'He's terrific between the balance sheets, so it means I can have everything I want, but I'm getting a bit fed up playing Tinker, Tailor with the caviar . . .'

I giggled.

'Where's Rory?' she said.

'Out painting.'

She looked at me closely. 'You look tired. Has Rory been giving you a hard time?'

'Of course not,' I said firmly.

'Don't get sore, I'm not being critical, just realistic. Rory's divine-looking, he exudes sex-appeal the way other men breathe out carbon dioxide, and he's got terrific qualities.' She paused as if trying to think what they were. 'But he can be difficult. Where other people make scenes, Rory makes three-act plays. When he's upset he takes it out on other people, he always has. My brother, Finn, is difficult, but in a more predictable way, and he's not spoilt like Rory, or bitchy either. Rory's always trying to send Finn up, but it doesn't work because Finn couldn't care less. And although Rory's always had everything, somehow Finn makes him feel inadequate. They hate each other's guts, you know,' she added in satisfaction. 'There's bound to be fireworks – the island isn't big enough for both of them.'

She got up and wandered round the room. I

looked at that wild, unstable loveliness, and wondered what had possessed her to marry an old man when she could have had anyone.

'Why don't you both come to dinner on Thursday?' I said.

'That'd be lovely, but you'd better ask Rory first.'

At that moment Rory walked in.

'Hello, Rory,' she said softly, and then when he didn't answer immediately, she went rattling on.

'It would be nice if you could learn to say hello sometimes, Rory. With six months' practice you might even learn to say, "It's a lovely day".'

I steeled myself, wondering what sort of mood he was in now, but he turned round, then came over and kissed me on the mouth, quite hard.

'Hello, baby, have you missed me?'

'Oh yes,' I said, snuggling against him, feeling weak with relief.

Then he looked across at Marina, and ice crept into his voice. 'Hello, Mrs Buchanan, how's marriage? Still making Hamish while the sun shines?'

I giggled. 'We've been having a lovely gossip. I've asked Marina and Hamish to dinner here on Thursday.'

9

I was determined the dinner party would be a
success. For the next three days I cooked, polished
and panicked, determined Rory should be proud of
me. On the afternoon of the day they were coming,
I was well ahead; the house gleamed like a telly ad.,
all the food was done. The only thing we needed
was lots of flowers. There were none in the garden,
but I'd noticed some gorgeous roses in a garden
down the road. I set off, still in my nightie – flimsy
and black. I'd been so busy I hadn't even bothered
to get dressed.

It was a warm day for the time of year, the wet
grass felt delicious beneath my bare feet. I ran past
ancient fruit trees and overgrown shrubberies, and
started to pick great armfuls of roses.

I was just bending over, tearing off one huge red
rose with my teeth, when I heard a furious voice
behind me.

'What the hell do you think you're doing?'

I jumped out of my skin and spun round, aghast,
the rose in my teeth like Carmen. A man towered
over me. He must have been in his early thirties,
he had dark red hair curling over his collar,
a battered, freckled, high-complexioned face, a

square jaw, a broken nose, and angry hazel eyes. His face was seamed with tiredness, his mouth set in an ugly line – but it was still a powerful, compelling, unforgettable face.

'Don't you realize this is private property?'

Then I twigged. This must be Finn Maclean. I stared at him, fascinated. It was not often one came face to face with a legend.

'Didn't you know you were trespassing?'

'Yes, I did. I'm terribly sorry, but no-one's ever picked any flowers here before. It seems such a waste to leave them. I didn't know you'd turn up.'

'Evidently,' he said, taking in my extreme state of undress. 'Who are you, anyway?' he asked.

'Emily,' I muttered. 'Emily Balniel.'

For a second there was a flicker of emotion other than anger in his face. Was it pity or contempt?

'I'd have thought Rory was rich enough to afford his own roses. I suppose you've picked up all his habits of doing and taking exactly what you like?'

'No, I haven't, and you can keep your rotten roses,' I said, and threw the whole lot at his feet.

10

Although I was seething with rage, I didn't mention the incident to Rory when I got back; he was in too bad a temper. I started tidying the drawing-room.

'I wish you wouldn't hum nervously when you do things,' he said. 'Stop fiddling with those leaves, too, they look awful enough as it is.'

'You only notice them because Marina's coming.'

I went into the kitchen and slammed the door. First Finn, now Rory. I thought I was going to cry, but it would only make my eyes red, so I took a large swig of cooking wine instead. Then I suddenly realized I hadn't put out any napkins, and had to rush upstairs, pull them out of the laundry basket and iron them on the carpet.

Maddeningly, Marina and Hamish arrived twenty minutes early, so I had no time to tart myself up. I wondered if Marina did it deliberately. She looked staggering in a slinky, backless blue dress which matched her eyes. But even I was unprepared for Hamish. He must have been close on sixty, with nudging eyes, an avid grin and yellow teeth. But he'd got himself up like an out-of-date raver: thinning grey locks clustering over his forehead and down his back, sideboards laddering his wrinkled cheeks, a white chamois leather smock, lots of beads and jeans several sizes too small for him. He looked like an awful old goat. Rory, who looked devastating in a grey satin shirt, couldn't stop laughing.

'Marina, darling, what have you done to him?' he said in an undertone. 'He looks like an octo-genarian ton-up boy.'

'I've made an old man very hippy,' said Marina, and giggled.

'Don't you like his smock? A touch of white is so flattering close to the face when you reach a certain age.'

They were convulsed with mirth. I think I would have been shocked by their malice if Hamish hadn't been so awful, lecherous and pleased with himself.

We all drank a great deal before dinner.

'I'm thinking of growing a beard,' Hamish said.

'I don't like beards on boys or girls,' said Marina.

'Are you still taking singing lessons?' Rory asked Marina.

'I drive over to Edinburgh once a fortnight. It's a long way, but worth it. I usually stay the night. It gives Hamish a break.'

'To get up to mischief,' said Hamish, giving me a wink that nearly dislocated his eyelid.

No-one really noticed the dinner, not even when one of my false eyelashes fell in the soup. Marina ate nothing; Hamish was obviously frightened his trousers were going to split. Rory never ate much, anyway. I cleared the plates and served each course; I might have been a waitress. Walter Scott was having a field day finishing up in the kitchen.

There were strange undercurrents. I felt as though I was watching a suspense story on television where I'd missed the beginning and couldn't quite work out what was going on. Hamish rubbed his skinny leg against mine. Any moment he'd get a fork stuck into it.

After dinner Marina turned on the gramophone. She and Hamish danced. Hamish looked absurd, flailing about like a scarecrow in a gale. Marina moved like a maenad, her red hair flying, her face transformed by the soft light.

Rory sat watching her, his face expressionless. He had been drinking heavily all evening.

Finally she flopped down beside him on the sofa.

'Did you ever finish that water-colour of the harbour?'

He nodded. 'It's in the studio.'

'May I come and see it?'

They went next door.

Hamish looked dreadful now, grey and exhausted. He went off to the loo and I wandered into the studio to see the painting they were talking about.

Suddenly, I froze with horror. They hadn't bothered to turn on the studio light, and were standing near the window in the moonlight.

Marina stood there vibrating, a foot away from Rory; her face glowed like a pale flame.

'Why did you marry her?' Her voice dropped an octave.

'Oh come on,' Rory said, 'let's say I wasn't wanted any more.'

'To punish me, to put me on the rack. You can't believe I married Hamish for anything but his money, but she's something entirely different.'

She turned on her heel and was coming towards me; it was as though I was frozen in some terrible nightmare.

'Marina, wait,' I heard Rory say.

'Oh go to hell,' she said, but the longing and ache in her voice were quite unmistakable.

She didn't see me as she came into the drawing-room. 'Hamish, I want to go home,' she snapped.

Her face was turned away from him, only I could see it was wet with tears. Rory didn't even bother to come out and say goodbye to them. I went back into the studio, my legs hardly holding me up.

'Rory,' I said, 'I think we ought to have things out.'

'I've nothing to have out, nothing.'

I realized he'd reached that pitch of drunkenness that was about to explode into violence, but I didn't care.

'What's going on between you and Marina? Why was she hanging around when we arrived? It was she who sent the wreath, wasn't it? And her whom you rang up the first night of our honeymoon? I want to know what it's all about.'

'Nothing, nothing. We were brought up together, that's all. Anyway,' he snarled, 'you asked her to dinner. Now get out of my way.' He pushed me aside. 'I'm going to sleep in the spare room, and don't come crawling into my bed in the middle of the night.'

11

I didn't sleep at all. I lay trembling with panic,
clutching Walter Scott's solid body, my mind reeling from possibility to possibility. At dawn I tried
to be rational. Rory and Marina had probably been
childhood sweethearts, and he'd been piqued when
she married Hamish. After all, it was me he'd
married.

Next morning I came down, washed up, and
tried to be brave about my hangover.

What would please Rory most? I decided to
clean out his studio.

He came down at midday. He looked terrible.
He must have been hungover down to his toes, but,
glass in hand, he was making a nice recovery. I was
standing on a ladder dusting a shelf.

'Hello, darling,' I said, brightly.

'What are you doing?'

'Dusting.'

'Why the hell can't Miss Mackie do that? You'll
only muddle everything up, for Christ's sake.'

'Please don't let's quarrel. I'm sorry for the
things I said. I didn't mean them. I couldn't bear
another night like last night.'

'You can always leave,' he said brutally.

'I don't want to leave. I love you.'

His face softened. 'Do you now? Well come down off that stupid ladder then,' and, catching my ankles, he ran his hands slowly up my legs.

'I'll just dust this last folder,' I said, steadying myself on the shelf.

'Put that down,' said Rory, his voice suddenly icy.

Startled, I swayed on my high ladder.

'I said put it down.'

Purely out of nerves, I let the folder slip from my hands and crash to the floor. Hastily I scrambled down and knelt to pick it up.

Rory reached it at the same time as me, his hand on my arm like a vice.

'Ow!' I yelped.

'Leave it,' he snarled, but it was too late.

Spilling out of the folder were the most beautiful drawings. The naked model smiling that secret, comehither smile was unmistakably Marina.

We looked at the paintings scattered round our feet. Marina in her lush beauty mocked me a hundred times over.

'Well?' I said.

'It's your fault. I told you not to touch that file.'

'They're very good, very life-like indeed,' I said slowly, trying to keep my voice from trembling. 'I'm sure you didn't paint these from imagination.'

'Of course I didn't. I wanted to do some nudes last summer, and there are only a limited number of people on the island who'll take their clothes off. You can hardly see Buster or Hamish stripping down to the buff and sitting around for hours on end. Anyway, as I've said before, it's damn all to do with you what I did before I was married.'

'Or what you do after you're married,' I said bitterly.

Rory drained his drink and poured himself another one.

'Rory,' I said slowly, 'this is important. Do you love me at all?'

Rory looked bored. 'Depends how you define love.'

How could I explain that he was the most beautiful man I'd ever seen, that my tongue suddenly got stuck in my throat when I saw the set of his shoulders, that I spent all day wanting him.

'Oh Rory,' I said, appalled. 'Can't you try and be a bit more loving?'

'Why?' he said, logically.

'Why did you marry me then?'

He looked at me reflectively, 'I'm beginning to wonder.'

I gave a gasp. God, he could be vicious.

'What shall we do about it, then?' I said.

'Do?' he exploded. 'Do let me work, that's enough for me.'

'But not enough for me!' I screamed, and brushed blindly past him.

'Where are you going?' he said.

'Out.'

'Well, for God's sake come back in a less destructive mood.'

And so our marriage began to deteriorate. It wasn't helped by the rain which started to fall the next day, and continued for weeks. Rory passed the time in painting, I in sulking, then in trying to win Rory round, then in sulking again.

I suppose I was pretty disagreeable myself, I complained steadily about the weather and how bored I was. At first I made an attempt to stop myself, then I didn't try to stop myself, then I found I couldn't. Emily – the fishwife.

That crack about being lousy in bed had gone home too. I wrote off to London for a sexy black cut-out nightie, and a book on how to undress in front of your husband. It showed you how to swing your bra round like a football rattle, and slide your pants off in one go.

I tried it on Rory one evening, but he merely raised his eyebrows and asked me if I'd been at the gin. As the weeks passed, he didn't lay a finger on me. I was desperately unhappy and cried a great deal when he wasn't around. I kept telling myself that when he'd assembled enough canvases for the exhibition we'd be like a couple of love birds, but I didn't really believe it.

I spent most of my time corrupting Walter Scott. Rory was a great believer that dogs should be treated like dogs and kept outside. I kept bringing him in and feeding him in between meals and cuddling him – I needed a few allies.

Gradually Walter invaded the house. He started off sleeping in the kitchen, then moved to the foot of the stairs, then to the landing outside our bedroom. At dawn he would steal in and try to climb on our bed. Invariably Rory, who was a light sleeper, would wake up and throw him out.

'Walter Scott suffers from being an only dog,' he was fond of saying.

'Blood is thicker than Walter,' I said.

'Nothing is thicker than Walter,' said Rory.

12

In November, later than expected, Coco and Buster came back.

Buster brought his new private plane, which he landed perilously on the sward outside the castle, terrifying the life out of the islanders and the local sheep, and nearly depositing himself, three labradors, gun cases, rod boxes and several hundred tons of pigskin luggage, in the sea.

'Pity,' said Rory. 'Never mind, there'll be plenty of other opportunities. In the old days he used to come up by train from Euston and take the dogs to lamp-posts as the train waited interminably at Crewe.'

Coco arrived in rip-roaring form and swept Rory and me into a round of gaiety, meeting people on the island and the mainland. It was a frightful strain trying to keep up the appearance that I was blissfully happy.

A few days later, Marina and Hamish asked us back to dinner. I was amazed and irritated to discover she was a very good cook, and had decorated Hamish's huge, stark house with a wild elegance I could never achieve in a million years of poring over *House and Garden*.

The drawing-room had grey silk walls and flame-red curtains, and I felt sure, had been chosen to compliment Marina's colouring.

'Oh it's lovely,' I said wistfully, 'you ought to go into interior decorating.'

'Emily's an inferior decorator,' said Rory.

In my attempt to make our bedroom more feminine, I'd started painting it but had got bored in the middle. The colour, too, was disastrous. It looked all right on the chart but once on the wall turned out an appalling E-K directory pink.

I felt very overdressed that evening, too. Trying to compete with Marina, I'd put on a see-through blouse and a long skirt. Marina of course was wearing jeans.

There was another couple to dinner – Deirdre and Calen Macdonald. She was a commanding, big-boned woman with a ringing voice. He had a handsome, dissipated face, roving grey eyes, and had obviously married her for her money. He turned out to be a shooting friend of Buster's and made an absolute dead set at me.

'I can't claim to be a gentleman, but I've always preferred blondes,' he said, cornering me on the sofa as soon as we were introduced, 'and you really are gorgeous.'

The intensity with which he gazed at my see-through blouse threw me off balance – I folded my arms firmly to cover up what I could.

'Er – do you do anything for a living?' I said, casting around for something to say.

'Good God, no. I realized very early on that I was quite incapable of supporting myself, so I married old Deirdre instead; she's a pretty full time job, but I do get the odd afternoon off while she's sitting on committees. How about you?'

'I've only been married seven weeks,' I said firmly.

'So disillusion hasn't set in yet. Pretty tricky customer Rory, I admire you if you can handle him. He runs rings round poor Buster. Is he still drinking too much?'

'Hardly at all,' I said, out of the corner of my eye watching Rory go to Marina's sidetable, and help himself to a second very large glass of whisky.

'Very loyal and proper,' said Calen. 'I must say you really are extremely attractive, I wish you'd stop sitting with your arms folded like a rugger player so I could appreciate you properly. Promise me that if you ever decide to be unfaithful to Rory, I can have first refusal.'

I tried to look disapproving, but after Rory's indifference of the past few weeks, it was such heaven to be chatted up. I was sure Marina had invited Calen on purpose. But although he flirted outrageously with me all evening, I felt terribly depressed that Rory wasn't betraying a spark of jealousy.

'So nice for you to find someone of your own mental age to play with, Emily,' was all he said afterwards.

As the weeks passed, we often encountered Marina and Hamish at parties. Marina and Rory so studiously avoided each other that I wondered if they were meeting on the sly.

Occasionally I saw her loathsome brother, Finn Maclean, driving round the island, obviously far too preoccupied with building his beastly hospital to waste time on parties.

*　　*　　*

In December, Coco slipped down some steps at the castle after a boozy evening and sprained her ankle. Next day she rang up, saying she was bored, would I come over and see her. On my way I drove into Penlorren to find her some nice escapist novel from the bookshop.

Having parked my car in the main street, I started browsing through some romances. Oh dear, the lovely things that happened to those heroines. Why didn't Rory feel like that about me?

Finally, I heard a cough behind me. The owner wanting to shut up shop.

Hastily I bought the book and wandered dreamily into the main street, through the mist and rain. A man was standing by my car. There was something heroic about the way he stood, the massive breadth of the shoulders, the hair curling over the collar of his battered sheepskin coat like Michelangelo's David.

Instinctively, I unhitched the long lock of hair from behind my ear and let it fall seductively over my eyes. Then I realized the man was Finn Maclean, and he was blazingly angry.

'Is this your car?'

'Yes . . . at least, it's Rory's.'

'Can't you read?'

He seized my arm and swung me round to face a notice on a garage door. It said, *Doctor's car, please leave free.*

'Oh,' I said. 'Well, in London, people often put notices like that on their garage doors even if they're not doctors, just to keep people away.'

'This is not London,' he snapped, and in terms of the most blistering invective, proceeded to tell me exactly what he thought of Londoners who came to live in the country, and me in particular, and didn't I realize that people could be dying because people like me parked their cars in places like this. Finally I got fed up.

'It strikes me,' I said, 'that while you've been rabbiting on and on and on about my criminal responsibility, at least twenty more people could have died. Admittedly, a few of them may have been Chinese. In fact, if all the people who died while people like you were blowing their cool all over the islands were laid end to end . . .'

'Don't be fatuous,' snapped Finn. 'There's obviously no point in trying to get anything through to you. You'd better move your car.'

Of course, the beastly thing wouldn't start. Eventually I remembered to let out the clutch, and it shot forward in a series of agonizing jerks.

'Louse, swine, monster,' I muttered to myself, as I drove to the castle. No wonder Rory and he couldn't stand each other.

13

I found Coco lying in bed looking beautiful as always, but very tired. Someone had brought her some lilies, and she'd buried her face in them. Her nose was bright yellow with pollen. She was obviously in considerable pain, but greeted me with her usual zest.

'Help yourself to a drink, chéri, and get me one. Buster has gone shooting. Every day now he shoot, pop, pop, bang, bang. I find it very boring. I 'ave live in Scotland nearly thirty years, and still I do not find the plus-four sexy. Admittedly, Buster 'ave very good legs. A seagull excruciated on his coat just as he was leaving. He was very angry.'

I giggled. Coco could always cheer me up. We gossiped for half an hour, then I reverted to the subject I could never ignore for long, even though it crucified me to talk about it.

'Have you seen Marina?' I asked.

Coco raised her eyes to heaven.

'Yes I 'ave. That's a marriage going on the rocks. We had dinner with them the other night, she and Hamish. I gave her a lecture. I said "You are not making Hamish happy like Emily is making my Rory happy." (I winced at that bit.) And Marina laugh in my face. Sometimes I think she is a bit touchy in her head. She is so different from her brother, Finn. He's so kind and down-to-earth, and such a wonderful doctor.'

That moment a maid banged on the door.

'Dr Maclean's here, madam,' she said.

'Show him in,' said Coco, excitedly.

'Oh God, he was as mad as a boiled squirrel last time I saw him,' I said.

But Coco wasn't listening, she was too busy combing her hair and spraying on scent.

In marched Finn Maclean.

'Talk of the devil,' said Coco in delight. 'I was just singing your praises to Emily, telling her what a wonderful doctor you were – so kind and under-standing. I shouldn't think anything rattles you, does it, Finn?'

'No,' I said acidly, 'I should think it's always Dr Maclean who does the rattling.'

Finn turned round and saw me. His face hard-ened slightly. 'Oh it's you,' he said.

'I didn't know you knew Emily,' said Coco. 'Isn't she pretty? And so good for Rory.'

'I'm sure they're ideally matched,' said Finn.

The sarcasm was entirely lost on Coco, who beamed at us both.

'Let's have a look at your ankle,' Finn said.

Coco stretched out one of her beautiful, smooth, brown legs. The ankle was very black and swollen. Although Finn handled it with amazing delicacy, she drew her breath in.

'Sore is it?' he said gently.

She nodded, catching her lip.

'Poor old thing. Never mind, you've still got one perfect ankle,' he said, getting up. 'No reason why

76

the other shouldn't be as right as rain in a few weeks.'

'What's right about rain?' I said gloomily, looking out of the window.

'Still, I'd like to X-ray it,' Finn went on, ignoring me. 'I'll send an ambulance to pick you up later. It'll jolt you less than a car.'

'I must go,' I said. 'I've got to cook Rory's supper.'

'Finn will give you a lift,' said Coco.

'I've got a car,' I said quickly.

It was very cold outside and I shivered: I didn't want to leave the cosy warmth of the castle for one of Rory's black moods. Finn Maclean got something out of the pocket of his overcoat.

'I should have thought it was a bit early on in your marriage to escape into tripe like this,' he said, handing it to me. It was the romantic novel I'd intended to give Coco.

14

Coco's ankle was X-rayed, bound up and she was ordered to rest it. Just before Christmas, however, Maisie Downleesh (one of Coco's friends) decided to give a ball to celebrate her daughter Diney's engagement. We were all invited.

There is something about the idea of a ball that lifts the spirits, however low one is. I suppose it's the excitement; buying a new dress, new make-up, a new hairstyle and settling down in front of the mirror in an attempt to magic oneself into the most glamorous girl in the room. In the past, a ball had offered all the excitement of the unknown, opportunity knocking. This time, I hoped, it would be a chance to make myself beautiful enough to win back Rory.

The ball was being held at the Downleeshes' castle on the mainland. Coco, Buster, Rory and I were all to stay there. In the morning I took the car across the ferry and drove to Edinburgh to buy a new dress. In the afternoon I had to pick up a couple who were coming to the dance from London, then drive back and pick up Rory from the Irasa Ferry, and then drive on to the Downleeshes'.

I was determined that a new me was going to emerge, so gorgeous that every Laird would be mad with desire for me. I spent a frenzied morning rushing from shop to shop. Eventually in a back street I tracked down a gloriously tarty, pale pink dress, skin tight over the bottom, slashed at the front and plunging back and front.

It had been reduced in a sale because there was a slight mark on the navel, and because, the assistant said with a sniff, there was no call for that sort of garment in Edinburgh.

I tried it on; it was wildly sexy.

'A little tight over the barkside, don't ye thenk,' said the assistant, who was keen to steer me into black velvet at three times the price.

'That's just how I like it,' I said.

It was a bit long too, so I went and brought new six-inch high shoes, and then went to the hairdressers and had a pink rinse put on my hair. I never do things by three-quarters. All in all it was a bit of a rush getting to the airport.

The Frayns were waiting when I arrived – I recognized them a mile off. He was one of those braying chinless telegraph poles in a dung-coloured tweed jacket. She was a typical ex-deb, with flat ears from permanently wearing a headscarf, and a very long right arm from lugging suitcases to Paddington every weekend to go home to Mummy. She had blue eyes, mouse hair and one of those pink and white complexions that nothing, not rough winds nor drinking and dancing till dawn, can destroy. They were also nauseatingly besotted with one another. Every sentence began 'Charles thinks' or 'Fiona thinks'. And they kept roaring with laughter at each other's jokes, like hyenas. She also had that terrible complacency that often overtakes newly married women and stems from relief at having hooked a man, and being uncritically adored by him.

She was quite nice about me being late, but there was a lot of talk about stopping at a telephone box on the dot of 6.30 to ring up Nanny and find out how little Caroline was getting on; and did I think we'd get there in time to change?

'It's the first time I've been separated from Caroline,' she said. 'I do hope Nanny can cope.'

She sat in the front beside me, he sat in the back; they held hands all the time. Why didn't they both get in the back and neck?

It was a bitterly cold day. Stripped, black trees were etched on the skyline. The heavy brown sky was full of snow. Shaggy forelocked heads of the cows tossed in the gloom as they cropped the sparse turf. Just before we reached the ferry to pick up Rory and Walter Scott, it started snowing in earnest. I had hoped Rory and I could have a truce for the evening – but I was an hour late which didn't improve his temper.

Fiona, who had evidently known Rory as a child, went into a flurry of what's happened to old so and so, and who did so and so marry.

Rory answered her in monosyllables; he had snow melting in his hair and paint on his hands.

'Too awful,' she went on. 'Did you know Annie Richmond's father threw himself under a taxi in the rush hour in Knightsbridge?'

'Lucky to find one at that hour,' said Rory, looking broodingly at the snowflakes swarming like great bees on the windscreen.

I giggled. Rory looked at me, and then noticed my hair.

'Jesus,' he said under his breath.

'Do you like it?' I said nervously.

'No,' he said and turned up the wireless full blast to drown Fiona's chatter.

Suddenly she gave a scream.

'Oh look, there's a telephone box. Could you stop a minute, Rory, so I can telephone Nanny.'

Rory raised his eyes to heaven.

She got out of the car and, giving little shrieks, ran through the snow. Through the glass of the telephone box I could see her smiling fatuously, forcing 10p pieces into the telephone box. Rory didn't reply to Charles' desultory questions about shooting. His nails were so bitten that his drumming fingers made little sound on the dashboard.

A quarter of an hour later, Fiona returned.

'Well?' said Charles.

'She's fine, but she's missing us,' she said. 'She brought up most of her lunch but she's just had two rusks and finished all her bottle, so Nanny thinks she's recovered.'

Rory scurled off through the snow, his hands clenched on the wheel.

'What b-awful weather,' said Fiona, looking out of the window. 'You really must start a family very soon, Emily,' she went on. 'It gives a completely new dimension to one's life. I think one's awfully selfish really until one has children.'

'Parents,' said Rory, 'should always be seen and not heard.'

Punctuated by giggles and murmurs of 'Oh Charles' from the back, we finally reached the turrets and gables and great blackened keep of

Downleesh Castle. The windows threw shafts of light on to the snow which was gathering thickly on the surrounding fir trees and yews. The usual cavalcade of terriers and labradors came pounding out of the house to welcome us. Walter Scott was dragged off protesting by a footman to be given his dinner in the kitchen.

In the dark panelled hall, great banks of holly were piled round the suits of armour, the spears and the banners. We had a drink before going upstairs. Diney, Lady Downleesh's daughter, who'd just got engaged, fell on Fiona's neck and they both started yapping about weddings and babies.

We were taken to our bedroom down long, draughty passages to the West Tower. In spite of a fire in the grate, it was bitterly cold.

I found when I got there that my suitcase had been unpacked and all my clothes laid out neatly on the mildewed fourposter, including an old bone of Walter Scott's and a half-eaten bar of chocolate I had stuffed into my suitcase at the last moment. On the walls were pictures of gun-dogs coming out of the bracken, their mouths full of feathers.

I missed Walter. Sometimes in those awful long silences I had with Rory I found it a relief to jabber away to him.

'Can he come upstairs?' I said.

'No,' said Rory.

In the bookshelves was a book called *A Modern Guide to Pig Husbandry*. 'Perhaps I should read it,' I said, 'it might give me some advice about being married to a pig.'

Across the passage were the unspeakable Frayns. They had already hogged the bathroom, and judg-

82

ing from the sound of splashing and giggling, it wasn't just a bath they were having. I realized I was jealous of their happiness and involvement. I wanted Rory to start every sentence. 'Emily says' and roar with laughter at my jokes.

I took ages over dressing, painting my face as carefully as Rory painted any of his pictures. My pink dress looked pretty sensational; I put a ruby brooch Coco had given me over the mark on the navel. It was certainly tight, too, everyone would be able to see my goose-pimples, but on the whole I was pleased with the result – it was definitely one of my on days. The only problem was that when I put on my new tights, the crotch only came up to the middle of my thighs. I gave them a tug and they split irrevocably, leaving a large hole, so I had to make do with bare legs.

I was just trying to give myself a better cleavage with Sellotape when Rory announced that he was ready. Even I, though, was unprepared for his beauty, dressed up in a dark green velvet doublet with white lace at the throat and wrists and the dark green and blue kilt of the Balniels. Pale and haughty, his eyes glittering with bad temper, he looked like something out of *Kidnapped*; Alan Breck Stuart or young Lochinvar coming out of the West.

'Oh,' I sighed. 'You do look lovely.'

Rory grimaced and tugged at the frills at his neck.

'I feel like Kenneth McKellar,' he said.

'Never mind, you've got exactly the right hips to wear a pleated skirt,' I said.

Rory put a long tartan muffler thing on the dressing-table. 'This is for you,' he said.

83

'I'm not thinking of going out in this weather,' I said.

'You wear it indoors,' he said, draping it diagonally across my shoulders, 'like this, and pin it here.'

'But whatever for?' I moaned.

'It's the Balniel tartan,' he said evenly. 'Married women are supposed to wear their husband's tartan.'

'But it completely covers up my cleavage.'

'Just as well, you're not at some orgy in Chelsea now,' said Rory.

'Do I really have to, it's a bit Hooray for me.'

Very sulkily I arranged it; somehow tartan didn't go with skintight pink satin, and brooches on the navel.

I wanted to fiddle with my hair and make-up a few minutes longer, but Rory was sitting on the bed, staring at me coldly, making me nervous.

'Why don't you go on down?' I said.

'I'll wait here,' he said.

I combed a few pink tendrils over my shoulders.

'What made you go crazy with the cochineal?' said Rory.

'I thought I ought to change my image,' I said, sourly. 'My old one didn't seem to be getting me very far.'

Downstairs in the huge drawing-room people were having drinks. The host and hostess stood near the door repeating the same words of welcome to new arrivals. Looking round I realized I looked better than most of the women but infinitely more tarty. Most of them were big, raw-boned deb types in very covered-up clothes, the occasional mottled purple arms were the nearest they got to *décolletage*. Very tall, aristocratic men in kilts stood talking in haw haw voices about getting their lochs drained and burning their grouse moors. Fishes in glass cases and mounted stags' heads stared glassily down from the walls.

Fiona and Charles were standing near the door. She was wearing a blue dress and absolutely no eye make-up.

'What a pretty dress,' I said, with desperate insincerity.

'Yes, everyone likes it,' she said, 'blue is Charles' favourite colour.'

Charles was gaping at my pink hair, his mouth even more open than usual. Fiona started trying to bring Rory out about his painting.

'Do you do all that funny abstract stuff?' she said.

'No,' said Rory.

'Some young man – he had a beard actually – painted my sister Sarah. She sat for two hours and all he had drawn after all that time were three figs and a milk bottle.'

She gave a tinkle of laughter, Rory looked at her stonily.

'Charles paints quite beautifully too, I feel it's such a shame his job in the City is so demanding he doesn't have time to take painting up as a hobby – like you, Rory.'

'Rory *does not paint* as a hobby,' I said furiously, 'it's his profession.' But I spoke to deaf ears, Rory had turned on his heel and gone off to get himself a drink. Charles and Fiona were suddenly shrieking at a couple who had just come into the room.

I was extremely pleased therefore that the next

moment Calen Macdonald bore down on me and kissed first my hand, then my cheek, then both my bare shoulders.

'I was just saying to Buster I wished I could see more of you,' he said, pulling down my tartan sash and peering at my cleavage, 'and now I have. I must say that dress is very fetching, pink looks like bare flesh if one shuts one's eyes.'

'Where's Deidre?' I said.

'Oh, she's stalking in Inverness.'

I giggled.

'So I've got the whole evening off and I'm going to devote it entirely to you.'

Two matrons with red-veined faces stopped discussing herbaceous borders and looked at us frostily.

At that moment a voice shouted 'Emily!' and there was Coco, dripping with sapphires as big as gull's eggs, wearing a glorious midnight blue dress. She was lying like Madame Recamiers on a red brocade sofa, surrounded by admirers.

Rory sat at her feet.

'I didn't see you,' I said, going over and kissing her.

'You look very nice, doesn't she, Rory,' said Coco.

'A bit prawn cocktail,' said Rory.

I bit my lip.

'I think she looks tremendous,' said Buster giving me a warm look. 'In the pink, I might say,' he laughed heartily.

The room was filling up. Buster and Calen were joined by some ancient general, and they were soon busy recounting to each other the number of creatures they had slaughtered in the last week.

'Grouses, and twelve bores, and twenty bores, and million bores, that's all men can think about up here,' said Coco. She began talking to me about shoes.

There was a sudden stir and a whisper ran through the room. The old general straightened his tie and smoothed his moustache.

'What a beautiful girl,' he said.

A swift flush mounted to Rory's pale cheeks. With a sinking heart, without turning my head, I knew it must be Marina.

'Hello, everyone,' she said, coming over and kissing Coco, 'how's your poor leg, darling?'

She was wearing a pale grey chiffon dress, smothered in two huge pale grey feather boas. With her flaming red hair it made one think of beech woods in autumn against a cloudy sky. I noticed she had no truck with Hamish's tartan across her bosom. I supposed it was Rory's tartan she was after. Sadly I realized that if I spent a million years on my face and clothes, I would never be as beautiful as Marina. Hamish, all done up in black velvet and frills, looked awful.

'Mutton dressed as cutlet,' said Rory to Marina under his breath. Even worse was to come. Following her into the room came Finn Maclean in a dinner jacket, with a sleek brunette.

'Oh God,' said Rory, 'here comes the virgin surgeon. Diney,' he added, turning to the daughter of the house, 'what the hell is Doctor Finlay doing here?'

'He was absolutely wonderful about Mummy's ulcer,' said Diney, her eyes shining.

'Probably gave it to her in the first place,' said Rory.

'Well, I must say, I think he's rather super myself,' said Diney.

'I'm surprised at you,' said Rory, 'one really shouldn't know one's doctor socially.'

Finn came up to Coco.

'How's it feeling?' he said.

'Much better,' said Coco.

'Maybe, but there must be no dancing on it,' he said firmly.

'Who's that with him?' I whispered to Calen Macdonald.

'I think she's one of his nurses,' said Calen.

'She's pretty,' I said.

'Not my type,' said Calen, and started whispering sweet everythings into my ear. I, however, was much more interested in seeing how Rory and Finn reacted to each other.

'Look, Rory,' said Coco, 'here's Finn.'

Rory, just lighting a cigarette, paused, eyeing Finn without any friendliness.

Finn nodded coldly, 'Hello, Rory,' he said.

'Good evening, Doctor,' said Rory – he smiled but his eyes were cold, his face as pale as marble. There was an awkward pause.

'Isn't it nice Finn's back for good,' said Coco brightly to the assembled company.

'Not for my good, he isn't,' said Rory.

'This is Frances,' said Finn, ignoring him and introducing the sleek brunette. 'She works at the hospital.'

'Oh, a staff outing,' drawled Rory, 'what fun. Did you come here by charabanc with a crate of beer, or is it part of the SRN syllabus – a dazzling night of dancing and passion in the arms of Doctor Maclean?'

'Only for very privileged nurses,' said Frances, smiling at Finn.

'I'm surprised you've been able to drag him away from delivering babies and darning up appendices,' said Rory.

Frances was obviously uncertain how to take Rory.

'Dr Maclean certainly doesn't allow himself enough free time,' she said warmly.

'Quite so,' said Rory, his eyes lighting up with malicious amusement. 'He's an example to us all. I gather that's the reason your marriage came unstuck, Finn. I heard your ex-wife couldn't cope with the short hours, or wasn't your double bedside manner up to scratch? However,' he smiled at Frances, 'you seem to be consoling yourself very nicely.'

I turned away in embarrassment; if only he wouldn't be so poisonous. Rory grabbed my arm.

'You haven't met Emily, have you, Finn?'

'Yes, he has,' I said quickly.

'Oh?' Rory raised an eyebrow.

'We met at Coco's one day,' I said, 'when Finn came to see her about her ankle.' Rory held out his glass to a passing waiter to fill up.

'Are you still trying to paint?' Finn said.

'He's got an exhibition in London in April,' I said hotly.

'Doesn't really need one,' said Finn. 'He's been making an exhibition of himself for years,' and taking Frances by the arm, crossed the room to talk to his host.

'Scintillating as ever,' said Rory, but his hand shook as he lit one cigarette from another.

'Do you like dancing reels, Emily?' said Marina.

'If I have enough to drink,' I said, draining my glass, 'I reel automatically.'

We went in to dinner.

The leathery, sneering faces of ancestors looked down from the walls. The candlelight flickered on the gleaming panelling, the suits of armour, the long polished table with its shining silver and glasses, and on the pearly white shoulders of Marina.

'I hope there's a huge flower arrangement in front of me so I don't have to sit staring at Doctor Maclean,' said Rory.

I was horrified to see that he and Marina were sitting next to each other on the opposite side of the table. I was next to Calen, who ran his fingers all over my bare back when he pushed my chair in. And now the bad news. On my other side was six feet four inches of Titian-haired disapproval – Finn Maclean.

'Hello, Finn,' said Calen, 'how are things, have you met this steaming girl?'

'Doctor Maclean isn't one of my fans,' I said.

'Maybe not,' said Calen, 'but he's tall enough to see right down your front, unless I rearrange that sash. That's better, don't want to give you blood pressure, do we Finn? Always get swollen heads, these quacks, think all the nurses and women patients are nuts about them.'

I laughed, Finn didn't.

'It must be exciting, running your own hospital,' I said to him. He was about to answer when someone shoved a steaming great soup ladle between us. 'Great fun running your own hospital,' I went on. Then it was his turn to help himself to soup.

'What's the disease people suffer most often from round here?' I asked.

'Verbal diarrhoea,' muttered Calen.

I was just warming to my subject, asking Finn all the right questions about the hospital and the operations he would perform there, when Calen lifted up the curtain of hair hanging over my left ear and whispered: 'Christ, I want to take you to bed.'

I started to laugh in mid-sentence, then blushed:

'I'm awfully sorry,' I said to Finn, 'it's just something Calen said.'

Finn obviously thought we were too silly for words and turned his huge back on me and started talking to the girl on his right.

Footmen moved round the table, the clatter of plates mingled with the clink of knives and glasses and the hum of various animated conversations. Lady Downleesh sat at the end of the table, a large imposing woman who must once have been handsome. Only Marina and Rory sat mutely side by side, talking little, eating less. They appeared to see and hear nothing of what was going on around them. Suddenly I felt panicky. They were probably playing footy-footy. I imagined their cloven hoofs entwined. Calen and Finn were temporarily occupied with other conversations. I dropped my napkin and dived under the table to retrieve it. It was very dark. I hoped my eyes would soon become accustomed to it, but they didn't; not enough carrots when I was a child I suppose. I couldn't see which were Rory's or Marina's legs. I grabbed someone's ankle, but it was much too fat for Marina's and twitched convulsively – cheap thrill!!! All the same, I couldn't stay here for ever exciting dowagers. I surfaced again.

'Are you all right, Mrs Balniel?' said Lady Downleesh, looking somewhat startled.

'Fine,' I squeaked, 'absolutely marvellous soup.'

'Everyone's waiting for you to finish yours,' said Finn in an undertone.

'Oh I have,' I said, 'I've got a tiny appetite, I never eat between males.'

Finn didn't laugh. Pompous old stuffed shirt.

Everyone started to talk about fishing as the soup plates were moved.

'You're not a bit alike,' I said, 'you and Marina.'

He shot me a wary glance.

'In what way?'

'Well, she's so wild and you're so well controlled. I can't see you as a medical student putting stuffed gorillas in college scarves down Matron's bed.'

He gave me one of those big on-off smiles he must use all the time for keeping people at a polite distance.

'I was working too hard for that.'

'Are all the people in this room your patients?' I asked. 'Must be funny to look round a table and know what every single woman looks like with her clothes off.'

'Calen does anyway,' said Finn. 'What do you do with yourself all day?'

'Not a lot, I'm not very good at housework. I read and grumble, sometimes I even bite my nails.'

'You ought to get a job, give you something to do,' he went on. 'What did you do before you met Rory?'

'Oh, I mistyped letters in several offices, and I did a bit of modelling when I got thin enough, and then I got engaged to an MP. I don't think I would have been much of an asset to him, and then Rory came along.'

'It's a full moon tonight,' said a horse-faced blonde sitting opposite us. 'I wonder if the ghost'll walk tonight. Who's sleeping in the west wing?'

'The Frayns,' said Diney Downleesh, lowering her voice, 'and Rory and his new wife.'

'What ghost?' I whispered nervously to Calen.

Calen laughed. 'Oh, it's nothing. There was a Downleesh younger son a couple of centuries ago, who fell in love with his elder brother's wife. The wife evidently had a soft spot for him as well. One night, when her husband was away, she invited the younger brother into her bedroom. He was just hot-footing along the West Tower where she was sleeping (all tarted up in his white dressing-gown), when the husband came back, and picking a dirk off the wall, he stabbed him. The younger brother is supposed to stalk the passage when there's a full moon, trying to avenge himself through all eternity for not getting his oats.'

'How creepy,' I said with a shiver.

'I'll take care of you,' said Calen, putting his hand on my thigh and encountering bare flesh.

'Christ,' he said.

'My only pair of tights split,' I said.

Finn Maclean pretended not to notice. Calen filled my glass over and over again.

Eventually we finished dinner and the ball began. The host and hostess stood at the edge of the long gallery welcoming latecomers. Every time the front door opened you could feel a blast of icy air from outside. It was terribly cold in these big houses. The only way to keep warm was to stand near one of the huge log fires that were burning in each room, then two minutes later you were bright scarlet in the face. I could see exactly why Burns said his love was like a red, red rose.

Rory came up to me. 'What was Finn Maclean talking to you about?' he said suspiciously.

'He was stressing the importance of getting one's teeth into something,' I said.

'If he got his teeth into me, I'd go straight off and have a rabies jab,' said Rory.

'On with the dance,' I said. 'Let Emily be unconfined.'

'Come on, Rory,' said Diney Downleesh, coming over to us, 'we need two more people to make up an eightsome over there.'

We couldn't really refuse.

Dum-diddy Dum-diddy Dum-diddy-diddy-diddy went the accordions. The men gave strange, unearthly wails, like a train not stopping at a station. We circled to the left, we circled to the right.

'Wrong way,' hissed Rory, as we swung into the grand chain. When it was my turn in the middle, I made an even worse hash of it, setting to all the wrong people and doing U-turns instead of figures of eight, and whooping a lot. 'For Christ's sake stop capering around like the White Heather Club,' said Rory under his breath. 'Women don't put their hands up, or click their fingers, or whoop.'

The next dance, thank God, was an ordinary one. I danced it with Buster, who squeezed me so hard, I thought I'd shoot out of my dress like toothpaste.

'Why don't any of them look as though they're enjoying themselves?' I said.

'You can never tell until they fall on the floor,' said Buster.

On the other side of the room Marina was dancing with Hamish. She looked so glowingly beautiful and he so yellow and old and decayed I was suddenly reminded of Mary Queen of Scots dancing and dancing her ancient husband into the grave.

The evening wore on. I wasn't short of partners. I danced every dance.

A piper came on, well primed with whisky, and assaulted our ear-drums for a couple of reels. My reputation as a reel-wrecker was growing. I messed up Hamilton House and then the Duke and Duchess of Perth, and then the Sixteensome. On the surface I must have appeared rather like a loose horse in the National, potentially dangerous, thoroughly enjoying myself and quite out of control. But through a haze of alcohol and misery I was aware of two things, Rory's complete indifference to my behaviour and Finn Maclean's disapproval. Both made me behave even worse.

I danced a great deal with Calen. I came into my own when they stopped doing those silly reels.

'Did your wife dance professionally?' I heard a disapproving dowager say to Rory, as I came off the floor after a gruelling Charleston. Calen and I went into the drawing-room for yet another drink. I put my glass down on a gleaming walnut table. When I picked it up two minutes later, there was a large ring on the table.

'Oh God,' I said, 'how awful.'

'Looks better that way,' said Calen, 'looks more lived in somehow.' He led me back on to the floor. The music was slow and dreamy now.

'You are the promised breath of springtime,' sang Calen laying his handsome face against mine.

I snuggled up against him for a few laps round the floor, and then I escaped to the loo. Big-boned girls stood around talking about Harrods and their coming-out dances. Really, I thought as I gazed in the mirror, I look very loose indeed. Tight dress, loose morals, I suppose.

I wandered along the long gallery so I could watch the people on the floor. A double line of dancers were engaged with serious faces in executing a reel. Marina and Rory faced one another, expressionless. God they danced beautifully. I was reminded of Lochinvar again:

So stately his form and so lovely her face
That never a hall such a galliard did grace . . .
And the bride's maidens whispered, 'T'were
    better by far
To have matched our fair cousin with young
    Lochinvar.

Oh dear, I thought in misery. In this case young Lochinvar seems to have missed the boat, arriving too late and finding his love married to Hamish.

The dance ended. The couples clapped and spilled out into the hall. If only Rory would come and look for me. But it looked as though I'd have to wait for a Ladies' Excuse Me before I had a chance to dance with him again.

I heard footsteps behind me. I felt two hands go round my waist, I turned hopefully, but it was Calen.

'I've got a bottle,' he said, 'Let's go and drink it somewhere more secluded.' He dropped a kiss on to my shoulder and led me downstairs along a long passage into a conservatory.

Chinese lanterns, hanging round the walls, lit up the huge tropical plants. The scent of azaleas, hyacinths and white chrysanthemums mingled voluptuously with the Arpège I'd poured all over myself. The sound of the band reached us faintly from the hall.

'You are the promised breath of springtime,' sang Calen, taking me in his arms.

'There isn't any mistletoe,' I said.

'We don't need it,' said Calen, his grey, dissipated eyes gazing into mine.

You're rotten to the core, I thought. Mad, bad and dangerous to know. Bad from the neck upwards, and not at all good for Emily. Not that Rory was doing much good for me either.

'God, I want you,' said Calen undoing the top button of my dress. He bent his head and kissed the top of my cleavage, and slowly kissed his way up my neck and chin to my mouth.

I didn't feel anything really, except a desire to slake my loneliness. God, it was a practised kiss. I thought of all those hundreds of women he must have seduced. Hands travelled over my bare back, pressing into every crevice. Suddenly a light flicked on in the library next door.

'Calen,' said a voice, 'you're wanted on the telephone.'

'Go to hell,' said Calen, burying his face in my neck, 'don't be a bloody spoilsport, Finn.'

Over Calen's head, our eyes met. 'It's Deidre,' Finn said.

'Oh God,' sighed Calen, as reluctantly he let me go. 'You see before you the most henpecked husband in the Highlands. Good night, you dream of bliss.' He kissed me on the cheek and walked somewhat unsteadily out of the conservatory. Finn and I glared at each other.

'You are beyond the pale,' I snapped, 'beyond a whole dairyful of pales. Why do you have to rush around rotting up people's sex lives? I thought you were a doctor, not a vicar.' I lurched slightly without Calen to hold me up.

'You won't get Rory back that way,' said Finn. 'Getting drunk and going to bed with Calen doesn't solve anything.'

'Oh it does, it does,' I said with a sigh, 'it gets you through the next half an hour – and half an hour can be an eternity in Scotland.'

I wandered into the library and discovered a glass of champagne balanced on a stag's head. I drank it in one gulp.

'I'll take the high road and ye'll take the low road,' I said, 'and I'll be inebriated before ye. Tell me, Doctor, you know the area better than I do, what gives between Rory and your sister?'

'Nothing,' he said roughly. 'You're imagining things, and you're not making things any better behaving like this.'

I stared at him for a minute. 'My mother once had an English setter who had freckles like yours,' I said, dreamily. 'They looked really nice on a dog.'

We went into the hall which was fortunately deserted. 'What about your friend Frances Nightingale,' I said, swinging back and forth on an heraldic leopard that reared up the bottom of the banisters. 'Isn't she missing you?'

'That's my problem,' he said.

'Look,' I said, 'I'm not usually as silly as this. It's a pity you're not as good at mending broken hearts as broken bones.'

'I suggest,' said Finn, 'you go straight up to bed without making a fool of yourself any further. Take three Alka-Seltzers before you go to sleep, you'll feel much better in the morning. Come on.' He moved forward to take me upstairs, but I broke away.

'Go and jump in the loch,' I snarled, and ran away from him up the stairs. I fell into bed, preparing to cry myself to sleep, but I must have flaked out almost immediately.

In the middle of the night, it seemed, I woke up. I didn't know where I was, it was pitch black in the room. The fire had gone out. Where the hell was I? Then I remembered – Downleesh Castle. I put out a hand – groping for Rory. He wasn't there, I was alone in the huge four-poster. Suddenly the room seemed to go unnaturally cold, the wind was blowing a blizzard outside, the snow still falling heavily. As the windows rattled and banged and the doors and stairs creaked, it was like being on board ship. Then I felt my hair standing on end as I remembered the ghost in the white dressing-gown that walked when the moon was full. I gave a sob at the thought of him creeping down those long, musty passages towards me. I was trembling all over. Getting out of bed, I ran my hands along the wall, hysterically groping for a light switch. I couldn't find one. The room grew even colder. Suddenly I gave a gasp of terror as the curtain blew in, and I realized to my horror the window was open. I leapt back into bed. Where the hell was Rory? How could he leave me like this? Suddenly my blood froze as, very, very gently, I heard the door creaking. It stopped, then creaked again, and, very, very gradually, it began to open. I couldn't move, my voice was strangled in my dry throat, my heart pounding.

Oh God, I croaked, oh, please no! I tried desperately to scream as one does in a nightmare, but no sound came out.

Slowly the door opened wider. The curtains billowed again in the through draught from the window, and the light from the snow revealed a ghostly figure wrapped in white, gold hair gleaming. It suddenly turned and looked in my direction, and slowly crept towards the bed. Panic overwhelmed me, I was going to be murdered.

Someone was screaming horribly, echoing on and on through the house. The next minute I realized it was me. The room was flooded with light and there was Buster, standing in the doorway, looking very discomfited in a white silk dressing-gown. I went on screaming.

'Emily, my God,' said Buster. 'I'm so sorry, pet. For Christ's sake stop making that frightful row. I got into the wrong bedroom, must have got the wrong wing for that matter.'

I stopped screaming and burst into noisy, hysterical sobs. Next minute Finn Maclean barged in, still wearing black trousers and his white evening shirt.

'What the hell's going on?' he said.

He was followed by the Frayns. She had tied her hair up with a blue bow.

'Where's Rory?' I sobbed, 'where *is* he? I'm sorry, Buster, I thought you were the ghost. I was so frightened.' My breath was coming in great strangled gasps. Buster patted my shoulder gingerly.

'There, there, poor Emily,' he said. 'Got my

wings muddled,' he added to Finn. 'She thought I was the Downleesh ghost.'

'I'm not surprised after all the liquor she shipped,' said Finn. 'I'll go and get something to calm her down.'

Once I started crying I couldn't stop.

'Do try and pull yourself together, Emily,' said Fiona. 'Oughtn't you to slap her face or something?' she said as Finn came back with a couple of pills and a glass of water.

'Get these down you,' he said, gently.

'I don't need them,' I sobbed, then gave another scream as Rory walked in through the curtains, snowflakes thick on his hair and his shoulders.

'What a lot of people in my wife's bedroom,' he said blandly, looking round the room. 'I didn't know you were entertaining, Emily. You do keep extraordinary hours.' A muscle was going in his cheek, he looked ghastly.

'Where have you been?' I said, trying and failing to stop crying.

'Having a quiet cigarette on the battlements,' said Rory. 'Pondering whether there was life after birth. Hello, Buster, I didn't see you, how nice of you to drop in on Emily. Does my mother know you're here?'

'She was quite hysterical,' said Fiona, reprovingly.

'I'm not surprised,' said Rory, 'with all these people in here.' He came over and patted me on the shoulder. 'There, there, lovie, pack it in now, everything's all right.'

'I thought Buster was a ghost,' I explained, feeling terribly silly. 'I could only see his dressing-gown and his hair.'

'You what?' For a minute Rory looked at Buster incredulously, and then he leant against the wall and started to shake with laughter.

'I got into the wrong wing,' said Buster, looking very discomfited. 'Perfectly natural mistake in these old houses, thought I was going into my own bedroom.'

Rory sniffed, still laughing. 'I didn't know ghosts reeked of after-shave. Really, Buster, next time you go bed-hopping, you should take an A-Z. Just think if you ended up in our hostess's room.' He looked round the room. 'Well, if you've all finished, I'd quite like to go to bed.'

Finn Maclean glared at Rory for a second and then stalked out of the room, followed by Buster followed by the Frayns.

'What an extraordinary couple,' I could hear her saying, 'do you think they could be a bit mad?'

Still laughing, Rory started pulling off his tie. There was a knock on the door.

'Probably Buster wondering if he's forgotten someone,' said Rory. Sure enough, Buster stood on the threshold. 'Rory, dear boy, just like a word with you.'

'Knowing you, it'll be several words,' said Rory.

'Don't say anything to your mother about this, will you?' I heard Buster saying in a low voice. 'She's been under a lot of strain with her ankle, just taken a sleeping pill, wouldn't want to upset her.'

'You're an old goat, Buster,' said Rory. 'But your secret is safe with Emily and me. I can't, alas, vouch for Doctor Maclean, who is the soul of indiscretion, or for that appalling couple we gave a lift to.'

'Goodness,' I said after he'd gone. 'Do you think he was being unfaithful to Coco?'

'Probably,' said Rory. 'He and my mother trust each other just about as far as they can throw each other, which always seems a good basis for marriage.'

'But whose bedroom was he trying to get into?' I asked.

'Probably taking pot-luck,' said Rory.

'Marina's perhaps,' I said, then could have bitten my tongue off.

'Marina left hours ago, she and Hamish aren't staying here,' said Rory. 'They were having the most frightful row when they left. They should lay off arguing occasionally, a short rest would recharge their batteries for starting again.'

So he hadn't been with Marina. Instead he'd been on the battlements by himself in a blizzard, driven by what extremes of despair. Somehow that seemed even worse. He got into bed, put his arms round me and kissed me on the forehead. I could never understand his changes of mood.

'Sorry you were frightened by Buster,' he said, and the next moment he was asleep. I lay awake for a long time. Towards dawn he rolled over and caught hold of me, groaning, 'Oh my darling, my little love.' I realized he was asleep and, with a sick agony, that it certainly wasn't me he was talking to.

15

For the first time I dreaded Christmas. At home it had been our own, cosy, womb-like festival, but with Rory there wasn't likely to be peace on earth, or goodwill towards men. Half-heartedly I chose a fir tree from the plantation behind our house and set it in a tub, put holly on the walls, strung a bit of mistletoe from the drawing-room light.

On Christmas Eve I went into Penlorren to do last-minute shopping and buy some little presents for Rory's stocking. I left Rory cleaning his gun for the shoot Buster had arranged for Boxing Day.

When I got back, weighed down with parcels, there was a car parked outside the gate. I let myself in and was just about to shout I was back, when I heard raised voices from the studio. I tiptoed closer so I could distinguish them. One was like rough sand with a pronounced Scottish accent, the other aristocratic, drawling, silken with menace. Through the door I could see Finn and Rory facing each other, like a huge lion and a sleek, slim, black panther, obviously in the middle of a blazing row. Neither of them heard me.

'Well, Doctor?' said Rory, the words dripping

with insolence. 'Why are you hounding me like this?'

'Because I've got several things I want to say to you.'

'Well, don't say them now. Emily'll be back any moment.'

'I don't know what devilish game you're up to this time,' said Finn, 'but you'd better stop playing cat and mouse with my sister. Leave her alone, you've done enough damage.'

I felt my throat go dry. I held on to the door handle for support.

'Marina's over twenty-one. Surely she's old enough to take care of herself,' said Rory.

'You know she can't,' thundered Finn. 'You of all people must know how near the edge she is. Don't you ever think of Hamish?'

'Not if I can help it,' said Rory in a bored voice.

'Or Emily?'

'Leave Emily out of it. She's my problem. You should really visit us more often, Finn. You're like a breath of fresh air.'

'You damned little rat,' roared Finn. 'You're going to carry on as before, aren't you?'

'Well, things are slightly more complicated now, but on the whole, Doctor, you've got a pretty clear view of things.'

'You know I can put the police on you, don't you?' said Finn.

Suddenly Rory lost his temper. He went as white as a sheet, his black eyes blazed.

'You wouldn't dare,' he hissed. 'Your family would come out of it as badly as mine.'

'I don't care.'

Their faces were almost touching in their rage.

Then Rory's control seemed to desert him. He sprang at Finn, howling abuse, his fingers round Finn's throat. At one moment it seemed as though Finn was going to be murdered. The next, Rory had gone down before a crashing blow on the jaw, and Finn was standing over him, fists clenched, about to kick Rory's head in.

'No!' I screamed. 'No! Don't touch him.'

Finn swung round, his yellow eyes blazing. Then he looked down at Rory.

'That's only the beginning, Rory,' he said. 'I won't be so gentle with you next time.'

And he was gone.

'Are you all right?' I said.

'Fine,' Rory said. 'I do love Christmas, don't you? It brings out those delightful histrionic qualities latent in all of us.'

I didn't laugh.

'I suppose you're going to tell me he was talking nonsense,' I said, 'that there wasn't any truth in his accusations.'

Rory poured himself a drink and downed it in one, then he banged the glass down.

'What do you think, Emily? That's what matters.'

'I don't think anything,' I said, biting my lip to stop myself crying. 'I just know you haven't made love to me for nearly three months and it's driving me crazy. Then Finn comes here and says all these things, and they seem to add up.'

Rory picked up the gun from the table and examined it. 'So, you're not getting your ration,' he said softly.

'Put that thing away,' I said nervously.

'Does it frighten you? Poor, frustrated Emily.'

He lifted the gun, his finger on the trigger.

'Don't!' I screamed.

He aimed the gun upwards. There was a muted explosion, the crash of a light bulb, and the studio was in darkness. The next minute a wedge of muscle and flesh hurled itself against me, knocking the breath out of my body, pinioning me to the carpet. Then Rory's mouth ground against mine with such intensity our teeth clashed. I struggled helplessly like a fly against a wall, trying to push him away.

'No, Rory, no,' I shrieked.

'You wanted it,' he swore. 'You're bloody well going to get it.'

It was over in a few seconds. I lay on the floor, rocking from side to side, my hands over my mouth. My ribs felt as though they'd crack with agony from the dry sobs I couldn't utter.

Rory flicked on the side light and shone it in my face.

'That's what you wanted, wasn't it? You don't seem pleased.'

I gazed at him dumbly, I could feel the tears welling out of my eyes.

'You hate my guts, don't you?' I whispered.

'It's your lack of guts, I hate,' he said.

Then, suddenly, he put his arms round me and pulled me against him. I jerked my head away.

'Oh, Emily, Emily,' he muttered, 'I'm so miserable, and I've made you miserable, too. Forgive me, I don't know what gets into me.'

Running a dry tongue over my lips and tasting the blood congealing there, I digested this outburst.

I should have tried to comfort him, to find out what drove him to these black, uncontrollable rages. But I didn't feel up to it. Without a word, I shook him off, got to my feet, and walked out of the room, banging the door shut.

16

Looking back on a time of intense unhappiness, one fortunately remembers very little. Our marriage was into injury time. Somehow we got through Christmas and the next month; hardly speaking, licking our wounds, yet still putting up a front to the outside world. Over and over I made plans to leave, but could never quite bring myself to. In spite of everything I still loved Rory.

February brought snow, turning the island into a place of magic.

Coco's ankle recovered and she decided to give a birthday party for Buster.

Rory went to Glasgow for the night to stock up with paint, but was due back at lunchtime on the day of the party.

I went to sleep and had the most terrible nightmare about Marina and Rory, lying tangled in each other's arms, asleep on the floor. I woke up in floods of tears, with the moon in my eyes and the screaming horrors in my mind. I groped for Rory beside me, and then remembered he wasn't there. I was too frightened to go back to sleep again. I got up and cleaned the house from top to toe (my charwoman had been off for several weeks with rheumatism), and spent hours cooking Rory a gorgeous lunch to welcome him home. Then I went out and bought two bottles of really good wine. From now on I decided I was going to make a last effort to save my marriage.

At twelve o'clock the telephone rang. It was Rory. He was still in Edinburgh. He'd be back later, in time for Coco's party.

'Why bother to come back home at all?' I said, and slammed down the telephone, all my good resolutions gone to pot. How the hell was I to fill in the time until he got back? I refused to cry. I decided to drive into Penlorren and buy Buster a present.

Two miles from home I suddenly realized I'd come out without my purse, and decided to turn round and get it. The road was icy and inches deep in snow. My U-turn was disastrously unsuccessful. The next thing I was stuck across the road, the wheels whirring up snow every time I pressed the accelerator.

Suddenly, around the corner, a dark blue car came thundering towards me, going much too fast even without ice on the roads. I screamed with terror but was absolutely powerless to move. There was no way it could brake in time. Then by some miracle of steering, the driver managed to yank the car to the right, slithering into a sixteen-yard skid, missing my car by inches, before juddering to a halt in a snowdrift.

Trust my luck. It was my old enemy Finn Maclean who got out of the car, all red hair and lowered black brows, jaw corners and narrow, infuriated eyes. 'What the blazes do you think . . .' he began, then he realized it was me, took a deep

110

breath and said, 'God, I might have known.'

He looked me over in a way that made me feel very small, and hot and uncomfortable.

'I couldn't help it,' I blurted out, still shaking from shock.

'That's what I'm complaining about,' he said wearily. 'I'm sure you couldn't help it; only an imbecile would have attempted to turn a car around here.'

'I've said I'm sorry,' I said, colouring hotly. 'Anyway, you were driving much too fast and my car skidded. No-one could have moved it.'

'Get out,' said Finn brusquely.

I got out. He got in and turned the car immediately. Then he got out and held the door open for me.

'Nothing to it,' he said, infuriatingly. 'You were just using too much choke.'

It was the last straw. I got into the car, just looked at him and burst into tears; then, crashing the gears, I roared off home. God knows how I got back with the whole countryside swimming with tears.

I don't know how long I cried, but long enough to make me look as ugly as sin. Then I noticed the potted plant Coco had given me for Christmas. It looked limp and dejected.

'Needs a bit of love and attention, like me,' I said dismally, and getting up, I got a watering can and gave it some water.

Then I remembered someone had once told me if you watered rush mats it brought out the green. I heard a step. I must have left the door open. Hoping by some miracle it might be Rory, I looked up. It was Finn Maclean.

'Don't you come cat-footing in here,' I snarled.

Then I realized how stupid it must look, me standing there watering carpets in the middle of the drawing-room.

'I'm not quite off my rocker,' I said weakly. 'It's meant to bring out the green in the rushes.'

Finn began to laugh.

'Whenever I see you you're either tearing up roses with your teeth, trying to block the traffic, or watering carpets. How come you're such a nutcase?'

'I don't know,' I muttered. 'I think I was dropped as an adult.'

'You're going to water the whole floor in a minute,' he said, taking the watering can away from me.

For a minute he looked at me consideringly. Aware how puffy and red my eyes were, I gazed at my feet.

Then he said, 'I came to apologize for biting your head off this morning. I was tired, I hadn't been to bed. Still, it was no excuse, and I'm sorry.'

I was so surprised I sat down on the sofa.

'That's all right,' I said, 'I had a lousy night too, otherwise I wouldn't have cried.'

'Where's Rory?'

'In Glasgow.'

'I'm going over to Mullin this afternoon to see a patient, why don't you come too?'

'I get sick on planes,' I said quickly.

'You can't land a plane there. I'm taking the speedboat. I'll pick you up in half an hour. We needn't talk if we don't want to.'

17

It was a beautiful day: the sun shone and the hills glittered like mountains of salt against an arctic blue sky. The gloom was still on me as we ploughed over the dark green water, but I found it easier to endure, particularly when I found Finn and I could talk or not talk, with a reasonable amount of ease. When we moored and I leapt on to the landing-stage, he caught me, and his hands were steady and reassuring like a man used to handling women.

As we walked up the mountainside to a little grey farm-house, the bracken glittered white like ostrich feathers of purest glass, snow sparkled an inch on every leaf, icicles hung four feet deep. Suddenly, an old woman, her arm in plaster, came running out of an outhouse beside the farm.

'Doctor!' she screamed, 'thank God ye've come, it's me wee cow.'

'Careful, you'll slip,' said Finn, taking her good arm.

'What's the matter with her?'

'She's started calving and things dinna look too well. Angus went to the mainland for help, but he's not back yet.'

'I'll have a look at her,' said Finn, going into the outhouse.

A terrified, moaning, threshing cow was lying in the corner.

'Easy now,' said Finn soothingly, and went up to her. He had a look then called, 'She's pretty far gone, Bridget.'

The old woman promptly started crying and wailing that it was their only cow.

'Go back to the house,' Finn told her, 'I'll do what I can. You'll only be a hindrance with that arm. Come on,' he added to me, 'you can help.'

'I can't,' I squeaked. 'I don't know anything about cows. Shall I take the boat back to the island and get help?'

'It's too late,' said Finn, rolling up his sleeves. As he spoke, the cow gave another terrified moan of pain.

'Oh, all right,' I said sulkily. 'Tell me what to do.'

'Hold on to the calf's legs,' said Finn, 'and when I say "pull", pull hard.'

'Gawd,' I muttered. 'What a way to spend a Thursday.'

The straw was already sticky with blood and there was only one 30-watt bulb to work under. Finn barked out instructions.

'Haven't you got any Pethedine for her?' I said.

Finn didn't answer. I supposed he was used to delivering babies. But women in labour don't usually flail and lurch around like cows do.

'I'm sure she'd be less uptight if the bull had been present at the birth,' I joked weakly, as I picked myself up from the stinking straw for the third time.

114

After that I stopped making jokes, but just gritted my teeth and followed Finn's instructions, aware that despite his Herculean strength, he could be surprisingly gentle. Then, at last, a thin, long-legged calf was lying safe on the straw, being proudly licked by its mother.

'Oh, isn't it sweet?' I said, tears pricking my eyelids.

'Well done,' said Finn. I felt as though he'd given me the Nobel Prize. 'Come inside and have a wash. Bridget'll give us a cup of tea.'

On the boat home he said, 'You look absolutely whacked.'

'It isn't often I spend the afternoon playing midwife to a cow,' I said.

'Come along to the surgery tomorrow,' he said. 'I'd like to have a look at you.'

I blushed, absurdly flattered at his concern.

'How's the hospital going?' I asked.

'Fine. Three wards completed already.'

'You must be run off your feet.'

He shrugged his shoulders. 'I've got a new intern starting next week which'll help.'

'What's he like?'

'It's a she.'

'Oh,' I said, momentarily nonplussed. 'What's she like?'

'Very attractive. I chose her myself.'

'For yourself?'

'Bit early to tell. I'm a romantic, I suppose. All part of the Celtic hang-up. I don't think the man-woman thing should be conducted on a rabbit level.'

The lights were coming on in Penlorren now,

pale in the fading light. I felt stupidly displeased at the thought of some glamorous woman doctor working with Finn. I saw her with slim ankles, and not a hair out of place, white coat open to show an ample cashmere bosom.

'What happened to your marriage?' I asked.

'My wife liked having a Harley Street husband, and giving little dinner parties in the suburbs with candlelight and sparkling wine.'

'Oh dear,' I said, giggling. 'Not quite your forté?'

'On the contrary, I look very good by candle-light. It was my fault as much as hers. She was beautiful, capable and absolutely bored me to death. I married her without really knowing her. Most people don't love human beings anyway. They just love an idealized picture in their heads.'

I looked at his face, softened now. I've never liked red hair, but Finn's was very dark and thick and grew beautifully close to his head. I've never liked freckles either, or broken noses, but he had extraordinary eyes, yellow-flecked, with thick black lashes, and his mouth, now it wasn't set in its usual hard line, was beautiful. The wind was blow-ing his trousers against his hard, muscular legs. He was in great shape, too. In spite of his size, he moved about the boat like a cat.

'Are you coming to Coco's party tonight?' I asked.

'I might,' he said. 'Depends what's up at the hospital.'

'Please come,' I said, then blushed. 'I mean, if you're not too busy.'

18

Rory was in the bath when I got back, wearing my bath cap but still managing to look absurdly handsome.

'Come in,' he said. 'I'm indecent. Where have you been?'

'Out and about,' I said. 'Can I have that bath after you?'

I went into the bedroom. I didn't want to tell him about Finn.

He followed me, dripping from the bath.

'Where's my white silk shirt?' he asked.

'Oh, er, I'm glad you asked that question.'

'Is this it?' he said, pulling a crumpled pink rag of a shirt out of the pillowcase of washing on the bed.

'Well, it could be,' I said.

'God,' said Rory. He went on pulling crumpled pink shirts out like a conjurer whipping out coloured handkerchiefs. 'How do you manage it?' he asked.

'I left one of my red silk scarves in the machine by mistake,' I said, miserably.

'Next time you want to do some dyeing, just count me out,' he said, and starting to get dressed, he put both feet into one leg of his underpants and fell over, which didn't improve his temper.

'How was Edinburgh?' I said, knowing that Marina had her singing lesson there once a fortnight.

He paused a second too long. 'I've been to Glasgow,' he said, evenly.

Rubbed raw with rancour, we arrived at the party. It was a dazzling affair, all the locals done up to the eyeballs in wool tweed. I was wearing about a quarter as much clothing as everyone else.

'Pretty as a picture,' said Buster, coming and squeezing me.

'Happy Birthday,' said Rory. 'I thought of buying you a book, Buster, but I knew you'd already got one.'

I heard someone laugh behind us. It was Marina, looking ravishing in a high-necked, amber wool dress with long sleeves. I'd forgotten about her being so beautiful. Since Christmas, she had become, in my tortured imagination, a sort of man-eating gorgon, with snakes writhing in her hair and corpses strewn about her feet. She smiled into Rory's eyes and went over to say hello to Coco.

Even the high-necked dress couldn't conceal two dark bruises under her chin.

'She's got love bites all over her neck,' I hissed at Rory out of the corner of my mouth.

'I suppose you recognize the teeth marks,' he hissed back.

'Well, they couldn't be Hamish's,' I said. 'He hasn't got any teeth left.'

'E-m-ilee,' said Rory quietly, 'you've got very bitchy since I married you.'

'You were bitchy before I married you!' I snapped.

'It must be catching.'

The party was a roaring success.

Everyone drank a great deal too much. I was sitting on the sofa with Rory several hours later, when Marina came up and sat down beside us.

'Hello darlings. I've decided to give up Hamish for Lent. Do you think Elizabeth's dress quite comes off?' she added, pointing at a fat blonde.

'It will do later in the evening, if I know Elizabeth,' said Rory.

Buster came up and filled up our drinks.

'Hello, Emily,' he said. 'You look a bit bleak. Not having words with Rory, I hope.'

'Rory and I don't have words any more, we just have silences,' I said, getting somewhat unsteadily to my feet.

'Come back,' said Rory. 'Buster wants to look down your dress.'

But I fled out of the room, falling over Buster's labrador who took it in extremely bad part. Why didn't Finn come? Every time the doorbell rang I hoped it was him. People were dancing in the dining-room now. I talked for hours to some dreary laird with a haw-haw voice and a come-hither look in his eye.

Hamish came up to us. He looked greyer and more haggard than ever, but his eyes had lost none of their goatish gleam.

'Emily,' he said, 'I haven't talked to you all evening. Come and dance.'

How could I refuse? On the dance floor, Rory and Marina were swaying very respectably, two feet apart. It was just the way they were looking at each other, like souls in torment.

'Just like lovebirds, aren't they?' said Hamish bitterly.

I looked at him startled.

'On second thoughts,' he said, 'it's time you and I had a little chat.'

He led me into a study off the hall, and shut the door. My heart was thumping unpleasantly.

'What do you want?' I said.

'Just to talk. Doesn't that little ménage upset you?'

'What ménage?' I said quickly.

'My lovely wife and your handsome husband. We've each been dealt a marked card, darling. Neither of them gives a damn about us.'

'I don't want to listen,' I said, going towards the door.

'But you must,' he said, catching my arm, his face suddenly alight with malevolence. 'It's quite a story. When Marina married me six months ago, I was foolish enough to think she cared for me. But, within weeks, I realized she only wanted me for my money.'

'If she was after money,' I said, 'why didn't she marry Rory? He's just as rich as you are.'

'Just as rich,' said Hamish. 'But Rory, if you remember, only inherited his money after he married you. That was one of the conditions of Rory's father, Hector's, will. Rory wouldn't get a bean until he was safely married.'

'Then why didn't he marry Marina?'

'That was another condition of the will. Hector made another condition that if he married Marina, he wouldn't get a penny. It would all go to charity.

So he married you to get his hands on the cash.'

I felt myself go icy cold.

'But I don't understand,' I whispered. 'That doesn't sound like Rory at all. If he'd really wanted to marry Marina, he wouldn't have cared a damn about not inheriting the money. He could easily have got a job, or earned money from his painting, if he'd wanted to.'

'Oh, my poor child,' said Hamish mockingly. 'What a lot you've got to learn. Can't you understand that it's not possible for Rory ever to marry Marina, money or no money?'

'Why not?' I said.

'Because they're brother and sister.'

'What!' I gasped in horror. 'They can't be.'

'I'm afraid so. Hector, laird of the island, Lord Lieutenant, pillar of respectability on the surface, was an old ram on the side. Like claiming *droit de seigneur* and all that. He was very keen on Marina's mother for a long time. I'm afraid the result was Marina.'

I felt as though I was going to faint.

'Brother and sister,' I whispered again.

'Well, half-brother and -sister. Hardly a healthy union. Particularly as there's always been a strong strain of insanity in Hector's family. But it doesn't seem to deter them, does it?

'How long have they known?' I muttered.

'Only about a year. There's always been a blood feud between the Balniels and the Macleans, as you know. So when Rory and Marina fell in love, they didn't exactly broadcast the fact, until one night Rory got drunk and had a row with Hector (they never really got on) and told him he was going to marry Marina. Hector nearly burst a gut. The next day he told Rory the truth, and that under no circumstances could he marry Marina. Rory went berserk with rage. The shock killed Hector. He died that night of a heart attack. But the will still stood.'

'My God,' I said, dully.

'So Marina married me in a fit of despair,' Hamish went on. 'And Rory went south and married you, which drove Marina mad with jealousy. And now, as you see, they're up to their old tricks.'

My brain was reeling. I felt as if I'd been kicked in the gut. Marina and Rory, brother and sister: Byron and Augusta Leigh, star-crossed lovers, a union so fatally seductive because it was impossible.

'Oh, poor Rory,' I breathed, 'now I understand. Oh, poor, poor Rory.'

'Poor you and me,' breathed Hamish in my ear.

He was standing very close to me, one hand fondling my wrist, his eyes fixed on my face in a greedy way. I could feel the warmth of his body, his hand stealing up my bare arm, his hot breath on my shoulder.

'You mustn't be shy of me, little Emily,' he said caressingly, slipping his arm round my waist. 'I think you're very pretty, even if Rory doesn't. Why don't we console one another?'

'No!' I screamed. 'No, no, no! Go away, you revolting old man. Don't touch me!'

I leapt to my feet, ran across the room, wrenched open the door and went slap into Finn Maclean.

'Hello,' he said. 'I've been looking for you.' Then he looked at me more closely. 'Hey, what's the matter?'

'Nothing, everything,' I sobbed, and shoving him violently aside, I fled past him.

I ran out into the garden. It had been snowing again, the drive was virginally white in the pale moonlight. All was deathly silent. The snow lay soft and tender on the lawn. Crying great, heaving sobs, I ran to the edge of the cliffs. The sea stretched out, opaque, black and star-powdered. The lighthouse flashed like a blue gem, the rocks gleamed evilly two hundred feet below.

'Oh, Rory,' I sobbed. 'I can't go on, I can't go on.'

But as I took a step forward, my arm was caught in a vice-like grip.

'Don't be a bloody little fool,' said a voice. 'Nothing's that important.'

It was Finn.

'Let me go,' I sobbed. 'I want to die.'

He held on to my arm and finally I collapsed against him.

'Oh, Finn,' I sobbed. 'What am I going to do?'

He held me for a minute, then, putting an arm round my shoulders, he half carried me across the snow to the stables where Buster kept his horses.

I collapsed on to a pile of hay, still sobbing bitterly. Finn let me cry; he just sat there stroking my shoulders. Finally I gulped, 'It's not true, is it, Marina and Rory both being Hector's children?'

Finn paused, his hand tightening on my shoulder, then he said, 'It is, I'm afraid.'

'Oh, God,' I said. 'Why didn't anyone tell me?'

'No-one knew except me and Rory and Marina. Marina must have told Hamish. Even Coco doesn't know about it.'

'How long have you known?' I said dully.

'As long as I can remember. I got back from school early one afternoon. I heard laughter coming from the bedroom and went in and found my mother in bed with Hector. My father was away at the time. I ran and hid in the woods. My father came home that night and sent out a search party. When they found me, my father thrashed me for worrying my mother. I never told him the truth. I suppose kids have a sort of honour even at that age. But I never forgave Hector, and he never forgave me for discovering what an old fraud he was.'

'So you always knew Rory and Marina were brother and sister?'

He nodded. 'About a year ago, I came back from London for a weekend and discovered, to my horror, they'd fallen in love and were thinking of getting married. I tried to stop Marina, but she'd got the bit between her teeth by then, so I went to Hector and told him he'd got to tell Rory the truth.'

'Not a very pretty story, is it?' I said.

'That's why I've been behaving like a policeman, trying to keep them apart,' said Finn. 'With insanity on both sides and a blood tie between them, it would be absolutely fatal if Rory got Marina pregnant.'

I sat numbly, trying to take it all in. Finn was holding me in his arms now, stroking my hair, soothing me like a child. I felt the hardness of his body, the gentleness of his hands. It was so long since I'd been in a man's arms. I've always said I have no sense of timing.

His mouth was so near to mine. Almost instinctively, I put my face up and kissed him. The next moment he was kissing me back.

'Heavens,' I said, wriggling away, absolutely appalled. 'I'm terribly sorry.'

'Don't be,' he said softly. 'It's one of the nicest surprises I've ever had,' and he kissed me again. This time it was a kiss that meant business. I tried to be frigid and unyielding, but could feel the warm waves of lust coasting all over me. I felt my body go weak. I was torn between desire and utter exhaustion.

'Strange things happen in stables,' I muttered weakly. 'One moment I'm a midwife, next moment I'm bowling towards adultery. Talk about My Tart Is In The Highlands.'

Finn smiled, got up and pulled me to my feet.

'Come on, I'm taking you home.'

'Please don't,' I said.

'Listen,' he said. 'I never meant this to happen when I brought you in here. I want you very much, but I think now is neither the time nor the place. You're slightly drunk and you're suffering from severe shock. I'm not going to let you do anything you might regret in the morning.'

He drove me home. Outside the house he burrowed in his bag and produced a couple of sleeping pills.

'Take them tonight, immediately you get in, and come and see me at the surgery tomorrow at eleven. Then we can talk things over.'

When I got in I hardly had the strength to undress. I fell, rather than got, into bed, pulled the sheets like a curtain over my head and dropped into a deep sleep.

19

I woke up next morning feeling ghastly, went straight to the loo and was violently sick. I had a blinding headache, took four Alka-Seltzers and was sick again. Rory was still fast asleep.

I tiptoed around the bedroom getting my clothes on. I only just managed to make it to Finn's surgery.

There was only one woman in there when I arrived. Finn came out. He looked tired, but he smiled at me reassuringly.

'I'll just see Mrs Cameron first,' he said. 'She won't take long.'

I gazed unseeingly at magazines and wondered why I was feeling quite so awful. Finn's receptionist eyed me with interest.

Mrs Balniel looking like a road accident, she must have been thinking.

Mrs Cameron came out, thanking Finn effusively, and I went into his surgery.

It was large, and rather untidy, and amazingly comforting. Finn shut the door and leant against it. Then he came across the room and kissed me. It was a different kiss from last night. That was alcohol and pent-up emotion. This was slow, measured, tender, and left me just as weak with lust.

'Aren't we doing fearful things to the Hippocratic Oath?' I said, flopping on to a chair.

'I couldn't give a damn. You aren't my patient yet, though you ought to be, you look terrible!'

'Thanks,' I said.

'And infinitely desirable. Nothing a few weeks away from Rory wouldn't cure.'

'I was as sick as a dog all morning,' I said. 'Nerves and booze, I suppose.'

'I'll tell Miss Bates to shove off, then I'll give you a going over.'

'You'd better wipe that lipstick off first,' I said.

Finn laughed.

He wasn't laughing half an hour later.

'You're pregnant,' he said.

I was stunned by the news. 'But I can't be pregnant!' I gasped. 'Rory hasn't laid a finger on me for months.' Then I remembered. 'Oh, God,' I said.

'What's the matter?' asked Finn.

'After that row on Christmas Eve when you knocked Rory over, he was so mad with rage, he sort of raped me.'

'That must have been it,' said Finn.

My brain was whirling. Me – pregnant with Rory's child! What sort of chance would a baby have with Rory not loving me, and me fancying Finn absolutely rotten all of a sudden? I had a nightmare vision of Rory and me shouting at each other across the baby's cot, of the baby crying all day, and Rory going spare because he couldn't work.

'Oh, heavens,' I said shakily.

Finn went to a cupboard in the corner of the room and got out a bottle of brandy and two glasses. 'We'd better have a drink,' he said.

As I watched him fill the glasses, I was filled with a ridiculous mawkish sadness. I'll never be able to memorize every freckle on his face now, I thought, or see the grey hairs gradually take the fire out of that red mane.

He put a glass beside me, then took hold of my frozen hands. His were warm and strong and comforting; I felt an irresistible urge to collapse in tears on his shoulder.

'It's a hell of a mess,' he said gently, 'but it doesn't matter, we'll sort something out.'

'Can we?' I asked dolefully.

'Look,' he went on. 'You and Rory are washed up. Anyone can see that. Do you want to keep the baby?'

I thought for a minute. 'Yes I do. Very much.'

'That means you'll stay with Rory?'

'What else can I do?' I said bitterly. 'I'm signed up for this gig and I've got to play.'

'You can move in with me.'

The room reeled. For a moment all I could think of was the blissful sanctuary of Finn taking care of me.

'Oh, Finn,' I said, the tears welling up in my eyes, 'I'd drive you round the twist.'

'I wouldn't think so. We can always try.'

'But what about the baby?'

He shrugged his shoulders.

'It's Rory's,' I said, taking a slug of my brandy and nearly choking. 'You'd hate that, you'd keep seeing all the things you hate about Rory in its character. And your reputation on the island would be absolutely ruined – your worst enemy's wife shacking up with you, and pregnant to boot.'

'*My* reputation can take it,' said Finn.

'Is it because you want to score off Rory by taking me away from him?' I blurted out.

It was a terrible thing to say. Rory would have certainly hit me for it, but Finn merely looked at me consideringly.

'I don't know,' he said. 'I thought about that for a long time last night, after I'd dropped you off. Of course there's an element of truth. I don't have any compunction about taking you away from Rory. I know he's made you miserable and unhappy. But even if you were married to my best friend, I don't think it would make any difference. I'd still want you. It's one of the unattractive things about loving someone – one just suspends all moral values.' Then his face softened. 'But there are an awful lot of attractive things about it. Come here.'

'No,' I said desperately. 'Please, no.'

He held out his hands. 'Why not? I want you.'

'It's very noble of you to make the offer, but I couldn't.'

'Noble! What the hell are you talking about?'

'I know why you're asking me. It's from motives of altruism. Marina's your sister and you feel guilty about the way she and Rory have fouled up my life.'

Finn drained his glass. 'Emily, will you please stop talking nonsense! I'm the least altruistic person alive. Apart from being a doctor, I never do anything to please anyone except myself.'

'You took me sailing yesterday . . .'

'Look,' said Finn, 'I took you sailing yesterday

because I thought you needed a break. Now I realize I've wanted you since the first moment I saw you – pulling up my roses with your teeth – in a black see-through nightie.'

'Oh,' I felt myself blushing furiously. 'How kind of you to put it like that.'

'And you don't believe a word of it?'

'No, you'd never have asked me to move in with you if I hadn't been pregnant.' I searched feverishly for a tissue and mopped my eyes.

'Of course I wouldn't,' said Finn. 'I'd have taken it more slowly.'

'There's absolutely no point in shacking up with someone one hardly knows, who one's not in love with,' I said shakily. That stopped him.

'I suppose not,' he said grimly.

I gave my eyes a final wipe.

'I'm sorry. I don't mean to keep crying – it's the shock of the baby, and finding out about Rory and Marina last night. And, besides, I'd be hopeless for you – I mean long-term. I don't have the right face for greeting patients, and I'd forget to pass on messages about cardiacs and things.'

'We can still go on seeing each other.'

'No,' I said. 'When you're pregnant you can't go around carrying on with other people. I mean it turns you into a sort of nun, having a baby.'

Finn laughed, but bitterly. 'You know, do you? From your quarter of an hour's experience. You'll still have to come in for check-ups. If you don't want to see me, I suppose Jackie Barrett can look after you.'

'Who's she?'

'My new intern.'

Oh, God, I minded about her. I minded like hell.

130

I fought back the tears. I didn't dare kiss Finn, or I might have broken down.

'Goodbye and thank you,' I said.

Finn looked suddenly tired and defeated. 'All right, go back to Rory if you want to, but remember I'm here. You've only to pick up a telephone and I'll come and take you away.'

20

Which wasn't a very good basis for trying to rebuild a marriage. When I got home, I was all screwed up to tell Rory about the baby, but he was so immersed in slapping blue paint on a huge canvas, absolutely lost to the world, that I funked it and so, having not told him, I found it more and more difficult.

In fact, he was so obsessed with work for the next few weeks, he hardly noticed me at all.

I thought endlessly about the baby. No more staying in the cinema to see the film once again – got to get home to the baby-sitter. No more running away to sea. I thought of dirty nappies and sleepless nights, and maternity bras, and getting bigger and heavier, and less attractive to Rory.

But somehow, I felt excited too. Growing inside was something that, when it arrived, would really need me. Something I could love totally and unashamedly, as I wanted to love Rory, as circumstances had stopped me loving Finn.

I kept wanting to tell Rory. I bought a bottle of champagne, and day after day took it out of its hiding place at the back of a drawer, then funked it and put it away.

I made a concerted attempt to win Rory over sexually, but it had been 'God, I'm tired', for days now. As soon as I got into bed, he'd switch off his light, turn his back on me, and pretend to be asleep.

And I'd lie beside him, tears sliding into my hair, listening to the sea washing on the rocks below and thinking of Finn, who was probably still working, going out to deliver a baby or soothing a restless patient. His harsh, beautifully ugly face would swim before my eyes, and I would wonder how much longer I could hold out.

I went to every party on the island too, in the hope that I might see him, but he never turned up. Which meant I drank too much and was even sicker the morning after.

I did see Miss Barrett, the new intern, though. I couldn't resist having a gawp. I went in for a check-up and had a great shock. She was naturally blonde, and slim – one of those women who look marvellous without make-up – deep, subtle, competent, able to keep her mouth shut. The antithesis of me.

Did I imagine, too, an added warmth in her voice when she talked about Finn? Dr Maclean likes things done his way. Dr Maclean doesn't approve of pregnant women putting on too much weight. Dr Maclean recommends these vitamin pills.

'And Dr Maclean recommends me,' I wanted to shout at her. 'He's mine, and trespassers will be very much prosecuted.'

The weeks passed. Slowly I sank into despair. I could hardly bring myself to get up in the morning and get dressed. One Sunday morning, however, when I was trying to keep down some toast and marmalade, I suddenly caught Rory looking at me.

'You look awful,' he said. 'What are you trying to turn yourself into?'

Then followed a ten-minute invective about my general attitude towards him and everyone else on the island. I was lazy, childish, stubborn, stupid and unco-operative. Why didn't I do something instead of slopping around all day?

'What do you think I should be doing? Going to evening classes, exchanging meaningful glances over the basket-work and all that?' I said.

'Maybe; you could go out more, see people. Buster offered you his horses anytime you wanted to ride. Anything but this plastic tomb you've sealed yourself into.'

'Have you finished?' I whispered.

'Yes, for the time being. I'm sorry I came on so strong. I didn't mean to be quite so vicious, but I'm fed up with sharing a house with a zombie.'

I got up without looking at him and dragged myself upstairs. He was right. One look at myself in the mirror sent me yelping to the bathroom to wash my hair.

Then I rang Buster and asked if I could come and ride with him that afternoon. Rory was absurdly pleased and even rubbed my hair dry for me.

'Stay over at the castle when you've finished,' he said. 'I'll come over and take you all out to dinner.'

For the first time in months he kissed me.

Buster and I rode up the lower slopes through beech trees between mossy rocks. Walter Scott ran about, snorting and chasing rabbits. Finally we reached the top.

'Hospital's finished now,' said Buster, pointing

his whip at the new building on the right. 'Finn's got it up jolly fast. Have you been inside?'

I shook my head.

Buster's voice – the usual mixture of sex, gin and a dash of bitters – flowed on. 'Have you seen Finn's new popsy?'

I stiffened. 'Popsy?'

'Dr Barrett,' went on Buster. 'She's an absolute smasher. Took my lumbago to see her last week – can hardly keep my hands off her.'

'Are she and Finn having a walk-out?' I asked.

'Why do you think he brought her up here?' said Buster, as though it were a matter of course. 'Finn isn't daft.'

Black gloom overwhelmed me as I rode back down the hill. Finn in love with someone else. That left Rory and me, didn't it?

'I think I'll go straight home now,' I said.

'Isn't Rory taking us out to dinner?' asked Buster.

'He is,' I said, 'but there's something I want to tell him first. And I want to change too.'

We stabled the horses, and as I drove back home I decided now was the time to tell Rory about the baby.

'We'll have to face the music together, mate,' I said to the child inside me. 'Maybe he'll surprise us and be delighted after all.'

I went into the house and tiptoed upstairs to get the champagne. The bedroom door was open.

And I caught them red-handed.

21

Marina and Rory in bed. For a second all I could think was how beautiful they looked on my dark blue sheets – her glorious mass of red hair cascading all over the pillows. Just like a Hollywood film. Two people too beautiful for real life.

Then I screamed and they looked round. Marina recovered from the shock first.

'I'm sorry, Emily,' she said. 'But you had to know some time.'

'Oh, I've known,' I said. 'I've known for ages and I've known too about your being brother and sister.'

That rocked them.

'I mean, it's nice your keeping it in the family,' I went on, 'but that sort of thing is rather frowned on in the prayer book and by the law, I should think.'

I ran out of the room, locked myself in the loo and started to cry. After a few minutes someone came and rattled on the door.

'Go away!' I screamed. 'Use the other loo. This one's engaged.'

'Emily, it's me. Marina's gone. For God's sake come out. I want to help you.'

'Help me?' I felt my tears escalating into hysterical laughter. 'Help me? What can you do to help me?'

'Let me in, or I'll break the door down.'

'No!' I screamed. 'No! No!' There was a silence, and then an explosion.

I screamed again. The door was swinging and Rory was standing in the doorway, a smoking gun in his hand. He'd shot the lock out.

'Now, come out!' he said, grabbing my arm and dragging me into the bedroom. Walter Scott sat whimpering in the corner.

'I know why you married me,' I hissed. 'Just to release the cash from Hector's will, to give you a front of respectability so you could carry on with Marina, your dear little sister.'

Rory was trembling. 'Who told you all this?' he said.

'Hamish did,' I said.

'He's a swine,' said Rory.

'He's unhappy,' I said. 'He didn't want anyone to be left out. He certainly hasn't behaved any worse than you.'

'When you're desperate, you suspend any kind of morality,' Rory said, echoing Finn's words of two months before.

Then he told me, quietly and without any emotion, that when he'd first met me, he'd been very attracted to me, had thought I was so gentle, loving and understanding, that we might even make a go of it. He said he had intended, had tried desperately hard, to break it off with Marina, but had failed to do so. And there was nothing he could plead by way of excuse or justification. Volcanoes of invective and abuse kept boiling up inside me, and sinking down again. It was his detachment that paralysed my powers of speech. But for the cold, fixed shadows in his eyes, and his deathly pallor, he seemed his normal self.

'Marina and I do realize we're social pariahs, in the wilderness for good and all. She's upset, of course, because she can't have my children.'

'She's upset,' I breathed. 'Oh, boy, do I feel sympathy for her. I suppose it's more exciting, doing it here in our bed. It's much more exotic than turning on ten miles away where I couldn't possibly catch you.'

He looked at me. Did I imagine there was a flicker of despair in his eyes.

Then he said the fatal words.

'I'm sorry, Em.'

'Get out,' I hissed. 'Get out! Get out.'

He stood irresolute for a minute.

'I don't want to spend another minute under the same roof as you,' I said.

I suppose that was the cue he wanted. Within two minutes he'd thrown his things into a suitcase and Walter and he were gone.

Whimpering with terror, I rushed to the telephone.

I recognized Jackie Barrett's voice immediately. There was music in the background.

'Can I speak to Dr Maclean?' I said.

'Just a minute.' How cool and off-hand she sounded. 'Is it urgent? He's very tied up at the moment.'

'Yes it is. Very urgent.'

'Who's that speaking?'

'It's personal.'

'Finn, darling,' she said, and I could just imagine

her turning up her palms in a gesture of helplessness. 'I'm afraid it's for you.'

I slammed down the receiver.

Rory gone. Finn obviously taken care of by Dr Barrett. That left the baby and me.

'You're the only thing I've got now,' I said numbly.

It wouldn't take me long to pack my suitcase, either. If I hurried I could catch the seven o'clock ferry.

I rang for a taxi.

When the doorbell rang I grabbed Rory's dark glasses to hide my swollen eyes, gathered up my two suitcases and walked to the top of the stairs. I suppose I must have missed the top step. The next moment I was falling. The pain was something I'd never known or could ever have imagined. The rest was blackness.

22

Through a haze of pain, I kept dreaming of Marina and Rory in bed together, writhing like snakes on those navy-blue sheets.

Then I heard a familiar voice say, 'The doses have been exceptionally strong, but her reflexes are much better.'

A woman's voice said, 'It's unlikely we'll get a peep out of her for twenty-four hours.'

Painfully, battling with nausea, I opened my eyes and there, miraculously, was Finn standing at the end of the bed talking to a nurse.

The image of Rory and Marina floated back in front of me, and I screamed.

Finn moved like lightning.

'Darling Emily, it's me.'

I went on screaming and yelling incoherently. He had his arms round me. 'I'll deal with her,' he said. The nurse melted away.

I sat rigid. 'I remember everything that happened,' I said.

'It's Finn, Emily darling.'

I stopped screaming and collapsed against him. 'Oh, Finn! Help me!'

'You've had a bad dream.'

'I remember everything.' My lips began to tremble. 'You promise not to do anything to find Rory? Not anything!'

'Don't worry,' he reassured me.

He persuaded me to lie back on the pillows, but kept a firm grip on my hand.

'Don't go away,' I whispered.

'I'm staying right here.'

'I thought you didn't want me any more, and then I found Rory and Marina . . .'

'Steady, darling, don't think about it. You're going to get better.'

'But I saw them in bed together! I saw them!'

The edge of the cliff began to crumble. I started to scream and lash about. The nurse came back with a hypodermic syringe. I tried to struggle, but Finn held me still. Whatever it was they gave me worked instantly.

Next time I surfaced, I was calmer. I was in an ugly, fawn but sunny room. A fat nurse was arranging some daffodils in a blue vase. There were flowers everywhere. 'Is this a funeral parlour?' I asked.

She rushed over and started fumbling with my pulse.

'Where am I?'

'In hospital.'

'Good old hospital. With hot and cold housemen in every bedroom.'

'I'll get Dr Maclean,' she said, and belted off. I heard mutterings in the passage about 'still being delirious'. Finn walked into the room.

'Jump in, Doctor,' I said, 'we'll be delirious together.'

'It sounds as though she's recovered,' Finn said to the nurse.

He was one of those rewarding men who can betray emotion in public. His yellow eyes were filled with tears as he looked down at me.

'Hello, baby.'

'Hello,' I said.

'Don't try to talk.'

'I missed you,' I said, 'I missed you horribly.'

He smiled. 'I suppose you must have. You talked enough in your sleep.' He looked absolutely grey with tiredness. The dope they'd given me had removed every vestige of my self-control. 'I do love you,' I said. 'You've got such a lovely face.'

They kept me under gradually reduced sedation for the first forty-eight hours, bringing me back to earth slowly. I can't remember when the baby drifted back into my consciousness, but I remember suddenly saying to Finn in panic, 'The baby? It's all right, isn't it?'

He took my hand. 'I'm afraid you lost it. We tried to save it, darling, you must believe that.'

I felt gripped by a piercing sadness. Then I said, 'Where's Rory?'

'He's fine.'

I said: 'Where's Rory? Tell me the truth, Finn.'

The yellow eyes flickered for a moment. 'He hasn't come back. He must be on the mainland somewhere.'

'With Marina?'

He nodded. 'I presume so. She disappeared the night you fell down the stairs. Neither of them has been seen since.'

23

I lay in my hospital bed for I don't know how many days, dully watching the beauty of the Highland spring. Among this building of nests and mating of birds and animals, I felt alien and outcast. I ached for the baby I had lost. A brisk, bossy nurse looked after me, Nurse McKellen. She had come-to-bedpan eyes, and tried to fill me up with pills and pretty revolting food.

'Couldn't I have a nurse with a sense of humour?' I asked Finn.

'Not on the Health Service,' he said.

I longed inordinately for his visits. He used to pop in during the mornings or late in the evenings after visiting hours and just sit holding my hand and telling me about his day, or letting me rave on about Rory and the baby, if I felt like it.

Once, when Jackie Barrett came in, he didn't even let go of my hand.

'She's getting better,' he told her.

'Good,' she said crisply. 'You gave us all a fright,' she added to me.

I thought I detected a few chips of ice in her blue eyes.

'I thought you were having an *affaire* with her,' I said after she'd gone.

Finn looked surprised.

'She answered the telephone the night I rang, and sounded awfully proprietorial.'

'She had no need to,' said Finn. 'We were only watching some medical programme on television.'

After that I felt much happier. I slept a lot. Finn still wouldn't allow me any visitors and I didn't want any. But at the back of my mind was a great deal of dread and expectation. I didn't have to wait long.

Two days later I was lying in bed half asleep.

Suddenly there was a commotion outside and a familiar voice saying impatiently, 'Where is she?'

Immediately I was awake and drenched with sweat, my pulses pounding.

'Don't be so bloody stupid,' continued the voice. 'I'm her husband!'

Then Nurse McKellen's voice, anxious and flustered. 'I'm sorry, Dr Maclean's orders are that she has no visitors.'

'Then I'll go through the wards waking every patient till I find her.'

'You dinna understand, sir, Mrs Balniel's been verra ill. She had severe concussion and internal haemorrhage as well, and she's been very depressed since she regained consciousness, learning about losing the baby, poor wee lassie.'

'The what?' Rory's voice was like the crack of a whip. 'What did you say?'

'Since she lost the bairn. You must have been disappointed too, sir?'

Then Rory's voice hissing through his teeth. 'Where is she, damn you?'

And Nurse McKellen's high-pitched shriek. 'Don't you lay your hands on me, young man! All right, Mrs Balniel's in there, but I'll no answer for Dr Maclean when he comes back.'

I heard a quick step outside. A moment later the door was flung open and in strode Rory. 'So there you are.'

'Hello, Rory,' I croaked.

He was beside the bed, black eyes blazing, his face deathly pale against the black fur of his coat.

'What's this about a baby?' he demanded. 'Is it true?'

I nodded.

'How long had you known?'

'About two months.'

'Why the hell didn't you tell me?'

'I tried to,' I said miserably. 'I wanted to so badly. I just didn't feel up to it.'

'And you threw me out without even letting me know of its existence!'

'I didn't think you'd be interested.'

'Not interested in my own child?'

'Mr Balniel.' It was Nurse McKellen again, her starched bosom heaving. 'We mustn't disturb Mrs Balniel.'

Rory didn't turn his head.

'Get out, you fat bitch,' he said.

Then, when she didn't he turned on her. One look at the murderous expression on his face and she scarpered.

'How did it happen?' he asked.

'I was wearing your dark glasses. I must have missed the top step of the stairs and conked out when I hit the bottom.'

145

'I suppose you don't remember anything about it?' he said.

'Not much,' I said slowly, 'but I remember very vividly what happened before.'

Rory side-stepped the issue. 'Why the hell couldn't you have told me about the baby before?' he said. 'It was criminally irresponsible of you, I hope you realize that?'

'I knew you were in love with Marina,' I said feebly. 'If I'd told you about the baby you'd have thought I was trying to trap you.'

'That's the most fatuous remark I've ever heard,' snapped Rory. 'I suppose it *was* my child?'

I burst into tears. At that moment Finn walked in. He was livid. You could feel the hatred sizzling between the two men like summer lightning.

'What's going on?' Finn said to Nurse McKellen.

'Make him go away,' I sobbed.

'Leave her alone,' thundered Finn. 'Get out of here. Do you want her to have a complete relapse?'

'She's my wife,' said Rory, 'I'm entitled to stay with her.'

'Not if you're going to make her ill. Look at her.'

Finn sat down on the bed and put his arms round me. 'There lovie, it's all right.'

'I can't take any more,' I sobbed into Finn's shoulder. 'Please make him go away.'

Finn looked up. Rory was ashen, his fists clenched.

'Now are you going to get out?' said Finn.

Rory walked out, slamming the door behind him.

24

Next day Finn flew round the island to visit his patients, and Rory rolled up at visiting time. He looked tired, sulky, unshaven, but still illogically handsome.

Oh, please, don't let me fall under his spell again.

He brought with him a huge bunch of lilies-of-the-valley, two tins of *pâté de foie gras*, a pornographic novel and a bottle of Lucozade.

'The meat paste is from my mother,' he said. 'Buster sent the piece of porn. He said he enjoyed it, which is no great recommendation. They all send love.'

Then he handed me the Lucozade bottle.

'This should get you through the long evenings. It's whisky and water actually, but if you keep the top on I defy even Dr Maclean to tell the difference.'

I giggled. 'How did you get in here?' I said. 'I should have thought Finn would have put blood-hounds on the gates.'

'I batted my eyelashes at a rather formidable blonde called Dr Barrett. She said I could see you for a quarter of an hour.'

'That figures,' I said.

'How are you?' I asked.

'I'm fine,' said Rory.

'Who's looking after you?' I said, then blushed furiously. 'I mean . . . I didn't mean to pry.'

'No-one's looking after me,' he said.

I was dying to ask where Marina was, but suddenly I felt exhausted, like a hostess at the end of a party when no-one's enjoyed themselves.

'You don't have to stay,' I said. 'It's awfully boring visiting people in hospital.'

'Sick of me already, are you?'

I looked up and he was staring at me, as if for the first time. He went on staring until I dropped my eyes in embarrassment.

He got up to go. 'I'll come back tomorrow,' he said. 'I'm sorry about the baby.'

Then he did the strangest thing. He leant forward and did up the four undone buttons of my nightie.

'I don't want Finn looking at your tits,' he said.

He turned up every day after that. Neither of us mentioned Marina. I was surprised how nice he could be – not mocking, not bored, but I found his visits a terrible strain. If Finn knew about them, he didn't say anything.

One day, a week later, a heavily pregnant girl was rushed into the room next door to have her baby. She was very young and frightened, and her husband looked even younger and more scared. But their tenderness for one another made me once again realize what I had lost.

When Finn came in later in his overcoat, just off on his rounds, he found me in tears.

He understood at once. 'Is it the girl next door?' he asked.

I nodded miserably. 'It's just triggered off memories,' I said.

'Don't be unhappy,' he said, putting his arms around me. 'There's years ahead for you to have babies.'

The door opened. I jumped and looked around. Rory stood in the doorway looking distinctly menacing. Going absolutely scarlet, I leapt away from Finn; then thought, why the hell should I after the way Rory's treated me?

'I thought you weren't coming until later,' I stammered.

'So I notice,' he snapped. 'Shall I leave you to it?'

'Don't be stupid,' I said. 'Finn's just off on his rounds.'

'I'm quite happy to stay here if you think you'll need protection,' Finn said.

Rory set his teeth and strolled into the middle of the room. A muscle was pounding in his cheek.

Before he could speak, I quickly said, 'I'm able to take care of myself, thanks.'

Rory glared furiously at Finn until he was out of the room. 'If you don't want me to smash the hell out of him, you'd better not start necking with him any more. OK?'

'Quite OK,' I said. 'But quite honestly, you're being fatuous. Only jealousy could merit such rage, and as you self-confessedly don't love me, why the hell should you be jealous?'

'I believe in protecting my own property,' said Rory.

'Anyway, he wasn't necking with me,' I said. 'He was comforting me. I was miserable about losing the baby.'

Rory came towards me, holding out his

arms. 'It's me who ought to comfort you,' he said gently.

I shrank away from him, terrified. I started to cry.

'Oh, for Christ's sake,' he snapped.

'I'm not up to rows,' I bleated.

He prowled up and down the room. 'What a horrible place this is,' he said. 'It's time you came home.'

'I can't!' I yelped. 'I've been very ill. Finn says I'm not strong enough to go home yet!'

25

Later that evening I tried to read Buster's pornographic novel while the little girl had her baby next door. I held my ears to blot out her screams, and the voice of her husband trying to reassure her. Finally, I heard the lusty yelling of the new-born baby.

Later, going out to the loo, I saw the husband outside the room, tears pouring down his face.

'Is she all right?' I asked.

He nodded. 'She's wonderful, and the baby's fine. A wee boy. We're going to call him Finn after Dr Maclean.'

'How would you like some whisky?' I said.

'I wouldna say no to a drop.'

I took him back to my room and got out the Lucozade bottle. An hour later we were sitting on my bed as tight as two ticks, laughing immoderately over passages in Buster's novel. It was Nurse McKellen who discovered us. She was absolutely appalled.

I escaped to the loo, giggling feebly. I felt very peculiar. 'At least I've got some colour in my cheeks,' I said, looking at my flushed, wild-eyed face in the mirror.

Outside, I found Finn. I looked down the passage. There was no-one there.

'Hello, darling,' I whispered.

'What have you been up to?' he said. 'Nurse McKellen's spreading terrifying tales of drunken orgies.'

I giggled and collapsed against him.

'You have been drinking,' he said.

'On the emptiest stomach in the Western Isles,' I said, 'and it's gone right down to my toes. I've been celebrating the birth of little Finn the second, and reading porn. So I feel fantastically sexy.'

Finn tried to look disapproving, and then laughed. I wound my arms round his neck and kissed him. After a minute's hesitation, he kissed me back, long and hard, until the blood was drumming in my head and I thought I was going to faint.

'Wow, do I feel sexy,' I murmured.

'How the hell do you think I feel?' he said.

A telephone shrilled in the next room.

'I'd better answer that,' he said. 'I'll deal with you later.'

'I've got you under my sk-in, I've got you de-heep in the heart of me,' I sang as I swayed down the passage, slap into Rory standing in the shadows. He must have seen everything.

'Oh, God,' I said, going briskly into reverse. He caught my arm and held on tightly.

'You bloody phoney,' he hissed. 'You bloody little phoney. All that *Dame aux Camelias* act. Not feeling well enough to get out of bed, you said. Depends on whose bed, doesn't it? Doctor Maclean won't let you leave. I bet he won't. You're having a ball together, aren't you – *aren't you*!' he yelled.

I looked around for a convenient second-floor window to jump out of.

'You don't understand,' I muttered.

'Oh, I do, baby, I understand only too well.'

The whole thing was getting too much for me. With a sigh I forced myself to look at him. I'd never seen him so cold with rage.

'You're coming home tonight, before you get up to any more tricks,' he said.

That moment Finn came out of the side door. I thought they'd have a right old set-to, but I was wrong. Finn had other things on his mind now.

'A petrol ship's blown up outside the harbour,' he said. 'They're bringing the survivors back in the life-boats. Most of them are likely to have second- or third-degree burns.'

'So you'll be needing all the beds you can get,' said Rory.

'Yes, we will,' said Dr Barrett, coming down the hall.

'I'll take Emily home then,' said Rory.

'That's an excellent idea,' said Dr Barrett warmly – the scheming cow.

Finn looked as though he was about to protest, then thought better of it. 'If you can take her to the castle,' he said, 'where there's someone to look after her. See that she rests as much as possible.'

'Of course,' said Rory. 'Do you need any help?'

'I'll ring you if we do, but most of the poor bastards will have had it.'

'The ambulance is leaving, Finn,' said Jackie Barrett, going towards the stairs.

'Just coming,' said Finn. He looked at me as though he wanted to say something, but I could feel him sliding away, both mentally and physically.

'I'll ring tomorrow and see how you're getting on,' he said. Then he was gone.

I felt overwhelmed with desolation and fear.

'And now, Emily dear,' said Rory softly, 'I think it's time you came home.'

We didn't speak on the way back from the hospital, but as the castle loomed into view, Rory shot straight past it.

'Finn said you were to take me to the castle,' I bleated.

'You're coming home,' snapped Rory, 'where I can keep an eye on you.'

'You can't force me to stay with you.'

'I can – even if I have to strap you to the bed.'

'Go directly to jail,' I chanted. 'Do not pass go, do not collect £200.'

I steeled myself for chaos when we got home. But the house looked marvellous. Someone had obviously been having a massive blitz. Rory steered me into the studio. The canvases had all been stacked neatly into one corner, a huge log fire blazed, and the smell of wood smoke mingled exotically with the scent of a big bowl of blue hyacinths on the window-sill.

'Anyone would think you were expecting company,' I said.

'I was,' said Rory grimly. 'You. I came to the hospital to collect you.'

'Oh, very masterful,' I said, collapsing on to the divan in the corner.

Rory poured himself a good mahogany-coloured whisky.

'I'd like one, too,' I said.

'You've had enough,' he said.

He leaned against the mantelpiece, a long stick he had been about to throw into the fire in his hands. The expression on his face scared me – he was quite capable of beating me up.

'Now,' he said, 'just how long have you been having an affair with Maclean?'

'I haven't,' I said.

'Don't lie to me,' he thundered.

'Affairs begin below the waist,' I protested. 'All Finn has done is kiss me – three times, to be exact.'

'You counted them?'

'Yes I did! Because they mattered.'

'And where did all this restraint take place?'

'Finn looked after me the night I found out you and Marina were brother and sister. But the next day, as soon as I discovered I was pregnant, we stopped seeing each other. Tonight I'd been at the whisky and Buster's porny novel, so when I met Finn in the passage, I suddenly fancied him rotten.'

There was a crack – Rory had snapped the lath in his hands. He was silent for a minute, his face strangely dead, then he threw the broken sticks on the fire. 'You're nothing better than a tart,' he said.

'I don't want to be better than a tart,' I said. 'Men seem to rather like them.'

'Well it's got to stop,' said Rory.

'You have the teremity . . .' I said.

'Temerity,' interrupted Rory.

'I'll say teremity if I like. You have the terem . . . or whatever it's called . . . to carry on with Marina behind my back, and then kick up a dog-in-the-manger rumpus, just because I seek a little consolation from Finn. You're only livid because

155

you hate Finn, not because you care a scrap for me.'

'Shut up,' said Rory. 'You're drunk – you'd better go up to bed.'

'No!' I shrieked. 'I can't do it.'

'Do what?'

'Sleep in that bed. Not after seeing you and Marina . . . I get nightmares night after night . . . I couldn't sleep there, I couldn't!' My voice was rising hysterically.

Rory caught my arm. 'Stop it, Em! You're behaving like a child.'

'Let me go!' I screamed. 'I hate you. I hate you!'

After that I said every terrible thing I could think of, and then started hysterically beating my fists against his chest. Finally, he was reduced to slapping me across the face, and I collapsed, sobbing, on the divan.

26

I awoke next morning with an awful head. I lay for a moment with my eyes closed. Slowly, painfully, I pieced together the happenings of the night before. I looked around me, wincing. I was in the studio.

Then, suddenly, I remembered Rory had hit me. 'The louse,' I muttered, getting unsteadily to my feet. In the mirror above the fire, I examined my face. Not a bruise in sight – how infuriating. My eyes lit on Rory's oil paints on a nearby table. Why shouldn't I paint in a black eye myself?

Soon I was busy slapping on blue and crimson paint – now a touch of yellow. Rory wasn't the only artist round here. Within five minutes I looked exactly like Henry Cooper after a few brisk rounds with Cassius Clay. Hearing a step outside, I hurriedly jumped into bed.

Rory came in, carrying a glass of orange juice.

'Awake, are you?' he said. 'How are you feeling?'

'Not very good,' I quavered.

'Don't deserve to, after all that liquor you shipped.'

Then he caught sight of the bruise.

'Heavens! Where did that come from?'

'I think you must have hit me,' I said in a martyred voice. 'I don't remember much about it – it must have been quite a blow. But I can't really believe you would have thumped me on my first night home – me being so weak and all. Perhaps I bumped into a door.'

Rory looked as discomfited as I've ever seen him.

'You were hysterical,' he said. 'It was the only way to shut you up. I'm sorry, Em. Does it hurt?'

'Agony,' I said, closing my eyes. A flood of vindictiveness warmed my blood.

'Let's have a look,' he said.

'Don't come near me,' I hissed.

He put a hand under my chin and forced my face up.

'Poor Em,' he said shaking his head. 'What a brute I am.'

'You should be more careful in future,' I said.

'I will, I will,' he said getting to his feet. He looked the picture of contrition. 'And next time don't add so much ochre. Bruises don't usually go yellow till the second day.'

I opened my mouth, shut it again, and started to giggle. I giggled till the tears, and the bruise, ran down my cheeks, until Rory started laughing too.

After that I slept for most of the day. When I woke up, Rory was painting and it was dark outside.

'What time is it?'

'About six.'

Six o'clock – suddenly I wondered what had happened to Finn.

'Did anyone ring?' I asked.

Rory had his back to me. There was a pause, then he said nastily, 'Your boyfriend did telephone about half an hour ago. I told him you were asleep. I'm just going down to the village for some cigarettes,' he added. 'Don't start getting out of bed, or making a bolt for it. I'd track you down in no time, and if you put me to the bother, you wouldn't find me in a very nice mood.'

27

As soon as he'd gone, I leapt out of bed and rang the hospital. Finn sounded relieved to hear me, but somehow detached.

'Are you OK, darling?'

'I'm fine,' I lied.

'Rory said you were asleep.'

'I was – but, oh, Finn, he's as touchy as gunpowder. I do need you – can't you come over later?'

'I can't, lovie, some of those poor sods from the petrol tanker are in pretty bad shape.'

'Oh, God.' Why did Finn always make me feel slightly ignoble? 'What a horrible, self-centred little bitch I am. I'd forgotten all about them.'

'I hadn't forgotten about you,' said Finn, then someone said something in the background. 'Look, darling, I've got to go. I'll try and come and see you tomorrow.'

The receiver clicked. At that moment Rory walked through the front door and stood in the doorway looking murderous.

'Have you gone quite mad?' he said softly. 'Standing in a howling draught when you're supposed to be in bed? Who were you talking to?'

'Coco. I was just letting her know I'm home.'

'She happens to be in London,' said Rory acidly. He walked towards me, put his hands on my shoulders, and gazed down at me for a minute. The fury seemed to die out of his eyes.

'Look,' he said, 'you think you're hung up on Finn, but he isn't the answer for you. He's married to his work, always has been. He's a man with no nonsense about him,' and for a minute his face softened. 'And you're a chick with an awful lot of nonsense about you, Em. Now go and get into bed and I'll bring you something to eat.'

I went back to bed and thought about Finn – but at the back of my mind, like an insistent tune, the thought kept repeating itself: if Finn had really loved me, he'd never have let me leave the hospital. He'd have whisked me back to his flat. Rory didn't love me at all, he loved Marina but even so, he'd been utterly single-minded about getting me home and keeping me there. I felt very confused and uncertain of my feelings. I wanted my mother.

Next morning the telephone rang. 'That was your Doctor friend,' said Rory when he'd put the receiver down. 'He's coming round to see you in half an hour.' He went back to his easel rummaging noisily about for a tube of burnt sienna that he'd mislaid. Finally he gave up looking and poured himself a drink and started painting.

I was dying to go and tart up for Finn. Surreptitiously I levered myself out of bed.

'Where are you going?' said Rory, without turning round.

'To the loo,' I said.

'Again?' said Rory. 'You've just been.'

'I've got a bit of an upset stomach,' I said, sliding towards the door.

'I should have thought it was hardly necessary, then, to take your bag with you,' said Rory.

'Oh,' I said, blushing and putting my bag on the table.

In the bathroom there was nothing to do my face with. I washed and took the shine off my nose with some of Rory's talcum powder, and tidied my hair with Walter Scott's brush. I got back into bed. Rory was still painting ferociously. Very cautiously I eased my bag off the table and just as cautiously opened it. Of course, my bottle of Arpège was at the bottom. I'd scrabbled my way down there, managed to unscrew the top, and was just about to empty some over my wrists when Rory turned round and my bag, plus all its contents and the unstoppered scent bottle, fell with an appalling crash to the floor.

Rory was not amused. We were in the middle of a full-dress row when Finn rang the doorbell. Rory went to let him in. I shoved the bag and all its contents under the bed. The whole room stank of scent like a brothel.

Finn came in, looking boot-faced, but he smiled when he saw me. Rory went and stood with his back to the fire, his eyes moving from Finn to me.

'All right, Rory, I won't be long,' said Finn dismissively, and picked up my wrist.

'I'll stay if you don't mind,' said Rory.

'Well I do,' I snapped. 'I feel like a biology lesson surrounded by medical students with you both in here.'

'I'll turn my back if you like,' said Rory, 'but

keep your thieving hands off her, Doctor,' and he gazed out of the window, whistling Mozart.

'How are you feeling?' said Finn gently. 'Are you eating all right?'

'Like a horse,' said Rory.

'I am not,' I snapped. I grabbed Finn's hand.

'No need to feel Finn's pulse, Emily,' said Rory.

'Oh shut up,' I said.

Finn was a bit like a dignified cart-horse with a couple of mongrels rowing between his legs.

'It's not fair,' I said to Rory afterwards. 'Look at the way you and Marina carry on.'

'We're not talking about me and Marina,' said Rory, his eyes glittering with strain and exasperation. Walter Scott was noisily eating a coat-hanger in the corner.

'Walter thinks your behaviour is appalling,' I said, 'and he knows all about dogs in the manger.'

28

A week went by. I corrected the proofs of the catalogue for Rory's exhibition. He was painting frantically; wild, swirling, self-absorbed canvases of savage intensity: babies with no arms or legs, feeling their way into life; the agonized features of women giving birth. They were ghastly, hideous paintings but of staggering power. For the first time it occurred to me that Rory might have minded my losing the baby.

He was like a mine-field: one would inadvertently tread on him and he'd explode and smoulder for hours. He was always worse after the times Finn came to see me.

Each time I found Finn increasingly more remote. I couldn't even talk to him because Rory stayed in the room all the time, scowling. It was horribly embarrassing.

Then one night I woke up to find Rory standing by the bed. The fire was dying in the grate. Outside the window the sea gleamed like a python.

'W-what's the matter?' I said nervously.

'I've finished the last painting.'

I sat up sleepily. 'How clever you are. Have you been working all night?'

He nodded. There were great black smudges under his eyes.

'You must be exhausted.'

'A bit. I thought we ought to celebrate.'

He poured champagne into two glasses.

'What time is it?' I said.

'About five-thirty.'

I took a gulp of champagne. It was icy cold and utterly delicious.

'We ought to be sitting on a bench in a rose garden, after a Ball,' I said with a giggle. 'You in an evening shirt all covered in my lipstick, and me in a bra-strap dinner frock and a string of pearls.'

He laughed and sat down on the bed. Suddenly I was as jumpy as a cat in his presence – it was as if I were a virgin and he and I had never been to bed together.

He leaned forward and brushed a strand of hair back from my forehead – and it happened. Shocks, rockets, warning bells, the lot, and I knew, blindly, that the old magic was working and I was utterly hooked on him again. Emily the push-over – lying in the gutter with a lion standing over her.

Rory, however, seemed unaware of the chemical change that had taken place in me.

'Oughtn't you to get some sleep?' I said.

'I've got to pack up the canvases,' he said. 'Buster's taking them down to London in his plane.' Then he said, not looking at me, 'He's giving me a lift to Edinburgh.'

Panic swept over me. It was Thursday. Marina's singing lesson day. Oh, God, oh, God, Rory was obviously going to meet her.

'What are you going to Edinburgh for?' I said in a frozen voice.

'To see an American about an exhibition in New York. And a couple of press boys want to talk to me about the London exhibition.'

'When are you coming back?' I said.

'Tonight. My mother's giving a party for my aunt. She's arriving from Paris this evening – you're invited. I think you should come. They're pretty amazing, my aunt and my mother, when they get together. It'd do you good to get out.'

I lay back in bed trying to stop myself crying. Rory bent over and kissed me on the forehead.

'Try and get some more sleep,' he said.

29

Mrs Mackie, our daily woman, came to look after me while he was away. Her gossiping nearly drove me insane. I washed my hair and shut myself away in the studio to get away from her.

Suddenly there was a knock on the door.

'Someone to see you,' said Mrs Mackie.

And Marina walked in.

I felt weak with relief, as though a great thorn had been pulled out of my side. So Rory hadn't gone to Edinburgh to see her. I wanted to fling my arms round her neck.

'Hello,' I said, grinning from ear to ear.

She seemed shattered by the warmth of my reception.

'Are you going to Coco's party tonight? Hamish wants to, but I'm not sure if I can face it.'

'Oh, I am,' I said, suddenly feeling I wanted to sing from the rooftops. 'It should be a giggle – if Coco's sister's anything like her.'

Marina looked terrible. Her eyes were hidden behind huge amber sunglasses, her face chalky. She looked like someone who was shaking off gastric 'flu.

'Are you all right?' I said suddenly, feeling sorry for her.

'Not very,' she said. 'I'm suffering from a broken heart. Can I have a drink?'

I gave her a huge slug of Rory's whisky. She looked at the golden liquid for a minute, then said: 'Has Rory said anything about me?'

I shook my head.

'Oh, God.' She put her head in her hands. 'I've spent days and days waiting for the Master to ring, but the Master did not ring. He obviously doesn't wish to avail himself of the service.'

'Are you still . . . well, crazy about him?'

'Of course I am!' she screamed, her eyes suddenly wild. 'And he's crazy about me. Nothing will ever cure that.'

I didn't flinch – I was making great strides in self-control these days.

'He's crazy about me, but he feels guilty about you losing the baby. He thinks you've had a lousy deal, so he's got to grit his teeth and try and make a go of it.'

'Charming,' I said, combing and combing my wet hair. She took off her dark glasses. Her eyes were suddenly alight with malevolence.

'Look, you don't love Rory a millionth as much as I do. You wouldn't be playing around with Finn if you did. Finn's crazy about you, and he's a much better proposition than Rory is, he's straight and utterly dependable. You're not tricky enough for Rory, he needs someone who can play him at his own game. You drive him round the bend.'

'It's absolutely mutual,' I said acidly.

'All you've got to do is go to Finn,' said Marina.

'Why doesn't he come and take me away?' I said. 'He's got a car.'

'Because he's had a rough time; he's had one broken marriage, and when he wanted you to leave Rory before you wouldn't go. He wants you to come of your own free will.'

'How idealistic,' I said, sulkily. 'For someone who throws his weight around as much as Finn does, he's very diffident when it comes to sex.'

'He doesn't want to go through hell again, he's got the hospital to consider, and if you don't hurry, Dr Barrett will snap him up. Anyway, can't you realize that if Rory wasn't my brother, he'd drop you like a hot coal?'

Suddenly her face crumpled and she burst into tears. 'I can't stand Hamish any more,' she sobbed. 'You don't know what it's like waking up to that awful old face on the pillow every morning.'

I turned away with a sense of utter weariness. I felt as though I'd been struggling for hours up a hill, and just as I reached the top, my hold had given way and I was pitching headling into darkness.

After she'd gone, I told Mrs Mackie to go home. I couldn't stand her chatter any more.

Half an hour later, Finn's car drew up outside. I watched him get out and lock it. What the hell did he have to lock it for round here, I thought irritably. There was no-one to pinch any dangerous drugs, except a few sheep.

'Go away,' I said miserably to Finn, refusing to open the door.

'Five minutes,' he said.

'What for?' I said.

'I don't like unfinished business.'

'Is there unfinished business?'

'Come on, stop messing about, let me in.'

'Oh all right,' I said, sulkily, opening the door. He followed me into the drawing-room.

'Do you want a drink?' I said.

'No, I want you,' he ran his hands through his hair, 'I haven't been able to get you on your own since Rory took over.' He looked almost as bad as Marina. Deep lines were entrenched around his mouth and his eyes. He seemed to have aged ten years in as many days.

'You haven't tried very hard,' I said.

'I've been run off my feet – two men from the petrol ship died last night, another early this morning.'

'Oh I'm so sorry,' I said, horrified, 'did they suffer a lot?'

'Yep,' said Finn. 'It hasn't been very pleasant at the hospital – in fact it's been hell.'

'Did you get any extra help from the mainland?' I said.

'I've got another doctor arriving this evening – at least it'll give Jackie a break, she's been marvellous.'

'I'm sure she has,' I said. 'Oh dear, she's far more suitable for you than I am.'

'Maybe she is,' said Finn, 'but it happens to be you that I love. You certainly need more looking after than she does; what the hell are you wandering about with bare feet and wet hair for?' He picked up a towel. 'Come on, I'll dry it for you.'

'No, it'll go all fluffy.' Finn took no notice. Christ, he rubbed hard.

'I won't have any scalp left,' I grumbled.

After that, the inevitable happened and I ended

up in his arms, and I must confess that I did like kissing him very much. It was one of the great all-time pleasures, like smoked salmon and Brahms' second piano concerto. Then I started getting nervous that Rory might walk in, so I wriggled out of his grasp.

'Who told you Rory was away?' I said.

'Marina did.'

'She has been busy,' I said. 'She was here earlier telling me how much she and Rory still love each other, and how noble Rory had been coming back to me.'

'Rory,' said Finn, kicking a log on the fire, 'has never done anything noble in his life. This little display of territorial imperative is sheer bloody-mindedness because he doesn't want *me* to get you. It's only *me* he's jealous about. Did he ever give a damn when Calen Macdonald made a pass at you?'

'No,' I said, plunging back into the depths of gloom.

'Why don't you leave him? You know how much I want you to.'

'The downward path is easy,' I said, 'but there's no turning back. When your dear, scheming sister was telling me how mad Rory is about her it hurt me so much I couldn't speak, but when she started dropping dark hints about you and Doctor Barrett, it irritated me but it didn't tear me in pieces at all . . . QED. I love Rory, not you.' I suddenly felt a great sense of loss. 'I'm wildly attracted to you, physically,' I said, 'I expect I always will be, but I'm stuck with loving Rory.'

'Even if he doesn't love you?'

I nodded. I played my last card:

'The only way it might work is if we went away

together, away from Irasa, and Rory and Marina, and all those associations – but that would mean your leaving the hospital.'

'Darling, I can't abandon it at this stage,' said Finn. 'You know I can't.'

I could see the pain starting in his eyes. I went over and put my arms round his neck, breathing in his strong, male solidarity.

'Oh Finn,' I whispered, 'I'm so sorry it's not you.'

30

All in all I didn't feel in a very festive state for Coco's party. Numb misery would have just about summed it up. Rory had noticed my red eyes when he got home, and demanded to know what was the matter. I'd refused to tell him, and he'd got extremely bad tempered.

I was wearing a very sexy red dress, but in my current condition I felt about as sexy as a pillar-box.

'At least it matches your eyes,' said Rory.

Coco's party was the usual noisy success, but everyone seemed even more anxious to get drunk than usual.

'My sister arrives later,' Coco told me. 'She says she is bringing me a surprise. I think I am too old to be surprised by anything, but perhaps it will be something that amuses Buster.'

Marina was wearing a beautiful white dress: everything about her shimmered and glimmered softly as though the material had been woven of candle beams. But inside it she looked like a stricken masquerader. Hamish was there, too, looking dreadfully old and ill. I hadn't seen him since the night he told me Rory and Marina were brother and sister.

Rory was drinking steadily and talking to Buster about fishing – Buster was in a very good temper, having landed a huge salmon that afternoon.

I was being the death and soul of the party.

About ten o'clock, after supper, a crowd of us were in a little room off the hall, playing roulette. Rory was winning, Hamish was losing heavily. Buster was still talking about his salmon. 'Amazing fish, the salmon,' he said, placing four chips on Rouge. 'They live for years in salt water, and then always come back to the same freshwater spot to breed.'

'Not surprising,' said Marina, and she looked at Rory and laughed. 'As you'd know, Buster, if you'd ever suffered the agony of making love in salt water.'

'I really thought the bugger had got away,' said Buster, not listening at all.

'Not surprising,' said Rory, 'if he saw you hauling on the other end of the line.'

Then, just as there was a pause in play, and Buster was raking in counters, Hamish looked at Rory.

'I hope you've been keeping a pretty close guard on your wife lately,' he said.

Rory stopped in the middle of lighting a cigarette.

'Shut up, Hamish,' I snapped.

'Hush, darling,' Rory put his hand on my arm. 'Hamish is about to explain himself.'

'All I'm saying,' said Hamish, flashing his false teeth evilly, 'is that patients often fall in love with their doctors, and it's nice to know I'm not the only cuckold in Irasa.'

His words brought an uneasy silence.

'Belt up, Hamish,' said Buster. 'You don't know what you're saying.'

'Oh, I do, Buster, old chap. All I'm saying to Rory is that next time he goes to Edinburgh, and my wife disappears to join him, he should realize that while he's away, pretty Mrs Balniel will be amusing herself with Dr Maclean.'

'That's not true,' I squeaked.

'Are you going to take that back?' said Rory through clenched teeth.

'No, dear boy, I'm not. Your wife is as big a whore . . .'

He got no further. Rory had chucked his drink into Hamish's face.

'And that's a waste of good whisky,' he said.

Hamish, whisky dripping from his face, made a lunge at Rory.

Buster pulled him off.

The doorbell rang noisily, bringing us back to our senses.

'Buster, Rory,' shrieked Coco from the hall, 'I think it must be Marcelle.'

'Excuse me,' said Buster, and hurried out.

Hamish wiped the whisky off his face. I dared not look at Rory or Marina.

The next minute, Coco swept into the room with her sister, Marcelle.

We all tried to act normally and everyone kissed everyone on both cheeks. Marcelle was not as pretty as Coco, younger and brassier, but pretty high voltage all the same.

She said, with a touch of malice: 'I've brought you your surprise, chérie. He's putting the car away and feeling a little shy, too.'

'Why don't you go and get him, Buster?' said Coco.

Buster trotted out obediently.

'Who can it be?' said Coco excitedly. 'I have so many skeletons in the wardrobe.'

I'd had my share of surprises, too. I was still shaking from Hamish's accusations. I sat down on the sofa. The next moment Buster came through the door. For once he'd lost his superb indolence. He looked shattered. He went up to Coco.

'Darling,' he whispered. 'This is going to be something of a shock.'

'I hope it's a nice one,' said Coco, patting her curls and arranging her breasts in the low-cut black dress. Someone else stood behind Buster in the door, a tall thin figure.

Alerted by everyone's faces, Buster swung round.

'For Christ's sake,' he snapped. 'I told you to wait.'

I watched, fascinated, as the man came through the door. He had unruly black hair streaked with grey, high cheek bones, formidable, contemptuous black eyes above grey pouches, and a haughty thin-lipped mouth. He was dressed theatrically in a black cloak with a gold earring hanging from one ear. He looked around slowly, taking everyone in. He must have been at least fifty – but he was still sensationally attractive. And I knew positively that I'd met him somewhere before.

There was a pause, then Coco turned as white as a sheet. 'Alexei,' she said in a frozen tone. Then she gave a strange little laugh that was almost a sob, and running towards him, flung her arms round his neck.

The odd thing was the silence. Everyone in the room looked stunned.

'You're still very beautiful, Coco,' Alexei said softly. 'How did I ever let you go?'

Coco seemed to recover herself.

'I was not rich enough for you,' she said unromantically.

'You haven't been properly introduced to my husband, have you, Alexei?' said Coco. 'Alexei was a great boyfriend of mine before I married Hector,' she said.

'So it seems,' said Buster.

'I seem to have stumbled on a little family gathering,' said the stranger with amusement.

Oh, where had I seen that arrogant, equivocal smile before?

'You must also meet my son, Rory,' said Coco.

Rory got to his feet.

Very carefully, they looked each other up and down.

I looked from Rory to the stranger. The resemblance was unmistakable.

'Did you say Alexei was a boyfriend of yours before you married my father, or afterwards?' Rory said softly.

Coco shrugged her shoulders, 'Well, a bit of both, darling.'

Alexei turned to Rory. 'Your mother and I were very much in love but, alas, we neither of us had any money. So she married Hector, and I, alas, martyred in the arms of . . .'

'A fat American heiress,' said Coco.

Then Rory started to laugh. He got a drink and raised it to Hector's portrait, kilted and bristling, over the fire. 'So the bastard wasn't my father after all,' he said, and turning to Alexei, 'I do hope you don't expect me to call you Daddy?'

Coco smiled. 'You do not mind, chérie?'

Rory shook his head. 'As long as his references are all right.'

Alexei grinned in genuine amusement. 'Oh, they're extremely good, my dear. I'm Russian; white, of course, and can trace my ancestry back to centuries before Peter the Great.'

His glance wandered in my direction. He had exactly the same way of stripping off all one's clothes that Rory had.

'This is Rory's wife,' said Coco.

Alexei sighed and bowed over my hand. 'What a pity,' he said, 'I suppose that puts her out of bounds?'

'I wouldn't let that worry you,' I said in a shaking voice. 'Incest has never deterred anyone in this house.'

I'll never understand any of them, I thought hopelessly. Only Marina was beginning to generate a fitting amount of emotion.

The next moment she had rushed up to Rory and flung her arms round his neck.

'Don't you see, darling?' she cried wildly. 'That lets you and me off the hook.'

The room swam before me.

31

The next moment I blacked out. I remember coming to and seeing a sea of faces and hearing Rory shouting at everyone to get out of the way and give me some air.

'She looks terrible,' said Coco. 'Are you all right, *mon ange*?'

'She got up too soon,' said Buster.

'She ought to see someone,' said Coco.

'I can see at least ten people already,' I joked feebly.

'Shall I call Finn?' said Marina.

'No,' snapped Rory, 'that's the last thing she needs,' and picking me up, he carried me upstairs.

'You'll rupture yourself,' I grumbled, as he stumbled on the top step. Thank God I'd lost some weight in hospital.

Rory kicked the door of the best guest room open. A fire was blazing in the grate. The purple-flowered sheets of the bed were turned down. The scent of freesias filled the room.

'But it's all ready for Marcelle,' I said feebly.

'She can sleep somewhere else,' said Rory, depositing me on the bed. He started to undo the zip of my dress.

'I'll do it,' I stammered, leaping away. He looked at me, frowning.

'Do you hate me so much you can't even bear me to touch you?'

'No – I mean . . .'

'What do you mean?' The tension was unbearable.

'I can't explain.' He shrugged his shoulders.

'All right, if that's the way you want it. I'll get you a couple of my mother's sleeping pills.'

I sat down on the bed, burying my face in my hands. I felt sick. How could I explain to him that I couldn't bear him to touch me because if he did, I'd only collapse, gibbering with lust, telling him I couldn't live without him, that I loved him – all the things he hated.

Coco's sleeping pills must have been very strong. It was mid-day when I woke up. The sun was streaming through the curtains, everything was quiet, except for a persistent thrush, and the occasional click of Buster hitting a captive golf-ball in the garden.

The fire had been re-lit in the grate. The scent of freesias was stronger than ever. Walter Scott lay sprawled across my feet. It was such a pretty room. For a moment I wallowed in the voluptuous euphoria created by the sleeping pills, then, bit by bit, the events of the last night came filtering back. Coco's sister arriving and then that glorious Russian turning out to be Rory's father, and Rory not being Marina's brother after all, and there being nothing now to stop them getting married – and having hordes of ravishing black-eyed, red-haired children or ravishing blue-eyed, black-haired children. Oh, God, God, God, I writhed on the pillow – a bad business paid only with agony.

What the hell was I to do next? The last month had been difficult certainly, Rory and I living together with no sex, but at least we'd had a few laughs, and I felt somehow that even if he didn't love me in the white-hot way he loved Marina, he was making very real efforts to make a go of it. Then Marina's words of yesterday came back to me: 'If he weren't my brother, he'd drop you like a hot coal.'

I lay feeling suicidal for a bit, then got up and drew back the curtains. It was a marvellous day, the sea sparkling, the larches waving their pale green branches against an angelically blue sky. I felt the sun warming my hair and smoothing away the marks of the sheets on my skin.

Buster, hearing the curtains draw, looked up. I moved out of range and examined my body in the mirror. The only advantage about being miserable is you do lose weight. For a minute I forgot my gloom and admired my flat stomach and my ribs, then I sucked in my cheeks, and putting on a haughty model's face, stood up on my toes.

'Very nice,' said a voice at the door, 'you'll make the centrefold of *Playboy* yet.' It was Rory. I gave a squeak of embarrassment and grabbed a towel to cover myself. 'Don't,' he said, shutting the door. He looked extremely pleased with himself. I wondered, with a flash of despair, if he'd spent the night celebrating with Marina.

'You look better,' he said, coming towards me. I backed away.

'Oh for God's sake, Em, stop behaving like a frightened horse.'

He was wearing a dark blue sweater, and an old

pair of paint-stained jeans; his hair was ruffled by the wind: he looked so unspeakably handsome, I felt my entrails go liquid. I lowered my eyes in case he read the absolutely blatant desire there. I wanted him so much I had to turn away and jump back into bed, pulling the sheets up to my neck.

'That's a good girl,' said Rory. 'It seems a pity to get up on such a lovely day.'

'Where is everyone?' I asked.

'Wandering around the house in various stages of undress, groaning about their hangovers.' He sat down on the bed and lit a cigarette. 'Do you still feel sick, does the smoke worry you?'

I shook my head in surprise, fancy Rory bothering to ask that.

'How are you getting on, adjusting to your new – er – father?' I baulked on the word.

Rory grinned. 'I quite like him, but he's an old phoney; he's already tried to borrow money off me, but then my mother always did have frightful taste in men. I'm very glad he didn't bring me up, I'd have been cooling my heels in Broadmoor by now.'

'Is he as grand as he makes out?' I said.

'I don't think so, he looks degenerate enough, but I don't believe those claims about tracing his ancestry back to Peter the Great. It does appear in fact that I've been born on the wrong side of an awful lot of blankets. Do you mind having an illegitimate husband?'

'Do *you* mind?' I said cagily.

'Not at all, I never understood how Hector could be related to me anyway. His favourite painter was Peter Scott. There's only one slight problem now to tax the ingenuity of the family solicitor. Have I any right any more to Hector's money?'

'Are you worried about it?'

'Not particularly, I quite like the thought of starving in a garret.' He shot me a glance under his eyelashes. 'How about you?'

'I haven't tried it,' I said carefully. 'How's your mother taking it?'

'Medium. I think she's a bit put out. Buster and Alexei have taken to each other like drakes to water, great bounders think alike I suppose. Alexei, like all foreigners, has a great reverence for English upper-class institutions. His ambition, like Buster's, is to murder as much wildlife as he can. He's so heartbroken the grouse shooting season is over that Buster has promised to take him pigeon shooting this afternoon.'

'Are you going?' I said.

'I might – for a laugh. So my mother is rather irritated about the whole thing. She's not gaining an ex-lover, she's losing a husband. Alexei is between marriages at the moment, I think he and Buster might do very well together.'

'But he's old enough to be Buster's father,' I said.

'Probably is, if I know that lot,' said Rory. I burst out laughing. Rory took my hand. 'You haven't laughed much lately, Em. I think we ought to have a talk.'

I snatched my hand away. 'People always say that,' I said in a trembling voice, 'when they're about to say something awful.'

'I've made you very unhappy since I married you, haven't I?' said Rory. 'I'm sorry, you must have had a pretty bloody six months.'

Panic swept over me. 'Come on,' he said in an exaggeratedly gentle voice, 'come here.' He held out his arms to me.

'No,' I said desperately, 'no, no, no.'

I knew exactly what he was about to say, that he'd made me so unhappy I obviously didn't want to stay married to him any longer, so why didn't we have an amicable divorce? If he touched me, I knew I'd cry.

'Is it that bad?' he said.

I nodded, biting my lip.

'I gather Finn Maclean was round to see you yesterday,' he said in a flat voice. 'Are you still hooked on him – come on, I want the truth.'

I felt defeated, my eyes filled with tears. There was a knock on the door. 'Go away,' howled Rory. In walked Finn. 'My God,' exploded Rory, 'why the hell can't you ever leave us alone? What do you mean by barging in here, who the hell asked you?'

'I've come to have a look at Emily,' said Finn.

'You've had a bloody sight too many looks at Emily recently,' said Rory.

'She happens to be a patient of mine.'

'Among other things,' said Rory. 'She's perfectly all right.'

'She looks it,' said Finn. He bent down to stroke Walter Scott who thumped his tail noisily on the floor.

'And stop sucking up to my dog,' snarled Rory.

'Oh, please,' I said, 'leave Finn and me for a few minutes.'

Rory scowled at both of us. 'All right,' he said, going towards the door, 'but if you put a finger wrong, Finn, I'll report you to the medical council and get you struck off the register.' And he slammed the door so hard, all the windows rattled.

Finn raised an eyebrow. 'What was that little tantrum in aid of?'

'He was trying to give me the sack,' I said miserably. 'And you interrupted him. You've heard that his real father's turned up?'

Finn nodded.

'So there's nothing to stop Rory and Marina now.'

'It's not going to be as easy as that, there's Hamish to be considered. I doubt if he'll give Marina a divorce.'

'It's funny,' I said, feeling very ashamed of myself, 'none of us ever thinks of Hamish, do we?'

Finn gave me some tranquillizers. 'Look,' he said, 'I'm off to a conference in Glasgow this afternoon. I'd cancel it, but I've got to speak. I'm not too happy about the current situation. Marina's in a highly overwrought state. So, obviously, is Rory, and I'm worried about Hamish. I want you to stay in bed today. I'll be staying at the Kings Hotel tonight, don't hesitate to ring me if you need me. Here's the telephone number.' He dropped a kiss on the top of my head. 'Don't look so miserable, little one, things will sort themselves out.'

Knocking back tranquillizers like Smarties, I decided to disregard Finn's advice and get up. When I finally made it downstairs, I found a noisy and drunken lunch had just finished. The debris of wine glasses, napkins and cigar butts still lay on the dining-room table. Buster was bustling about organizing his pigeon shoot. I went into the kitchen and opened a tin of Pedigree Chum for Walter. Then wandered into the drawing-room where I found Alexei well entrenched, chewing on a large cigar, drinking port and reading a book called *The Grouse in Health and in Disease*.

'Ah, my enchanting daughter-in-law,' he said, getting to his feet and kissing my hand with a flourish. Oh God, I hoped my fingers didn't smell of Pedigree Chum. 'Come and sit down,' he patted a rather small space on the sofa beside him, 'and tell me about yourself.'

Predictably I couldn't think of anything to say, but Alexei had obviously had enough to drink for it not to matter a scrap.

'Coco tells me you lost a baby recently – I am so sorry – you must have been very disappointed. You must have another one – as soon as you're strong again. You and Rory would have beautiful children.' It was not a subject I cared to dwell on.

'Do you have lots of children yourself?' I said.

'Yes, I think so, several that I know about and several that I probably don't, but none, I think, as talented as Rory. I have been looking at his paintings this morning. I am proud of my new son, he is a very good-looking boy, I think.'

'Yes, he is,' I said wistfully.

'And not unlike me, I think,' said Alexei with satisfaction. He got up. 'I must go and change for the shooting.'

'But it'll be dark in a couple of hours,' I said.

'We wait till dusk and catch the pigeons as they come home to roost,' he said.

'Poor things,' I said. 'Where's Rory?'

'Gone to fetch his gun. Hamish is coming too.' Suddenly, in spite of the centrally heated fug of the house, I felt icy cold. I didn't like the idea of that cast of characters going shooting.

Alexei went up to change. I turned on the television and watched a steeplechase. It all looked so bright green and innocent one couldn't really believe those horses falling at the fences were really hurting themselves.

A few minutes later, Rory arrived with Walter Scott. 'Who told you to get up?' he asked angrily. 'You look frightful.'

'I thought I might come and watch you all shooting,' I said.

'Absolutely not,' snapped Rory. 'You're supposed to rest – according to *your* doctor. Go back upstairs at once.'

At that moment Buster walked in, looking ludicrously like a French tart in rubber thigh boots and an extraordinary hat with a veil.

'Time's getting on, Rory,' he said, 'we ought to take up our positions at least an hour before dusk.'

'Is he getting married to Alexei already?' I said.

Rory laughed: 'It's supposed to stop the pigeons seeing his face when they fly over – a pity he doesn't wear it all the time. Come on,' he whistled to Walter Scott.

'Rory,' I said. He turned in the doorway. 'Be careful,' I said.

'Don't worry,' he said. 'It's all gun and no fear.'

I met Coco coming down the stairs.

''Ullo Bébé, how are you, I am fed up. I 'ope the presence of Alexei would make Buster jealous, and spend less time on his horrible bloody sports, but it only makes 'im worse. I like to have a good sleep in the afternoon, but what is the point if there is no-one to sleep with you? So Marcelle and I decided to go over to the mainland. You will be all right, *mon ange*?'

'Of course,' I said.

I tried to sleep but I was in much too uptight a state. I heard voices outside and crept to the window to see them go off. Poor Hamish looked iller than ever. Alexei was laughing at some joke of Buster's. Walter Scott, who was thoroughly over-excited by the whole proceedings, suddenly decided to mount Hamish's red setter bitch. Hamish went mad and rushed over and started kicking Walter in the ribs in a frenzy. Walter started howling and Rory turning on Hamish in fury. I couldn't hear what he was saying, but Hamish went absolutely spare with rage. I could see the white of his knuckles as his hands clenched on his gun. Then Buster came over and said something and they all set off, their boots ringing on the drive.

They crossed the burn and took the narrow, winding path up to the pine woods. I thought of the pigeons coming home after a long day to face the music: tomorrow they would be strung up as corpses in the larder, their destination pigeon pie.

I took more tranquillizers and tried to sleep, but it was impossible. I tried to read, Coco had left some magazines by the bed. I read my horoscope, which was lousy. Rory's horoscope said he was going to have a good week for romance, blast him, but should be careful of unforeseen danger towards the weekend. I should never have let him go shooting.

An explosion of guns in the distance made me jump nervously. Then I heard a crunch of wheels on the gravel and looked out of the window again. It was Marina, Miss Machiavelli herself. She parked her blue car in front of the house and switched off the engine, then combed her hair, powdered her nose, and put on more scent – the conniving bitch. God, how I hated her.

She got out of the car, fragile in a huge sheepskin

coat and brown boots, her red hair streaming in the breeze, and set off down the track the guns had taken.

No wonder Rory had been so insistent about my staying in bed and keeping out of his way. Drawn by some terrible fascination to see what they were getting up to, I got up, put on an old sheepskin coat of Coco's and set off after her.

The guns popped in the distance, like some far-off firework party. It was getting dark, the fir trees beetled darkly, a rabbit scuttled over the dead leaves frightening the life out of me. The sweat was rising on my forehead, my breath coming in great gasps. I ran on, ducking to avoid overhanging branches. There was the ADDERS – PLEASE KEEP OUT sign Buster had put up to frighten off tourists. I could hear voices now; the colour was going out of the woods; in the distance the sea was darkening to gun metal.

Suddenly I rounded a corner and, to my relief, saw Buster's gamekeeper, then Marina's red hair, and the guns strung out in a ring; Buster still wearing that ludicrous veil, Alexei next to him, then Rory, then Hamish, with Marina standing between them, but slightly behind. She was lighting one cigarette from another. I hoped they wouldn't see me, then I stepped on a twig and she and Rory looked round. He looked absolutely furious. Buster smiled at me, waving and indicating to me to stay quiet. Walter Scott sat beside Rory, quivering with excitement, trying to look grown up. Marina tiptoed back and stood beside me. On closer inspection she didn't look so hot, her skin pale and mottled, her eyes sunken and bloodshot. Even so, there was plenty of the old dash about her.

'I thought you were at death's door,' she said. 'It's been quite exciting, Alexei has already tried to shoot a couple of sheep and nearly killed Hamish – I wish he'd tried harder.'

'What are they waiting for?' I asked.

'The pigeons,' she said, 'they're late back. I had the most cataclysmic row with Hamish last night,' she said, lowering her voice. 'I ended up throwing most of the silver at him. We started at four o'clock in the morning and went on till just before he came out. This is half-time, I ought to be sucking oranges and thinking what to do in the second half. He said I behaved atrociously last night,' she went on, her eyes glittering wildly, 'and that he absolutely refuses to divorce me. Has Rory spoken to you?' she said, suddenly tense.

'He tried to this morning,' I hissed, 'but your dear brother walked in in the middle.'

'The trouble is,' whispered Marina, 'that Rory feels frightfully guilty about you because everything's worked out for him, now he can marry me. If you went off with Finn it would make things much easier for everyone.'

'I don't want to go off with Finn,' I said, my voice rising. 'What the hell do you think you're doing, riding roughshod over everyone's lives, don't you ever think that Hamish and I might have feelings?'

Marina turned her great headlamp eyes on me: 'I'd never hang around being a bore to a man who couldn't stand me – I've got too much pride, you obviously haven't.'

'Shut up you two,' said Buster.

We were silent but the whole forest must have heard my heart thudding.

Then suddenly the pigeons came sailing into view over the pine tops, and with a deafening crash the guns went off. It was like being in the middle of a thunderstorm, except that the sky was raining pigeons. The deafening fusillade lasted about three minutes.

Some of the birds escaped unscathed, others came down directly. The guns charged about looking for booty. Dogs circled, cursed by their masters. Alexei stood proudly with two birds in each hand. There were congratulations and verdicts. Walter Scott rushed grinning up to me, his mouth full of feathers.

'Must be some more in here,' said Buster, disappearing into the undergrowth. A minute later his great red face appeared and he said in a low voice, 'Rory, come here a minute.' Rory, followed by Walter Scott, went into the undergrowth.

There was a pause, then Rory came out, his face ashen in the half light, shaking like a leaf.

'What's the matter, darling?' Marina ran forward. 'What's happened?'

'It's Hamish,' said Rory. 'There's been an accident. I'm afraid he's blown his brains out.' His face suddenly worked like a small boy about to cry. 'Don't look, Marina, it's horrible.'

Marina gave a scream and rushed into the wood after Buster. Rory disappeared to the right: next moment I heard the sound of retching.

Marina emerged a minute later, her eyes mad with hysteria. 'There, you see,' she screamed at me, 'Rory killed him, he killed him for me, because he thought Hamish wasn't going to let me go. Now who do you think Rory loves?'

'Don't be bloody silly, Marina,' said Buster,

coming out of the copse. 'Of course Rory didn't kill him, poor old boy obviously did himself in.'

Rory, having regained his composure, had returned.

'I didn't, Marina,' he said, as she ran forward and collapsed in his arms. 'I swear I didn't.'

'Well, it's my fault then,' she sobbed. 'I told Hamish to do it, I told him how much I loathed and hated him, how much he disgusted me. I goaded him into it. Oh, Rory, Rory, I'll never forgive myself.'

I turned away. I couldn't bear the infinitely tender way he was holding her in his arms, stroking her hair, and telling her everything would be all right. Suddenly there was an unearthly wailing: everyone jumped nervously, then we realized it was Hamish's red setter howling with misery.

'She was the only one,' said Rory, 'who gave a damn for the poor old bugger.'

32

I can't really remember much of getting back.

Rory took me home; he was in a terrible state, shaking like a leaf. He came in and poured a stiff whisky and downed it in one gulp.

'Look, I must go to her.'

I nodded mechanically. 'Yes, of course you must.'

'I'm frightened this will unhinge her; I feel sort of responsible, do you understand?'

'Yes, I do.'

'Do you want to come too?'

I looked at him for the last time, taking in the brown fur rug on the sofa, the yellow cushions, the gold of his corduroy jacket, his dark hair and deathly pale face, the smell of turpentine, the utter despair in my heart. I shook my head, 'I'd rather stay here.'

'I won't be long,' he said, and was gone.

So Hamish had loved Marina after all. What was it that Marina had said that afternoon – that she'd never hang around being a bore to a man who couldn't stand her.

So the game had ended that never should have begun. I'm not a noble character, but I know when I'm licked.

For the second time in two months I packed my suitcase. I had no thought of going to Finn. Finn fancied me, but he didn't really love me. Not as Rory understood love. And now I couldn't have Rory, I didn't want second best.

I left a note.

'Darling,
Hamish has set you and Marina free, now I'm going to do the same. Please be happy and don't try and find me.

Emily.'

Mist swathed the Irasa hills, the lochs lay about them like steel and silver medallions in the moonlight. A small, chill wind whispered among the heather. I walked the narrow track that twisted down the hill to the ferry. I caught the last boat of the day. There was scarcely anyone on it. I stood on deck, and watched the castle and everything I loved in the world getting dimmer and dimmer until they vanished in a mist of tears.

I shall never remember how I got through the next ten days. I went to ground in a shabby London hotel bedroom. I couldn't eat, I couldn't sleep. I just lay dry-eyed on my bed like a wounded animal, shocked by incredulous grief and horror.

I toyed with the idea of going to see my parents, or ringing up Nina, but I couldn't bear the expressions of sympathy, then the whispering, and later, the 'I told you so's', and 'We always knew he was a bad lot', and much later – the 'Pull yourself togethers'. Sooner or later I knew I would have to face up to life, but I hadn't got the courage to get in touch with them yet, nor could I face the bitter disappointment I would feel if Rory hadn't rung them and tried to contact me.

But why should he contact me? He must be blissfully happy now with Marina. The idea of them together rose black and churning. Sometimes I thought I was going mad. Even my unconscious played tricks on me. Every night I dreamed of Rory and woke up in tears. In the street I saw lean, dark, tall men and, heart thumping, would charge forward, shrinking away in horror when I realized it wasn't him.

I hoped I would find it easier as the days went by, but it got much worse. What I hadn't anticipated was going slap into the infinitely bosky lushness of a late London spring. Everything was far further on than it was in Scotland. Outside my bedroom window the new lime-green leaves of the plane trees swung like little cherubs' wings, ice-cream pink cherry trees were dropping their blossom on the long grass. Huge velvety purple irises and bluebells filled the Chelsea gardens. Everywhere, too, there was an atmosphere of sexiness, of sap rising, of pretty girls walking the streets in their new summer dresses, of men whistling at them, of lovers entwined in the park, everything geared to ram home my loss to me.

'He's gone, he's gone, and when thou knowest this thou knowest how dry a cinder this world is.'

The day of the opening of Rory's exhibition came and went. With heroic self-control, I stuck to the hotel and didn't hang around in the coffee bar opposite in the hope of getting a glimpse of him. I couldn't face the anguish of seeing him with Marina.

But next morning I dragged myself up and went

out and bought the papers, and crept back to the hotel to read them. The reviews were very mixed: some of the critics loathed the paintings, some adored them, but everyone agreed that a dazzling new talent had arrived. There were also several pictures of Rory looking sulky and arrogant, and impossibly handsome. The Nureyev of the Art world, the gossip columns called him.

I cried half the morning, trying to decide what to do; then the manager presented me with my weekly bill, and I realized I could only just pay it. Next week I should have to get a job.

I had a bath and washed my hair. I looked frightful, like one of those women that wait for the bodies at the pit head – even make-up didn't help much. I can't even make any money as a tart now, I said dismally – I'd have to pay *them*.

When I got to Bond Street, I felt giddy. It struck me I hadn't eaten for days. I went into a coffee bar and ordered an omelette, but when it arrived I took one bite and thought I was going to throw up. Chucking down a pound I fled into the street. Four doors down, I went up the steps to the agency that used to find me work in the old days. How well I remembered that grey-carpeted, grey-walled, potted-plant world that I hoped I'd abandoned for ever. I started to sweat and tremble.

Audrey Kennaway, the principal, agreed to see me. She greeted me in an immaculate, utterly awful primrose yellow dress and jacket. Her heavily made-up eyes swept over me.

'Well, Emily,' she said in cooing tones, 'it's nice to see you. How are you enjoying your new jet-set life? Are you on your way to Newmarket or the Cannes Film Festival?'

'Actually, neither, I'm looking for a job,' I blurted out.

'A job?' She raised eyebrows plucked to the edge of extinction. 'Surely not, but I thought your handsome husband was doing so well, he had such a success in the papers this morning.' Her red-nailed fingers drummed on the table.

'That's all over,' I muttered. 'It didn't work out.'

'I'm sorry,' she said. I'm not surprised, I could see her thinking, she's let herself go so much. Her manner had become distinctly chillier.

'There's not a lot of work about at the moment, people are laying off staff everywhere,' she went on.

'Oh dear,' I said feebly. 'In my day, they were always laying on them.'

Audrey Kennaway smiled coolly.

'You'll have to smarten yourself up a bit,' she said.

'I know, I know,' I said. 'I haven't been very well. I used to type a bit, do you remember?' I went on. 'And when I was thin, you sometimes got me television commercials or a bit of modelling. I'm much thinner than that now.'

'I don't think I could find you anything in that field at the moment. Let's see if there's any filing clerk work.' Her long red talons started moving through the cards in a box on her desk. I felt great tears filling my eyes. I struggled to control myself for a minute, then leapt to my feet.

'I'm sorry,' I said, 'I couldn't do a filing job. I can't even file my nails without setting my teeth on edge. It's a mistake for me to have come here. You're quite right, I couldn't hold a job down at the moment. I can't hold down anything.' Bursting into tears, I fled out of the office, down the stairs into the sunshine. Two streets away was Rory's gallery. Gradually, as though pulled by some invisible hand, I was drawn towards it. I went into a chemist's to buy some dark glasses with my last pound. They weren't much help, they hid my red eyes but the tears kept trickling underneath. Slowly I edged down Grafton Street, No. 212, here it was; my knees were knocking together, my throat dry.

There was one of Rory's paintings of the Irasa coast in the window. Two fat women were looking at it.

'I don't go for this modern stuff,' said one.

I entered the gallery, my heart pounding. Then, with a thud of disappointment, I realized Rory wasn't there. I looked around, the paintings looked superb, and so many already had red 'sold' stickers on them. By the desk an American was writing out a cheque to a chinless wonder.

I wandered round the room, proud yet bitterly resentful that people should be able to buy something that was so much a part of Rory.

The chinless wonder, having ditched the American, wandered over.

'Can I help you?' he said.

'I was just looking round,' I said. 'You seem to have sold a lot.'

'We did awfully well yesterday, and we sold four more this morning – not, I may add,' he whispered darkly, 'through any assistance on the artist's part.'

'What do you mean?' I said, startled.

The chinless wonder smoothed his pale gold hair.

'Well, he's talented, I admit, but quite frankly,

he's an ugly customer. Doesn't give a damn about the show being a success.'

He put stickers on two more paintings.

'Always thought the fellow was pretty cold-blooded,' he went on. 'Didn't seem to care about anything, but he's certainly cut up at the moment. Apparently his wife's left him. Can't say I blame her. Only been married six months. He's absolutely devastated. I mean, he was a dead loss at the private view on Thursday. I'd lined up a host of press boys to meet him, and he wouldn't speak to any of them. Just hung around the door, hoping she might turn up.'

I leant against the wall for support.

'D-did you say his wife has just left him?' I said slowly. 'Are you sure it's his wife he's cut up about?'

'Certain,' said the chinless wonder. 'I'll show you a picture of her.'

We moved into a second room, where I steeled myself to confront one of Rory's beautiful voluptuous nude paintings of Marina.

'There she is,' he said, pointing to a small oil opposite the window. I felt my knees go weak, my throat dry – because it was a painting of me in jeans and an old sweater, looking incredibly sad. I never knew that Rory had painted it. Tears stung my eyelids.

'Are you sure that's the one?' I whispered.

'That's her,' said the chinless wonder. 'I mean it's a great painting, but she's not a patch on that gorgeous redhead he was always painting in the nude. Still, I suppose there's no accounting for tastes. I say, are you feeling all right? Would you like to sit down?'

Then he looked at the painting – and at me.

'I say,' he said, absolutely appalled, 'how frightfully rude of me. That painting – it's you, isn't it? I really didn't mean to be rude.'

'You haven't been,' I said, half laughing, half crying. 'It's the nicest, nicest thing anyone's ever said to me in my life. Do you possibly know where he's staying?'

33

I ran towards the tube station, rocked by conflicting emotions. It was the rush hour. As I battled with the crowds, I tried to calm the turmoil raging inside me. It couldn't be true, it couldn't be true. Then suddenly, as I reached the bottom of the steps, I was absolutely knocked sideways by an ecstatic, whining, black heap leaping up and licking my face, its tail going in a frenzy.

'Walter,' I sobbed, flinging my arms round his neck. 'Oh Walter, where's your master?' I looked up and there was Rory.

'Come here, you bloody dog!' he was shouting from the other side of the crowd. His slit eyes were restless, ranging from one person to another, sliding towards me. Then, as if drawn by the violence of my longing, they fastened on me, and I saw him start in recognition.

I tried to call his name, but the words were strangled in my throat.

'Emily!' he yelled.

The next moment he was fighting his way through the crowd.

'Oh, Emily, Emily, darling,' he said. 'Don't ever run away again.'

And pinning me against the wall, hunching his shoulders against the pressure of the crowd, he began to kiss me greedily, angrily, as tears of love and happiness streaked my face.

After a few minutes I drew away, gasping for breath.

'We can't stay here,' said Rory, and dragged me in my tearful blindness, muttering incoherently, out into the street and across the road to his hotel, where he kissed me all the way up in the lift, utterly oblivious of the lift man. Walter Scott jumped about trying to lick my hands.

'What the bloody hell,' said Rory, as he slammed the bedroom door behind us, 'do you mean by running away like that?' That sounded more like the old Rory. 'I've had the most frightful ten days of my life. And poor Walter,' he went on, 'how do you think he's enjoyed being the victim of a broken home?'

'I didn't think you loved me,' I said, collapsing on to the bed.

'Jes-us,' said Rory, 'I tried to tell you enough times. Didn't I wear myself out trying to fend off that smug bastard Finn Maclean? I nearly put a bullet through him that night I found him kissing you in the corridor at the hospital. And I've been driven absolutely insane with jealousy these last few weeks, having him rolling up to the house all hours of the day, acting as though he owned you.

'I played it as cool as I could when you came back from hospital. I didn't want to rush things, but whenever I tried to talk things over and explain how I felt, you leapt away from me like a frightened horse.'

'I thought you were trying to tell me you

202

couldn't live without Marina. That you were only staying with me because you felt guilty.'

'Christ no, that's all over, it was over that night you caught us in bed together, and threw me out. We went to Edinburgh, but it was hell, actually living with her; she got on my nerves so much I wanted to wring her neck, yacking away all the time, and never letting me think. All I could think of, actually, was you, and what a sod I'd been to you.

'Then my prodigal father turned up, and I discovered I wasn't even related to Marina, and there was no reason why I shouldn't marry her, particularly now poor old Hamish has kicked the bucket. I realized the only person in the world I wanted to be married to was you.'

'But,' I said, blushing crimson with pleasure, 'that day you all went shooting, Marina said you'd been trying to talk to me that morning to ask me for a divorce.'

'The truth was never one of Marina's strong points,' said Rory. 'She knew I was going to talk to you, we sat up half the night discussing the situation after you'd gone to bed. She said you were still crazy about Finn, and that I should let you go. I said sod that for a lark.'

He came and sat on the bed and pulled me into his arms. 'You're not still keen on him, are you? He's so pompous and self-righteous and such a bore. I was scared stiff, when you pushed off, that you'd gone to him. I borrowed Buster's plane that night and landed it in a park in Glasgow – there's been a bit of a row about that – and routed him out of his hotel bed. He was pretty angry.'

'I bet he was,' I said in awe. 'Did you really?'

'I really did,' said Rory. 'And I wonder just how much longer I am going to have to go on trying to convince you that I love you. I shouldn't think it's ever happened before in Irasa – someone falling helplessly, ludicrously in love with their own wife, after they've married them.' I felt myself blushing even more, and gazed down at my hands.

'For God's sake, Em darling, look at me.'

I picked up his hand and pressed it to my cheek.

'I've been so unhappy,' I said, 'then, in the gallery, I saw the painting you did of me. They said it was the only one you wouldn't sell.'

'I couldn't bloody well find you,' said Rory. 'I've been telephoning your mother and Nina for news every five minutes since you left.'

'Oh my God,' I said, 'I didn't ring them in case you hadn't.' I looked up and he was smiling at me and with a jolt I realized it was the first time he'd smiled without mockery; and close-up, how wan and heavy-eyed he looked, as though he hadn't slept for weeks.

'You *have* missed me,' I said in amazement. 'I really do believe you love me after all.'

'And now I'll prove it to you,' said Rory triumphantly, starting to slide down the zip of my dress.

'I'm terribly out of practice,' I muttered, suddenly shy. 'I haven't done it for ages.'

'Don't worry, it's like riding a bicycle or swimming, you never really lose the art. Get off, Walter,' he said, pushing a protesting Walter Scott on to the floor. 'This is one party you're not invited to.'

As his lips touched mine, we both began to tremble. A feeling of reckless happiness overwhelmed me. I felt his heart beating against mine and his kisses becoming more and more fierce, and the sounds of the traffic outside grew dim as they gave way to the pounding in my ears.

By the time we'd finished it was dark outside.

'God, that was lovely,' I sighed, 'we should do it more often.'

'We will,' said Rory, 'all day and all night for ever. Darling,' he said, looking suddenly worried, 'do you think you'll be able to put up with my absolutely bloody nature for the next sixty years?'

'I might,' I said, 'if you compensate from time to time with performances like the one I've just experienced.'

Rory laughed softly and rubbed the back of my neck. He lit a cigarette and lay down in the bed, pulling me into the crook of his arm.

'Rory,' I said a few minutes later, 'I know it's a terrible thing to say at a time like this, but I'm starving.'

'So am I,' he said.

'Shall we go out?'

'No, I might want you between courses, which wouldn't do in a restaurant. I'll send down for something.'

Later, as he was opening a bottle of champagne, he said, 'Darling, do you mind awfully if we don't live in Irasa any more?'

'Do I mind?' I said incredulously, 'of course I don't.'

'I'm bored with painting sheep and rocks,' he said. 'I want to paint you in the sun and give you half a dozen babies to look after to stop you having thoughts about pushing off and leaving me any more.'

'But you love Irasa.'

'It's lost its charms,' said Rory. 'I don't want you

within a million miles of Finn Maclean for a start and Marina's a bloody troublemaker, and I've had enough of my mother and Buster for a few years, and lastly my new father is still there – house guestating.'

'What does he find to do all day?' I said. 'Is he still in love with Buster?'

'Yes. They're both addicted to whisky and highly-coloured reminiscences, but Alexei now seems to have other fish to fry. In the old days when Marina wanted to bug me she always used to say what she wanted was an older man. Well, Hamish was a bit too old, but Alexei looks a bit like me, and when I left he was making a marvellous job comforting her in her bereavement.'

'My goodness,' I said, staggered, 'how extraordinary. You don't mean . . . ?'

'Well, not yet. Marina fancies herself in black far too much to give it up for at least a year, but I think now that she's so rich, and Alexei is so poor, it's very much on the cards.'

'You're not jealous?' I said anxiously.

'Not at all.' He bent over and kissed me. 'But I really don't fancy Marina as a stepmother.'

THE END

BELLA

Jilly Cooper

CORGI BOOKS

To Laura with love

Author's Note

I have always wanted to write a novel about an actress and I started writing *Bella* in 1969. However, at that time I wrote it as a novella, called it *Collision* and it was serialized in *19*. Only now am I able to fulfil my original wish and present the story as a full-length novel – *Bella*.

BELLA

1

Bella read faster and faster until she came to the final page then, giving a howl of irritation, hurled the book across the room. Narrowly missing a row of bottles, it fell with a crash into the waste-paper basket.

'Best place for it!' she said furiously. 'How corny can you get?'

She escaped completely into every book she read, identifying closely with the characters. This time she was incensed because the heroine had slunk dutifully home to her boring husband instead of following her dashing lover up the Amazon.

She shivered and toyed with the idea of letting the water out and running more hot in, but she had done this four times already. Her hands were wrinkled and red from the dye of the book, and the sky that filled the bathroom window had deepened since she'd been in the bath from pale Wedgwood to deep indigo, so she knew it must be late.

She splashed cold water over her body, heaved herself out of the bath and stood, feeling dizzy, on the bath-mat. The bath was ringed with black like a football sweater, but the char would fix that in the morning.

Taking her wireless, she stepped over the debris of her clothes, picked up the second post which was lying in the hall, and wandered into the bedroom.

She turned up the music, danced and sang a few bars, then caught sight of herself in the mirror, hair hidden in a mauve bath-cap, body glowing red as a lobster.

The Great British Public would have a shock if they could see me now, she thought wryly.

She pulled off her bath-cap and examined herself more carefully. She was a big girl with a magnificent body and endless legs. Her mouth was wide and her large sleepy yellow eyes rocketed up at the corners. A mane of reddish-blonde hair spilled over her shoulders. The overall impression was of a sleek and beautiful racehorse at the peak of its condition.

She opened her letters. One was from a journalist who wanted to interview her, another an ex-boyfriend trying to come back and several forwarded by the BBC from fans:

'Dear Miss Parkinson,' wrote one, in loopy handwriting, 'I hope you don't mind my writing. I know you must lead such a busy, glamorous life. I think it's marvellous the way there's never any breath of scandal attached to your name. Could you possibly send me a signed full-length photograph and some biographical details?'

Oh, God! thought Bella, feeling slightly sick, if only they all knew.

The last letter was practical. It was headed the Britannia Threatre, and was from the Director, Roger Field, who had written:

'*Dear Bella,*

If you're late again, I shall sack you. Can't you see how it unnerves the rest of the cast? Stop being so bloody selfish.

Love, Roger.'

Roger, Bella knew, would be as good as his word. She looked at the alarm clock by the bed and gave another howl of rage. It was twenty past six, and the curtain went up at seven-thirty. Dressing with fantastic speed, not even bothering to dry herself properly, she tore out of the flat and was fortunate to find a taxi almost at once.

The Britannia Theatre Company was one of the great theatrical successes of the decade. It specialized in Shakespeare and more modern classics and generally had three plays running on alternate nights and three in rehearsal. Bella had joined the company a year ago and had risen from walk-on parts to a small speaking part in *The Merchant of Venice*. She had recently had her first real break playing Desdemona in *Othello*. The critics had raved about her performance and the play had been running to capacity audiences for three nights a week.

Lying back gazing out of the taxi window at the trees of Hyde Park fanning out against a rust-coloured sky, Bella tried to keep calm. From now until her first entrance she would be in a nervous sweat, stage fright gripping her by the throat like an animal. She deliberately always cut it fine because it meant that she would be in such a hurry dressing and making up, she wouldn't have time to panic.

And yet, ironically, the only time when she felt

really secure was when she was on stage, getting inside someone else's personality.

The taxi reached the theatre at five past seven.

'Evening, Tom,' said Bella nervously, scuttling past the man at the door.

He put down his evening paper and glanced at his watch. 'Just made it, Miss Parkinson. Here's a letter for you, and there're some more flowers in your room.'

Not bothering to glance at her letter, Bella bounded upstairs two steps at a time and fell into the dressing-room she shared with her best friend, Rosie Hassell, who played Bianca.

'Late again,' said Rosie, who was putting on eye make-up. 'Roger's been in once already, gnashing his teeth.'

Bella turned pale. 'Oh, God, I couldn't get a taxi,' she lied, throwing her fur coat on a chair and slipping into an overall.

'I think Freddie Dixon's after me,' said Rosie.

'You think that about everyone,' said Bella, slapping grease-paint on her face.

'I don't – and, anyway, I'm usually right. I know I am about Freddie.'

Freddie Dixon was the handsome actor playing Cassio. Both Bella and Rosie had fancied him and been slightly piqued because he'd shown no interest in either of them.

'You know the clinch we have in the fourth act?' said Rosie, pinning on snakey black ringlets to the back of her hair. 'Well, last night he absolutely crushed me to death, and all through the scene he couldn't keep his hands off me.'

'He's not meant to keep them off,' said Bella. 'I expect Roger told him to act more sexily.'

Rosie looked smug. 'That's all you know. Look, you've got more flowers from Master Henriques,' she added, pointing to a huge bunch of lilies of the valley arranged in a jam jar on Bella's dressing table.

'Oh, how lovely,' cried Bella, noticing them for the first time. 'I wonder what he's on about to-night.'

'Aren't you going to read his letter?' said Rosie.

Bella pencilled in her eyebrow. 'You can – since you're so nosey,' she said.

Rosie took the card out of its blue envelope.

' "Dear Bella," ' she read. 'That's a bit familiar. It was "Dear Miss Parkinson" last time. "Good Luck for tonight. I shall be watching you. Yours, Rupert Henriques." He must be crazy about you. That's the eighth time he's seen the play, isn't it?'

'Ninth,' said Bella.

'Must be getting sick of it by now,' said Rosie. 'Perhaps he's doing it for "O" levels.'

'Do you think he's that young?'

'Expect so – or a dirty old man. Nobody decent ever runs after actresses. They've usually got plenty of girls of their own.'

Bella fished a fly out of her bottle of foundation and had another look at the card. 'He's got nice writing though,' she said. 'And Chichester Terrace is quite an OK address.'

There was a knock on the door. It was Queenie, their dresser, come to help them on with their costumes. A dyed-in-the-wool cockney with orange hair and a cigarette permanently drooping from her scarlet lips, she chattered all the time about the 'great actresses' she'd dressed in the past. Bella, who was sick with nerves by this stage, was quite happy to let her ramble on.

'Five minutes, please! Five minutes, please!' It was the plaintive echoing voice of the callboy.

Bella looked at herself in the mirror, her smooth, young face belying the torrent of nerves bubbling inside her. Then she sat down on the faded velvet sofa with the broken leg in the corner of the room and waited, clasping her hands in her lap to stop them shaking.

'Beginners, please! Beginners, please!' The sad echoing voice passed her door again.

Rosie, who didn't come on until later, was doing the crossword. Bello took one more look round the dressing-room. Even with its bare floor and blacked-out windows, it seemed friendly and familiar compared with the strange brightly lit world she was about to enter.

'Good luck,' said Rosie, as she went out of the door. 'Give Freddie a big kiss.'

They stood waiting by the open door under a faded orange bulb – Brabantio, Cassio and herself. Wesley Barrington, who was playing Othello, stood by himself, a huge handsome Negro, six and a half feet tall, as nervous as a cat, pacing up and down, murmuring his lines like an imprecation.

The three of them left her. Help me to make it, she prayed.

Othello was speaking now in his beautiful measured voice: 'Most potent, grave and reverend signiors'.

In a moment she would be on. Iago came to collect her.

'Come on, beauty,' he whispered. 'Keep your chin up.'

It had begun. She was on. Looking round the stage, beautiful, gentle, a little shy. 'I do, perceive here a divided duty,' she said slowly.

She was off, then on again, flirting a little with Cassio, and then Othello was on again. Here, where she found life a thousand times more real than in the real world, she had words to express her emotions.

But all too soon it was over. The appalling murder scene was ended and the play had spent its brief but all too vivid life.

And as she took her curtain calls, she had nearly reached the limits of her endurance. Three times Othello and Iago led her forward and the tears poured down her cheeks as the roars of applause increased.

'Well done,' said Wesley Barrington in his deep voice.

Bella smiled at him. She fancied him so much when they were acting, but now he was Wesley again, living in Ealing with a wife and three children.

Bella would now go out for a cheap dinner with Rosie and in the morning she would lie sluttishly in bed until lunchtime. She avoided the busy, glamorous world that her fans imagined she lived in. It was a question of conserving her energy for what was important.

In their dressing-room, however, she found Rosie in a fever of excitement. 'Freddie's asked me out.'

'I expect he wants to discuss the way you've been upstaging him,' said Bella. She collapsed on to a chair and felt depression descending on her like dust on a polished table.

Not that she wanted Freddie to ask her out. She'd long ago decided his curly hair and neon smile weren't for her. But if he started up a serious affair with Rosie, there'd be no more cosy little dinners, no more Rosie and Bella, united and gossiping together against the rest of the cast. Still, it was nice for Rosie.

'Where's he taking you?'

'Somewhere cheap. He's amazingly mean. Do you think one ear-ring looks sexy?'

'No, silly. As though you'd lost the other one.'

There was a knock on the door. It was Tom, the doorman.

'There's a Mr Henriques downstairs, Miss Parkinson. Wonders if he could come up and see you.'

'Oh,' said Bella, suddenly excited. 'What's he like?'

'Looks orl right,' said Tom, fingering a five pound note in his pocket.

'Not a schoolboy?'

Tom shook his head.

'Nor a dirty old man?'

'No, quite a reasonable sort of bloke. Bit of a nob really. Plum-in-the-marf voice and wearing a monkey suit.'

'Oh, go on, Bella,' said Rosie. 'He might be super.'

'All right,' said Bella. 'I can always tell him to go if he's ghastly.'

'Great!' said Rosie. 'I'll finish off my face in the loo.'

'No!' yelped Bella, suddenly nervous. 'You can't leave me.'

At that moment Queenie, the dresser, appeared at the door.

'You'd better get out of that dress before you spill make-up all over it,' she said to Bella.

Bella looked at herself in the mirror. Against the low-cut white nightgown, her tawny skin glowed like old ivory.

Let's knock Mr Henriques for six, she thought.

'Can I keep it on for a bit, Queenie?' she asked.

'And I'm supposed to hang about until you've finished,' said Queenie sourly.

'Come on, you old harridan,' said Rosie, grabbing her arm and frog-marching her out of the room.

'You can have a swig of Freddie's whisky to cheer you up.'

Bella sprayed on some scent, then sprayed more round the room, arranged her breasts to advantage in the white dress and, sitting down, began to brush her hair.

There was a knock on the door.

'Come in,' she said huskily in her best Tallulah Bankhead voice.

As she turned, smiling, her mouth dropped in amazement. For the man lounging in the doorway was absurdly romantic looking, with very pale delicate features, hollowed cheeks, dark burning eyes, and hair as black and shining as a raven's wing. He was thin and very elegant, and over his dinner jacket was slung a magnificent honey-coloured fur coat.

They stared at each other for a moment, then, smiling gently, he said: 'May I come in? I hope it's not a nuisance for you.'

221

He had an attractive voice, soft and drawling. 'My name's Rupert Henriques,' he added as an afterthought.

'Oh, please come in.' Bella stood up, flustered, and found that her eyes were almost on a level with his.

'You're tall,' he said in surprise. 'You look so small on the stage beside Othello.'

Embarrassed, Bella tipped a pile of clothes off the red velvet sofa.

'Sit down. Have a drink.' She got out a bottle of whisky and a couple of glasses. She was furious that her hand shook so much. She rattled the bottle against the glass and poured out far too large a drink.

'Hey, steady,' he said. 'I'm not much of a drinker.'

He filled the glass up to the top with water from the washbasin.

'Do you mind if I smoke?'

She shook her head and was pleased to see his hand was shaking as much as hers when he lit his cigarette. He wasn't as cool as he looked.

As she sat down she knocked a jar of cold cream on to the floor. They both dived to retrieve it and nearly bumped their heads.

He looked at her and burst out laughing.

'I believe you're as nervous as I am,' he said. 'Aren't you used to entertaining strange men backstage every night?'

Bella shook her head. 'I'm always frightened they might be disappointed when they meet me in the flesh.'

'Disappointed?' He looked her over incredulously. 'You must be joking.'

Bella was suddenly conscious of how low her dress was cut.

'The flowers are heavenly,' she said, blushing. 'How on earth did you manage to get such beautiful ones in winter?'

'Rifling my mother's conservatory.'

'Doesn't she mind?'

'Doesn't know. She's in India.' He smiled maliciously. 'I'm hoping an obliging tiger might gobble her up.'

Bella giggled. 'Don't you like her?'

'Not a lot. Do you get on with your parents?'

'They're dead,' said Bella flatly, and waited for the conventional expressions of sympathy. They didn't come.

'Lucky you,' said Rupert Henriques. 'I wish I were an orphan – all fun and no fear.'

He had a droll way of rattling off these remarks which made them quite inoffensive. All the same, she thought, he's a spoilt little boy. He could be quite relentless if he chose.

He picked up his drink. 'You were even better than usual tonight.'

'Don't you get bored seeing the same play night after night?'

He grinned. 'I'm glad it's not a Whitehall farce. You're the only reason I've been so many times.'

There was a knock on the door.

'Hell,' he said. 'Do we have to answer it?'

It was Queenie.

'I won't be a minute,' Bella said to her. 'I'm sorry,' she added to Rupert, 'I shall have to change.'

He drained his glass, got up and moved towards the door.

'I was wondering if you'd have dinner with me one evening next week,' he said.

It's Monday now, thought Bella. He can't be that keen if he can wait at least a week to see me!

'I'm very tied up,' she said, untruthfully.

'Tuesday?' he said.

'I'm working that night.'

'Wednesday then?'

She paused just long enough to get him worried, then smiled: 'All right, I'd like to.'

'I don't suppose you like opera.'

'I adore it,' lied Bella, determined to keep her end up.

'Great. There's a first night of Siegfried next Wednesday. I'll try and get tickets.'

As he left he said, 'I'm sorry I had to make your acquaintance in this rather gauche fashion, but I didn't know anyone who knew you, who could have introduced us, and the only other alternative would have been to have bought the theatre.'

It was only later that she discovered he was only half-joking. The Henriques family could have bought every theatre in London without batting an eyelid.

2

Promptly at six-thirty on Wednesday he picked her up.

'You look gorgeous,' he said, walking round her.

'You don't look so bad yourself,' she said.

He was wearing a very dark green suit with a red silk shirt.

'You like it?' he said, pleased. 'My tailor only finished it on Monday; that's why I couldn't ask you out last week.'

An Aston Martin was waiting outside; music blasted out of the slot stereo; the heat was turned up overpoweringly.

Bella wound down her window surreptitiously as they drove off. She didn't want to be scarlet in the face before she started.

As they stopped at the traffic lights, Rupert turned and smiled at her. 'You shouldn't have made me wait so long to see you,' he said. 'I've been in such a state of anticipation I've been unbearable to everyone.'

Even in the thick of a first-night audience with the diamonds glittering like hoar frost, everyone turned to stare at them. Rupert seemed to know lots of people, but he merely nodded and didn't stop to chat.

The curtain hadn't been up for five minutes before Bella decided that Wagner wasn't really her. All those vast men and women screaming their guts out. She glanced at her programme and was appalled to see she was expected to sit through three acts of it.

Somehow she managed to endure the first act. It seemed so strange to be on the other side of the curtain.

'Is it all right? Are you enjoying yourself?' asked Rupert as he fought his way back to her side with drinks during the interval.

'Oh, it's great,' she lied enthusiastically.

Rupert looked dubious. 'Well, I don't know; they make a frightful row. Say as soon as you're bored and we'll leave.'

Two earnest-looking women with plaits round their heads turned to look at him in horror.

During the second act Rupert became increasingly restless, but cheered up when Brünhilde made her appearance.

'She looks just like my mother,' he whispered loudly to Bella, who gave a snort of laughter.

A fat woman in front turned round and shushed angrily. Rupert's shoulders shook. Bella gazed firmly in front of her but found she couldn't stop giggling.

'I say,' said Rupert a minute later, 'shall we go?'

'We can't,' said Bella horrified. 'Not in the middle of an act.'

'Will you be quiet,' hissed the fat woman.

'My wife feels faint,' Rupert said to her and, grabbing Bella by the hand, he dragged her along the row, tripping over everyone's feet.

Outside the theatre they looked at each other and burst into peals of laughter.

'Wasn't it awful?' he said. 'I wanted to impress you, taking you to a first night, but this really was the end.'

As they picked their way through Covent Garden's debris of cabbage leaves and rotten apples he took her hand. 'We'll have a nice dinner to make up for it.'

They dined in Soho; very expensively, Bella decided. Crimson velvet menus with gold tassels, and rose petals floating in the finger bowls. They sat side by side on a red velvet banquette, rather like being in the back row of the cinema.

'What do you want to eat?' Rupert asked her.

'Anything except herrings.'

He laughed. 'Why not herrings?'

Bella shivered. 'My mother forced me to eat them when I was young. I was locked in the dining-room for twelve hours once.'

Rupert looked appalled. 'But I've never had to eat anything I didn't like.'

'This is a nice place,' said Bella.

'It's a haunt of my father's,' said Rupert. 'He says it's the one place in London one never sees anyone one knows.'

'Rupert, darling!' A beautiful woman with wide-set violet eyes was standing by their table.

'Lavinia.' He stood up and kissed her. 'How was Jamaica?'

'Lovely. I can't think why I came home.'

'Have you met Bella Parkinson?'

'No, I haven't. How do you do?' She looked Bella over carefully. 'I've read all about your play, of course. Macbeth isn't it? I must come and see you.'

She turned back to Rupert and said, a little too casually, 'How's Lazlo?'

'In Buenos Aires.'

She looked relieved. 'That's why he hasn't rung. When's he coming back?'

'Next week some time.'

'Well, give him my love and tell him to ring me before my sun-tan fades.' She drifted off to join her escort at the other end of the room.

'She's beautiful,' sighed Bella, admiring her beautifully shod feet. 'Who is she?'

'Some bird of Lazlo's.'

'Who's he?'

'My cousin.' He lowered his voice. 'Evidently Lazlo complained her bed was too small, so she went out to Harrods and bought one three times the size.'

'She's *mad* about him. Is he attractive?'

'Women think so. I know him too well. We work together.'

'What at?'

'Banking. We've got a bank in the City. But most of our business is tied up in South America. My father's chairman but Lazlo really runs it.'

'You look a bit Latin yourself.'

'My father's South American. My mother, alas, is pure English. She's coming home next Friday, worse luck. I'm hoping someone will hi-jack her plane. She keeps sending me postcards telling me not to forget to water the guides.'

Bella giggled. 'Who?'

'One of her interests along with the Blind, the Deaf, the Undernourished, and any other charity

228

she can poke her nose into. Alas, there's no charity in her heart. Her life is spent sitting on committees and my father.' He looked at Bella. 'What were your parents like?'

Bella's palms went damp. 'My father was a librarian,' she said quickly. 'But he died when I was a baby, so my mother had to take a job as a school mistress to support me. We were always terribly poor.'

Poor but respectable. She'd told the same lies so often that she'd almost come to believe them.

Their first course arrived – Mediterranean prawns and a great bowl of yellow mayonnaise. Bella gave a little moan of greed.

Later, when she was halfway through her duck, she suddenly looked up and saw that Rupert was staring at her, his food untouched.

'Bella.'

'Yes.'

'Will you have dinner with me tomorrow?'

'Of course,' she said. She didn't even stop to consider it. The one thing that could have spoilt her evening was the sense of being a failure, that he'd get to know her a little and then decide she was a bore.

Later, they went back to her flat for a drink and Bella drew back the curtains in the drawing-room to show Rupert the view. Half London glittered in front of them.

'Isn't it gorgeous?' said Bella ecstatically.

'Not a patch on you, and you've got the most beautiful hair in the world.' He picked up a strand. 'Just like Rapunzel.'

'Who's she?'

'The princess in the tower who let down her hair and the handsome prince climbed up and rescued her. You must have read it as a child?'

Bella looked bleak. 'My mother didn't approve of fairy stories.'

Rupert frowned and pulled her into his arms. 'The more I hear of your childhood the less I like it,' he said.

Then he kissed her very hard. After a minute he pulled her down on to the sofa and began fiddling with her zip.

'No,' she said, stiffening.

'Why not?' he muttered into her hair. 'Christ, Bella, I want you so much.'

Bella took a deep breath and burst into tears. One of her greatest acting accomplishments was that she could cry at will. She had only to think of the poor unclaimed dogs at Battersea Dogs' Home, waiting and waiting for a master that never came, and tears would course down her cheeks.

'Oh, please don't,' she sobbed.

Rupert was on his knees beside her. 'Darling. Oh, I'm sorry. Please don't cry. I shouldn't have rushed things. I've behaved like a pig.'

She looked at him through her tears. 'You won't stop seeing me because I won't?'

He shook his head wryly. 'I couldn't if I tried now. I'm in too deep.'

After he'd gone she looked at herself in the mirror. 'You're a rotten bitch, Bella. God, you're in a muddle,' she said slowly.

She wanted men to want her, but once they tried to get involved she ran away, frightened they'd find out the truth.

3

Rupert arrived next evening, his arms loaded with presents.

'I've decided you missed out on a proper childhood, so we're going to start now,' he said.

In the parcels were a huge teddy bear, a Dutch doll, a kaleidoscope, a solitaire board filled with coloured marbles, a complete set of Beatrix Potter and *The Wind in the Willows*.

Bella felt a great lump in her throat. 'Oh, darling, you shouldn't spend all your money on me.'

Rupert took her face in his hands. 'Sweetheart, listen. There's one thing you must get into your head; there are a hell of a lot of disadvantages about being a Henriques, but being short of bread isn't one of them.' He held out his hands. 'We've got buckets of it. My father's worth a fortune and, since Lazlo put a bomb under the bank, we're all worth a lot more. I've got a private income of well over £25,000.'

Bella's jaw dropped.

'That's what's so lovely about you, Bella. Anyone else would know about the Henriques millions. I've never worried about money in my life, and when I was twenty-one last month I inherited . . .'

'Twenty-one?' said Bella quickly. 'You said you were twenty-seven.'

He looked shame-faced. 'I did, didn't I? I knew you wouldn't be interested in me if you knew how young I was.'

'But I'm twenty-three,' wailed Bella. 'I'm cradle-snatching.'

'No you're not,' he snuggled against her. 'Anyway, I'm crazy about old women.'

From then on they were inseparable, seeing each other every night, touring the smart restaurants and getting themselves talked about.

As spring came, turning the parks gold and purple with crocuses, Bella found herself growing more and more fond of him. He was very easy to like, with his languid grace, sullen pent-up beauty, and his appalling flashes of malice that were never directed at her.

But he could be moody, this little boy who had always had everything he wanted in life. His thin face would darken and she could feel his longing for her like a volcano below the surface.

The eternal late nights were taking their toll of his health too. He had lost pounds and there were huge violet shadows beneath his eyes.

One May evening they were sitting on the sofa in her flat, when he said, 'Don't you mind that I never take you to parties and things?'

She shook her head. 'The only parties I like are for two people.'

Rupert turned her hand over and stared at the palm for a minute, then said, 'Why don't we get married?'

Panic swept over Bella. 'No!' she said nervously. 'At least, not yet.'

'Why not?'

'We come from different backgrounds. I've always been a have-not, you've always been a have. Your family would loathe me. I haven't any background.' She gave a slightly shaky laugh. 'When I talk about the past, I mean yesterday.'

'Rubbish,' Rupert said angrily. 'Don't be such a snob. I love you and that's all that matters.'

'I love you too.' Bella pleated the folds of her skirt.

'You're making things impossible for me,' said Rupert sulkily. 'You won't marry me; you won't sleep with me. I'm going out of my mind.'

He got up and strode up and down the room. He looked so ruffled and pink in the face, Bella suddenly had an hysterical desire to laugh.

'There's someone else,' he said, suddenly stopping in front of her.

'How could there be? I've seen no-one but you for the last six months.'

'And before that?'

'Casual affairs.'

He caught her wrist so hard that she winced with pain.

'How casual? I don't believe you! You're as passionate as hell beneath the surface, Bella. One only has to see you playing Desdemona to realize that.'

Bella had gone white. She snatched her hand away from Rupert and went over to the window.

'All right. There was someone, when I was eighteen. He seduced me and I loved him, and he walked out on me the night my mother died.'

233

Rupert was unimpressed. 'But darling, one loves the most ghastly people when one's eighteen. You wouldn't be able to see what you saw in him if you met him now.'

Finally, Bella agreed to go and meet his family on her birthday, the following Thursday.

She lay in bed dreaming about Rupert the Monday morning before her birthday. I can't have been very easy these past weeks, she thought ruefully. Living on a permanent knife-edge wondering whether or not to tell him the truth about my past.

'I love you, and that's all that matters,' he'd said. Perhaps she would tell him, but could she bear to see the incredulity and contempt in his face? And if she didn't tell him, would he ever find out? No-one else had. She realized that, for the first time in years, she was beginning to feel secure and happy.

She idly wondered what to wear when she met his parents. She hoped she wouldn't be too intimidated by them. She ought to buy a new dress, but too many bills were flooding in.

She picked up the paper, glanced at the gossip page to see if she or Rupert were mentioned, then turned to the personal column – villas in the South of France, ranch minks, hardly worn, costing £3,000. If I marry Rupert, she thought, they'd be within my grasp.

And then she saw the advertisement, in bold-type, edged with black, and went cold with horror.

'Mabel, where are you? I've looked for you everywhere. I'll be waiting at the bar of the Hilton at seven o'clock. Steve.'

Suddenly, her heart was pounding, her hands clammy.

It must be a mistake. Lots of people communicated through the personal column – gangs of criminals, lost friends. It was a fluke. It couldn't concern her.

But all day long she couldn't get the thought of it out of her mind.

Next day, when she picked up the paper, she tried not to turn immediately to the personal column. But there was another advertisement, burning a hole in the page.

'Mabel, where are you? Why did you leave Nalesworth? Please come to the Hilton bar at seven o'clock tonight. Steve.'

Oh God! thought Bella, giving a whimper of horror. A feeling of nausea overwhelmed her.

On Wednesday, after a sleepless night, she found another message waiting for her.

'Mabel, where are you? I waited on Monday. Perhaps you can't get to London? Cable me at the Hilton. I shall wait for you. Steve.'

She was sweating with fear. After all these years, Steve was in London, had come back to claim her. The one man in the world who could rock the boat and bring down the precarious fabrication of lies and falsehoods that was Bella Parkinson.

4

On the morning of her birthday Bella was woken by the sun streaming through the window. For a moment she stretched luxuriously – then the sick feeling of menace overwhelmed her as she remembered Steve was trying to get in touch with her.

She jumped violently when the doorbell rang, but it was only the postman with a pile of letters and a registered parcel to be signed for. The newspaper was lying on the doormat. Willing herself not to look at it, Bella opened the parcel and gave a shriek of excitement. A pearl necklace was glittering inside. She put it on and rushed to the mirror. Even against a setting of mascara-smudged eyes and tousled hair, it looked beautiful.

'There is nothing to say except I love you,' Rupert had written in the accompanying letter. Bella gave a sign of happiness. It was as if someone had pulled her in out of the cold and wrapped her in a mink coat.

There were cards from the rest of the cast, and more bills. There were far too many of those crowding in lately.

The telephone rang. It was Barney, her agent.

'Happy Birthday, darling. Do you feel frightfully old?'

'Yes,' said Bella.

'I'll buy you lunch next week. We can't go on not meeting like this,' said Barney.

Bella laughed. Barney always cheered her up.

'Harry Backhaus is in London casting for Anna Karenina,' he said, in his nasal cockney drawl. 'He saw you on the box last week and wants to audition you this evening.'

'But I can't,' wailed Bella. 'Not tonight. I'm meeting Rupert's family.'

'I know sweetheart. As if you'd let me forget it. I've arranged for you to see Harry beforehand – at six. He's staying at the Hyde Park. Ask for his suite at the desk. He likes birds, so be yourself. You know, sexy but refined. And don't be late.'

Bella was elated. She'd worshipped Harry Backhaus for years. She rifled through her wardrobe for something to wear, but found nothing sexy enough. She'd have to go out and buy yet another dress. Afterwards she would come back and change into the discreet but ludicrously expensive black midi dress she'd bought for meeting Rupert's parents.

The telephone rang again. This time it was Rupert wishing her a happy birthday. She thanked him ecstatically for the necklace, then told him about the audition.

'I don't know who I'm more frightened of – Harry Backhaus or your parents.'

'It won't be just them,' said Rupert. 'Gay, my sister will be there with Teddy, her fiancé.'

'What's he like?'

'He's in the Brigade. If you take away his long

umbrella he falls over. His chin goes straight down into his stiff collar. Gay used to be an ally. Now all she can talk about is curtain material. I say, you'll never guess.'

'What?'

'She's pregnant.'

'My God! When did she find out?'

'Well, she only told me yesterday, so she'll have to carry a very big bouquet.'

'Was your mother livid?'

'Doesn't know. My father was very good. He walked once round the drawing-room then said, "Never mind, you always get a few shots fired before the 12th of August."'

Bella giggled.

'And as well as my pregnant sister,' Rupert went on, 'you're finally going to meet my glamorous cousin, Lazlo, and you're to promise not to fall for him; and his sister Chrissie's coming too. She's sweet. So there'll be some young people – as my mother calls them – for you to play with, darling.'

Dear Rupert, thought Bella fondly, as she put down the receiver. He loved her so much, Steve really couldn't hurt her any more. Casually, she picked up the paper. She must have been imagining things before.

But there it was – the first advertisement that caught her eyes when she turned to the personal column.

'Mabel, where are you? Why didn't you turn up at the Hilton? I shall wait again tonight. Steve.'

She felt a lurch of fear as a huge black cloud moved over the sun of her happiness.

She spent the rest of the day in a frenzy of activity – shopping and at the hairdresser. Anything not to think about Steve. She squandered a fortune on new make-up, a pair of impossibly tight blue jeans and a white frilly blouse that plunged to the waist. She also had her hair set in a wildly dishevelled style that made her look as though she'd just crawled out of bed.

She arrived twenty minutes late for the audition. Harry Backhaus turned out to be a lean, dyspeptic American who sucked peppermints all the time. He had been ruined, he said, by lunch at what was supposed to be the best restaurant in London.

'So you wanna play Anna, eh?' he said.

'I'd like to.'

'Know the book?'

'Adore it. I've read it over and over again.'

'So you've got all kinds of preconceived notions how the part should be played?'

'I could be talked out of them.'

'I picture Anna as dark. You'd have to dye your hair. You'd have to diet, too. And the boy we've got lined up for Vronsky is a good three inches shorter than you.'

Finally he said, 'We'll be in touch. Thanks for coming along.'

A beautiful tiny brunette was waiting to go in as she came out.

'Harry, darling! It's been too long!' Bella heard her say as she shut the door behind her.

Bella looked at her watch. It was twenty to seven. Enough time to go home and change before dinner. But she didn't go home. Across the Park she could see the Hilton gleaming like a liner at sea. Her flat was in the opposite direction but, as though mesmerized, she began walking towards the hotel.

You're mad, she kept telling herself. You're walking straight into a torture chamber. In five minutes you'll undo all the good of the last five years.

Just go and have a quick drink, said another voice inside her. See if it really is Steve and come away. Once you've seen him it'll break the spell.

Outside the hotel, to gain time, she bought some flowers for Rupert's mother.

Her heart was thudding like a tom-tom. Her hands were clammy as she went through the swing doors of the hotel.

The bar was very crowded. People turned to stare at her. Why couldn't she stop trembling? A tall, fair man who looked like a pig was giving her the glad eye. Surely he couldn't be Steve?

'Hullo, darling,' said a soft voice with an American accent in her ear.

She jumped like a startled horse and swung round. Her mouth was dry. The bottom seemed to fall out of her stomach as she looked into the bluest, most wicked eyes in the world.

'Oh, Baby,' he said, taking her hands. 'It's so good to see you.'

'Hullo, Steve,' she croaked.

'You made it. You really showed up. I can't believe it. Come and sit down.'

Bella felt the years melt away. She was eighteen again.

'We ought to celebrate by drinking that filthy sparkling hock which I always pretended to you was champagne.'

'I'd like some whisky,' said Bella stiffly.

'Two double Scotches,' Steve told the waiter.

He got out a packet of cigarettes and, as he lit hers, their fingers touched.

'Oh, honey,' he said. 'You've grown so beautiful. Look at me properly.'

With a great effort she raised her eyes to his. How insane she'd been to think he'd have gone off. If anything he was better looking – more seasoned. He'd lost his peachey, open, golden-boy look. There were lines now, fanning out at the corners of his eyes, and his hair was brushed forward in a thick, blond fringe to cover lines that might have developed on his forehead.

She lowered her eyes.

'I've looked for you everywhere,' he went on, as their drinks arrived. 'I wrote to Nalesworth over and over again, but they sent my letters back saying you'd gone away like a fox. I even went there to see if anyone had any news of you. Advertising in the personal columns was my last hope. What are you doing now – modelling?'

'I'm an actress.' She couldn't keep the pride out of her voice as she told him how well she'd done.

Steve whistled. 'You have gone places.'

'And I've just had an audition with Harry Backhaus for the lead in his new film.'

Lay it on thick, she thought. Damn you, Steve. I can get along without you.

'Darling, you're a star! I must come and see the play. What name do you act under? Surely not Mabel Figge?'

'No,' said Bella in a strangled voice. 'I . . . I changed my name to Bella Parkinson.'

She noticed that he was wearing a very well-cut suit and heavy gold cuff-links.

'You've made good too, Steve.'

He grinned. 'Can't complain. I've got a couple of clubs in Buenos Aires. One of the reasons I'm over here – apart from finding you, of course – is to find a site for a disco in London.'

He signalled to the waiter. 'Let's have another drink.'

'Not for me,' she said. 'I can't stay.'

But she didn't move, and when the drinks came he raised his glass to her. 'To us, baby.'

'There isn't going to be any "us"!' she snapped. 'I've got someone else.'

'Did have, you mean. Who is he?'

Again the temptation to brag was too much.

'You won't know him. He's called Rupert Henriques.'

Steve raised his eyebrows. 'Not the banking family?'

Bella nodded defiantly.

'Oh, sweetheart, you *are* piling yourself up riches on earth.'

'You know him?'

'I've run across his cousin, Lazlo, in Buenos Aires.'

'Everyone seems to know him. Rupert adores him. What's he like?'

'Ruthless, rather sinister. A strange mixture. Half Jewish – his mother is some Austrian opera singer. The City don't know what to make of him. They don't approve of his long hair and all that scent he wears. But they have to admit he pulls off deals with a panache no-one else can equal. He's got the kind of steel nerves that buys when the market's down. And he owns some pretty good horses.'

'Why isn't he married?'

'Doesn't believe in it. I think he got very badly

burnt over some married woman several years ago. Always has the most fantastic birds, though.'

There was a pause. Then Steve went on, 'But it's Rupert you're keen on?'

'Yes I am,' said Bella quickly.

'Then why did you come here today?'

'I wanted to lay a ghost. Steve, I must go.'

How idiotic those monosyllables sounded. She had to go home, change and go out to dinner with the Henriques, but she couldn't move.

'Darling,' Steve said softly, 'I know I behaved like a heel, walking out on you when you most needed me. But I owed bread everywhere. I'd have been arrested if I'd stayed in Nalesworth any longer.'

'And what about all those other girls every night?' Impossible to keep the shrill hostility out of her voice.

'I was too young to be tied down. I've grown up since then. I wouldn't cheat on you now, if that's what you're thinking.'

But she was only conscious of his big, sexy body lounging beside her, and the fact that she wanted him as she'd never wanted anyone else.

'You're no good for me, Steve. I want to marry someone nice and stable.'

'And I'm just nice,' sighed Steve. 'One has to specialize so young these days.'

He sat back and let one of his knees rub against hers. She jumped as though she'd touched a live wire.

'My, but you're edgy,' he said.

She laughed nervously.

'When did you develop that laugh?'

'What laugh?'

He imitated it, and Bella laughed again out of nervousness.

'Yeah, like that.'

'You haven't changed a bit,' she stormed. 'You always enjoyed sending me up.'

'Your voice has changed too,' he said. 'Stage school certainly ironed out all the Yorkshire accent.'

As she leapt to her feet, he grabbed her.

'Let go of my hand,' she choked.

'Come on honey, don't be mad at me.'

'Let me go,' her voice rose.

'Keep your voice down. Everyone's looking at us. Oh, come on!' He pulled her down beside him.

'Don't you understand! I've come thousands of miles to get you back. I'm the one who knows all about you, darling. I bet you haven't told Baby Henriques about life in the slums and your jailbird father, have you?'

'Shut up!' spat Bella, turning white.

'And that's only the beginning, as you well know. Now finish up your drink like a good girl and I'll drop you off wherever you want to go. But from tomorrow the heat's on. I'm not going to let the Henriques get their hands on you. You don't want to get mixed up with them, darling; you're batting out of your league.'

As the taxi drove towards Chichester Terrace, Bella frantically combed her hair and re-did her face.

'Stop fussing,' said Steve.

'But I'm so unsuitably dressed,' wailed Bella. 'I had this lovely little black dress.'

'You're an actress. The Henriques would be terribly disappointed if you turned up looking

244

straight. Just tell them Harry Backhaus kept you for hours, and only just let you go.'

They were driving along the Old Brompton Road now, the cherry trees dazzling white against the darkening sky.

'It's spring,' said Steve, taking her in his arms. 'Can't you feel the sap rising?'

For a moment she kissed him back, aware only of the appalling rightness of being in his arms.

'Don't go,' he whispered.

'No, Steve. For God's sake!' She pushed him violently away and sat back trembling, unable to speak until the taxi swung into Chichester Terrace.

He wrote her telephone number down on a cigarette packet.

'Don't lose it,' she was furious to find herself saying. 'I'm ex-directory. Oh God, you've sat on Rupert's mother's flowers.'

5

As she stood in the road, watching the taxi carry him away, she was overwhelmed by desolation. She ran past the big, white houses, set back from the road, their gardens filled with early roses and azaleas. Then she came to the whitest and biggest of all. Two stone lions with sneering faces reared up on either side of the gate. A maid answered the door, but before she could take Bella's coat Rupert rushed into the hall, his face white and drawn.

How ridiculously young and unfledged he looks beside Steve, she thought.

'Darling! What happened? It's after nine o'clock!'

Bella was not an actress for nothing. Suddenly she was the picture of distress and contrition.

'I'm so sorry! Harry Backhaus kept me waiting for ages, and then took hours over the audition, and then he made the most frightful pass at me.' Her eyes filled with tears. 'I wanted to phone, really I did, but it got so late it seemed more sensible to come straight here. I didn't even have time to change. Please forgive me.'

Any moment a thunderbolt will strike me down,

she thought wryly. But Rupert, at least, was convinced.

'Poor darling,' he said, seizing her hands. 'Of course it doesn't matter. Come in and meet everyone.'

They went into a huge unwelcoming room, a cross between a museum and a jungle full of gilded furniture and elegant uncomfortable chairs. On the wall, appallingly badly lit, hung huge paintings with heavy gold frames. Potted plants were everywhere.

'Poor Bella's had a terrible time,' Rupert announced. 'The damned director's only just let her go.'

'I'm so sorry,' Bella said, giving them her most captivating smile. 'He kept me waiting for hours, and then . . .'

'We heard you saying so outside,' said a large woman coldly.

'This is my mother,' said Rupert.

Constance Henriques was tall but not thin enough. Her face, with its large turned-down mouth and bulging, glacial eyes, resembled a cod on a slab. Her voice would have carried across any parade ground.

'It's nice to meet you,' said Bella, deciding it wasn't.

'I thought you told Miss Parkinson we always dress for dinner,' Constance said to Rupert.

Bella had had too many whiskies, 'And I've undressed,' she said, looking down at her unbuttoned shirt. And, almost unconsciously slipping into a mocking upper class accent, added, 'I'm most frightfully sorry.'

There was a frozen pause, then someone laughed.

'This is my father,' said Rupert, grinning.

Charles Henriques must once have been very handsome, but had long since gone to seed. There was a network of purple veins over his face and great bags under his merry little dark eyes, which ran over Bella's *décolleté* like a pair of black beetles.

'How do you?' he said, holding her hand far longer than necessary. 'Rupert has talked about no-one else for weeks. But even he didn't do you justice.'

He handed Bella a vast drink.

Rupert's sister, Gay, and her fiancé, Teddy, were a typical deb and a typical guards officer. They hardly broke off their conversation when Bella was introduced to them.

Bella couldn't resist staring at Gay's stomach. She didn't look at all pregnant – nor did Teddy look capable of fathering a mouse.

'I told you they were totally self-obsessed, didn't I?' Rupert said, squeezing her hand. 'And finally I want you to meet my cousin Chrissie, Lazlo's sister. She's my good angel.'

She'd be divine too, if she were happier, thought Bella. But Chrissie looked thoroughly out of condition. Her dark eyes were puffy, a spot glowed on her cheek, and she must have put on a lot of weight recently because the dress she was wearing was far too tight over her heavy bust and hips.

'How do you do?' Chrissie said. She had a soft, husky voice with a slight foreign inflection. 'How foul having an audition. They must be beastly things.'

'I always get into a state,' said Bella, 'but some people sail through them.'

Chrissie started to talk about a friend who wanted to go on the stage but, although her mouth smiled, her eyes looked at Bella with hatred.

Bella gulped her drink and looked round the room. That was certainly a Matisse over the fireplace and a Renoir by the door. Between the curtains there was a lighter square on the rose-coloured wallpaper.

'The Gainsborough usually hangs there,' said Constance, following Bella's gaze, 'But we've lent it to the Royal Academy. What can Lazlo be talking about all this time?' she added irritably to Charles. 'The telephone bills that boy runs up.'

'He's talking to some Arabs,' said Rupert. 'He's been trying to get through all day.'

'How exciting to have a wedding so soon,' Bella said brightly.

They all looked at her. I'd better shut up, she thought. My girlish approach is going down like a lead balloon.

'It's your birthday, isn't it? How old are you?' said Constance Henriques, her mouth full of potato crisps.

'Twenty-four,' replied Bella.

'Twenty-four? But Rupert's only twenty-one. I'd no idea you were so much older than him.'

'And you've just turned fifty-four, my dear,' said Charles Henriques mildly. 'So I think the less said about age the better.'

Bella giggled, which was obviously the wrong thing to do, for Constance Henriques had turned the colour of a turkey cock.

Fortunately there was the click of a telephone.

'That'll be Lazlo finished,' said Constance. 'We can eat at least. It's too much to expect the young to be punctual these days, but I do hate keeping the servants waiting.'

Bella flushed. Rupert's mother was a cow. Thank God Lazlo was going to join them now. Of all the Henriques family he was the one she felt she was going to get on with. She imagined a gay, laughing, handsome, more dissipated version of Rupert, with the same slenderness and delicate features. But as usual in such cases, she couldn't have been more wrong in her assessment.

For the man who came through the door was tall and as powerfully built as Steve. With his sallow complexion, hooked nose, thick black curling hair and drooping eyelids, it was difficult to tell if he looked more South American or more Jewish in his appearance. But there was certainly nothing of the Jewish fleshiness about his face, nor the melting softness of the Latin about his eyes, which were as hard and black as tarmac. He looked dangerous and incredibly tough.

Rupert bounded forward, 'Lazlo! Bella's arrived. Come and meet her.'

Wincing slightly at the pride in Rupert's voice, Bella gave Lazlo her most seductive smile. 'I've heard so much about you,' she said. 'I feel I know you very well already.'

For a second there was a flicker of surprise in his eyes. He certainly took his time to look her over. Then, with a smile that wasn't entirely friendly, he said, 'I can assure you you don't. How do you do?'

Then he turned to Constance.

'Sorry I took so long. This deal's reached a really delicate stage. If we pull it off though, Charles'll make enough bread to pay for Gay's wedding.'

Constance didn't look in the least mollified. But

at that moment a maid announced dinner was ready.

Until then Bella had drunk enough whisky to sail through any situation, but as they went into the dining-room she was overwhelmed with a fear so violent that she had to clutch on to the table to stop herself fainting.

What was that terrible sickly smell? Then she realized it was the lilies – a huge clump was massed on a Grecian pillar at the far end of the room and another great bowl filled the centre of the table.

Bella stared at them horrified, remembering the wreaths of lilies that had filled the house before her mother's funeral, just after Steve had walked out on her. And how closely, at the time, the white waxy petals had resembled the translucence of her mother's skin as she lay dead upstairs. She felt the sweat rising on her forehead. She was trembling all over.

Looking up, she saw Lazlo watching her. Immediately on the defensive she glared back, then cursed herself as he looked away. It would have been so much more politic to smile.

They sat down at a table that could easily have accommodated a couple of dozen people. Bella was between Charles and Teddy. Rupert was hidden from her by the centerpiece of lilies. A maid began handing round a great bucket of caviar.

Constance and Gay discussed the wedding.

'It's amazing how people cough up,' said Gay. 'The most unlikely relations have sent vast cheques.'

'When I was married,' said Constance, taking a far bigger helping than anyone else, 'all the West Wing was cordoned off to accommodate

the presents. I'd forgotten how much there is to do.
I'm quite exhausted. I've been tied up with the
bishop all afternoon.'

'How very uncomfortable for you both,' said
Lazlo gravely.

Constance ignored this. 'The bishop was most
impressed by our work for the blind,' she went on.
'Particularly with the number of new guide dogs
we've provided.'

Lazlo held up his wine so that it gleamed like a
pool of gold. 'You should start a society of Guide
People for Blind Dogs,' he said.

'Do you know Baby Ifield?' Charles shouted to
Bella down six feet of polished mahogany.

She shook her head.

'Should have seen her in her heyday. My word
she was a smasher. Used to go back stage and see
her. Often took her to the Four Hundred.'

Constance's lips tightened.

'I simply can't bear to discuss the mess this
government is making,' she said, and proceeded to
do so for half an hour.

Listening to her, Bella found herself becoming
more and more critical, and as her critical spirit
waxed, her tact and caution waned.

Constance switched to the subject of Northern
Ireland. 'If only they'd bring back hanging.'

'Why should they?' said Bella, her trained
actress's voice carrying down the table.

Constance looked at her as though one of the
potatoes had spoken.

'It'd soon stop them dropping bombs so casually,' said Constance.

'No way,' said Bella. 'There's nothing the
Irish like better than feeling martyred. Hanging

would only make them step up the campaign.'

Constance was revving up for a really crushing reply, when Lazlo said.

'How's Jonathan?'

'A case in point,' said Constance sourly. 'Young people today are allowed far too much freedom. His housemaster wrote to me only this morning saying Jonathan painted "Death to Apartheid" in red all over the chapel wall.'

Lazlo and Charles grinned. Rupert started to laugh.

'But that's great,' said Bella, whose glass had been filled for the fourth time. 'He's doing something positive.'

Constance stared at Bella, her cold eyes baleful. 'Have you ever been to South Africa?'

'No,' admitted Bella.

'I thought not. People who haven't first-hand knowledge of a country always make sweeping generalizations.'

'But one has only to read the papers . . .' Bella was thoroughly roused by now.

'I bought that chestnut filly I told you about, Charles.' Once more Lazlo had interrupted her in mid-sentence.

Suddenly, the table came to life. Horses were obviously a complete obsession where the Henriques were concerned.

The candles threw sharp daggers of light on to the table. Chrissie was talking to Rupert. Bella watched the rapt expression on the girl's face.

So that's the way the wind blows, she thought. No wonder she hates me.

Constance was rabbiting on about the game reserves. Lazlo was picking his teeth.

I was a fool to come, thought Bella miserably.
Steve was right about these people.

She felt both exhausted and depressed when they
left the men to their port and cigars. Chrissie sat
down at the grand piano and played Beethoven
extremely well.

She looks beautiful now, thought Bella, looking
at her softened face, the lamplight on the black
hair.

Constance and Gay talked more about the wedding, Constance sewing a piece of tapestry of a
Victorian lady with a hare lip.

Rupert joined them first and came straight over
to Bella, his face drawn.

'All right, darling?'

'Fine,' snapped Bella. 'Give me a cigarette.' She
was irritated that he hadn't stuck up for her at
dinner.

'Sorry we took so long,' he said. 'My father and
Lazlo were having rather a heated discussion about
devalution.'

But Lazlo didn't look heated as he came through
the door a moment later, smoking a large cigar and
laughing at some joke of Charles's, his saturnine
face lit up by the glitter of dark eyes and the flash
of very white teeth.

He ought to laugh more, thought Bella, as he
went over to the piano.

'All right, love?' Lazlo picked up a loose hair
from Chrissie's shoulder.

'Of course,' she said brightly.

'Good.' He smiled down at her, then crossed the
room and sat down beside Bella.

He's a womanizer, thought Bella. Maybe I'll try

and vamp him. She leaned forward to show him more of her cleavage.

'I met a friend of yours the other day,' he said.

'Oh, who?' said Bella, giving him a long, hot, lingering glance, which was immediately wiped off her face when he said, 'Angora Fairfax. She said you were at drama school together.'

Bella had always loathed Angora Fairfax. She had been the spoilt darling of immensely rich parents, always at parties and complaining how exhausted she was next morning. All her fellow students, except Bella, had been pixillated by her. Angora, in her turn, had been jealous of Bella's talent.

'I knew her slightly,' said Bella. 'What's she up to now?'

'A television series, I think. She talked a lot about you.'

'I'm sure,' said Bella coldly.

'She's extremely attractive,' said Lazlo, examining his whisky. 'Can she act?'

Bella nodded. She wasn't going to fall into the trap of being bitchy.

'I hear you had an audition tonight,' Lazlo went on.

Bella's early warning system wasn't working very well.

'Yes, I did.'

'And the director made a pass at you. How distressing for you.'

Sarcastic cat, thought Bella.

'Who was he?'

'Harry Backhaus.'

'Harry?' His eyebrows shot up. 'Unlike him.

255

He's only just got married again. We're lunching tomorrow. I'll give him a bollocking.'

Bella felt herself going hot, then cold, with horror.

'Oh, no! please don't,' she said, far too quickly. 'I expect he got carried away.'

Lazlo's smile was bland. 'Still, there's no excuse for that sort of thing.'

At half past eleven Bella got up to go.

'I'll drive you home,' said Rupert.

'I'll take her,' said Lazlo. 'I go straight past her door.'

'But it's not that way,' said Rupert mutinously.

'I'd like you to wait for another call from Sordid Arabia,' said Lazlo. 'You know the background.'

Wow! thought Bella, he's really pulling rank. And she willed Rupert to stand up to him. But Rupert opened his mouth, shut it again, and sulkily agreed.

As she left, Charles kissed her on both cheeks. 'We'll see you at the wedding next month, if not before,' he said.

Everyone stiffened. 'Have you sent Bella an invitation yet, Constance?' he added.

'We've run out,' said Constance coldly.

'Nonsense. There are at least a dozen left in your desk. We need a bit of glamour on our side of the church.'

When they were nearing Bella's flat, Lazlo said, 'I want to talk to you. Shall we go to your flat or mine?'

'I'm very tired,' snapped Bella. 'Can't we talk here?'

'No,' he said. 'It's important.'

'All right. We'd better use mine.'

Her flat was in chaos, clothes all over the drawing-room, unwashed breakfast things lying around. Bella kicked a bra under the sofa and went into the bedroom to take off her coat. In the mirror her eyes glittered with drink. Really, that blouse was too indecent for words. Perhaps Lazlo was going to make a pass at her. When she came back she found him sprawled in an armchair playing with the solitaire board.

He's got the face of a riverboat gambler, she thought, tough, cool, measuring up all the options.

'Did Rupert give you this?' he said.

Bella nodded.

'He's a nice boy,' said Lazlo.

'*I* think so,' said Bella. 'Do you want a drink?'

Lazlo shook his head. 'Rupert hasn't had an easy life,' he went on. 'Lots of spoiling but not much love. Constance has always been too tied up with her charities; Charles much too preoccupied with Old Masters and young mistresses. Rupert's pretty unstable as a result. He needs someone who can't only handle him, but who also loves him very much.'

'My,' said Bella with a nervous laugh, 'I didn't know you were that romantic.'

Lazlo didn't smile back. 'I'm not. I just hate waste.'

Bella took a deep breath. 'You don't want me to marry him, do you?'

'No, I don't.'

'Because I don't come out of the top drawer?'

'I don't care if you come out of the coal-hole! I just want Rupert to land up with someone who loves him.'

'Like your sister Chrissie, I suppose? Then you'd keep all your millions in the family.'

'Leave Chrissie out of it.'

'Why should I? What makes you think she loves Rupert more than I do?'

'She wouldn't have arrived an hour late to meet her future mother-in-law.'

'I told you I couldn't get away. I was stuck at the audition.'

'And not bothered to dress.'

'I didn't have time to change.'

'Or arrived three parts cut.'

'I was not. Americans just pour very strong drinks.'

'Or been rude to Aunt Constance on every possible occasion.'

'She was insufferable,' said Bella in a choked voice.

'I agree,' he said evenly. 'She's an uphill battle-axe. But if you loved Rupert you'd have put up with it.'

'What's it got to do with you, anyway?' Bella said furiously.

He had only a few marbles left now in the centre of the solitaire board. She watched his long fingers, mesmerized.

'All I'm saying,' he said softly, 'is that if you loved Rupert, you'd have arrived on time, sober, properly dressed, instead of swilling whisky in the Hilton Bar with one of your lovers.'

Bella turned green. 'W . . . what are you talking about?' she whispered. 'I was having an audition.'

'Maybe you were earlier in the evening, baby. But when I saw you, you were so engrossed with your handsome desperado, you didn't even notice I was sitting only a few tables away.'

Confusion and horror swept over her. Lazlo had seen her with Steve. How much had he heard of their conversation?

'He's an actor,' she lied quickly. 'We . . . er . . . we were discussing a play we're doing together next week.'

'Rehearsing all the love scenes,' said Lazlo dryly. 'If you gazed at Rupert with a tenth of that slavish adoration, I'd be only too happy for you to marry him.'

He was left with one dark green marble now. He looked at it for a moment, then, putting the board down, took out his cheque book.

'Now,' he said, in a businesslike tone. 'How much do you want? If I give you – oh, five grand, will you leave Rupert alone?'

Bella laughed in spite of herself. 'I never realized people really said things like that! No, I won't.'

'Because you adore Rupert and can't live without him?' he said acidly.

'I never said anything about love,' she said. 'It's you who keeps banging on about it. But since you want things spelled out – I don't intend to break it off!'

'Ten grand,' said Lazlo.

There was a pause. Bella looked out of the window.

Wow, the things I could do with ten thousand pounds, she thought. I wonder if it would be tax free? Then aloud she said, 'I don't want your rotten money. You'll have to think of something else.'

Lazlo put away his cheque book and got to his feet. The sheer size of him made her step back.

'Well, if you won't be sensible about it, I shall have to try other methods.'

'You can't stop me marrying Rupert.'

'I can't?' he said softly. 'You obviously can't be familiar with our family motto: "Scratch a Henriques and you draw your own blood." '

The long scar showed white on his swarthy skin. A shiver ran down Bella's spine.

He's like the devil, she thought.

'My family's got a lot of influence,' he went on. 'We can make things very difficult for you if you don't play ball.'

'You're threatening me?' she said.

'Yes, and I'd warn you, I fight very dirty. Are you sure you don't want that cheque?'

Bella lost her temper. 'Get out! Get out!' she screamed. And, picking up a blue glass bowl, she hurled it at him. But he ducked and it smashed on the wall behind him. He laughed and left.

Bella couldn't stop shaking after he'd gone.

Oh no, she wailed. Why did I blow my top? Loathsome, horrible bully. He's only bluffing. He wouldn't do anything really.

And yet . . . and yet . . . with all that money and power behind him . . .

She shivered with fear. Perhaps she ought to take the money and clear out with Steve. But Steve was unreliable, not to be trusted. And then, of course, there was poor Rupert to be considered.

Suddenly the doorbell rang, making her jump out of her skin. Lazlo again? Steve? Her heart was cracking her ribs. Whoever it was was leaning on the bell.

'Who is it?' she sobbed in terror.

'It's me, Rupert.'

She opened the door and, as he followed her inside, she burst into a storm of weeping.

'Darling! Hush, sweetheart! It went all right.' He pulled her down beside him on the sofa, stroking her hair. 'They're always bloody at first. You should have seen them with Teddy. Wasn't Lazlo nice to you?'

She shook her head. She hadn't meant to tell Rupert, but she couldn't control herself any more.

'He hates me,' she sobbed. 'More than any of them. He said he doesn't want me to marry you.'

'He doesn't? Probably fancies you, that's why he's so rude. Anyway, my father's crazy about you.'

How good it was to be held in his arms and comforted.

'I'm so rotten to you,' she muttered. 'Arriving late and cheeking your mother. I don't know why you put up with me.'

And you don't know the half of it, she thought miserably.

'There's nothing to put up with,' Rupert said. 'I love you ten times more than I did this morning. I'd kill anyone who hurt you.'

She moved away and looked at him. Harlequin's face, sad, pale, with great blue rings under his eyes.

'Bella, darling, please let's get married.'

And whether it was to spite Lazlo, or to escape from Steve, or because she was drunk, or because Rupert wanted her so much she never knew, but the next moment she was saying yes.

6

Bella woke next morning with a series of flash-bulbs exploding in her head. Scenes from last night's débâcle re-staged themselves with relentless accuracy – the disastrous audition with Harry Backhaus, the meeting with Steve, the catastrophic dinner party at the Henriques'. She was just wincing her way through that appalling moment when she'd hurled a glass bowl at Lazlo, when she sat bolt upright and gave a groan.

Jesus! She'd let herself get engaged to Rupert. But she didn't love Rupert. She loved Steve – and that snake Lazlo Henriques knew it too, and would pull out every stop to make her break it off with Rupert.

Oh God, she wailed, pulling the bedclothes over her head, what a terrible mess!

The events of the next weeks left her breathless. Rupert insisted on looking at dozens of houses, taking her on a triumphal round of his relations and showering her with presents – including a huge plastic pink, heart-shaped engagement ring because he knew it would irritate his mother.

Bella had expected Lazlo to come round breathing fire, but he did nothing, obviously biding his time. What really crucified her was that even though Steve must have read about her engagement – every paper splashed pictures of 'The Millionaire and the Showgirl' – he made no attempt to get in touch with her.

The sex side with Rupert hadn't been going well either. Now she was engaged, she could hardly refuse to sleep with him. Rupert, fobbed off for so long, wanted to spend every free moment in bed, then afterwards was desperate for reassurance.

'Was it all right, darling? Are you sure it was all right for you?'

'Yes, yes,' she would say, pulling him down on to her breast until he fell asleep, and she would gaze unseeingly at the ceiling, her body twitching with unsatisfied desire and longing for Steve.

A week later, after a performance at the theatre, she slumped down in front of her dressing-room mirror, cheers echoing in her ears. She had acted superbly. Now she was all in.

Rupert had gone to a dinner in the city and wasn't meeting her until later. It gave her a breathing space.

Convincing him how blissfully happy she was to be marrying him put more of a strain on her than anything else.

Dully, she reached for a pot of cleansing cream to take off her make-up. There was a knock on the door.

'Come in,' she said, listlessly.

Then her heart gave a sickening lurch. Steve stood in the doorway – lazy, smiling, impossibly blond and handsome.

'How did you get in here?' she gasped.

'The doorman's a mate of mine.' He shut the door and leaned against it. 'Well?' he added softly.

'Well, what?'

'I thought I told you not to get tangled up with Rupert Henriques.'

'It's nothing to do with you!' There was a sob in her voice. 'A lot you care. You haven't even rung me.'

'I thought I'd leave you on slow burn for a week or two,' he said.

He walked towards her and put a hand on her bare shoulder. Funny how Rupert could maul her for hours and nothing happened, but just a touch from Steve sent a thousand volts through her. The warm hand crept slowly up her shoulder round to the back of her neck.

Then he laughed. 'You were fantastic as Desdemona, honey. I'd no idea you were that good.'

Happiness flooded through her. 'Oh! Did you really think so?'

'Yes. Absolutely bowled me over,' he said, bending his head and kissing her.

Bella was kissing him back. His hand was edging down the front of her dress and everything was getting quite out of control when, suddenly, to her horror, she heard the door burst open and a voice saying, 'This must be Bella's room.'

Colour flooding her face, she leapt away from Steve – but it was too late. Standing in the doorway was Lazlo Henriques and Bella's old enemy from drama school, Angora Fairfax.

'Bella. You are frightful,' said Angora with a giggle. 'You've only just got engaged to Rupert and here you are being unfaithful already with this stunning man.' She raised her huge blue eyes to Steve. 'I think you should call him out,' she added to Lazlo.

'Rupert can fight his own battles,' said Lazlo, looking amused. 'Hello, Bella. How are you?'

Bella was speechless. It was Steve who came to the rescue.

'I'd better introduce myself. My name's Steve Benedict,' he said, grinning.

'And I'm Angora Fairfax. And this foxy individual here is Lazlo Henriques,' said Angora.

She was as pretty as a kitten, incredibly slim with tiny wrists and ankles, cloudy dark hair, purply-blue eyes and pouting red lips which didn't quite meet over her slightly protruding teeth. Angora, said one of her stage school colleagues, was the sort of girl who could get away with asking a man if he could 'possibly carry this frightfully heavy match box'.

'Bella, darling,' she said. 'Do stop looking so pink in the face. It was a lovely performance. You were so good – though they shouldn't have given you that terrible set in the last act. I mean you were hopping all over the place like the Grand National. Lazlo was awful. He went to sleep in the second and third acts, but he's had a rough day. Gold bullion's gone down a half-penny or something. Have you anything for us to drink?'

'Yes, of course,' said Bella, grinding her teeth. She'd forgotten Angora's ability to make her feel a complete idiot. 'There's a bottle of whisky in the cupboard. Perhaps you'd do the honours, Steve.'

When Steve had poured out four very large drinks, Lazlo raised his glass to Bella. 'To you and Rupert,' he said, with a nasty glint in his eye.

'Yes, to the lovebirds,' said Angora. 'You must be in a daze of happiness, Bella. Such a relief to be settled and know one won't end up a terrible old maid keeping cats in a garret.' She looked at Lazlo under long, sooty black lashes.

'Don't fish, Angora,' he said.

She giggled. 'I'm sorry, but I'm a bit over-excited. Harry Backhaus has signed me up for the lead in his new film.'

'That's great,' said Steve, flashing her his devastating smile. 'How did you pull that off?'

'Strings really, darling. Lazlo took me and Harry out to a long, drunken lunch today. I gather you went after the part too, Bella darling? But as they start shooting in a fortnight, I knew you wouldn't want to be parted from Rupert so soon.'

'Of course I wouldn't!' said Bella. And she smiled at Lazlo, her heart black with hatred.

'What about you then?' Angora said to Steve. 'Where did Bella dig up something as lovely as you from?'

'Buenos Aires,' said Steve. He turned to Lazlo. 'Actually, we've met. I own the Amontillado Club. You've been in once or twice.'

'One of my favourite haunts,' said Lazlo. 'It's so dark I can never remember who I've come in with.'

'Is it nice out there?' asked Angora.

'It's nice anywhere,' said Steve and, laughing, he refilled Lazlo's glass.

Bella suddenly felt twitchy. If Lazlo learned from Steve the real truth about her past, heaven knows what use he'd make of it.

Angora was rabbiting on and on about acting. Steve and Lazlo had moved on to business.

'Money, money, money!' said Angora finally. 'I can see you two are going to be very bad for each other.'

Bella felt a stab of jealousy. In a quarter of an hour they'd accepted Steve as they'd never accept her.

He was talking to Angora now, turning on his *homme fatal* act, dropping his voice several semitones, flashing his teeth all over the place.

Finally, Angora stretched. 'Lazlo, darling. If I don't eat I shall fall over.'

'Let's go then,' said Lazlo, stubbing out his cigar. 'why don't you come, too?' he added to Steve.

'Won't I be *de trop*?' said Steve.

'Not at all,' said Angora. 'Lazlo will melt into a telephone box and magic up some amazing looking girl for you, then we'll go on the town. Thanks for drinks, Bella. See you at Gay's wedding. Lazlo had some crazy scheme for us all to go down to the country the next day, then we can go to Goodwood. If you like horses,' she added to Steve, 'you'd better come too.'

And they drifted out, hardly bothering to say goodbye, leaving Bella jibbering with misery and impotent rage. Lazlo's nasty grin stayed with her, like the Cheshire Cat, long after he'd gone.

She had even more cause to be angry with him in the next few days. Two television plays and a commercial she'd considered certainties suddenly fell through. Her bank manager wrote a vitriolic letter complaining about her overdraft.

She was also due to play Nina in the Britannia's production of *The Seagull*, which was going into rehearsal next week. Suddenly, Roger Field, the director, sent for her and told her he wanted her to play Masha, the frumpy, frustrated school-mistress instead.

Bella lost her temper. 'Lazlo Henriques is behind this!' she stormed.

'Who's he?' said Roger unconvincingly. 'I make the decisions round here. I feel you'd be better as Masha.'

7

As usual, Bella left buying something to wear to Gay's wedding to the last minute. She knew she shouldn't buy anything at all. There were stacks of hardly worn dresses in her wardrobe and, with the present intransigence of her bank manager, he was bound to bounce the cheque anyway.

But for the last week she'd been spending money as though it was going out of fashion, almost as though she was determining her own destiny, forcing herself into such financial straits that the only way out would be to marry Rupert.

Anyway, she had to have a new dress. She knew that Steve had been asked to the wedding, and that he'd been seeing a lot of Angora, and that she must knock him for six by looking even more glamorous.

The shopping expedition was a disaster; half the shops seemed to have sales on. Everything she tried on looked perfectly frightful and she'd no idea how the weather was going to turn out. It was one of those grey, dull days that might easily get hot later.

'Puce is going to be very big in the autumn,' said a sales girl, forcing her into a wool dress and holding great folds of material in at the back to give it the appearance of fitting.

Bella winced at her washed out reflection. 'I look like something the cat brought in or up,' she said. 'I need a new face, not a new dress.'

By two o'clock, when she was getting desperate, she found a dress in willow green, sleeveless, low cut and clinging, with a wrap-over skirt. It was the only remotely sexy thing she had tried on.

'Do you think it's all right for a wedding?' she said desperately.

'Oh yes,' said the sales girl, raking a midge bite with long red nails. 'People wear anything for anything these days.'

By the time she'd found a floppy, coral pink picture hat and shoes to match she was really running out of time. But when she tried them all on later in daylight in her flat, she realized the coral looked terrible with her tawny hair.

She had an hour and a half before she had to be at the church. Her hairdresser was closed that afternoon. The only answer was to wash her hair and put a red rinse on it, but in her haste she forgot to read the instructions about not using it on dyed hair. The result was not a gentle Titian, but a bright orange going on Heinz tomato, and impossibly fluffy with it.

She soon realized too, that half a ton of eye-liners, blushers, shaders and all her skill at making-up wasn't going to do her any good. It simply wasn't an on-day.

Her skin looked dead, her eyes small and tired, and no amount of pancake could conceal the bags under them.

It was also getting colder. A sharp east wind was

flattening the leaves of the plane trees in the square outside. All her coats were too short to wear over her new dress. In the end she slung Basil, her red fox fur, round her neck.

'I need a few allies to face that mob,' she thought.

A large crowd had gathered outside the church to watch people arrive. Bella, hopelessly late, rolled up at the same time as the bridal car and fell up the steps in her haste to get in first.

'Drunk already,' said a wag in the crowd.

Lazlo helped her to her feet. With a flash of irritation she realized that he looked very good and that the austere black and white formality of morning dress suited his sallow skin and irregular features extremely well.

He looked at her hair and said, 'Oh dear, oh dear,' and then at her bare arms, and added in amusement, 'You're going to be bloody cold in church.'

She wanted to slip unnoticed into a pew at the back, but, grabbing her arm like a vice, Lazlo led her right up to the second row from the front,

'You're a member of the family now,' he said.

Rupert, looking glamorous, and almost as pale as the white carnation in his button hole, tried to sit next to her, but Lazlo stopped him.

'Uh-uh,' he said. 'You've got to sit in the front and look after Constance,' and sat down very firmly on the edge of the row, next to Bella. Bella moved quickly away from him, slap into a very lecherous-looking old man with long grey sideboards, on her other side.

'You haven't met Uncle Willy yet, have you Bella?' said Lazlo.

Beyond Rupert sat a scruffy, but nice-looking boy with a pudding basin hair cut. That must be Rupert's brother, Jonathan, let off from school.

Across the aisle sat Teddy and his best man. Teddy's pink and white cheeks were stained with colour as he alternately tugged at his collar and smoothed his newly cut hair.

'I comforted my mother,' said Rupert, 'that she wasn't losing a daughter, just gaining a cretin.'

Bella giggled. People were turning round and talking to each other and saying, 'Hello, haven't seen you for *years*.'

The organ was playing the same Bach cantata for the third time. Bella, sneaking a surreptitious look round, realized that as usual she was quite wrongly dressed. Everyone was in silk dresses or beautifully cut suits. And the competition was absolutely stependous. Lazlo was right; it was icy in church. Every goose pimple was standing out on her bare arms. Uncle Willy next door was gazing openly at her beasts. Irritably, to obscure his view, Bella shoved the fox's mask down the front of her dress.

'Gone to earth,' said Lazlo.

Bella gazed stonily ahead at the huge Constance Spry flower arrangement. Suddenly she realized that her wrap-over dress, which looked so respectable when she was standing up, had fallen open, revealing a large expanse of thigh and the pants with 'Abandon Hope All Ye Who Enter Here' printed on them, which Rosie had given her for her birthday. Hastily she covered herself up, but not before both Lazlo and Uncle Willy had had a good look.

I'll kill him, fumed Bella, I'll kill him, and afterwards I'll kick his teeth in.

Another old relation, sleeping peacefully behind them, suddenly woke up and said, 'Come on, buck up. Let's get cracking,' in a loud voice. There was a rustle of interest as Constance swept up the aisle looking like a double-decker bus in a dust sheet, waving graciously to friends and relations.

'She claims she's just discovered the tent dress,' Rupert whispered to Bella. 'But she needs a couple of marquees to cover her.'

Finally, when Bella was about to turn into a pillar of ice, the organ launched into 'Here Comes the Bride' and everyone rose to their feet.

Here was Charles, a fatuous smile on his face, wafting brandy fumes as he went. On his arm hung Gay, looking pale but well in control, and carrying a huge bouquet to conceal any evidence of pregnancy. Her progress was slow, for every few seconds she nearly had her head jerked off as one of the little bridesmaids trod on her veil.

Chrissie brought up the rear, wearing pink, a coronet of pink roses on her gleaming dark hair. She'd obviously had a professional make-up. She looked lovely, but suicidal. She halted just beside Lazlo. Rupert turned round and pulled a face at her, trying to make her laugh.

'Dearly beloved,' intoned the bishop.

Bella had to share a prayer book with Lazlo. Rigid with loathing, she looked down at his long fingers and beautifully manicured nails and tried not to breathe in the subtle musk and lavender overtones of the after-shave he was wearing.

'First,' said the bishop, 'it was ordained for the procreation of children.'

'You can say that again,' muttered Rupert with a grin.

'Second as a remedy against sin, for such people as have not the gift of continence.'

'I do hope you're taking all this in,' said Lazlo out of the corner of his mouth.

Bella was not listening; she was having a day-dream of standing in Gay's place, with long white satin arms, and hair drawn back to show a delicately blushing face, with an impossibly slender waist from a pre-wedding crash diet, with Steve beside her, devastatingly handsome, smiling proudly down at her, and putting a gold ring on her finger.

'To have and to hold, for richer for poorer, in sickness and in health, to love and to cherish till death us do part,' repeated Teddy in his strangulated hernia voice, after the bishop.

But would Steve ever stay with her? Was he capable of loving and cherishing anyone for very long? Would she herself ever be able to love and cherish Rupert the way Chrissie would?

Looking past Lazlo, she saw Chrissie staring fixedly in front of her, the tears pouring down her face. Oh, what a stupid muddle it all is, thought Bella.

'I feel sick,' said one of the little bridesmaids.

'Immortal, Invisible God only wise,' sang the congregation. Lazlo, next to her, sang the bass part loudly. He's just the sort of person who would embarrass his children singing parts too loudly in church, she thought savagely.

They all sat down for the sermon. The bishop was getting warmed up about fidelity and the need for steadfastness in the modern world when so many marriages crumbled.

Uncle Willy was rubbing his thigh against

Bella's. She couldn't move away or she would have been jammed against Lazlo.

She gazed furiously in front of her. Really, she was getting to know that flower arrangement extremely well. Suddenly, with the spontaneity that was so much part of his charm, Rupert turned round, took her hand and squeezed it. She was conscious of both Lazlo and Chrissie watching them. A deep blush spread over her face and down her shoulders.

Constance was crying unashamedly as they all went off into the vestry.

'It's not because she's losing Gay,' said Lazlo dryly, 'but the thought of all the money this is costing her.'

A reedy tenor began to sing, 'Sheep May Safely Graze.'

The wait was interminable.

'You'd think they were consummating the marriage, wouldn't you?' said Rupert. 'I wish we could smoke.'

Back came the procession. Teddy, crimson with embarrassment; Gay, looking relieved, grinning slightly as she caught the eyes of various relations.

'Hear you're an actress,' said Uncle Willy to Bella. 'Ever bin in Crossroads?' (He pronounced it Crawse.) 'Never miss it m'self, bloody good programme.'

For several minutes they were penned up at the top of the church while the photographers took pictures. As soon as he came out of his pew, Rupert squeezed Bella's arm.

'Christ, what a performance. Hullo, Aunt Vera. I'm not going through a bloody circus like this when we get married, darling. Hullo Uncle Bertie.

It's going to be in and out of Chelsea Registry office and straight off to London Airport to somewhere warm immediately afterwards.'

Bella put her hand lovingly over Rupert's. 'I agree,' she said, looking straight at Lazlo. 'And as soon as possible too. I've suddenly gone off long engagements.'

The reception was a nightmare. It was held in three huge marquees in the Henriques' garden and Bella had never felt more lonely or out of things in her life.

There was a strange assortment of people there. Teddy's grand, dowdy relations in their silk shirtwaisters and pull-on felts were almost indistinguishable from Constance's fellow committee workers, who included several Chief Guiders in uniform, who brayed to one another and drank orange juice. In one corner, two bus-loads of tenants from Teddy's father's estate sat with their legs apart, looking embarrassed. But by far the largest group of people there, Bella suspected, were Charles's and Lazlo's friends, members of the international set at their richest and most international. Even though some of them had turned up in jeans, they had that kind of bland self-assurance, the gilt-edged security that enabled them to be accepted anywhere. Everywhere you looked ravishingly pretty women had emerged from their winter furs like butterflies and stood jamming cigarettes into their scarlet lips, knocking back champagne, refusing asparagus rolls and smoked salmon for the sake of their figures, and chattering wittily to the suave, handsome, expensive-looking men who surrounded them. Bella had never seen so many people who seemed to know each other, or, even if they didn't, would discover a host of friends they had in common.

Rupert did his best to look after her, but he was constantly being grabbed by Constance or Charles, or particularly by Lazlo, to go and look after someone else, or see to something.

She tried to scintillate and be amusing, but because she was nervous and unsure of herself, her voice came out far more artificial and affected than it would normally. Putting up a front to cover up her desperate insecurity, she knew she was appearing phoney and as hard as nails. Rupert kept introducing her into a group of people, but it was like feeding a screw into the hoover. Five minutes later they'd spew her out again.

God, they were noisy too. Half the conversations were being carried on in foreign languages, full of laughter and exclamation marks, like the talking bits in Fidelio.

She couldn't even get drunk because she had a performance that evening. In her misery, she ate five éclairs, then felt sick.

Suddenly, as though someone had stamped a branding iron on her back, she was aware of Chrissie standing behind her, her eyes glittering with misery and loathing.

'Pink really suits you,' Bella said nervously. 'And you've lost so much weight! You really look ravishing.'

'But not quite ravishing enough,' snapped Chrissie, and, turning on her heel, she disappeared into the crowd. Even talking to Uncle Willy would have been preferable to standing by herself, but he was hemmed in by some aunts in a corner.

Where on earth were Steve and Angora, Bella wondered. It was almost impossible to find them in this crowd.

She couldn't stay leaning against a pillar for ever – like a small boat launching itself on a rough sea, she began fighting her way across the marquee again – and, suddenly, there like something on the big screen, was Angora, wearing a navy blue straw hat which framed her cloudy dark hair and a parma violet suit, which emphasized her huge, purply-blue eyes.

She was surrounded by men, but lounging by her side was Steve in a grey morning suit, cracking jokes, deflecting any competition, very much master of the situation. Admire her, but keep your distance, he seemed to be saying. They made a sensational pair.

Angora was laughing at something he said, throwing back her head to show her lovely white throat when, in mid-laugh, suddenly she saw Bella.

'Belladonna! Come here – at once.'

As there was nowhere else to go, Bella went up to them.

'Darling, you've gone orange. How brave of you. Is it for a new part, or are you doing a soup commercial?'

The men around Angora looked at Bella without interest.

'You've all met Rupert's fiancée, haven't you?' said Angora. 'You know Steve of course, Bella, and this is Timmie, and this is Patrick, and this is . . . oh God, I can't remember your name.'

Bella was looking at Steve. Her heart was pounding.

'Yes, I know Steve,' she said. 'Or I thought I did. How are you?'

'Fantastic,' said Steve, giving her that curiously opaque, shutters-down look she knew of old. 'Where's Rupert? Getting some aunt out of mothballs?'

'I'm glad you've brought Foxy,' said Angora, patting Bella's fox fur. 'He looks as though he needs an outing. Why don't you give him some Bob Martins?'

Everyone laughed. Bella blushed. Why can't I think of some witty crack to make back, she thought miserably.

Rescue, however, was at hand, in the not very steady shape of Charles. 'Bella, darling,' he said, kissing her on both cheeks. 'I've been looking all over for you. They ought to page people at this party. I wonder if you'd be terribly kind and give a word of advice to a young niece of mine. She's awfully keen to go on the stage and I thought, being such a star, you were the person to talk to.'

Bella got a slight satisfaction in seeing a look of annoyance flicker across Angora's face. She obviously felt she was the one who ought to be consulted.

'I'd love to,' said Bella and, without even saying goodbye to Steve, she followed Charles back into the crowd.

The stage-struck niece had a horse face and half Chelsea Flower Show on her head.

'It must be amazing to be acting at the Britannia,' she said. 'I suppose you pulled strings.'

'No,' said Bella, 'not even a tiny thread, but I had a lucky break. Have you had much experience?'

'No. I played Juliet in the school play. Everyone said I was awfully good.'

Oh God! Bella groaned inwardly. 'Have you tried to get into any of the drama schools?' she said.

'No. Perhaps you could give me a list of names. And perhaps you could introduce me to your director. I gather he's very charming.'

'Very,' said Bella. Her mind started to wander.

The horse-faced niece droned on and on.

'Incredible, fantastic, amazing,' said Bella at suitable intervals. Then she said, 'How marvellous'. The horse-faced girl looked at her in surprise.

'How marvellous,' said Bella again.

'I said Mummy was in Harrods when the bomb went off last week,' said the girl.

'Oh God, I'm sorry,' said Bella. 'I misheard you. There's such a din going on.'

Next moment one of Horseface's friends came up and they started shrieking at each other. Bella escaped, but not before she heard Horseface saying, 'That's Rupert's fiancée. I don't think she's quite all there.'

Bella retreated to a pillar again and ate three more éclairs, malevolently surveying the rest of the crowd.

'Don't look so horrified,' said a voice. 'You chose to marry into this lot.'

She jumped nervously. It was Lazlo.

'They're a load of junk,' she snapped. 'They should be driven over a cliff with pitch forks.'

Lazlo laughed. 'I'm glad you're enjoying yourself.'

A waitress came by with a tray.

'Have an ice,' he said. 'Children are supposed to like them, aren't they?'

'I hate ices,' her voice rose shrilly, 'more than anything else in the world except you.'

At that moment Teddy came up, looking distraught.

'Hullo, Bella,' he said. 'I say, Lazlo, I thought pregnant women only threw up in the morning. Gay's puking her guts out upstairs. I'm sure Constance is going to smell a rat. She wants us to cut the cake now. She's terrified everyone is going to drink too much.'

'Poor old Teddy,' said Lazlo, 'But you did go into this with your flies open.'

'I certainly did,' sighed Teddy. 'It's hell being a bridegroom. No-one talks to you because they all think you ought to be talking to someone else.'

He wandered off, looking miserable, and they were immediately joined by a smooth looking man with auburn hair and heavy-lidded eyes.

'Lazlo!'

'Henri my dear, how are things?'

'Pretty rough. I've had to sell half my horses and I've had to sell off the land, but at least they've let me keep the shooting. Hope you'll come and stay for the twelfth.' He held out his glass to be filled by a passing waiter.

'I say,' he went on. 'Where's this chorus girl Rupert's got himself mixed up with. One hears such conflicting views. Charles is evidently rather smitten, but he always liked scrubbers. The rest of the family seem to think she's absolute hell.'

Bella went white.

'Judge for yourself,' said Lazlo. 'This is Bella.'

'Oh God,' said the red-headed man, looking not at all embarrassed. 'Trust me to put both feet in it.' He gave Bella a horse-flesh-judging once-over, then said, 'I must say I'm inclined to agree with Charles. You're bound to get opposition if you marry into this lot; they're so bloody cliquey. It'll be your turn next, Lazlo. One of those pretty girls you run around with will finally get her claws into you.'

'Hardly,' said Lazlo. 'Just because I enjoy a good gallop it doesn't necessarily mean I want to buy the horse.'

The red-headed man laughed.

'Cold-blooded sod aren't you? I must say you've got a pretty smart crowd here today. Aren't those a couple of Royals I see through the smoke?'

'My Aunt Constance,' said Lazlo, 'would get blue blood out of a stone. I suppose I'd better go and organize someone or we'll be here till midnight.'

Gay, looking pea-green but fairly composed, reappeared to cut the cake. Rupert fought his way over to Bella's side.

'God, what a hassle. The most terrible things are happening. Uncle Willy's just exposed himself to one of Teddy's female tenants. Has Lazlo been taking care of you?'

'I'm sure he'd like me taken care of,' said Bella.

Someone rapped the table. The speeches were mercifully short.

Lazlo stood up first to propose Gay's and Teddy's health. He was the sort of person who could quieten a room just by clearing his throat.

'I'm sorry,' he said, in his husky, slightly foreign voice, 'that so many of you have had to miss Goodwood. We all appreciate the sacrifice.' He then proceeded to read out the Goodwood results.

God, that laid them in the aisles. They were all in stitches.

'Bloody funny,' said Rupert.

In a corner Uncle Willy was so drunk he was trying to light an asparagus roll.

Lazlo then told a couple of jokes – Bella had to admire his timing – before raising his glass to Gay and Teddy. Everyone round her drained empty glasses. The drink, due to Constance's parsimony, was running short.

Teddy got up.

His heart was in his mouth, he said, and, as his old Nanny had told him never to talk with his mouth full, he'd better shut up. God, they fell about at that too. I wish I played to audiences like that, thought Bella.

He just wanted to thank Constance and Charles, he added, and toast the jolly pretty bridesmaids. The best man replied briefly and the room became a great twittering aviary again. Children were beginning to get over-excited and run through people's legs. Grandmothers retired to the sidelines to rest their swelling ankles. Suddenly, there was a loud bang on the table and Bella turned hearing Charles's voice.

'I won't keep you a moment,' he said, his voice slurring, his eyes glazed.

'Pissed as a newt as usual,' said someone behind Bella.

'I won't keep you a minute,' he said again. 'But I just wanted everyone to know how absolutely delighted Constance and I are that our son, Rupert, has just announced his engagement to a very talented and beautiful girl.'

'Charles,' thundered Constance, magenta with rage.

'Pissed as a newt,' said the voice again.

'I want you to drink to Bella and Rupert,' said

Charles. 'I know she'll be an asset to us all.'

Half the marquee had started mumbling. 'Bella and Rupert,' when Chrissie suddenly said, very loudly, 'It's not true. She's not an asset. She's horrible, horrible. She's the biggest bitch that ever lived.'

There was a dreadful, embarrassed silence.

'Shut up, Chrissie,' snarled Rupert.

'What's that, what's that?' everyone was saying.

Lazlo had crossed the room in a flash.

'Come on, baby, that's enough. Upstairs with you.'

'You don't understand. No-one understands anything,' said Chrissie and, wrenching her arms away from Lazlo, she fled out of the marquee.

Bella had also had enough. She fought her way out into the street and immediately found a taxi. Just as she had got in and was telling the driver to take her to the theatre, Rupert appeared at the window.

'Bella darling, please wait.'

'No, I will not,' she hissed. 'I've had enough of you and your bloody family for one afternoon. I'm not going to stand around getting insulted any more. Go on,' she said to the driver. 'Get going.'

'Darling,' pleaded Rupert, 'for Christ's sake let me explain.'

As the taxi moved off he reached in to grab her arm, but caught hold of the fox's tail instead, which promptly came off in his hand.

Bella leaned out of the car,

'And I'll report you to the RSPCA for cruelty to foxes,' she screamed back at him.

8

She couldn't wait to get to the theatre to pour out all her miseries to Rosie Hassell.

When she arrived, she discovered Rosie was off with 'flu and an understudy was taking her place. The poor girl was absolutely sick with nerves and needed all the boosting Bella could give her.

Here I am at twenty-four, a real trouper with a Manx Fox, thought Bella, and she started to giggle helplessly. All the same, she gave a terrible performance. She couldn't concentrate and she kept drying up and fluffing her lines.

Rupert rang her in the interval. It took all his powers of persuasion to get her to come out that evening.

'Chrissie was tight,' he said. 'She's been on a diet, hasn't eaten properly for days, and she's got this sort of crush on me. She passed out when she got upstairs. She'll be absolutely mortified in the morning.'

'She's not coming out with us tonight?'

'I don't think so – just Angora, Steve, Lazlo and one of his birds.'

'The Heavy Brigade,' said Bella.

But she couldn't resist another chance to get at Steve.

She made a real hash of the last act. Wesley Barrington had to carry her the whole way. There was a great deal of applause at the end, both for him and the understudy.

'Roger's out front,' said Wesley, out of the corner of his mouth, as bowing and smiling, they took the last curtain call.

'Oh God,' said Bella. 'I'd better make myself scarce.'

Roger, however, came back-stage immediately.

'Well done,' he said to the understudy, his square freckled face breaking into a smile of approval. 'That was a lovely performance. Now clear out and get changed somewhere else.'

When she had gone, he shut the door and leant against it. 'That was a cock-up, wasn't it,' he said grimly. 'I suppose you got tight at the wedding.'

Bella shook her head. 'Not enough. That was the trouble.'

'Hell – was it?'

'Hell would seem like a day at the seaside compared with that little bunfight. The Henriques really don't like outsiders, do they? Trespassers are very much persecuted.'

She lit a cigarette with a trembling hand.

'Putting the heat on, are they? Are you sure you're doing the right thing, marrying this boy?'

'Oh, not you too,' groaned Bella. 'I thought you were my friend.'

'I am, and one of your greatest fans too. I know you can make it really big, but not if you go on giving lousy performances like this evening. You're in bad shape, angel. If I touched you, you'd twang.

And you look frightful too. No-one looking at you could see any reason why Othello should have the hots for you.'

'Thanks a lot,' said Bella, and started to laugh.

'That's better. Now you've got three days off, haven't you? For God's sake get some sleep. What are you going to do?'

'Spend the weekend at the Henriques' country hot seat.'

'You'll enjoy that. It's very plushy. Hot and cold servants in every bedroom, and the country is absolutely magical.'

'If that's supposed to cheer me up,' said Bella, 'it's an experience I would gladly forgo. You know how I hate the country.'

It was only when she got out of her costume that she realized she'd brought nothing to wear. She hated the willow green dress as she hated hell pains. The only alternative was a T-shirt with a picture of Clark Gable on the front and a crumpled pair of black knickerbockers which had been at the bottom of her cupboard for weeks and smelt of old mushrooms.

Oh well, she thought, tugging them on, I've got the top batting average for wearing the wrong clothes, why spoil the record?

It was four o'clock in the morning and the night had fallen to pieces around her. They had gone from disco to disco, and ended up in one of Rupert's haunts, where the musicians played cool jazz.

Chrissie had cried off, pleading a headache.

She can't stand seeing me and Rupert together, Bella thought wryly. And Lazlo had brought a ravishing Spanish girl with him, with a long black plait trailing down her beautiful brown back.

Steve had ignored Bella all evening. It was as though a sheet of glass had risen between them. Not once did he ask her to dance.

She was dead with exhaustion, but some masochistic streak wouldn't allow her to go home.

They were all dancing now, Steve still laughing with Angora. Rupert, his cheeks flushed, his hair tousled over his face like some Bacchante, was pressing his body against Bella's, muttering endearments into her ear. Lazlo was kissing his beautiful Spaniard, his hands slowly caressing her brown back, which was arched towards him in ecstatic submission, the two of them exuding so much white-hot sexuality it rubbed off on everyone else.

I can't stand it, thought Bella in agony, and wrenching herself away from Rupert, she fled into the loo and burst into a storm of weeping.

After a few minutes she managed to pull herself together and looked at her face in the mirror. It was pale grey. She rubbed some lipstick onto her cheeks. The effect was horrible.

And you can stop grinning too! she snarled silently at Clark Gable, who was baring his teeth across her bosom.

Rupert was dancing with the Spanish girl when she got back to the table. Lazlo was smoking a cigar. Bella sat down as far away from him as possible and gazed into her drink.

'You won't find the truth in the bottom of a shot of Johnnie Walker,' he said.

The light from an opening door suddenly lit up the long scar down the side of his face.

Curious, in spite of herself, Bella asked, 'Where did you get that scar?'

'In Buenos Aires. A man called Miguel Rodriguez pulled a knife on me.'

'What for?'

'He thought I was having it off with his wife.'

'What did you do?'

'I killed him!'

Bella shivered. 'But why?'

'He'd have killed me otherwise, and I was – er – quite fond of his wife.'

'There must have been a frightful scandal.'

'Frightful. But there have been worse since. People soon forget.'

She started to laugh scornfully but, somehow, the laugh got out of hand and went on and on.

'This isn't doing you any good, is it?' he said.

'I'm all right,' she snapped.

He picked up her hand and examined it. 'Maybe, but bitten nails do not denote serenity. The woods are deep and dark and full of tigers. You'd be very wise to pack Rupert in.'

'Over my dead body,' she hissed, snatching her hand away from him.

Then the inevitable happened. Steve and Angora were no longer there.

Lazlo gave Rupert and Bella a lift. The top of the car was down, the night all warm, and Bella looked up at the endless stars, trying to convince herself her life wasn't over.

Rupert put his arm round her.

'Don't maul me,' she yelled, suddenly at breaking point.

There was a shocked silence. Rupert went white. 'Take it easy, darling,' he said gently.

'I'm sorry, love,' said Bella, a moment later taking his hand.

But in the driving mirror, she saw a glint of satisfaction in Lazlo's eyes.

9

As a result of hangovers, none of them had gone down to the country until late on the day after Gay's wedding. They all felt jaded. The only answer seemed to start drinking again.

It was Angora, probably at Lazlo's instigation, who suggested they play table-turning. Everyone, except Bella, agreed with alacrity. A polished table and a glass were found; the lights were dimmed.

At first the glass produced no messages for anyone; then, chided by Chrissie that the spirits would not work unless they stopped fooling about, they started to concentrate.

The glass hovered a bit, then spelt out that Lazlo was going on a journey, which impressed everyone because he was flying to Zurich tomorrow night, and it told Angora she was due for measles.

Then it spelt Mabel.

'We don't know anyone called Mabel,' said Angora.

'Yes, we do,' said Steve. 'Bella, of course.'

'Bella?' said Rupert in surprise. 'But she's Isabella.'

'No, she's not. I've known her longer than you

and her name's not Bella. She was born Mabel Figge, to be exact.'

Bella blushed scarlet.

Angora gave a crow of joy. 'You're never called Mabel Figge!' And she went off into peals of laughter. Chrissie grinned delightedly.

'Shut up, Angora!' snapped Rupert. 'Let's go on with the message for Bella.'

They all put their fingers on the glass.

'G-o h-o-m-e' it spelt out slowly. Then, suddenly, taking on a life of its own, it veered around the table, spelling out 'T-w-o t-i-m-i-n-g g-o-l-d d-i-g-g-e-r.'

There was a long pause.

Then Bella screamed, 'Someone's pushing that glass!'

'Darling,' Rupert protested, 'it's only a game.'

'And you can shut up!' she shouted at him, and, jumping to her feet, she caught her bag on the edge of the table. Everything cascaded on to the floor, her mirror breaking.

'And I hope it brings you all seven hundred years' bad luck!' she screamed.

She gave a sob and fled upstairs, locking herself in her bedroom and lying on her bed, crying just loudly enough for people to hear.

Later, Rupert came upstairs and banged on her door until she let him in.

'You're over-reacting,' he said. 'They're only teasing.'

'Throwing darts into a maddened bull, more likely,' she stormed.

He started kissing her; then followed the inevitable row because he wanted to make love to her. Suddenly, the fight went out of her.

'Oh well, go on if you must, I don't care,' she said listlessly.

Rupert stared at her for a minute.

'Thanks,' he said coldly, 'but I never accept charity,' and walked out of the room, slamming the door behind him.

It was early dawn when she finally fell asleep, and late dawn when she woke up, head splitting, gravel behind her eyes.

Desperate for aspirins, she got up and wandered down the passage to the bathroom she shared with Angora.

There were no pills in the cupboard, only bath salts and cologne. She weighed herself on the scales. God, she was putting on weight. She must stop all this misery eating.

She got off the scales and turned them up seven pounds. That would screw up Angora and her flaming slimming diets.

On the way back, she paused outside Angora's bedroom. The door was ajar. She peered in, uneasily breathing in the smell of French cigarettes, nail-polish and expensive scent. Then her nails bit into her palms as she realized there was no-one sleeping in the bed. Angora must be with Steve. Until now, Bella had nurtured a faint hope he was just chasing Angora to goad her into breaking it off with Rupert.

Now she imagined his suntanned hands caressing Angora's body, her cloudy black hair on the pillow, her little gasps of excitement, her head threshing back and forth like a meningitis victim, as Steve drove her to the extremes of pleasure that Bella knew of old he was capable of. Then, later, the low laughter, the private jokes, the exchanged cigarettes, the sleeping in each other's arms.

She sat on her bed for a few minutes, whimpering. It was impossibly hot already.

She got up and opened the shutters and stepped out on to the balcony.

The fields were white with dew, a heavy mist hung over the lake at the bottom of the lawn. The white climbing roses on their tall arches were touched with pink. On the tennis court birds were chasing worms; in the distance a train chugged.

The beauty of the view only intensified her misery. A light breeze caressed her bare legs and lifted her hair off her shoulders.

Suddenly, she heard a scrunch of wheels and, leaning over the balcony, she saw the ivy green Mercedes draw up in front of the house. Lazlo got out. He was wearing a red and white striped shirt and dark grey trousers, and carrying his jacket and tie.

Bella stepped out of his line of vision, but, through a crack in the shutter, she watched him yawn and stretch, breathing in the morning air. Then, whistling, he set off across the dew-soaked lawn towards the stables.

The next moment, she heard a door shut quietly and saw Angora, wearing a white silk dressing gown, steal across the drive and then the lawn, after him. Then she called his name. He turned round, smiled and walked back towards her.

There was a quivering expectancy about Angora, as though she was longing for him to take her in his arms. For a minute they talked in low voices, with Bella nearly falling off the balcony in her efforts to hear. Then Lazlo picked up a loose strand of hair which had fallen over Angora's forehead and smoothed it behind her ear. She seemed to be arguing now; then he patted her cheek and nodded towards the direction of the house. Reluctantly she came running back across the grass and disappeared through the front door.

Bella opened her door slightly, but Angora didn't come back to her room. Had she gone to Steve's bedroom, or Lazlo's?

10

A beautiful blazing day soared out of the mist. Bella lay by the swimming pool, trying to learn her lines. It was mid-morning. Out in the park, the sun touched the pale green shoulders of the elm trees, cattle grazed contentedly in the lush grass beside the lake, and Lazlo's two golden retrievers frolicked on the lawn.

It was impossible to imagine a view more serene, yet Bella felt sick with terror.

Anxious to avoid Rupert, she had got up early and gone to buy some aspirins at the local shop. She knew one of the fleet of servants would have provided them, but she wanted an excuse to get out of the house.

Just as she was leaving, a window box crashed from one of the balconies, missing her by inches.

The gardener, of course, was profuse in his apologies.

But twice later, as she wandered along the narrow country lanes, a large blue car roared past her, driving so close that she would have been run over if she hadn't leapt on to the verge.

Lazlo's behind this, she thought. He's capable of getting rid of Miguel Rodriguez because he'd got in his way; why not me too?

She tried to concentrate on learning her lines for *The Seagull*. She was playing Masha, the plain and ageing spinster, loved by the schoolmaster, but, in her turn, hoplessly in love with the son of the house. Every line she read seemed to parallel her own set-up:

'*I am in mourning for my life, I am unhappy . . . It isn't money that matters, a poor man may be happy . . . Oh, nonsense, your love touches me but I cannot return it . . . Help me, help me, or I shall do something silly. I shall make a mockery of my life and ruin it. I can't go on . . . I am miserable. No-one knows how miserable I am. I love Konstantin.*'

She might have been speaking about her situation with Rupert and Steve. 'I shall make a mockery of my life and ruin it,' she repeated.

A shadow fell across her book. She jumped violently, then realized it was Steve.

It was the first time she'd been alone with him since that evening in the theatre. Even in the blazing sunshine he looked brown.

He was wearing navy blue bathing trunks and a pair of dark glasses, so she couldn't read the expression in his eyes as he looked down at her.

As always, she felt her stomach go liquid with desire.

'Hi stranger,' he said softly. 'May I talk with you?'

He sat down beside her.

'I don't know what game you're playing,' she blurted out.

'What game, honey? You tell me.'

'Telling me one moment you wanted me to break

it off with Rupert because you were so crazy about me, then ignoring me the next. Sending me up. Telling the others my real name. Blatantly chatting up Angora just to hurt me.'

'I've been doing a little more than chatting up,' he said, pinching one of her cigarettes.

'Do you love her?'

'I don't understand words like love; they're not in my vocabulary, but she's extremely attractive. Let's say we enjoy each other.'

'Maybe you do,' said Bella steadily. 'But not enough to stop her slipping out at dawn to have a private confab with Lazlo.'

Just for a second Steve paused.

'How do you know?'

'I couldn't sleep. I opened my shutters. Lazlo came home about six, no doubt from shacking up with some of the local talent. Within ten seconds, Angora was out of the house. She'd obviously been waiting for him. They had some kind of hassle, then he persuaded her to come back into the house.'

Steve shrugged his shoulders. 'She's entitled to a commercial break if she wants one. The programme was good enough.'

'But don't you see,' Bella went on desperately, 'they're in cahoots together. Angora's simply being manipulated by Lazlo. He's pulled off a marvellous film deal for her. She's very ambitious. He's probably been knocking her off as well, and, in return, she's agreed to lure you away from me. She's pretty formidable when she pulls out the stops. I defy anyone, even you, to resist her. And Lazlo knows what I feel about you. That seeing you and Angora together is driving me round the twist. That it's the one thing that'll make me break it off with Rupert.'

Steve yawned so hard he nearly dislocated his jaw.

'You always had too much imagination,' he said. 'And keep your trap shut, the others are coming. Hi Chrissie. Hi Rupe. The midges are terrible. You'd better come up and see my itchings sometime.'

Bella flopped down on her lilo in despair.

Rupert sat down beside her. Even on the hottest day of the year, he still had the look of a hothouse plant exposed to a killing draught. He was wearing a black shirt with the collar turned up, as if against some imagined storm, and looked at Bella with bruised, troubled eyes, and eyelids swollen from lack of sleep.

How he'd changed from the cool, bitchy self-confident little boy she'd met six months ago.

She put out her hand to stroke his face. He imprisoned it and held it against his cheek.

'Oh, darling, we must stop fighting. I can't stand another night like last night.'

I can't go on torturing him much longer, she thought unhappily. I must break it off with him, but not yet. I'm not going to give Lazlo the satisfaction of thinking he directly engineered it.

Chrissie, very white, and too fat for her scarlet bikini, sat down under an umbrella, and started the *Daily Mail* crossword.

Steve dived into the pool, his muscular arms coming out of the bright turquoise water as he did a leisurely crawl to the other side.

'It's lovely once you get in,' he called to Chrissie.

And eventually, after a lot of badinage, he persuaded her to join him in the water, where he chased her round the pool, tickling her, diving for her ankles, making her shriek with laughter and fear.

Rupert edged away as a particularly violent piece of splashing soaked his shirt.

'I detest horseplay,' he said. 'And I don't feel much more kindly towards Mr Benedict.'

Giggling frantically, Chrissie clambered out of the pool and ran along the edge to take refuge under the umbrella. Steve picked up a towel and, catching up, began to dry her, laughing down at her, his eyelashes stuck together with water, his blue eyes rivalling the drained sapphire of the sky. Gradually, in his arms, she calmed down and stopped giggling.

'I'm going to oil you,' he said. 'And you're going to lie in the sun and stop hiding your very considerable lights under a bushel.'

'I'll oil her,' said Rupert sharply, getting to his feet and almost snatching the bottle of Ambre Solaire from Steve.

Bella felt a stab of guilt as she saw the ecstasy in Chrissie's face as Rupert rubbed it into her back.

She returned to her lines, little red spots leaping in front of her eyes.

'*Oh nonsense,*' she whispered. '*Your love touches me but I cannot return it.*'

'What's the largest organ in the body, five letters?' said Chrissie.

'Penis,' said Angora, drifting towards them in her white silk dressing-gown, carrying a photograph album, a cigarette dangling from her scarlet lips.

Chrissie giggled. 'It can't be. Did you sleep well?'

'I didn't do much sleeping, thank you, darling. But I had a lovely night.'

'You made a bloody awful din,' said Rupert.

'Steve likes to hear the sound of his own vice,' said Angora, dropping a kiss on Steve's shoulder.

Steve's eyes met Bella's. See! his triumphant expression seemed to be saying.

Angora lay down on a lilo, stretching out her scarlet painted toes, admiring her sleek brown legs. Her almost Japanese slenderness always made Bella feel like a carthorse.

'Hullo, Belladonna,' she said. 'You look a bit peaky, darling. Shouldn't go to bed so early. What you need is a few late nights.'

Bella ignored her.

'*I can't go on*,' she repeated in a whisper. '*I'm miserable, no-one knows how miserable. I love Konstantin.*'

'Who?' said Angora. 'Oh, I see, you're learning lines. You are virtuous. I haven't had a script from Harry Backhaus yet, and we start shooting next week some time. I gather the costumes are heaven. I do hope I'm not expected to take mine off. The set always gets so crowded.'

God, she's hell! thought Bella. How can Chrissie look at her with such admiration.

'Don't you get tired of people asking you to be sexy all the time?' said Chrissie.

'They don't have to ask,' said Steve, lobbing a pebble onto Angora's back.

'Well it's not something I mind,' said Angora, 'like being bitten by midges. Steve, darling, do light another fag and drive them away. Now I want you all to gather round and look at this photograph album.'

'Is it yours?' said Chrissie.

'No – yours, but guess who keeps cropping up in it.'

She flicked a few pages.

'There's Rupert. Wasn't he an adorable baby? And there's Chrissie on a pony, and Gay at her first teenage party. It was the Hunter-Blake's firework party. And look who's over there.'

'My God! It's you,' said Steve.

'Wasn't I awful? Only fourteen then and still a virgin. Look who couldn't wait for it.'

Steve examined the photograph more closely:

'You weren't that bad. I wish I'd been around at the time. I'd have sorted you out.'

Angora turned over another page. 'There's Lazlo; not so hot in those days was he? Bit thin and beaky-nosed. And look, there's Constance getting her OBE.

'And there I am at fifteen, at the Bullingdon Point to Point, not a virgin any more. Look a lot happier, don't I? I was wearing falsies, although you wouldn't know it under all that heather-mixture tweed. And there's the guy who did it, Jamie Milbank. He's married with three children now.'

'Jamie Milbank!' said Chrissie, 'but he's so respectable.'

'I was his final fling. And there I am again, at Gay's coming-out dance. Isn't it amazing how one crops up in other people's photograph albums?'

I never do, thought Bella wistfully. Once more she felt miserably conscious of being out of it.

'There's Lazlo again,' said Angora. 'Looking much more glamorous now, and there he is with a bird. And there's Rupert making a duck in the Eton

302

and Harrow match. You look disgustingly pleased, Rupe darling. I suppose you were dying to get back to the bar.

'There's Lazlo with yet another bird. What's so extraordinary is he and I never met until this year.'

Steve looked at the photograph and whistled. 'Some chick. How does he manage to get all those broads?'

Angora giggled. 'Well, I'm only going by hearsay darling, but they tell me he's the fastest tongue in the West.'

Everyone howled with laughter until a dry voice behind them said, 'You talk too much, Angora.'

It was Lazlo, wearing dark glasses and black bathing trunks. He was carrying the morning papers and a large drink.

'What are you drinking?' said Chrissie.

'It says whisky on the bottle.'

'At this hour?' said Angora in mock horror.

'It says so all the time,' said Lazlo.

'You'll ruin your looks that way,' said Angora.

'Very probably,' said Lazlo. And sitting down on the edge of the pool, he turned to the racing pages.

Bella had to admit, reluctantly, that he was in extremely good shape.

She was pouring with sweat. She longed to swim, but it would make her hair even more fluffy than ever, and she was damned if she was going to ask Chrissie or Angora if she could borrow their rollers.

'How many horses have you got running this afternoon?' said Steve.

'Two,' said Lazlo. '*The Times* seems to think one of them's going to win.'

'You know Isidore, who fixes everyone's

divorces,' said Angora. 'He's sold all his horses, he's so terrified of the wealth tax.'

'Any minute now,' said Lazlo, 'the man in the street's going to go into the betting shop and find there aren't any horses to bet on.'

It was too hot – to hell with her hair. She got up and walked to the edge of the pool.

Conscious suddenly of the highly charged atmosphere, she tried to dive in gracefully, but promptly did a belly flop.

As she swam up and down, she was aware of Lazlo's sardonic, appraising eyes watching her, looking for chinks in her armour, presumably wondering, like the chief torturer in the Spanish Inquisition, what refinement to try next.

I'll end up with my feet in cement at the bottom of this pool if I stay here much longer, she thought.

She got out and dried herself and looked round for her script. Lazlo was reading it.

'*Your love touches me, but I can't reciprocate it. Help me, or I shall do something silly.*' He read softly, so only she could hear.

'Can I have it back, please?' snapped Bella.

'Of course. Do you realize now how much better you'll play Masha than Nina?'

Bella's yellow eyes narrowed.

'So you *were* behind that little chess move,' she said.

'Naturally,' he said. 'Why don't you admit you've had enough?'

'I bloody well won't.'

'That's a nice ring,' he said admiring the gold band studden with seed pearls on her little finger. 'Where did you get it from?'

'Rupert gave it to me,' she said.

'I might have known it,' he sighed. 'It's the only jewellery in remotely decent taste I've ever seen you wear. Although,' his eyes travelled over her body, 'I must confess in a bikini you look more chic than I've ever seen you.'

Angora, who disliked anyone's attention to be off her for very long, started reading out the horoscopes in the paper. 'What are you, Lazlo?' she said.

'Scorpio,' said Chrissie.

'Oh very passionate,' said Angora. 'Ruled by the privates.'

Everyone laughed. 'It says you're going to have a tricky weekend, so play things close to the chest. What's Bella?'

'Taurus,' said Rupert.

'Um.' Angora's eyes ran down the page. 'People around you just aren't too co-operative, but be prepared to stick to your guns and argue things out.'

Bella looked up, met Lazlo's eyes, flushed and looked away again.

'And now Rupert, what's he?'

'Aquarius,' said Chrissie promptly. She knew at once, thought Bella, and I haven't a clue.

'Oh dear,' sighed Angora. 'What a pity you've decided to marry Bella. Taurus and Aquarius are terrible together. You've got an awfully stormy marriage ahead, darling. You'd better think twice about it.'

'So you keep telling us, Angora,' said Rupert angrily. 'Would you bloody well mind getting off our backs?'

'Go and get ready, Angora,' said Lazlo. 'I know you're governed by double summer time, but unless you get moving, we'll be two hours late for the first race.'

He got up and dived into the water. Bella experienced the same surprise that she would have felt seeing a big cat allowing itself to get wet.

11

Bella was not on any sort of terms with Chrissie or Angora to ask them what was worn at Goodwood. It was far too hot to wear stockings, and her legs weren't brown enough to go without, but it seemed stupid to waste the sun, so she put on a pair of dungarees in dark blue denim, superbly cut to show off her long legs. She wore nothing else on top. The straps and bib made a pretty good job of covering her breasts if she didn't leap about too much.

Of course, she was the last out. They were all standing beside the Mercedes, like some magnificent five: Chrissie and Angora both in pretty flowery dresses, Rupert and Steve in lightweight suits. Lazlo, however, in an impeccably cut pin-stripe suit with a dark red carnation in the buttonhole, made everyone else look sloppy by comparison.

He laughed when he saw Bella. 'Have you come to mend the boiler?' he said.

Steve and Angora sat in the front beside Lazlo. To make more room, Steve sat slightly sideways, his arm along the back of the seat, his elbow resting against Angora's hair. His hand lay just in front of

Bella and she had to resist a constant temptation to touch it.

Angora adjusted her hat in the driving mirror. 'Do you think I ought to cut my hair, Lazlo?' she said.

'No,' said Lazlo. 'I hate short hair.'

Life is just a bowl of cherries, Bella sighed, until you break your teeth on the stones.

She was turned on by the whole ambience of the racecourse, the heavy smell of hot horse, leather and dung, the shrill neighing from the stables.

She was surprised how done up everyone was. The women, very upper class, displaying thoroughbred ankles. The men were even better looking. The members' enclosure was crammed with Yock Yocks in light checked suits, with the kind of curly brimmed hats you put in rollers every night.

Bella found she got some pretty odd glances, and some wolf whistles too. It gave her considerable satisfaction that people were gazing at her more than Angora, and that two people came up and asked her for her autograph.

'We saw you on television the other day. We thought you were so good.'

That annoyed Angora too.

In the paddock, the horses were circling for the first race.

Bella admired their scarlet nostrils, rolling eyes and impossibly fragile legs, and realized how exactly right the artists had drawn them in those old sporting prints.

'That's Lazlo's horse, Chaperone, over there,' said Rupert, pointing to a chestnut, gleaming like a furniture polish advertisement. 'She looks well, doesn't she?'

'Beautiful,' sighed Bella, as the filly walked by, nuzzling at her groom, proudly flaunting the green and black rug, with the initials L. C. H. on the corner.

'She's the only one who's walking out,' said Steve approvingly.

Who with? wondered Bella.

Out came the jockeys. How tiny they looked with their shrill voices and Jack Russell jauntiness.

Lazlo went into the paddock. Trainers, owners and jockeys stood in isolated islands, discussing last minute tactics, the trainers telling jokes and making reassuring noises to the jockeys, like the bride's father before the trip up the aisle.

'Will the jockeys mount please,' said the loud-speaker.

Chaperone was led in. She dropped her head on Lazlo's shoulder in a friendly fashion, leaving a large smear of green froth on his suit.

'I must go and wish him luck,' said Angora, about to duck under the rails.

'I wouldn't,' said Rupert. 'He's busy. Racing's the only thing he takes really seriously.'

Apart from getting rid of me, thought Bella.

'That's Lazlo's jockey, Charlie Lamas, getting up now,' Rupert went on. 'Lazlo brought him over from South America.'

Bella watched the little man with a leathery face and mournful dark eyes being hoisted up on to Chaperone's back. He swore at her, as she gave two light-hearted bucks, and sent her clattering down the tarmac after the other horses.

'Just time to place our bets,' said Rupert, taking Bella's arm.

They all backed Chaperone, except Bella who, out of sheer cussedness, backed an outsider, Hera's Pride.

From the members' stand they could see the heat haze shimmering on the rails, as the horses cantered down to the start.

Down below them, rumour and speculation seethed, cauldron-like round the bookies, with their knowing, magenta faces. The tic-tac men gesticulated frantically.

A minute before the start, Lazlo joined the party, looking louche and piratical, and chewing on his cigar.

'Good luck,' said Angora.

'They're under starter's orders,' said Rupert, raising his binoculars.

'They're orf,' said the loudspeaker.

Bella found herself watching Lazlo, rather than the race.

She had to admire his sang-froid as the field rocketed up the centre of the course, like mercury up a thermometer plunged into boiling water.

His hands clenched slightly on his binoculars. He puffed slightly faster on his cigar as he watched the filly flare promisingly into the lead for an instant, then slip to the back of the field as they streamed past the post.

There were no histrionics, no effing and blinding. He just moved away from the cries of sympathy that showered down on him, unable to speak for a minute from disappointment.

'Who won?' asked Bella, a minute later.

'Hera's Pride,' said Steve. 'I can't imagine anyone backing it.'

'I did,' said Bella. 'To my mind she was the only one who was walking out,' and, laughing in his face, she skipped down the steps to collect her winnings.

Her euphoria was short-lived. She lost a fiver on each of the next two races.

The high event of the day was the ladies' race, sponsored by the Bond Street jewellers who make those diamond brooches with ruby conjunctivitis, which rear up on smart racing women's lapels.

'Let's go and look at the gels,' leered a whiskery old gentleman with a purple face.

'Lazlo's got a horse in this race called Baudelaire,' said Rupert. 'It's a bit green, but Lazlo's got very high hopes for it. It's the black colt over there. He bought it in Ireland. They think black horses are unlucky there, so he got it cheap.'

Baudelaire, rolling his eyes wickedly, and snorting, marched round the paddock, snatching at his bit.

'They've had a devil of a problem getting weight on him,' said Rupert. 'He won't sleep; walks his box all night.'

'Sounds rather like his master,' said Angora.

Out came the women jockeys, one tall girl with blonde hair and very green eyes, the rest small and very slight. Binoculars were immediately focused on the transparent breeches which clung to the girls' svelte figures in the heat.

Chrissie looked at them enviously.

'Lazlo says if I lose two stone, he'll buy me a racehorse,' she said.

'Which is Lazlo's jockey?' said Steve.

'The prettiest one, of course,' said Chrissie. 'The tall one with green eyes.'

'Do you think he's banged her yet?' said Rupert.

Angora's eyes narrowed for a second, then she said lightly, 'If he hasn't, it won't be long.'

The start was in a different place this time, but Bella was determined to place her bet with the same bookie on the other side of the track.

'I'll meet you in the members' enclosure,' she called to Rupert.

'Bella, wait, you'll get lost,' he shouted after her.

She was returning across the course when, just as she reached the white railings, she realized she'd dropped her betting slip.

Turning, she saw it lying in the middle of the course. Without looking to left or right, she ran back to get it.

Suddenly there was a thundering in her ears and the ten runners had come out of a side gate and were galloping towards her down to the start.

Terrified, she stood frozen to the spot, then tried to run back to the rails, but it was too late; they were on top of her. She screamed. They must crush her to death. Then, miraculously, Lazlo's black horse had swerved frantically to the right to avoid her, depositing his blonde rider on the grass, and galloping off down to the start.

The next moment Lazlo was picking her up. She'd never seen him so blazing angry before.

'What the fucking hell do you think you're doing? Trying to sabotage my horse?'

'What the hell are you doing, trying to kill me?' jibbered Bella. 'She was riding straight at me, no doubt at your instructions, and if it hadn't been for that darling horse swerving out of the way, I'd be a dead duck now.'

'Don't be bloody fatuous,' said Lazlo. 'Get off the course.'

He went over to pick up the blonde, who had staggered to her feet, shocked but unhurt.

Baudelaire, having shed his rider, was now having a high old time. Black tail straight up in the air, reins trailing on the ground, he cantered round the course, using up valuable energy.

To the delight of the crowd, and the shredded nerves of Lazlo, the stable lad and his blonde rider, he resolutely refused to be caught.

Rupert fought through the crowd to Bella's side. 'Darling, are you all right?'

'Of course I am. I just dropped my betting slip and your dear cousin's jockey rode straight at me.'

'She couldn't do much else,' said Rupert. 'They haven't got very good brakes, these horses.'

'He's doing marvellously now,' said Bella admiringly, watching Baudelaire scampering away from a couple of stewards and come cantering back down the course. 'He's got real star quality.'

'He's going to trip over the reins. They've got legs of glass, these horses,' said Rupert in anguish.

At last, after ten minutes cavorting, Baudelaire got bored and came to a violent, slithering halt in front of Lazlo, uttered a long, rolling snort through flared nostrils, and started eating grass.

The blonde girl was put up again. Rupert, Lazlo and Bella went back to the stands to watch the race.

'Hasn't got a hope in hell now,' said Lazlo angrily.

They were off, and for Bella it was the same old

rat race. Listening to the whisper of 'Here they come, here they come' growing into a great roar, not being able to recognize any of the horses in the shifting kaleidoscope of colours.

'My God,' said Rupert, 'she's going to do it.'

And suddenly the tall blonde, crouched over Baudelaire's ears like a Valkyrie, by sheer force of personality and leg muscle, seemed to shake off the rest of the field and drive the black horse first past the post.

The stand erupted in excitement.

'Christ, what a finish. What a turn-up for the books,' said Rupert.

Back in the winner's enclosure, a great cheer went up as Baudelaire came in.

The blonde girl looked as cool as a cucumber; the other girls dripped with sweat, puce in the face, their mascara running as though they'd just come out of the sauna.

Baudelaire, his coat covered with the kind of subdued lather you get after the first application of shampoo, marched round the enclosure, still rolling his eyes and laughing in his equine way. Congratulations were being showered on Lazlo like confetti.

12

A great deal of champagne was drunk after that, and Bella got separated from Rupert, and was eventually driven back home by a lot of Lazlo's racing cronies.

Chrissie, who'd come back with Rupert, had changed for dinner by the time Bella arrived. She looked prettier than Bella had ever seen her, wearing black, with a huge diamond glowing between her breasts.

'That's gorgeous,' said Bella, hoping to conciliate her, and picked up the diamond between finger and thumb.

'It's called the Evening Star,' said Chrissie, ignoring Bella and speaking directly to Angora. 'It's one of the most famous diamonds in the world. My mother would have a fit if she knew I was wearing it.'

Dinner finished, everyone discussed what to do next.

'We could play sardines,' said Angora. 'Or why not murder? I haven't played that since I was a child.'

'When was that?' said Steve. 'Yesterday?'

Angora pulled a face at him.

Lazlo looked at his watch. 'I've got to leave for the airport in an hour,' he said.

'Never mind,' said Chrissie, looking really excited for the first time in days. 'We can play a couple of rounds before you go.'

Oh no, thought Bella, not another of their horrible tribal games.

Angora dealt out the cards.

'Good.' Lazlo waved the King of Spades. 'I'm the detective. I can stay down here and drink brandy.'

'Wait till we get upstairs, Lazlo,' said Chrissie. 'Then turn the lights off at the main. We must do it properly.'

'I don't want to play,' said Bella quickly.

'Come on, don't be a spoilsport,' said Angora, taking her arm.

'Well, I'm going to stay with Rupert then.'

'No, you're not,' said Angora relentlessly as they climbed the main staircase. 'You go along that passage, Bella. Rupert go this way, and the rest of us will fan out towards the West Wing.'

As soon as she was alone, Bella quickened her pace. If she could find some room and lock herself in, she'd be safe.

She started to run, then, suddenly, everything was plunged into suffocating darkness as the lights went out. She fell over a chair, then found a door. It was locked. Whimpering with terror, she crossed the passage and found another door. That was locked, too.

Then she heard footsteps behind her – slow, relentless. She gave a sob. Slimy terror gripped her. She crashed across the passage again, found another door. It was open.

She shot inside and pulled it shut behind her. But

316

there was no lock. Her heart pounding, she leant against it.

The footsteps grew closer, then stopped outside. Panic-stricken, she bolted across the room, crashing into more furniture, trying to find the window. Then she heard someone stealthily opening the door, then, equally stealthily, closing it. Someone was in the room with her.

'Who is it?' she croaked in terror.

Then, suddenly, as a waft of scent reached her, she nearly fainted with relief. She'd recognize that smell anywhere. It was Steve's aftershave.

'Steve!' she sobbed. 'Oh, Steve!'

'Are you by yourself?' came the whisper.

'Yes. I'm so frightened!'

She stumbled forward and, the next moment, she was in his arms and bursting into a flood of tears.

'I can't bear it! I can't bear it! Stop torturing me like this!'

He kissed her as he'd never kissed her before – as though he wanted to devour her and overwhelm her with the force of his passion. He must love her to kiss her like that.

'Why have you been so horrible to me?' she moaned, when she could speak.

'I had to make you come to heel. You can't marry Rupert. You know that.'

'Yes! Yes!'

'Promise you'll speak to him this evening?'

'I promise! Anything, anything. Just kiss me again.'

He pulled her down on to the bed. They erupted against each other.

'I want you,' he whispered. 'I want you – now.'

Any moment he'd be raping her and she didn't care.

It was a few seconds before they realized someone was screaming horribly.

'Bloody hell! Someone seems to have been murdered,' he said.

'Don't go! Don't leave me!'

He started to kiss her again, but the screaming went on, echoing unearthily through the house.

'I'd better go and see what's going on. I'll sort you out later, but not until you've packed it in with Rupert.' And he was gone.

When the lights came on she realized she was in a strange bedroom, probably belonging to one of the maids. In a daze of happiness, she re-did her face and staggered downstairs. Steve loved her! She wasn't looking forward to breaking it off with Rupert, but it was no good marrying him if she really loved Steve.

She felt so free, she wanted to swing from the chandeliers.

Downstairs she found everyone standing round Chrissie, who was in hysterics.

'It's gone!' she screamed 'It's gone!'

'What's gone?' said Lazlo sharply. 'Pull yourself together!'

'The Evening Star. I was upstairs. Someone put their hands round my neck and the next moment the diamond was gone. Oh! What will Mummy say?'

Bust a gut, thought Bella, and winked at Steve. But he didn't smile. He looked the picture of concern.

'Don't panic. I guess someone's playing a joke.'

'Bloody silly joke, whoever's playing it!' snapped Lazlo.

'I'm going to call the police,' said Chrissie.

'Don't be crazy,' said Lazlo. 'Come on, let's look for it.'

But although they searched all the passages and rooms, no-one could find any trace of the stone.

Lazlo looked at his watch. 'I've got to catch that plane. I must go. I'll ring you tomorrow,' he said, as he kissed Chrissie. 'And whatever you do, don't get the police in.'

And that, thought Bella, looking at Lazlo's broad departing back, is the last I'll ever see of that snake.

'I'm going to call Aunt Constance,' said Chrissie, going upstairs. But when she came back, ten minutes later, her eyes were glittering. 'I've rung the police,' she said defiantly. 'They'll be round any moment.'

Rupert frowned. 'That's a bit extreme, isn't it?'

Angora giggled. 'How exciting,' she said, starting to re-paint her lips a brilliant scarlet. 'Do you think they'll search me?'

'Sure to,' said Steve, rumpling her hair.

They smiled into each other's eyes.

Can't he let up even now, thought Bella; then she relented. Let him have his little game of taunting her; he'd be hers as soon as she broke it off with Rupert.

All the same, she felt twitchy. She hated the police. She hoped they wouldn't ask too many awkward questions. If they found out about her background, they might suspect her. Thank goodness she'd been with Steve all the time, and had a proper alibi.

*   *   *

When the police arrived, Chrissie talked to them first, then Steve, who stayed in there a long time, then Angora, Rupert, Lazlo's various racing cronies and, finally, Bella.

The CID man had a smooth, pink, deceptively homely face. After a few enquiries, he said politely, 'Your real name's Mabel Figge, isn't it, Miss Parkinson?'

She caught her breath. 'Yes – yes, that's right.'

'And your father died in prison, doing time for murder and robbery.'

'Yes.' She clasped her hands together to stop them from shaking.

After a few more questions it was quite obvious they knew all the appalling details of her past.

Who could have told them? Steve? No. Steve loved her. It must have been Angora or Chrissie, probably clued up by Lazlo.

'Where were you when the theft took place?'

Now she was on safe ground. 'I went up the main staircase and turned left towards the servants' quarters, and slipped into a room along that passage. Mr Benedict followed me.' She blushed under the detective's scrutiny. 'We – er – spent the rest of the time together.'

'That's odd. Mr Benedict says he was with Miss Fairfax, all the time, and she bears this out.'

Bella gave a gasp of horror. 'He's lying! He was with me.'

'He claims he was with Miss Fairfax in Miss Fairfax's bedroom. There was a lot of Miss Fairfax's lipstick on the shirt he was wearing.'

'It must be mine!'

'You don't wear bright scarlet lipstick, Miss Parkinson.'

'He's lying!' her voice rose.

'I've also got to warn you Miss Henriques claims that the person who put their hands round her neck and stole the diamond wore bracelets that jangled.' He looked at the three heavy gold rings on Bella's wrist.

'But that's absurd! Other people were wearing bracelets.'

'Not ones that jangled.'

'She's trying to frame me,' Bella whispered. 'She's madly in love with Rupert and he's engaged to me. They all hate me! They'd kill me rather than let me marry their darling Rupert. Oh, God!' She clasped her clenched fists to her mouth. She was badly out of control, on the verge of tears.

The pink-faced detective looked at her. Then, to her amazement, he said, 'All right, Miss Parkinson, you can go now.'

It was two o'clock in the morning, but she still made Rupert drive her straight back to London. She couldn't bear another moment under that roof. She didn't know what Steve was up to, but she knew the only way to get the Furies off her back was to break it off with Rupert.

As they were driving down the Bayswater Road, she took a deep breath and said, 'I'm sorry, Rupert. I know this sounds totally ridiculous and insane, but I can't marry you. I really can't. I'm afraid I'm in love with someone else.'

She had no idea how he took this because she was staring down at her hands.

'How long have you known this other chap?'

'Ages – but, well, he only came back into my life about a fortnight ago – the night, in fact, I was late for dinner, the first time I met your parents, I was with him.'

'And you still felt it was all right to get engaged to me?'

'I thought what I felt for you was the real thing, and that I was just infatuated by him, but now I know I can't live without him. I don't like him very much, but it's driving me out of my mind! I'm sorry, darling, I've not been thinking of you at all. I know I've been a bitch. I just thought I might grow to love you . . .' Her voice ran out in a thin line of drivel.

The car slowed down outside her flat. The pale green trees were lit up by the street lamps. Rupert looked quite calm, but he was as white as a sheet.

'We'd better talk about it upstairs.'

Outside Bella's flat, however, stood two men. 'Miss Parkinson?' said one of them.

'Yes!' snapped Bella. 'What do you want?'

'We're police officers, sir. We have a warrant to search Miss Parkinson's luggage.'

'Don't be bloody stupid!' said Rupert.

'It's all right,' said Bella. 'There's nothing in there. You're quite welcome to search it.'

But in the pocket of the smaller suitcase, wrapped in one of Bella's petticoats, they discovered the Evening Star.

'Someone put it there!' Bella screamed. 'I've been framed! I didn't take it!'

'I'm sorry, Miss Parkinson,' said the policeman imperturbably. 'I'm afraid we'll have to take you into custody.'

13

Bella, when she looked back later, could recall very little about her spell in prison. She remembered Rupert making the most appalling scene when the police arrested her and, later, beating her fists against the door of her cell. She remembered appearing in court the following morning, nearly fainting with horror when the magistrate refused her bail, and finally being gripped by hysterical panic at finding herself locked in a cell in Holloway.

One of the wardresses had brought her some revolting stew, and a sardonic doctor with rimless glasses had asked her endless questions about herself. Afterwards, she lay on a hard, narrow bed trying to control her mounting desperation. Why had Steve denied being with her during the murder game? Who had betrayed her to the police? Was it Chrissie, Angora or Steve? Who had planted the diamond in her suitcase? Would the papers get all the details of her past? If they did, her career was finished. At intervals, the thought of Lazlo rose, black and churning, choking her like a wave of nausea. He's behind this, she thought, he's the one who cooked my goose.

I'm innocent, she said over and over again but, in spite of the stifling heat in the cell, she couldn't stop shivering.

Then a key turned in the door.

'The Prison Governor wants to see you,' said the wardress.

The Prison Governor had a kind, sheep-like face. She looked embarrassed. For a minute she played with a paper knife.

Then she said, 'I'm afraid there's been a mistake. The evidence was very conclusive against you, but the police have now discovered you've been framed. The Henriques family have withdrawn all charges.

'We're very sorry for all the worry this has caused you,' said the Prison Governor, flashing her big teeth. 'But of course, all the papers will print the fact that you're innocent. It'll be wonderful publicity.'

Bella didn't smile back.

'Why wasn't I allowed bail?'

'There have been several big diamond raids in the past few weeks. Police suspect the same gang at work. For some reason they felt you were mixed up in it.'

'Have they arrested anyone else?'

'Not yet.'

Suddenly she couldn't stand the awful sheep-like face any longer.

'I want to get out of here – at once.'

'Of course. There's a car waiting to take you to the Court, where you'll be released immediately.'

When she came out of court an hour later and felt the hot sun on her face, she threw back her head and took a deep breath. Then a group of

324

reporters surged forward and started to bombard her with questions. Oh God! She hadn't thought they'd get on to the story so fast. Suddenly, a tall man in dark glasses grabbed her arm and pulled her down the steps into a waiting car. It was only after he'd driven off, leaving the reporters gaping, that she realized it was Lazlo Henriques.

'What the hell are you doing here?' she stormed. 'You're the last person I want to see. I thought you were in Zurich.'

'I was. Rupert rang me in hysterics this morning, begging me to come back and spring you from prison. The things I do for my family.'

'It was your rotten family who got me shut up in the first place.'

She was overcome by a terrible fit of shaking. Lazlo got out a packet of cigarettes, lit one, and handed it to her.

'Thanks,' she said, trying to get a grip on herself. 'Where's Rupert?'

'Gone to Zurich. Carrying on the deal I started. I thought it better if he was out of the way for a bit.'

'Just in case I might have second thoughts about getting re-engaged to him.'

Lazlo grinned. 'How perceptive you are, my dear.'

'Was it splashed all over the papers? My arrest?'

'It was too late for the dailies. But the evenings lead on it, with lots of pictures. By the final editions they'll be leading on your release. It'll look like a publicity stunt.'

'That's what the Prison Governor said.'

She started to relax. London in the blue haze of the late afternoon had never looked so lovely.

'Where are we going?' she asked.

'To my flat.'

'I want to go home.'

'Don't be silly. Once the big Press boys get on to this, they'll never leave you alone.'

'How did you manage to spring me, anyway?'

'Pulled a few strings, leaned on a few people.'

'I'd forgotten you were so influential. Who planted the diamond in my case?'

'I'll tell you the whole story when we get home.'

Lazlo's flat was a surprise. She had expected it to be as ugly and impersonal as the Henriques' London house. But it was sybaritic in the extreme, with grey silk walls, long fur rugs on the ground and brilliant scarlet curtains. Thousands of books and paintings covered the walls. Three large cats wandered up to welcome them.

Lazlo went straight to the drinks tray and poured Bella a vast brandy.

'Get that inside you.'

'I'm sorry, I'm still a bit stunned,' Bella said, taking the glass. 'Would you mind awfully if I had a bath?'

She soaked in emerald green scented water for a long time, and scrubbed and scrubbed herself to get every speck of prison dirt off. Later she pinched some of Lazlo's scent from the row of bottles near the bath. Odd that he used Black Opal like Steve.

She put on a dark green towelling dressing-gown that was hanging on the back of the door. In the kitchen she found Lazlo eating smoked salmon sandwiches and reading his mail.

'I've just weighed myself,' she said. 'I've lost five pounds in the last two days.'

Lazlo handed her the plate of sandwiches.

'Well, you'd better eat something. I'll get you another drink.'

'I'm not hungry,' she said. Then, realizing suddenly that she was ravenous, she wolfed the lot. The brandy was giving her heartburn, but a mild euphoria stole down inside her. She sat down on the sofa. A large ginger cat jumped on to her knee, and started purring and kneading her with his paws.

'How did you get me out?' she said.

'I told you, I leant on a few people.'

'But, *please*, who put the diamond in my case?'

A guarded look descended like a curtain over his face.

'Chrissie,' he said.

'Chrissie!' said Bella in amazement. 'What on earth for? It was *her* diamond.'

'She loves Rupert – to distraction. Seeing you and him together, when she knew you weren't in love with him, pushed her over the top. She thought – quite wrongly, as it turns out – that if you were arrested, Rupert would go off you.'

Bella thought for a minute. She'd gone through enough hell over Steve to understand exactly what Chrissie must have suffered.

'Oh poor, poor Chrissie,' she whispered.

For once Lazlo looked surprised. 'Well, it's nice of you to take it like that. The irony was that you broke it off with Rupert that evening anyway, so she needn't have bothered.'

'Did you tell the police she did it?'

He shook his head.

'How did you get me off then?'

'I said you were with someone else the whole time we were playing murder.'

Happiness flooded over her.

'Oh, so Steve's at last admitted that he was with me! Why on earth did he say he was with Angora?'

'He was with Angora,' said Lazlo in a level voice.

'For heaven's sake,' said Bella crossly, 'I know I was with him.'

'You weren't, you were with me.'

'Don't be ridiculous. I know it was pitch dark, but I couldn't mistake Steve. I recognized him by his aftershave, Black Opal.' Then she gave a gasp of horror.

'Oh no! It couldn't have been!'

'I'm afraid it was, darling,' said Lazlo. 'I was one of the stars of the Footlights when I was at Cambridge. It isn't very difficult to imitate Steve's American accent. I'm the same height and build as he is, our hair is more or less the same length. All I had to do was to douse myself in that rather noxious aftershave he uses – and, er, well, just leave the rest to nature.'

For a minute Bella was speechless, then she screamed, 'You bastard, you bastard! You tricked me into thinking Steve was still in love with me, and into breaking it off with Rupert, and what's more, I practically let you rape me.'

Lazlo laughed and helped himself to another drink. 'I must say I enjoyed that bit. I'd never have dreamt you could be so passionate. We must arrange an action replay some time.'

Bella gave a snarl of rage like a maddened animal.

'Dirty, lousy son of a bitch,' she shouted. 'You've ruined my life.'

'What play did you say that in?' he said, still laughing.

His amusement snapped her last thread of control. Gibbering incoherently, she jumped to her feet and leapt at him trying to claw his face.

'Stop it,' he said, catching her wrists. 'Unless you want your eyes blacked. I don't have any scruples about hitting women.'

For a moment she glared at him, then, realizing herself beaten, she tore her hands away and slumped on the sofa.

The door bell rang. Bella ran out into the hall and opened the door. Two men with hard, inquisitive faces stood outside.

'Miss Parkinson,' said one of them. 'Congratulations on your release. Can we ask you a few questions?'

'No, you can't,' said Lazlo.

He pulled Bella back into the flat.

'Mr Henriques, Mr Lazlo Henriques, isn't it?' said the second man in an oily voice.

'Get out,' said Lazlo icily.

They wilted as he slammed the door in their faces.

'How did you know I didn't want to talk to them?' Bella said furiously.

'You haven't got time.' He glanced at his watch. 'You're due on stage in an hour's time.'

'Don't be stupid, they'll have got an understudy.'

'They haven't. I rang Roger and told him you'd been let out!'

'But I can't go on, not after what's happened.' She collapsed on to a chair. 'I'm exhausted and my hair's dirty.'

'Don't be so bloody wet,' Lazlo said brutally. 'Whatever your faults, I thought you'd got guts.'

*　　*　　*

There was a crowd of reporters waiting outside the theatre, but Lazlo just elbowed them out of the way. If Bella hadn't loathed him so much, she would have been speechless that anyone could swear as fluently as he could.

In her dressing room Rosie Hassell was waiting in a petticoat and a fever of excitement.

'Bella, darling, what drama! How on earth did you get off so quickly?'

'That snake pulled strings,' Bella said, pointing at Lazlo, who was just behind her.

Roger Field popped in just before the five minute call.

'Bella, darling,' he said. 'Thank God you made it. How do you feel?'

'Utterly hellish,' said Bella through chattering teeth. 'I've just been sick.'

'All that smoked salmon and brandy,' sighed Lazlo. 'What a tragedy.'

Bella ignored him. 'I may be sick again any minute,' she said to Roger.

'It'll be your entrails next,' said Lazlo. 'Have you got any whisky, Roger?'

Before the performance Roger went on stage and told the audience Bella had been released and cleared of all charges. When she made her first entrance there were a few isolated claps. Then a storm of applause followed and the audience cheered their heads off. Bella nearly broke down.

At the end of the play she received the biggest ovation of her career. But she felt like a husk, completely exhausted, very near to tears. In a dream she received congratulations from the rest of the cast, and had just finished changing when Lazlo walked into her dressing-room.

'Can't you knock?' she said crossly.

'Don't be silly,' he said, taking her arm. 'Come on, we can't fend off the Press any longer.'

'I'm going home by myself,' she said, snatching her arm away, and, running down the stairs, she tugged open the stage door. Immediately, she was blinded by a volley of flash bulbs and the whirring of television cameras.

'There she is,' shouted a hundred voices.

'Oh, no,' she yelped in horror, and retreated, slamming the door.

In the end it was the same rat race as before, Lazlo protecting her with his arms and Roger Field fending off the crowd. Somehow Lazlo got her into his car, and again, almost before she could draw breath, they seemed to be out on the M4 steaming towards Oxford.

'Where are we off to now?' she asked listlessly.

'To stay with some friends of mine in the country.'

'I don't want to stay with any of your bloody friends, not if they're anything like you.'

'They're not,' said Lazlo calmly. 'She's a singer, he writes. You'll like them.'

'I haven't anything to wear.'

'You won't need anything. Cass'll lend you a bikini.'

He turned on the wireless and the hot summer night was suddenly flooded with Mozart. Bella listened to those lovely liquid notes pouring forth like a nightingale, and suddenly the terrible realization that Steve didn't love her any more swept over her. Unable to stop herself, she broke into a storm of weeping. Lazlo took absolutely no notice and let her cry.

Finally, when she reached the gulping stage, he said, 'There's a hipflask in the dashboard; help yourself.'

'No thank you.'

Heartless beast, she thought furiously. He tricked me, he pretended to be Steve. If Chrissie hadn't started screaming, he'd have certainly gone the whole hog and screwed me. A hot wave of shame swept over her at the thought of how much she'd enjoyed it at the time.

They had turned off the motorway into deep country now. Cow parsley brushed against the moving car, a huge moon was gliding in and out of transparent wisps of cloud. Finally, Lazlo drew up near a big rambling house, covered in wistaria. Almost at once a woman came running out.

'Darlings,' she shouted. 'You have made good time. How lovely to see you.'

'This is Bella,' said Lazlo. 'She's brought nothing with her, so you'll have to lend her everything. I'll just put the car away.'

The woman hugged Bella. 'My name's Cass,' she said. 'Lazlo tells me you've been having the most awful time. I do hate the Press when their blood's up.'

They went into a huge untidy room with crumbs all over the floor, bowls of drooping flowers and two grand pianos covered with books and music.

A man with spectacles on top of his head put down his book and came forward to welcome Bella.

'I escaped up to London for your first night. You were superb. Come and sit down and I'll get you a drink.'

Cass plonked herself on the sofa opposite Bella and stretched out fat legs, burnt red by the sun.

'Grenville's been in love with you for years, ever since he saw you on television once.'

Grenville blushed. 'I suppose we haven't got any ice, darling?'

'None at all,' said Cass cheerfully. 'The fridge is so frozen up I can't get the ice tray back in.'

When he had gone out she said, 'I didn't know the set-up, so I've put you and Lazlo in different rooms, but he's in a huge double bed so you can always join him.'

'Oh no!' said Bella, horrified into dropping her guard. 'I'd rather sleep with a cobra than Lazlo.'

'How are the children?' said Lazlo, walking into the room, his arms full of bottles of drink.

Bella went scarlet. How much had he heard of her last remark?

'The children are away this weekend, thank God,' said Cass. 'I do love them, but it's bliss when they're away. They're boys,' she added to Bella, 'ten, eight and seven.'

'I've brought them some gin,' said Lazlo. 'I know they like it.'

Cass laughed. 'What are you doing after *Othello*?' she said to Bella.

'*The Seagull* – we start rehearsing on Monday.'

For the first time in days she felt at home. So much so that half an hour later she wasn't too shy to ask if she might go up to bed.

14

She slept until lunchtime, then got up, bathed and washed her hair. To her annoyance the orange rinse still wouldn't come out and her hair had gone impossibly fluffy like candy floss. She found Lazlo in the garden, his feet up on a table, reading the racing news, drinking champagne and tearing a chicken apart. He was wearing only a pair of dirty white trousers, and his swarthy skin was already turning brown.

'Where are the others?' she said.

'Working. Have some chicken?'

'No thank you. I'm not hungry.' It was a lie. She was starving.

He poured her out a glass of champagne and said, 'I do hope you're not going to be boring and sulk the whole weekend. I'm about to ring my bookmaker. I fancy Bengal Freedom, Safety Pin and Happy Harry. Shall I put a fiver on each of them for you?'

Bella picked up the paper and scanned it.

'No,' she said coldly. 'I prefer Merry Peasant, Early Days, and Campbell's Pride in the four o'clock.'

'They haven't got a dog's chance,' said Lazlo.

'Still, if you want to waste your money.'

After he'd gone inside she skimmed the rest of the paper. On the front page was a picture of her and Lazlo leaving the theatre.

'Who stole the diamond?' screamed the banner headline. 'Henriques mystery thickens as Bella declared innocent.'

With a beating heart she read the rest of the story, but there was nothing mentioned about her past. Thank God her public image was still intact.

'I've backed your horses for you,' said Lazlo, returning with another bottle of champagne.

She put down the paper and pointedly picked up her book, trying to concentrate. Lazlo looked at the jacket. 'It's junk,' he said. 'How far have you got?'

'Page two hundred and fifty,' snapped Bella.

'Oh, yes, that's the bit just before page two hundred and fifty-one,' said Lazlo.

Bella ignored him.

She later had the indignity of watching the three horses Lazlo had backed romping home several lengths clear in three successive races. Her horses weren't even placed.

'You owe me fifteen pounds,' said Lazlo. 'I shan't press you for payment.'

Not trusting herself to speak, Bella went off for a walk. Even the bosky greenness everywhere couldn't cure her bad temper. By the time she reached the village shop, however, hunger overcame her and she bought two huge cream buns. She was just wandering back to the house, stuffing her face with one of them, when a dark green Mercedes glided down the road towards her. Choking with rage she turned her bulging cheeks towards the hedgerow.

'So glad you've recovered your appetite,' said Lazlo in amusement.

Cass cooked a marvellous dinner and, afterwards, Bella offered to wash up. Lazlo said he'd help her. But at exactly ten o'clock, after he'd given her back a third plate to wash because it still had mustard on the bottom, something snapped inside her.

Picking up the remains of the duck, she hurled it at Lazlo, missing him of course. Then she selected a very ripe peach and chucked it against the wall, then she kicked over Cass's music stand.

Lazlo started to laugh, 'Tell me, Bella, what are you going to do when you grow up?'

'Stop sending me up,' she screamed. Then she started breaking plates. That had Lazlo worried.

'Pack it in,' he snapped. Then, when she wouldn't, he slapped her extremely hard across the face. For a minute she glared at him, her eyes watering from the pain. She gave a sob and fled upstairs. In her bedroom her rage evaporated. Feeling bitterly ashamed of herself, she undressed and got into bed.

She lay still, listening to approaching thunder – her eyelids feeling as though they'd been pinned back from her eyes. She heard Cass and Grenville come to bed, laughing fondly. At last she drifted into an uneasy sleep.

It was the most terrifying dream she'd ever had. She was suffocating, drowning, unable to escape. Then she started screaming. Suddenly the room was flooded with light – Lazlo was standing in the doorway. The next moment he'd crossed the room and taken her in his arms.

'It's all right, baby, it's all right. It's only a bad dream.'

She could feel the warmth from his body. His fingers beneath her shoulder blades. What did it matter now that he was the person she loathed most in the world? He was at least a human being.

'I can't take any more,' she sobbed. 'I get this nightmare over and over again. I dream I'm drowning in blood – and I know it's my mother's. Oh God,' she buried her face in her hands.

'Come on. Talk about it.'

'I can't,' she whispered. Then, suddenly, everything came pouring out. She wasn't really talking to Lazlo, but to herself.

'I've always lied about my past,' she said in a choked voice. 'I was so ashamed of it. My mother was very respectable, the daughter of a Christian Science minister. But she fell in love with my father. He was divine, but as bent as a corkscrew. My mother didn't realize he'd been in prison four times for larceny even before she married him. For a bit he tried to go straight, but he kept getting sacked from different jobs. Then I was born. There was no money, and my mother was forced to go out to work.'

'Go on,' said Lazlo.

'She worked as a char, in other people's houses, but money finally got so short my father stole the church funds. My mother found the money under the floorboards, and she went straight to the minister, her father, and told him. That night they confronted my father and said they were going to the police. Can you imagine it? Grassing on your own family? My father made a bolt for it. There was a fight; my grandfather fell and hit his head on the fender, and later he died in hospital. My father got life inprisonment for murder. My mother never visited him. He died in prison ten years later, from TB.'

She paused and the faded mirror at the end of the room glinted gold with a strange rose-yellow flash. A violent crack of thunder split the air. Rain exploded from the sky.

'It was during the court case that my mother discovered my father was already married and I was il-il . . .' she gaged over the word.

'Illegitimate,' said Lazlo.

Bella nodded. 'My mother never smiled again. She moved to another part of Yorkshire, a little town called Nalesworth where no-one knew her. She went on working as a daily and saved enough money to send me to a good school. But I hated it. All the other girls laughed at my ugly clothes and my thick accent. My mother was continually terrified I was going to take after my father. I look like him, you see. She used to beat me and lock me for hours in a darkened room, while she sallied forth to church meetings.

'I grew to hate her.' Bella's voice was so quiet now against the hiss of the rain, that Lazlo could hardly hear it. 'I used to dream and dream of escaping to London and becoming an actress. When I was seventeen they discovered she had cancer. But being a Christian Scientist she wouldn't let them give her any drugs. She must have been in agony, and it made her far more vicious. She used to drag her body round the house, running her fingers along the furniture to see if I'd dusted properly. We hadn't any money so I had to leave school and take a job in the local draper's shop.

'And then I met Steve.' She paused. 'He was working at one of the local discos. He was the most beautiful man I'd ever seen. He seemed to exude Hollywood glamour, the bright lights and freedom. Needless to say, he seduced me the first time I went out with him. In the end my mother found out. She ranted and raved, but she was too weak to do anything about it.

'One morning I heard two girls gossiping in the shop about Steve, saying he was seducing half the West Riding and running up bills everywhere. I went mad. I rushed round to his digs and found he'd walked out without even saying goodbye to me. He'd left no address. I knew my mother was dying, but I spent all day and all night combing the town for him. I got home at four o'clock in the morning. Two neighbours were with my mother. She was in a coma. She never recovered.'

Bella was shaking like a leaf now, trying to stop herself from crying.

'They all hated me in the town,' she said. 'They drew their curtains and whispered behind their hands about how evil I was. For three days I was alone in the house, surrounded by all those damn wreaths of lilies. But I couldn't think about anything except Steve leaving me. I was half crazy with misery. It was only after a while that I realized what I'd done to my mother. Then the nightmares started.'

'What happened then?'

'I came South. There was a little money left when the house was sold. I got a scholarship to RADA, changed my name to Bella Parkinson, told everyone my father was a librarian, my mother a school-mistress. Lies I told so often I almost came to believe them.'

She looked down at her hands, 'Now you know everything.'

'I knew most of it already.'

'You did? But how? Did Steve tell you?'

'A little. I've got a good information service.'

Bella gave a hollow laugh. 'No wonder you didn't want me to marry Rupert. The bastard daughter of a murderer. Hardly Debrett is it?'

'I didn't care a damn about your background.'

She looked up in surprise. Lazlo didn't seem appalled, or angry or contemptuous, or any of the other things she'd expected anyone she'd ever told the truth to be. For once his dark mocking face looked completely serious.

'Look,' he said. 'It doesn't matter what happened before in your life. No-one minds except you. It's what you are – talented, funny.' He glanced down at her blotched, tear-stained face and smiled slightly. 'Yes, even beautiful, that's important. The Henriques have a pretty seamy past if you study it. Only four centuries back they were raping, looting and murdering to get the things they wanted. They just did it a few hundred years earlier than your father did. Besides, he wasn't a murderer. He just killed someone in a fight.'

'Like you did,' said Bella.

'Like I killed Miguel Rodriguez,' said Lazlo, his face hardening.

Gently, he laid her back in bed, and got to his feet. 'I'm going to get you a sleeping pill.'

It was only when he came back that she realized he was still dressed in the black shirt and dirty

340

white trousers he'd been wearing all evening.

'Why weren't you in bed?' she said.

'I was reading. I don't sleep a great deal. There's usually something, or – er – someone better to do.'

She suddenly realized she was only wearing a very transparent nightgown, and that Lazlo had been holding her in his arms, and that only two nights ago, when he'd pretended to be Steve, he'd practically raped her. She felt herself going scarlet and slunk down under the sheets.

'I'm sorry,' she muttered. 'I shouldn't have bored you with my problems.'

'Bella,' he said in amazement, 'you're apologizing to me. Are you sure you're feeling all right?'

'Don't tease me,' she said in a strangled voice. 'I'm not in the mood.'

He laughed. 'Hell being a woman isn't it? It's just not your century.'

15

She felt like a convalescent recovering from a very bad attack of flu the next day. She found herself impossibly shy of Lazlo, hardly able to meet his eyes. Most of the day she slept in the sun. And in the evening she sobbed herself stupid over *The King And I* on television. She also felt quite unnecessarily irritated when Angora telephoned Lazlo from France where she was filming, and he took the telephone into the other room.

Next day he'd driven Bella back to London to start rehearsals on *The Seagull*, and now here she was, three days later, sulking in the hairdresser's because he hadn't even rung her up to see how she was.

Bernard, her hairdresser, picked up a strand of her hair.

'That's a bit of a mistake, duckie,' he said. The pink rinse had turned green in the sun.

'I'll say,' said Bella crossly. 'I've decided to go back to my natural colour.' Bernard looked appalled, 'But what on earth is it?'

'A sort of dark mouse, not unattractive.'

'But, darling, you're crazy. You've been blonde

for years, no-one'll recognize you. It'll ruin your image.'

'I've got to play a very mousey girl in my next play.'

Alas, no woman is a dedicated artist to her hairdresser.

Bernard grinned slyly. 'Don't give me that, dearie. You've met some nice, straight bloke who you think doesn't like dyed hair.'

'Nonsense,' said Bella crossly. But she blushed crimson.

The weather grew even hotter. She had to rehearse all afternoon. It was impossibly stuffy in the theatre. She was just getting her teeth into her part when something happened to wreck her concentration. Five minutes later she was back in her dressing-room.

'What on earth's the matter?' said Rosie Hassell in alarm. 'It was going so well.'

'It's Johnnie,' stormed Bella, glaring at the handsome blond boy who played Konstantin, who was leaning against her dressing-table.

'Didn't you see him sneaking on to the stage and letting loose that toad. He knows I'm terrified of toads.'

Johnnie started to laugh. 'Bella, angel, the scene is played beside a lake. It should be absolutely crawling with frogs and toads and things. I was only trying to inject a little realism into the act.'

'You were not,' shouted Bella. 'You were trying to put the fear of God into me.'

'Oh well.' Johnnie shrugged his shoulders. 'If you're going to be stuffy.'

'I am. I bloody am.'

Roger Field stood in the doorway frowning. Two

of his leading players hurling abuse at each other cannot have been the most edifying sight, but Bella was past caring.

'I'll report you to Equity and get you kicked out,' she screamed at Johnnie.

'That's enough, Bella,' said Roger. 'The whole theatre can hear you.'

'I don't care,' Bella shouted. 'Do you know what he did? He put this toad . . .'

'All right, pack it in, Johnnie. Take that toad back to the Thames, or wherever you found it. I'll talk to you later.'

Grinning broadly, Johnnie slouched out of the room.

'I'll kill you, kill you, kill you!' Bella screamed after him.

'Stop bawling like a fishwife,' said Roger. 'There's someone to see you.'

'I don't want to see anyone,' snapped Bella. 'I want you to stop that horrible boy putting toads in my . . .' Her voice trailed off, for in the doorway stood Lazlo.

'I'll leave her to you,' said Roger. 'I hope you make a better job of calming her down than I did.'

Bella was speechless for a minute. Then she said, 'What are you doing here?'

'Watching your rehearsal,' said Lazlo. 'I was going to tell you how good you were, but I'm not sure if you deserve it. I'm glad you get abusive with other people besides me,' he said.

'It's not funny.' Bella slumped down in her chair and gazed at herself in the mirror. Mousey hair scraped back in an elastic band, shiny face without a scrap of make-up, shirt soaking with sweat, splitting jeans. Oh, damn, damn, damn. She'd meant to be so silken and beautiful next time she met him.

'What do you want?' she said, ungraciously.

'I was going to ask you out to dinner, but I won't if you're going to be so ratty.'

'Oh, well,' she blushed and shuffled her feet.

'I've got two Arabs to entertain, I'm meeting them at eight. Can you be ready in a quarter of an hour?'

'But I haven't got anything to wear,' Bella wailed.

Lazlo got to his feet. 'You'd better borrow something,' he said. 'I'm going to talk business with Roger. By the way,' he added, as he went out of the door, 'I like the hair. It's a distinct improvement.'

The Arabs were jolly and fat, and ate all Bella's potatoes and steak at dinner. She had borrowed a pair of shorts and an orange T-shirt from Rosie, which was much too tight across the bust.

Her suntan was beginning to fade. She kept wishing she could think of witty things to say.

The Arabs wanted to make a night of it and kept muttering about strip clubs, but Lazlo managed to extricate himself and Bella about midnight. They didn't speak as he drove across London. They stopped at a traffic light. Please make it stay red for ever, she prayed. She held her breath when they came to Hyde Park, but he turned left. She was appalled by the joy that flooded over her as she realized he was taking her back to his flat instead of hers.

As Lazlo poured out drinks for them both, she studied him carefully, examining the thick, black hair curling over his collar, the broad shoulders in the immaculate white suit, the sunburnt hands shooting soda into the glasses, and suddenly she felt quite giddy with lust.

What's happening to me? she thought in horror. Five days ago I was madly in love with Steve, and now all I can do is long and long and long to be in bed with Lazlo.

As he handed her a drink, their hands touched. Jumping as though he'd burnt her, she seized the glass and bolted over to the window. It's all right for him, she thought in panic. Riverboat gambler, with the morals of an alley cat, and a million light years of sexual experience under his belt. All he has to do is throw a little soft soap around and he'll have me eating out of his hand.

Lazlo took off his jacket and hung it on the back of a chair.

'You're very quiet,' he said. 'What's eating you?'

Bella took a deep breath. 'I know you're only being nice to me,' she blurted out, 'because you want me to fall for you. Just to make sure I won't go back to Rupert.'

Lazlo sighed. 'That's a very silly, childish remark. I did hope you'd given up making remarks like that.'

Bella looked mutinous. There was a pause.

Then she stammered. 'All right, I'm sorry. I was being ungracious.'

He smiled. 'Good girl to apologize. Come over here.'

'No,' said Bella in a strangled voice. 'I can't do it, I can't be another of your one-night-stands, just to amuse you for tonight because you can't sleep.'

'My dear child, what are you on about?'

The telephone rang. Lazlo took no notice.

'Hadn't you better answer it?' Bella said shakily.

'All right.' He picked up the receiver, not taking his eyes off her face.

'Hullo? Yes, Aunt Constance, *what* an unexpected pleasure.' He grinned at Bella and raised his eyes to heaven.

Suddenly the smile was wiped off his face.

'What's that?' he snarled. 'When did this happen? Why wasn't I told before? Have you told the police? All right, I'll come straight over.

The scar down the side of his face was like a livid gash as he put down the receiver. His eyes were blazing with rage.

'What's the matter?' said Bella.

'Chrissie. She's been kidnapped. They want two million pounds ransom.'

16

Lazlo stormed the great dark green Mercedes through the deserted London streets, shooting traffic lights, squealing the wheels round corners. Bella sat frozen with horror beside him.

'But how on earth did it happen?' she whispered.

'Chrissie went out to post a letter at half past six and didn't come back,' said Lazlo. 'Aunt Constance and Uncle Charles were out, and the first anyone realized she'd disappeared was when Steve turned up at nine to take her to some party, and she wasn't there.'

'Steve was taking her out?' Bella said sharply.

Lazlo shot her a sidelong glance. 'Now Angora's gone to France,' he said, 'Steve seems to have transferred his rather liberal affections to Chrissie.'

Bella flushed. 'What happened then?'

'The kidnappers telephoned at eleven-thirty, saying they'd got Chrissie and they'd release her unhurt as long as we paid up two million pounds and didn't call the police.'

Outwardly he was perfectly calm now. The harsh, swarthy face betrayed no emotion. But a muscle quivered in his cheek and his hand shook badly as he lit a cigarette.

If only I were Angora, thought Bella miserably, I'd fling my arms round him and find all the right things to say to comfort him.

She was further thrown by the fact that when they reached the Henriques' house the door was answered by Rupert. He had obviously just got off the plane from Zurich. His luggage littered the hall.

'Thank God you've arrived,' he said to Lazlo. 'Poor darling little Chrissie. What the hell are we going to do about her? Everyone's being absolutely useless. My mother's having hysterics at the thought of parting with two million pounds. My father's shipped enough liquor to float the *QE2* and that snake Steve is . . .' Suddenly he seemed to notice Bella and pulled himself together. 'Oh, hullo,' he said perfunctorily.

In the drawing-room they found Charles standing in front of the fire, with glazed eyes, and Steve on the sofa, drinking brandy, and managing to look completely at home and the picture of concern at the same time. Constance, massive in maroon satin, strode down the room towards them.

'Where on earth have you been, Lazlo? Out on the tiles as usual, I suppose,' she added sourly. Then she glared at Bella. 'And what's she doing here? You must talk some sense into Rupert and Charles. They won't call the police.'

'Quite right,' said Lazlo. 'The fewer people who know about this, the better.' He turned to Charles. 'We'd better work out the fastest way to get the cash together.'

Constance looked appalled. 'But we can't raise that amount. We shall be ruined. I have enough trouble making ends meet as it is. Why don't you let the police sort it out?'

'If you call the police,' said Lazlo brutally, 'you'll only panic the kidnappers into bumping Chrissie off.'

'Don't use those awful words,' said Constance. 'That child was like a daughter to me.'

'Oh, Gawd,' said Rupert rudely. 'Don't be such a hypocrite. You treated Chrissie like a slave. She never stopped running errands for you.'

Constance compressed her lips. 'It was Chrissie's fault in a way,' she said to Steve. 'I always told her if she went out without a hat she'd get picked up by undesirable types.'

'Those men were lying in wait for her,' said Rupert through clenched teeth. 'Don't be so bloody stupid.'

Constance turned purple. 'How dare you speak to me like that?' she said. 'I've had enough to cope with. All the strain of Gay's wedding, and then you getting engaged to that terrible . . .' Then she remembered that Bella was in the room, and just stopped herself in time. But before anyone could feel embarrassed, she launched into a further hysterical tirade against Rupert.

Lazlo looked at her reflectively, and then said, in a surprisingly gentle voice. 'This must be a terrible strain for you, Aunt Constance. You must be exhausted. I don't expect you've had any dinner either. Why don't you go to bed, and we'll get someone to bring you something on a tray.'

'How could you expect me to eat at a time like this?' said Constance, but she looked mollified. 'Perhaps I should keep my strength up. I suppose I could just manage a chicken sandwich.'

Steve got to his feet and gave Constance one of

his devastating smiles. 'I'll go and have a word in the kitchen,' he said.

'You're such a comfort to me, Steve,' Constance could be heard saying as she went up the stairs.

Lazlo, Rupert and Charles immediately settled down to discuss raising the money, but Charles was obviously having difficulty concentrating.

'I think I'll hit the hay, too,' he said, tottering towards the door. 'Thank you for coping so admirably with Constance, Lazlo.'

As Charles left the room, Steve came back.

'Half a capon and a vat of french fries are on their way upstairs to Constance. That should keep her quiet,' he said to Lazlo. 'I can't tell you how appalled I am about Chrissie. I've only known her a fortnight, but it's long enough to realize what a great kid she is.'

'You didn't realize anything of the kind,' snapped Rupert. 'You were just after her bread.'

'Shut up, Rupe,' said Lazlo, and went back to talking about money.

Bella studied Steve surreptitiously, and wondered how she could ever have loved him to such distraction. Everything about him revolted her now. He's just a handsome hunk of nothing, she thought. Then she turned to Rupert, sitting in the window seat, with his head in his hands, completely gone to pieces. Then she looked at Lazlo. That muscle was still pounding in his cheek, and she suddenly realized the titanic dependability and strength of the man – and how much it must be costing him in sheer teeth-gritting self-control not to give way to sniping and panic like the others.

As unexpected as an extra step at the bottom of

a flight of stairs, it came upon her. It was Lazlo she was in love with.

At that moment he looked at her. 'You're tired?' he said.

'I ought to go,' she muttered, terrified that he might read what was in her mind.

'I'll drive you home,' said Steve.

'Rupert'll take her,' said Lazlo. 'I want to pick your brains about raising cash in Buenos Aires, Steve.'

Bella didn't speak on the way home, desperately trying to control the raging emotions inside her. But when they reached the flat, she asked Rupert if he wanted to come up for a drink.

He shook his head. 'I must get back. Oh, hell, Bella, what am I going to do? I took Chrissie so much for granted, treating her like a tiresome kid-sister, and now, suddenly, she's gone . . .'

'You realize you're in love with her.'

He looked up, his face haggard. 'Yes, I am. I thought I was going to shoot myself last week because you wouldn't marry me, but now Chrissie's in such terrible danger, I know it's her I love, and I don't suppose I'll ever see her again.'

Bella put her arms round him. 'There, there, it's going to be all right. Lazlo'll find her for you.'

'Oh, he'll get her back if anyone can,' said Rupert. 'With all his mates in the underworld, he can pull strings like nobody's business, but I've got a horrible feeling this isn't a straight-forward money kidnapping, that it's all got something to do with Miguel Rodriguez.'

Bella's heart missed a beat. 'The man Lazlo killed?'

Rupert nodded. 'Miguel's brother, Juan, has been trying to pay Lazlo back ever since.'

'What was the real story behind it?'

'Miguel and Juan Rodriguez ran a vice ring in South America. They had Buenos Aires so completely sewn up. The police were terrified of them. Miguel had a much younger wife called Maria, whom he treated like dirt. She and Lazlo fell in love and had a raging affair. Miguel found out and pulled a knife on Lazlo in a bar. There was a fight. Miguel was killed.

'The next day – although no-one could pin it on him – Juan had acid thrown in Maria's face. Her beauty was ruined. She couldn't bear Lazlo to see her like that. A few days later she committed suicide. The police were too scared of Juan to do anything about it, but Lazlo and he have been stalking each other like a pair of tigers ever since. I think it's Juan's boys who have nicked Chrissie, and if they have, they'll never let her go alive, however much we fork out. That's what's crucifying Lazlo.'

'Was she very beautiful, Miguel's wife?' said Bella, trying to sound casual.

'Maria? Oh, absolutely ravishing. I don't think Lazlo's ever really got over her committing suicide.'

After she'd let herself into her flat, Bella sat for hours, lacerated with jealousy at the thought of Maria Rodriguez.

17

Two days dragged by with no news of Chrissie. Bella tried to throw herself into rehearsals, but she could think of nothing but Lazlo and the hell he must be going through. She also tried not to feel disappointed when he didn't telephone her. He must have far too much on his mind.

On the evening of the third day she came out of the theatre absolutely dead beat. She had rehearsed all day, followed by a gruelling performance of *Othello* in the evening. The audience had been as unreceptive as blotting paper, particularly a coach load from the Mothers' Union in the stalls who had talked and laughed through the last act.

It was a dark, hot, sultry night, with no stars and a suggestion of thunder. She was wearing only a skimpy red and white spotted dress. The smell of frying garlic and onions from a nearby Italian Restaurant made her feel slightly sick. She decided to walk part of the way home. She passed a telephone box and resisted the temptation to go inside and ring Lazlo to find out if he had any news of Chrissie. She would be too tongue-tied to do it properly.

You *must* stop thinking about him, she told herself angrily.

She turned right into a road only dimly lit by a few street lamps. Suddenly, she saw a cigarette glow in the dark and a figure stepped towards her.

She jumped nervously as a voice whispered, 'Bella.'

Then she saw a gleam of silver blond hair, and her nervousness turned to irritation. It was Steve.

'What the hell are you doing here?' she snapped.

'I *must* talk to you.'

'Well I don't want to talk to you. I've got nothing to say to you – nothing.'

'Honey,' he said urgently. 'For Pete's sake listen, I'm on the level. I've found out where Chrissie is.'

Bella turned towards him with a gasp.

'Are you sure? Is she OK?'

'I don't know. They're holding her in some deserted warehouse in the East End. It sounds like a pretty amateur job to me. One of the gang got cold feet and grassed to a mate of mine.'

'Have you told Lazlo?'

'I can't get hold of him. He went to the races this afternoon and hasn't been seen since.'

'Well, what are we waiting for?' said Bella, not stopping to think.

'I'm parked over there,' said Steve, pointing to a car under the trees.

Bella ran towards it.

'Come on. We mustn't waste any time.'

Her only thought was how pleased Lazlo would be if they found Chrissie.

Steve opened the front door for her, and she was just bending forward to get in when a voice in the back said, in a thick foreign accent, 'Don't try anything silly. We've got you covered.'

And she saw the gleam of a pistol butt.

Giving a scream, she backed out again, against Steve, but he shoved her violently into the car. The next moment something hard and metallic hit her on the head. And simultaneously it seemed, some-one reached in front of her, suffocating her with a sweet-smelling cloth. She had the feeling she was falling forward, crashing her head on the dash-board of the car as she went. Next moment all was blackness.

She had no idea how long she was unconscious. When she came to, there was an excruciating pain pounding through her head, and she realized she was in a moving car. There was thick cloth tied over her eyes, ropes were biting into her wrists and ankles, and she could feel the back of her head bleeding still, the blood dripping onto the back of her neck.

She groaned and retched.

'Steve, I'm going to be sick.'

No-one said anything, but the car slowed down. She was lifted out like a sack of potatoes and someone held her head while she retched and retched, sobbing with pain, humiliation and terror.

'Let me go, please let me go. I'm innocent. I haven't done anything.'

Next moment someone was forcing her mouth open. She struggled frenziedly as they poured liquid down her throat. They were trying to poison her. Then she realized it was only brandy. Her throat was burning. She thought she was going to throw up again.

They gave her another slug. She began to feel a bit better.

Hastily she was bundled back in the car. Still no-one spoke to her, and they set off again. Lulled by the brandy, she decided not to ask any questions. Why provoke them?

They must have driven about four hours after that. She kept worrying about the matinée next day, and how there was no way she was going to make it. And how the understudy would probably be much better than her. Then she thought of Lazlo and what he would think if he knew she'd been kidnapped – probably wouldn't care anyway.

But why should they snatch her? Perhaps if they still thought Rupert was crazy about her, she might pull in a bigger ransom. But Steve had been there the other night. It must have been quite obvious that Rupert was only crazy about Chrissie now, and wasn't in love with her any more.

Her mind reeled in turmoil. She'd never trusted Steve, but in all her dealings with him she'd never dreamed he was a gangster, perhaps tied up with a cold-blooded murderer like Juan Rodriguez. If it hadn't been for her, he would never have been able to meet the Henriques family and ingratiate himself into their good books and make off with Chrissie so easily. She was sure now he was behind Chrissie's kidnapping as well.

Then, with a shiver, she remembered Rupert saying that if Juan's boys nicked Chrissie, they'd never let her out alive. Perhaps she'd get acid thrown in her face like Maria Rodriguez.

The anaesthetizing effect of the brandy was wearing off. The pain in her head was excruciating.

Panic took over. 'Oh, Lazlo, help me, help me,' she whimpered.

Someone kicked her viciously in the ankle.

'Shut your bloody mouth,' said the same thick foreign accent, rough with fear and anxiety.

She could feel the tension in the car. Someone was beside her in the back, perhaps two in the front. She could tell they were really scared. There was a sickly sweet goat smell of sweat, and over and over again she heard matches flare as cigarettes were chain-smoked. Being blindfold, her whole nervous system picked up things quicker.

She had realized it must be nearly morning when someone turned on the wireless. It was the six o'clock news. She waited breathlessly.

Mrs Thatcher had taken Mr Wilson to task during a late night sitting in the House. Australia had devalued the dollar. A leopard had escaped from the Zoo. A Royal Princess had announced her engagement. The weather would be hot and sunny, although thundery showers were expected towards evening.

Bella slumped back in her seat in despair. No-one would ever find her.

They were driving fast now, presumably to reach their destination before too many people were about, storming along straight roads, squealing round corners. It was getting hotter. She was desperate to go to the loo.

Finally, the car stopped, and they took her out. She felt a warm breeze on her arms and legs, and a distant smell of salt and the sound of the waves pounding.

Suddenly she was panicking that they were high

up, near the sea, and they were going to push her over a cliff.

She was shaking uncontrollably. She started to cry again. Quickly someone put a hand over her mouth.

'Keep quiet,' snarled a voice, and she felt something cold and metallic jabbed in her back.

Then they sat down on the grass and took the ropes off her ankles, so she could walk. They must have moved her then a couple of miles. She felt people round her all the time, moving, walking and whispering. She could hear cows mooing, birds singing, and the hum of cars in the distance.

Now her feet were on gravel, crunching up a path. She could feel the relief of those around her, a lightening of tension.

She was stumbling over the threshold, a door slammed, a lock clicked. There was a smell of musty, unwashed house that took her straight back to her childhood in the slums. She felt the sweat pouring off her. Next moment someone ran downstairs and, taking her arm, dragged her upstairs and pushed her into a room.

Someone undid her hands. She felt her blindfold; it seemed to be held down with masking tape. The next moment someone had ripped it off, catching some of her hair. Her head was so tender, she screamed.

'Don't hurt her,' said the voice with the thick foreign accent.

She blinked in the half light. Two men stood in front of her. Both were masked. But she realized neither was Steve. One was very stocky with black hair, a black beard sticking out from under his mask, and massive shoulders.

The other was taller and slimmer, with thinning dark hair.

'Listen, baby,' he said. He also had a Spanish accent, but less strong than the other one. 'You're going to be here a long time. Don't do anything silly. If you want anything, we'll try and get it for you.'

'I must go to the loo,' said Bella desperately.

The taller one laughed. 'There's a bucket in the corner.'

She was flaming well going to wait till they'd gone.

'Where's Steve?' she said. 'Is he here?'

The taller one shook his head and showed her his gun.

'I repeat, don't try anything silly like escaping. There are five of us here guarding you.'

Suddenly Bella was terrified they'd taken off her blindfold, because she knew if one of them forgot their masks or if it slipped off they'd have to kill her.

They left her after that, and she had time to examine the room. It was very small, about ten feet by ten feet, and lit by a twenty watt bulb. A heavy wooden shutter was nailed over the window, the wallpaper was stained dirty brown, and thick dusty cobwebs hung from the smoke-grimed ceiling. The only furniture was a broken chair and the bucket in the corner.

She tried the bars on the window, but they were firmly nailed down. There were no weaknesses in the walls. Anyway, she'd bitten her nails so far down in the last few days they'd be no good for burrowing a hole.

A few minutes later another man came into the room to clean up the wound on the back of her head. He had long, blondish hair, was very thin, and had a quiet, soft voice with the same accent as the other two.

She found herself ridiculously grateful for the gentle way he handled her, warning her that the antiseptic was going to sting. She sensed he felt sorry for her. She noticed that he wore trousers that were too short, rather flashy yellow socks on his thin ankles and ill-fitting basket-weave shoes.

Afterwards she lay down and tried to make herself as comfortable as possible. Outside, she could hear them speaking to one another in Spanish. They *must* be Juan's boys.

Some time in the afternoon the thin blond boy brought her in a cup of tea and baked beans on a piece of bread on a greasy tin plate. Starving, she wolfed the lot, then, two minutes later, threw it all up, only just reaching the bucket in time.

Her head seemed to be splitting open. Clutching it, she crouched on the floor, sobbing. She must get out, she was going mad. Then she remembered reading somewhere that if you could survive the first forty-eight hours of a kidnapping, you could survive anything. She must get a grip on herself.

Our Father which art in Heaven, she began.

She noticed they hadn't risked giving her a knife and fork with her food. She examined her face in the spoon. Her eyes were huge, her face pale and streaked with blood.

She decided to try and recite the whole of *Othello* – anything to keep her sane; but as she got to the third act, as Othello's jealousy is slowly awakened by Iago, her mind kept straying to Lazlo, reliving the moments they'd spent together, the fights they'd had, the weekend in the country when he'd held her in his arms after the nightmare. What was it he'd said? That she was funny, talented and beautiful.

She looked at her reflection in the spoon again. He wouldn't think she was beautiful now. She felt a black churning hatred against Steve.

At last, out of sheer exhaustion, she fell into an uneasy sleep.

18

She was woken by crunching on the gravel outside. Light was no longer filtering through a crack in the shutters. She heard three knocks, then the front door being opened quickly and quietly, and then shut again, then whispered voices and a slight laugh and someone coming up the stairs past her door.

She still felt sick, but the pain in her head was receding a bit. She struggled to her feet, feeling stiff and dizzy. Her mouth tasted awful. She could feel a film of dirt when she ran her tongue over her teeth.

No Colgate ring of confidence for you, she thought, licking her fingers and trying to rub away the bloodstains on her cheeks.

Logic told her that if the kidnappers liked her and thought she was pretty they would be less likely to do her in.

She wondered who the latest arrival was, but she didn't have long to wait. Next minute the door opened and two men in masks came in, carrying guns. One was the stocky, bearded one; the other, whom she hadn't seen before, was taller, wearing very tight trousers over slightly overweight hips, and a dark blue shirt. He had a very large torso. She could see patches of hairy chest between each button.

'Come on, beauty,' he said, tying her hands up, in an oily, lisping voice that made Bella shiver. 'It's time for a little chat.'

They led her down the passage to a brightly lit room. In it were several chairs and a table covered with bottles, glasses and tins of food.

A man lounged on an old sofa. He was also masked, but Bella noticed he was wearing an expensive, if slightly too flashy, blue suit, expensive gold cuff-links and watch, a pale blue silk shirt and he smelt strongly of aftershave.

'Hi, Bella baby,' he said. 'What'll you drink?'

He had a nice voice, deep, slow and soft, with slight American overtones.

'We'll have her hands untied, too, Carlos,' he said to the stocky, bearded gunman.

'We don't want you to be any more uncomfortable than you need, and I guess we can trust you not to do anything silly.'

Why do they keep saying that, thought Bella, irrationally. Lazlo would say she was always doing silly things.

Carlos undid the rope with a bread knife. It had left purple marks on her wrists. The man on the sofa got up and rubbed them gently.

'You really shouldn't have tied them so tight,' he said reproachfully.

Bella was frightened by this soft approach. She could feel the sweat running down her sides.

'You'd like a drink,' he said. 'Scotch?'

Bella nodded.

'I'm afraid we don't run to ice.'

He poured her a large whisky and put the glass on a chair beside her.

She glanced round. The two guards leant against the door behind her, fingering their guns.

She picked up her glass, but her hand was shaking so much she could hardly get it to her mouth.

'You're frightened,' said the man in the blue suit. 'What are you afraid of?'

'Your mob haven't behaved with much gentleness so far.'

'You're afraid we might spoil your beauty. Forget it.'

He picked up the bread knife and started to cut the end off a cigar.

She noticed he had beautifully manicured hands, the nails slightly too long.

'Why have you brought me here?' she blurted out. 'It's tied up with Chrissie, isn't it?'

'Sure it is.'

'Is she OK?'

'She's just fine. Not bearing up under the strain as well as she might, but she's been cooped up longer than you have, and I guess she's led a much more cushy life than you – not used to roughing it. Not a great fan of yours, is she?'

Bella flushed. 'It's no business of yours.'

'Can't say I blame her. You took her boyfriend off her, didn't you?'

'I didn't,' said Bella, nettled, taking another slug of whisky. 'He came of his own accord.'

'I don't blame him,' he said, getting up from his chair, and running his hand down her face. 'You're very lovely,' he added softly as Bella flinched away. 'And I'm not surprised El Gatto's got the hots for you as well. He's been trying to cut Rupert out, hasn't he?'

Bella looked bewildered, then suddenly realized they meant Lazlo. 'No,' she said in a strangled voice. 'It's not true.'

Her early warning system wasn't working very well, but it seemed vital to convince him there was nothing between her and Lazlo – or she'd never get out alive.

'Is he going to be able to raise the dough?'

'Of course he will, but it takes time in the present economic climate.'

'Sure,' said the man in the blue suit.

'But he's got steel nerves, Lazlo,' Bella went on. 'He won't hand over a penny till he has assurances Chrissie's safe, and going to be handed back.'

'Well, to help him get his finger out, we'd like you to make a little tape tomorrow, telling him how much you're missing him and how miserable you are.'

Bella went white.

'No,' she said in a strangled voice. 'I couldn't do that.'

'I would if I were you. You'll find us very easy going as long as you agree to play ball.'

'Can I see Chrissie? Is she here too?'

'Sure, why not. She's in here.' He opened a door on the right and filled up her glass. 'Take your drink with you.'

Bella's first thought was how beautiful Chrissie had grown. She must have lost pounds. The black dress she'd been kidnapped in hung off her, her dark hair looked even darker because it was greasy, and her eyes were huge in her dead white face.

When she saw Bella she shrunk away.

'Go away!' she screamed. 'I don't want her near me. I hate her, I hate her!'

She collapsed on to the bed, sobbing hysterically. The door closed behind Bella; a key clicked in the lock. She bent over Chrissie, close to tears herself.

'Please don't cry. It's going to be all right. Lazlo's going to raise the cash.'

'He's not! He's not! Why hasn't he raised it before then? Everyone's deserted me, and now they bring you in here to torture me.'

Bella knelt down beside her.

'Here, have some whisky.'

'I don't want any of their horrible booze,' said Chrissie, clenching her fists in a sudden spasm of misery. 'I haven't eaten anything since I've been here. Trust you to suck up to them and accept their beastly drink.'

And, swinging round towards Bella, she knocked the glass out of her hand so whisky spilled all over the floor and Bella's dress.

'I *hate* you! *Hate* you!' she sobbed. 'Steve was your crooked friend. If you hadn't introduced him to us, this never would have happened. I wouldn't put it past you to be in this together.'

'I'm not anything to do with it,' said Bella, trying to be patient. 'I was as appalled as you to find that Steve was mixed up in it.'

'Then why have they grabbed you as well?' said Chrissie. 'I suppose they think Rupert would be more likely to persuade Lazlo to fork out two million pounds for you than he would be for me.' And she started to sob again.

'Look, please listen,' Bella said. 'It's all over between Rupert and me.'

Chrissie looked at her sullenly.

'You may have broken it off because you got bored with him, but he's still nuts about you.'

'He's not, I promise. He flew back from Zurich the night you were kidnapped. I've never seen anyone in such a state. Lazlo and I went round to Chichester Terrace the moment we heard the news. Lazlo started planning how to raise the cash. Constance was being her usual unspeakable self and Charles was too tight to be any use. But Rupert had gone completely to pieces. He absolutely tore a strip off Constance when she grumbled about raising so much money.'

'I don't believe you,' said Chrissie dully.

'Afterwards Rupert drove me home – only because Lazlo told him to,' she added hastily. 'He said he'd always taken you for granted because you'd always been there, a kind of kid sister ready to adore him. But now you were in danger, he realized it was you he loved all the time. He was absolutely demented with worry.'

'You're just saying it.'

'I'm not, I promise.'

Chrissie started to cry. Then like a child with a bedtime story, she said, 'Could you possibly tell me what you've just told me – all over again!'

Later Bella said, 'How the hell are we going to get out of here?'

'I don't think we can,' said Chrissie. 'They're all armed to the teeth. They scare the life out of me.'

'There was a blond one who was kind to me when he cleaned up the wound on my head,' said Bella.

'That's Diego,' said Chrissie. 'He's all right, but there's a spooky one called Pablo who hasn't said a word the whole time. He's got a finger missing on his right hand. And the really horrible one is Ricardo. He's the one who's bursting out of his shirts. Whenever he ties me up at night, he touches me far more than necessary. I'm sure he's going to try something soon – they all seem so jumpy and frustrated. I say, do you really think Rupert loves me?'

19

Three days passed with unbearable slowness. They listened to every news bulletin, but there was no mention of the kidnapping. Even Bella began to feel everyone had abandoned them. One of her greatest worries was stopping Chrissie from cracking up under the strain. But, in fact, it gave her something to do, fussing over the younger girl, seeing she ate something, keeping her cheerful. They talked incessantly, Chrissie babbling on about her childhood in South America, and about Rupert, and inevitably about Lazlo, Bella trying desperately not to appear too interested whenever his name was mentioned.

Now that Chrissie had lost so much weight, and her face had thinned down, she reminded Bella of him so poignantly. They had the same cheekbones, the same impassivity, the same smile that would light up a blacked-out city when suddenly they were amused.

On the second morning, the gunmen took Bella into the living-room and made her record a ridiculous tape to be sent to Lazlo and the family, begging them to raise the money as soon as possible, and not to contact the police. She had to read it over and over again, until they were satisfied with the stress and the timing.

'And at the end, say "I love you",' said Ricardo.

'I won't,' said Bella.

Ricardo held the gun to her temple, 'I would if I were you.'

'I love you very much,' whispered Bella.

'That should get El Gatto to pull his finger out,' said Ricardo.

Chrissie, who'd just been brought in to make her tape, overheard Bella's last remark.

'What the hell's going on?' she hissed to Bella as soon as they were locked up together again. 'You've been pulling a fast one all the time. Why did you say you loved Rupert just now. You are still after him.'

Bella found herself blushing. 'I'm not. The gunmen have got completely the wrong end of the stick. For some reason they're convinced Lazlo and I are mad about each other.'

Chrissie's mouth opened and shut, and then she started to laugh incredulously. 'You and Lazlo! God, they must be thick. If they only knew how much you loathe each other.'

Bella didn't wince. She was making great strides in self-control, but she found it very difficult not to react during the next day when Chrissie kept saying, 'You and Lazlo,' and going off into fits of laughter.

Chrissie, now she had Bella to protect her, slept a great deal. She had so many shocks in the last week to recover from. This left Bella plenty of time to observe her captors.

The smooth man in the light blue suit had left. He was probably, Bella decided, some henchman, fairly high up in the Rodriquez empire. Five others remained: Ricardo, the thug with the bulging muscles and the soft oily voice, Diego, the tall blond one with the gentle hands and voice, Carlos, stocky and dark with a beard, the very thin young boy, Pablo, with the missing finger, who never said anything, and, finally, Eduardo, the tall dark one with the air of authority, who seemed to be in charge of the operation. All of them, except Pablo, wore wedding rings.

There were always two of them on guard, one at the bottom of the stairs by the front door, one outside Bella and Chrissie's door. At night, a guard stayed in their room with a gun ready across his knee.

Ricardo was the most unpleasant. For long periods he'd be quiet, then suddenly get explosive and violently argumentative. Nor did she like the way he stared hungrily at Chrissie.

Diego, on the other hand, was very kind to them. One day, when she was crying, he got out a handkerchief and wiped her eyes. And often, when she got aches and pains from sleeping on the floor, he would rub her back for her. What really frightened her was the pity she frequently detected in his voice. He knows we're going to be killed, she thought in terror.

Physically she felt she was falling to pieces. Her red and white dress was filthy. So was she. She imagined her skin getting covered in blackheads, her eyebrows growing like bushes from not being plucked, her teeth rotting because she couldn't clean them. The stench in the room was terrible. She dreamed obsessively of Lazlo's ivy green bathroom and soaking in hot scented water.

On the fourth night the gunmen started quarrelling amongst themselves. They had been drinking and she could hear them shouting in the room next door. She wished she could understand what they were saying. Chrissie could understand Spanish, but she was asleep.

At midnight Ricardo took over the watch from Diego. He reeked of brandy fumes and stumbled over a loose floorboard. Bella pretended to be asleep.

The shouting died down in the next room and, soon, all was deathly quiet. Bella opened half an eye. In the half light, the gun gleamed across Ricardo's knee. Chrissie turned over and moaned in her sleep, her black hair flopped over her face, the top button of her black dress was undone, showing the marble whiteness of her breasts.

Ricardo's breathing became heavier, as suddenly he got up, stepped over Bella, and went towards the bed. Through half-shut eyes she saw him gazing down at Chrissie's full, voluptuous body, then, very slowly, he put his hand out and began to stroke her face. Chrissie moved again in her sleep, edging towards him, like a dog cuddling up to its owner. Ricardo went on stroking her cheek, then his hand moved slowly down her neck and began to undo the buttons of her dress.

Bella was frozen with horror, unable to move. Suddenly Chrissie woke up and gave a little gasp of terror at the sight of the masked face. Next moment, Ricardo's hand clamped over her mouth and then he was on top of her, clawing at her dress.

Bella reacted instantly.

'Leave her alone,' she yelled, picking up the broken chair, and the next moment she cracked it

373

over Ricardo's head. He gave a groan and collapsed on to the floor as Chrissie started screaming.

Bella was about to hit him again when the door burst open and in came Eduardo, Carlos and Pablo, all carrying guns.

'Put that chair down,' snarled Eduardo.

'He was trying to rape me,' sobbed Chrissie.

Bella, looking at the three gun barrels, dropped the chair. Pablo helped Ricardo to his feet.

'The bitch went for me,' said Ricardo, blood dripping from his head, and the next moment he'd turned on Bella, slapping her viciously across the face, back and forth, back and forth.

'That's enough,' said Eduardo. 'We'll teach her a lesson another way.' He gave instructions in Spanish over his shoulder to Pablo, who went out and came back with some rope with which he tied up both Bella and Chrissie.

They sat Bella down on a chair. She could feel the blood trickling down her cheeks where Ricardo's ring had cut her.

Then Carlos came in with a towel and put it round Bella's shoulders. Suddenly Bella remembered, terrified, how they'd cut off Paul Getty's ear.

'Oh please no!' she whispered.

'Shut up,' said Eduardo, lifting up her hair.

They were all standing behind her.

'No!' screamed Chrissie, 'please don't hurt her.' For she could see what Bella could not, that in Eduardo's hand was a razor blade glinting evilly in the dim light.

Bella jerked her head forward.

'Keep still,' swore Eduardo. 'Or you really will get hurt.'

She felt her hair being tugged backward, and sawed at, this way and that.

'Oh, no!' she wailed. 'Not my hair.'

Eduardo ran the razor blade gently down her cheek.

'Quiet,' he said softly. 'Or we really will give you something to remember us by.'

They cut her long mane off to a ragged three inches all over her head, short as a boy's, shorter than most boys, tugging and sawing till it lay in a heavy mass all over the floor.

Eduardo then told Pablo to gather it up.

'We'll parcel it up and send it to El Gatto. It might make him get off his arse about raising the dough,' said Eduardo.

After that, they took her next door and stood her up, with her hands and feet still tied and her head in a noose of rope hanging from the ceiling.

'Don't fall asleep or the rope will snap your head off,' said Ricardo, and he went out, locking the door.

Bella couldn't stop crying. Her only irrational thought was that now she'd finally lost Lazlo. She remembered him saying he only liked girls with long hair, not that she'd ever had him. But now, with short hair, there was no possibility that he could love her.

For four nights sleep had eluded her. Now that she had somehow to keep from dropping off, she felt overwhelmed with exhaustion. She *must* keep awake. She tried to remember all the snatches of poetry she had ever known, 'Farewell, thou are too dear for my possessing. And like enough thou know'st thy estimate . . . How like a winter hath my absence been from thee . . . How sad and bad

and mad it was, then. But, how it was sweet . . . Oh
heart! oh heart! if he'd but turn his head. You'd
know the folly of being comforted.'

The trouble with every poem was that it turned
her thoughts back to Lazlo, making her re-live the
moments they'd spent together. The last time she'd
seen him with his back to the fireplace, very suntanned in that dark blue shirt, with strangely
softened face, saying, 'Come here,' and her going to
him in spite of being frightened, and then the
telephone interrupting them just before she reached
him.

Then she allowed her thoughts to stray into the
dangerous fantasy of the telephone not ringing, of
being in his arms and hearing all the lovely things
he was saying, his voice husky with passion.

Oh God! she thought, it wasn't the racehorses or
the yachts or the fur coats she wanted from him, it
was the understanding, the kindness beneath the
mocking exterior, the protectiveness he displayed
to his family and people he loved.

She started to cry again, overwhelmed by utter
despair. Why not fall asleep and die? No! She
pulled herself together. Chrissie had to be looked
after. They'd got to get out.

Diego took over the watch at four o'clock and
was obviously appalled by what he saw.

'My God! What have those bastards done? Your
beautiful, beautiful hair.'

He untied the rope round her neck and feet and
hands, brushed away the hairs that were itching
down her back, and gave her a cigarette.

'What happened?'

She shrugged her shoulders.

'Ricardo tried to rape Chrissie.'

'And?'

'I went for him with a chair.'

'So he had to take his revenge. Is the kid all right?'

Bella nodded. 'Physically anyway. Where are the others?'

'Sleeping. I'll make you a cup of tea.'

He went out, leaving his gun on a chair. Bella could have picked it up and used it, but she felt too tired; and that Diego trusting her was her one chance of getting out. He came back with hot water and soap and washed her face and hands for her. Then he brought her a cup of tea and a pear, which he cut into quarters and peeled for her. Bella had never tasted anything so delicious in her life.

'You're so good to me, Diego,' she said. 'Do I look absolutely hideous like this?'

He shrugged. 'It was prettier long, but it will grow soon.'

'Will I be allowed to live long enough for it to grow?'

'Don't think about things like that. I don't know. I am only given orders.'

She took a gulp of the sweet, scalding tea. It seemed to give her strength.

'Why are you caught up in this racket?' she asked.

'Mine is a very poor country. The only way to make big money in a hurry is on the wrong side of the law.'

Then he told her about his son who was five, who had a very rare heart complaint.

'If he doesn't have an operation soon, he will die. We do not have your health service in my country.

Everything has to be paid for. This operation costs a lot of money.

'When this business is all over, and El Gatto pays up, I will have enough to pay for the operation, and be able to take my wife and children to live in a new country. They will arrange a new passport for us.'

'But won't the people who give the orders expect you to do other things for them?'

'No, only one job; that's the deal.'

'But can't you understand the kind of people you're dealing with?' said Bella. 'They'll never let you go once they get their teeth into you. You'll be doing jobs for them for the rest of your life, and one day you'll slip up and it'll be curtains.'

'Shut up,' said Diego. 'It's not true.'

Bella played her trump card.

'Juan Rodriquez is behind this, isn't he?'

Diego started. 'How do you know?'

'Lazlo knows it too, and he's not stupid. It won't be long before he tracks us down and, whether we're dead or alive, you'll have a long, long spell in jug.'

'You're bluffing,' said Diego, suddenly very agitated.

'Juan Rodriguez is hardly the sort of name I'd make up. Look, I know all about him, how powerful and vicious he is. He'll never let you go after one job. And if he bumps off Chrissie and me – which he intends to, doesn't he? – whether they get the cash or not, Lazlo will hunt the lot of you down until he gets his revenge. With two man-eating tigers on your tracks, you'll never get that peaceful life you want with your wife and child.'

Diego got up and began to pace about the room.

Bella's heart was pounding, but she tried to keep her voice calm:

'Look, Diego, I swear something – if you tip Lazlo off where we are, and it'll only take one telephone call, he'll look after you, he'll get your wife out of Buenos Aires, and he'll see your child gets the best medical treatment in the world. And you'll be able to live in peace for the rest of your life, not as a hunted man.'

'You're crazy,' said Diego. 'The Fuzz'll grab me the minute I get out of here.'

'You'll do a year at the most – particularly as it's your first offence – but probably Lazlo'll be able to fiddle it so you don't even do that – and at least your wife will be safe and your little boy saved.'

Diego sat down and picked up his gun and pointed it at her.

'Don't you realize the greatest crime among my people is *infamita*,' he said sternly. 'To talk to the authorities. If I shopped the others, Juan would make sure I was dead in a week.'

'Not if you had Lazlo's protection. They're not worth being loyal to, this lot. They're a bunch of cheap crooks. You're different, Diego. You're a good person, I can tell.'

'Don't talk to me like that. If the others heard you, it wouldn't be just your hair they'd chop off,' snapped Diego. 'Lie down and get some sleep.' He took off his coat and laid it over her shoulders.

'I ache all over,' said Bella, 'I can't sleep. Rub my back and tell me more about your little boy.'

20

Another day and night limped by. Pablo, feeling contrite, perhaps over his part in last night's shearing, gave her an old copy of *Woman's Own* to read. To Bella it was like stumbling on Chapman's Homer. Over and over again she read the cosy hints on crocheting and making lampshades, and the romantic stories with their happy endings. How her mouth watered as she pored over the pictures of Lancashire Hot Pot, and cheap ways with end of neck.

Best of all was being able to look at new faces. Apart from Chrissie, she'd seen nothing but masks for the last five days. But at the back of her mind was always the thought that time was running out, like High Noon. Do not forsake me, oh my darling.

The following morning Pablo was keeping guard in her room, smiling to himself as he polished his gun. Then shouting broke out next door.

'Get on guard,' she could hear Eduardo yelling. 'You know there should be two of you.'

'I need a drink.' It was Ricardo's chillingly oily whine.

'You've had your ration for the day,' snapped Eduardo. 'Go back to your post.'

'I want a drink.'

'There's only half a bottle left.'

'Well, someone's got to go out tomorrow and get some more.'

'It's too dangerous,' said Eduardo's voice, harsh with exasperation.

As the day crawled by, the atmosphere grew more and more tense, quarrels flaring up at the most innocent remarks. Carlos complained Ricardo hadn't put sugar in his tea. Ricardo hit the roof. Eduardo nearly got all the soup poured over him when he suggested there wasn't enough salt in it. If this inaction goes on much longer, thought Bella, they'll be at each other's throats.

At midnight, Diego took over the guard. At first he was offhand, and sullenly refused to talk to her.

'It must be very hot in Buenos Aires now,' said Bella.

Diego took no notice.

'Not much fun for a young mother looking after a sick child,' she went on.

'I don't want to talk about it,' exploded Diego.

'I was brought up in the slums myself,' said Bella. 'And I know what hell it is, and what it's like to escape and leave it all behind.'

'Ending up in a deserted farmhouse with a gun at your head, eh?' said Diego.

'That was just bad luck, but every child deserves a chance to get away, and one's own child most of all. Oh, Diego, don't you *love* him?'

'Of course I do,' he snarled. 'What do you think I did this for?'

'Then give him a chance to get better, and run in the sunshine, and go to a good school, and wear nice clothes.'

'Juan'll give me all that.'

'Rubbish. He's just put a noose round your neck, which he'll tighten if ever you don't play ball and do what he wants. Lazlo Henriques is a good man, whatever you've heard to the contrary,' she went on, her voice breaking slightly. 'He's tough but he knows how to look after his own people.'

'You love him, don't you?' said Diego softly.

Bella nodded, a great lump in her throat. 'And I'll probably never see him again.' The tears ran down her cheeks and she was overwhelmed by such despair that it was a few seconds before she realized what Diego was saying.

'If I contact El Gatto, how will he know I'm on the level?'

Bella's heart leapt. 'You're going to do it?'

'I don't know. Come on, how will he know?'

'I'll write him a note.'

'No, that's too dangerous.'

'Well, have this ring,' she slid the little gold ring studded with seed pearls off her finger. 'Rupert gave it to me. Lazlo always said it was the only thing he'd ever seen me wear that wasn't in appallingly bad taste. And use Black Opal as the password. Those are both private jokes that no-one would know anything about. Oh, Diego, you won't regret it, I promise you. Just tell him where we are and how to find us.'

'I haven't made up my mind yet,' said Diego, pocketing the ring.

Suddenly, there was a great crash from next door.

'They're quarrelling again. Probably about you,' said Diego, getting up and going out.

A few minutes later he was back.

'Ricardo's just knocked over the last of the whisky. Carlos slugged Ricardo. Tempers are running high.'

'Then you'll have to get some more supplies tomorrow,' said Bella.

'I don't promise anything,' said Diego.

The next day dawned hotter and more sultry. There were flies everywhere, the stench grew even more terrible. I wonder how nuns survive for years and years without washing, thought Bella. The hair was growing bristly on her legs.

'There'll soon be enough scurf in my hair to bread a veal chop,' she moaned. 'Oh God! I feel horrible.'

Diego's watch was taken over by Eduardo, who brought the wireless with him. At eight came the news. She could feel him tensing himself, but there was again no mention of the kidnapping. Everyone had forgotten them. So much for Lazlo's underworld connections.

When they played pop music, she got up and danced a few steps. Later she listened to *Waggoner's Walk*. It was hard to realize that outside life was going on as usual. People were making love, going to their offices, having toast and marmalade for breakfast.

For her breakfast she had tea without milk and a stale crust of bread.

'Is the service included?' she said.

'What?' said Eduardo.

'Oh forget it,' said Bella.

They were obviously running out of supplies.

About midday there was a lot of talking and whispering outside, and Pablo came in and tied her hands again. She was nervous; she dreaded changes in routine, but they only took her into Chrissie's room.

Chrissie seemed pathetically pleased to see her, but in bad shape.

'How much longer is this going on?' was her first question. 'I'm cracking up.'

'Sssh, something's bound to happen soon.'

'I'll go mad first. Why have they put us together again? They never do anything nice without an ulterior motive. I'm scared when they start softening up.'

'I think they're going off to get supplies, and we're easier to guard if we're both in the same room.'

Someone shouted something in Spanish outside.

Chrissie went pale.

'What are they saying?' said Bella.

'They said "Tell El Gatto if the money isn't raised by midnight tonight, it's curtains".'

'That means they're going to ring Lazlo,' said Bella.

'Oh, God! I know we're going to be killed,' said Chrissie.

Bella did her best to comfort her, but she was really worried by Chrissie's low morale and by her health. Her eyes were sunken, her cheeks were flushed and in spite of the stultifying heat of the day, she was shaking uncontrollably. She had also developed a tight, rasping cough.

She got Chrissie back on to the subject of Rupert, letting her ramble on and on.

Finally Chrissie said, 'I'm talking too much.'

'Talk all you want. There's nothing else we can do.'

'I've had a hell of a lot of time to think in the past twenty-four hours. I've been so vile to you because of Rupert. We all were, but me in particular, shouting at you at the wedding, then bitching you up over the weekend, and finally,' her voice cracked, 'putting the diamond in your suitcase.'

'It doesn't matter,' said Bella. 'If I loved someone, I'd have behaved just the same.'

'But you've been so good to me since I've been here. You're so strong and brave. You say you're ashamed of the kind of background you have, but it certainly makes you able to cope with a situation like this, standing up to them, going for Ricardo with that chair. I don't really know why you're doing it, but I just want to say thank you, and that I was quite wrong about you, and that I really love you, and I'm sorry I've been so bloody.'

Bella turned away so Chrissie wouldn't see she was crying. Ridiculous that when things were so grim, Chrissie saying those things should make her so happy.

'Lazlo's got you all wrong,' said Chrissie, 'and when we – I mean if we – one's so superstitious about presuming anything – get out, I'll tell him how lovely you are.'

She started to cough, on and on, until Eduardo brought her a glass of water.

'You'll have to get her something stronger,' said Bella.

'The others are going to bring back cough medicine,' said Eduardo.

21

The waiting was terrible. Bella read stories from *Woman's Own* out loud, acting out the dialogue, camping it up to make Chrissie laugh. Finally Chrissie fell into an uneasy sleep. It was amazing to Bella that her violent spasms of coughing didn't wake her up.

The two o'clock news still had no mention of the kidnapping, but, as the afternoon passed, Bella began to sense an increasing restlessness amongst the gunmen. Just after four o'clock there was a swift crunch on the gravel, three knocks, the front door opening and shutting, followed by raised, urgent voices.

Chrissie woke up.

'I can't stand it,' she sobbed. 'I can't bear being cooped up any more.'

'Hush,' said Bella sharply. 'I want to listen.'

She could recognize Carlo's thick accent, and Eduardo's deep, authoritative voice, and Ricardo's oily whine, but she couldn't hear Diego's light, gentle drawl. Her palms were soaking; she must keep calm.

The next moment the door was unlocked and in came Ricardo and Eduardo, looking thunderous,

and dragged her off into the living-room. Ricardo
seized her and forced her arm behind her back, his
fingers biting into her flesh.

'You've been talking to Diego, haven't you?' he
said. 'Where is he?'

'Ow, you're hurting me,' said Bella, joy bubbling up inside her. 'How should I know where
he is? I've been locked up all the time. Isn't he
here?'

Ricardo bent her arm even farther back.

'He liked you. He fancied you. You've talked
him round.'

'I have not,' said Bella indignantly. 'It's more
than my life's worth to talk to anyone here. Where
is he?'

'None of your business,' snapped Eduardo.

They cross-questioned her endlessly. Had she
talked to Diego? What was his mood last night?
Several times they gave her stinging slaps across the
face, but she was too elated to care.

Finally she asked if she could have a cigarette.

'We haven't got any,' said Ricardo. 'Diego's
done a bunk with all the supplies.'

She was thrown back into the rom with Chrissie.

'Don't get too excited, and don't ask me any
questions,' she muttered, 'but things are looking
up.'

'Tell me,' whispered Chrissie.

'Better if I don't,' said Bella. 'If you don't know,
they can't beat it out of you.'

Outside the door she could hear the panicking
getting worse. Hope grew inside her. If only they
didn't get frightened into becoming violent. She
re-read that damn *Woman's Own* over and over
again. She could crochet that matinée jacket in her

sleep now, but she had to force herself to do something or she'd go nuts.

Hours limped by, waiting for a crunch on the gravel that didn't come. She listened to every bulletin on the wireless, but there was still no reference.

Chrissie's cough was getting worse, and on Bella's nerves. She suddenly started panicking that they'd notice her ring was missing. There was a suntan band where it had gone. Could she say it had dropped off because she'd got so thin and she couldn't find it?

Back came Eduardo and Ricardo to cross-question her.

'What did he talk about last night? Tell us again.'

'Nothing much, mostly about his son. He was worried about his health. Maybe he's telephoned home and got bad news and made a bolt for it.'

'You know something?'

'God, I wish I did. I'd have hitched a lift if I knew he was going to do a bunk.'

'Stop fooling about,' said Eduardo.

'We're going to start cutting bits off you and send them to El Gatto through the post,' said Ricardo evilly.

Chrissie gave a sob.

'He should have got your hair by now,' said Eduardo. 'What shall we send him next?' He picked up her hand and examined her fingers. For a minute Bella froze with horror, then she realized it wasn't her seed pearl ring hand.

Ricardo was waving a razor, making patterns in the air. Then he ran it down Bella's face.

'Shall Eduardo and I play noughts and crosses?' he said.

'Come on, talk,' snapped Eduardo.

'I don't know anything,' Bella muttered, cringing away from him.

'Talk,' hissed Ricardo.

Suddenly Eduardo stiffened.

'Listen,' he said sharply.

And above the thumping of her heart, Bella could hear a faint droning, like a hoover in a far off room. Then it grew louder, buzzing like an angry wasp, coming nearer and nearer.

A helicopter, thought Bella. Thank God.

It was obviously taking its time, buzzing round and round overhead.

Eduardo swore softly. Both he and Ricardo went out to look. She could hear their anxious voices outside.

'I think,' she said to Chrissie, 'we've been located.'

Pablo came and sat on guard in their room and picked up his book, but Bella noticed he was reading with unnatural slowness, his eyes fixed on the same place. Occasionally his fingers drummed on the back of the book, and he kept darting fearful glances towards the window.

They're rattled, thought Bella joyfully. Really rattled.

Next door, she could hear Eduardo gabbling away to Ricardo in Spanish. It was too fast for her.

'What are they saying?' she asked Chrissie.

'They're arguing about whether to make a bolt for it now, or wait until dark,' said Chrissie.

Bella's red and white dress was drenched in sweat. It was impossibly hot. Suddenly there was a flash, followed by a huge clap of thunder, and the storm that had been lingering for days broke over the house. Flash after flash filtered through the boarded-up window. The rain was falling like machine-gun fire on the roof.

People were crashing about next door. Oh God, they're getting ready to move out, thought Bella. Perhaps we haven't been discovered at all. Maybe the helicopter was just a farmer going home, or a politician returning to his constituency. Ricardo, probably for something to do, returned to his taunting and questioning.

'We'll cut off your foot, I think,' he said. 'And send it through the post to El Gatto.'

'Wouldn't go through the letter box,' said Bella. 'Lazlo's always out anyway, so the Post Office'd have to send him one of those buff pieces of paper saying we have tried to deliver this foot several times; why not apply to Knightsbridge Post Office?'

She began to laugh hysterically, then clapped her hands over her mouth. She mustn't crack up, she mustn't.

Ricardo then tied up their hands and took them into the living-room. Everything had been tidied up, a couple of suitcases packed. Carlos was burning rubbish in the fireplace; Pablo was running a duster all over the furniture to remove the fingerprints.

There was a commercial on the wireless now, a girl's voice crooning about men loving her shining, lustrous hair.

Lucky thing, thought Bella wistfully, remembering her long mane. What would Lazlo think when he got the parcel, she wondered. Would he be sorry, or just think how ugly she must be now? It's what you are – funny, talented, beautiful – that matters. Oh, Lazlo, Lazlo. She felt the tears trickling down her cheeks.

Suddenly her musings were interrupted by the calm impassive voice of the news reader.

'News has suddenly come to light of a double kidnapping which began in London nine days ago, when Christine Henriques, the niece of Charles Henriques, chairman of Henriques Brothers, the banking firm, was seized as she was leaving her uncle's house in Chelsea. The kidnappers demanded a ransom of two million pounds, but warned the family to raise the money privately and not to notify the police. Three days later, actress Bella Parkinson, who is engaged to Rupert Henriques, the son of Charles Henriques, was also kidnapped on her way home from the theatre, and the kidnappers stepped up the demand.

'Today, however, there was a major break-through when one of the gang contacted the family with vital information about the whereabouts of the kidnappers and their victims. The men are all believed to be South American, and police have made important steps in tracing the men behind the kidnapping, both in England and South America. The kidnapping is not believed to be motivated by politics.'

There was a long pause, then everyone started shouting and swearing. Bella didn't dare look at Chrissie.

'They'll kill us in a minute,' said Chrissie in a shaking voice.

'I don't think so,' said Bella. 'We're the only card they've got left.'

'I can't stand the tension,' said Chrissie.

'You've got to,' said Bella. 'Don't upset them. All we can do now is wait.'

In the silence between thunder claps they heard the helicopter buzzing round again.

'Come on,' said Eduardo. 'We'd better get the hell out of here.' He put a blindfold over Bella's eyes, tied it tightly. Then she felt herself being led down the stairs.

Oh why doesn't Lazlo hurry, she prayed. If we leave here they'll never find us.

They paused at the bottom of the stairs. Bella could sense the tension around her. The storm seemed to have stopped.

'I'm going outside to see if the coast's clear,' said Carlos. He opened the door and shut it again.

'What's that?' said Ricardo.

There was a crackling and they all jumped at the sound of a loudspeaker.

'You are completely surrounded,' said a voice. 'Throw your guns out of the window. Send Bella and Chrissie out at once, alone and then come out one by one with your hands up. Do not attempt to escape, or you will be shot down.'

'They're bluffing,' said Eduardo. 'I'm going to have a look.' He put his head out of the door.

In answer, a semi-circle of floodlights flashed on, flaring between the trees in an arc nearly a hundred yards long.

'Jesus!' said Carlos. 'We're done for.'

'No we're not,' said Eduardo. 'They won't shoot into the house for fear of hitting Bella or Chrissie.'

A policeman moved forward from the lights. The next moment Eduardo opened up with a machine gun. Then he seized the terrified Chrissie, jammed the smouldering gun in her back and, dragging her upstairs, opened the window.

'Go on,' he hissed, jamming the gun further into her back, 'or I'll pull the trigger. Tell them to go away, that they're not helping, and they've got to do anything we ask.'

'Go away!' screamed Chrissie. 'They'll kill us, they'll kill us.' Her voice dried up on a screeched whisper.

'Tell them they've got to do what we tell them,' whispered Eduardo. 'We want a car to get out of here and a plane to take us to South America. Go on.'

'You've got to do what they tell you,' screamed Chrissie, repeating his message, then breaking down into hysterical coughing and sobbing.

There was total silence.

Eduardo pulled Chrissie inside and shut the window.

They all gathered in the living-room at the back, Bella and Chrissie tied up, Pablo keeping watch at the front, Ricardo with his gun trained on the two girls, Carlos and Eduardo discussing their next move.

Chrissie was still coughing and crying.

'Don't worry,' whispered Bella. 'They can't hold out much longer. It must be over soon.'

Carlos found a further news bulletin on another channel. The kidnapping was again the lead story.

'The hideout of the kidnappers has now been discovered,' said the announcer. 'A remote farm-house just outside Haltby on the Devonshire coast. It has been completely surrounded by the army and the police. Police also know the names of the four kidnappers, and realize they are only the front for a

393

much larger organization. Police and the army now have the whole area cordoned off and are preparing for a long siege.

'A quarter of an hour ago, one of the gang appeared at the front door and shot at the police. Later a gunman held Miss Christine Henriques out of a first floor window at gunpoint. In considerable distress she appealed to the police not to threaten the gunmen and to agree to anything they ask for.'

Chrissie was coughing non-stop now.

'For Christ's sake shut her up,' said Ricardo.

'Why don't you let her go?' said Bella. 'If she gets any worse, you'll have a murder on your hands without trying.'

There was another crackling over the loudspeaker. Another voice was speaking now in fluent Spanish. Bella's heart gave a lurch; she felt blood rushing to her face. It was Lazlo. Chrissie tried to struggle to her feet; Bella gave a gasp of excitement which turned to terror as Ricardo shoved a gun against her temple.

'Leave her alone,' snapped Eduardo, 'and listen. It's El Gatto's voice,' and she could feel the frisson of loathing around the room. These are men, she thought, with a shiver, who have been taught to hate the name Henriques at their mother's knee.

Lazlo's voice went on, softer, more persuasive now. It was too fast for her to follow.

'What's he saying?' she whispered to Chrissie.

'That the police know who all the men are,' said Chrissie. 'And have photographs of them, that there's no way the police are going to give them an aeroplane, or a car.' She listened for a minute, then caught her breath. 'Now he's saying Juan and Steve have both been pulled in, so there's no point them resisting any more. If they surrender they won't be harmed in any way.'

Bella wished she could see the gunmen's faces to see how they were reacting.

The loudspeaker crackled and stopped.

'Finally he said the police were in no hurry and intend to wait until the gunmen saw reason,' said Chrissie.

All very well, thought Bella, but this lot are human time bombs, liable to explode at any minute.

They were arguing violently now.

'Eduardo doesn't believe Juan or Steve have been arrested,' said Chrissie. 'He thinks Lazlo's bluffing. Ricardo agrees with him. Carlos is fed up and all for packing it in. Pablo, as usual, says nothing.'

'They've run out of booze and food and cigarettes,' said Bella. 'They can't hold out much longer.'

'If they get hungry, they'll get bloody-minded,' said Chrissie. 'If they starve them out, there'll be more chance of a shoot-out.'

There was no sound or sign of life from outside. The transistor was crackling like distant gunfire as they waited for the next news bulletin. It was the same as the one before, except it added that the police knew the gunmen had run out of food and drink, and included an interview with a doctor on the effects of long-term starvation.

'It is likely to sharpen the wits, but decrease physical efficiency,' said the doctor in a calm, flat voice.

'Great,' said Bella. 'We'll all be cracking jokes soon.'

'Then the pangs of hunger will give way to dull, painless lethargy, probably accompanied by headaches,' went on the doctor.

'How soon will the hostages be in any physical danger through lack of food?' said the interviewer.

'Man can live without permanent ill effects up to six weeks on water alone,' said the doctor.

'Jesus,' muttered Bella. 'It's a hell of a way to go on a crash diet.'

The voice faded and crackled again when Eduardo shook the wireless. The batteries are running out, thought Bella. She moved slightly. Her side ached where the floor boards were biting into her flesh.

She started on The Lord's Prayer. It was too serious a time to make bargains with God she couldn't keep. Please let me out, she prayed, and I'll try to be good for the rest of my life, and try not to want Lazlo too much if he doesn't want me.

The wind came in a sudden blast, rattling the trees against the roof of the house. Next moment, the arc lights went out.

'This is your chance,' said Carlos.

'They're trying to tempt one of us out,' said Eduardo.

Ricardo tiptoed downstairs and slowly opened the front door. The next moment the lights went on and a volley of bullets was fired over the house.

'Your blackmail has failed,' said the loudspeaker. 'Send the girls out at once if you want to save your lives.'

They heard whispering and breathing on the loudspeaker. Then everything went quiet.

22

Somehow it was dawn. It seemed to Bella that they had been left to their fate. She had terrible cramp down her side. The floodlights had lost their brilliance under the door. The loudspeaker had been silent for hours. She had even dozed fitfully. Even Chrissie, having coughed half the night, was asleep, snoring gently, perhaps dreaming of Rupert and her soft bed at home.

Carlos was dozing now, curled up like an embryo. Ricardo guarded the front door still, Eduardo the window. Pablo had his gun trained on her and Chrissie.

How can she sleep so peacefully, Bella wondered.

Eduardo reached out and switched on the transistor, but it spluttered and finally gave out.

They were arguing again now in low voices. Ricardo was obviously the one suffering most; he was desperate for cigarettes and alcohol, his nails bitten down to the quick.

The loudspeaker began again, making them all jump.

'Take the only way out and surrender. Take the only way out.'

'I must go to the loo,' said Bella.

Ricardo looked at Eduardo who nodded tersely. Ricardo undid Bella's legs and, at gunpoint, led her to the lavatory at the end of the passage. For a second, she was able to peer out of a crack between the boarded windows. The sight cheered her up. Across the grass on the edge of a wood she could see rows of policemen, motionless and intent, with revolvers raised to the window. Other policemen moved around behind rows of sandbags. Beyond were television cameras and television catering vans and hundreds of Special Branch men, and handlers with alsatians on leads, eyes alert, tails wagging expectantly.

She strained her eyes to catch a glimpse of Lazlo or Rupert.

'Come on, you've been in there long enough,' said Ricardo. Feeling slightly dizzy, she stumbled back to the living-room, where Chrissie had just woken up, and realizing where she was, had started the interminable coughing and crying. Bella felt her head; she was boiling hot with temperature.

'Why don't you let her go?' she said, turning furiously on Eduardo. 'You know you're finished.'

Ricardo raised his gun at her.

'Juan will rescue us,' said Eduardo quietly.

'Rubbish,' said Bella. 'Didn't you hear Lazlo saying he'd been arrested, and even if he hadn't been, you know the kind of man he is, that he'd disown you the moment things got awkward.'

'Not me,' said Eduardo, with sudden hauteur, 'Juan would never let me down, nor I him.'

The day began to take on a nightmare quality. Eduardo was constantly having to rally the others as, over and over again, the loudspeaker made offers of food and cigarettes in return for releasing one of the hostages, all of which were refused.

In all the big kidnapping cases Bella had read about recently, the besieged gunmen had eventually capitulated. But this is different, she thought. It's a hatred thing, all tied up with Eduardo's damn *machismo*. He'll never give in without a struggle.

At dusk the lights in the living-room went out. Carlos stumbled out to the hall and tried the light switch there. No light came on. 'They've turned the bloody electricity off,' he shouted.

For several hours they waited, trembling in pitch dark; then, suddenly, brilliant super arc lights blazed into the room, making them all cover their eyes. These lights were switched on, off, on, off, making sleep absolutely impossible. They all moved into one of the boarded-up rooms.

Chrissie seemed to have sunk into a dull torpor, which worried Bella far more than the coughing, sobbing and shivering.

The police are going about it the wrong way, she thought. We're going to crack before the gunmen.

Another dawn slowly reduced the power of the arc lights. Bella had lost the ability to feel anything.

Ricardo and Eduardo and Carlos were all at each other's throats. If they start offering them cigarettes today, thought Bella, Eduardo's going to have the devil's own job stopping them accepting.

The loudspeaker crackled.

Chrissie woke up. 'What's that?' she said listlessly.

'It's Lazlo,' said Bella.

He was talking in Spanish again.

'Tell me what he's saying.'

Chrissie wriggled into a sitting position and listened.

'He says he's got something of particular interest for both Ricardo and Carlos. Ricardo first. He wants them to listen carefully.'

Suddenly there was a woman's voice, pleading, sobbing, beseeching, choking with emotion. Intensified a hundred times by the loudspeaker, it sounded terrible.

Ricardo gave a groan and sat down with his hands over his ears.

'What's she saying?' Bella hissed to Chrissie.

'It's his mother,' said Chrissie. 'She's pleading with him to give himself up and let us go free. She says she's an old woman, and if he gets killed her life will be meaningless and, as she'll never be able to afford to come to England, she'll never see him again. Now she's asking him to think of his sister, who's about the same age as us. Now she's saying that Juan has been arrested, and what are five years in prison, which he'll get if he gives himself up, compared to death when he hasn't even said his confession.'

She finished speaking and started to cry.

Ricardo got to his feet. 'Stop it! Stop it!' he screamed. 'I can't stand it.'

'Pull yourself together,' said Eduardo icily. 'Can't you see she's been forced into doing it.'

'Not my mother,' hissed Ricardo. 'Never! She would never let herself be forced into anything.'

The loudspeaker began again. This time it was Carlos's wife. A quieter, more impassioned plea, asking Carlos to save himself because she and the children loved him, and they wanted him back. Again she told him to remember that Bella and Chrissie were only young girls who hadn't done anyone any harm.

Carlos reacted in a far less hysterical way than Ricardo, but Bella could tell from his still body and clenched fists that he was very much affected.

Nothing for Eduardo, she thought. Probably no-one loved him enough to plead with him to save his life. And what about the mute Pablo, standing motionless beside the door?

There was silence. Then a voice speaking Spanish. Not Lazlo's this time.

'We repeat, come out at once, and throw your guns out. Let the hostages out and come out yourselves, with your hands over your head, and you will not be harmed.'

'Don't take any notice of those lousy tapes,' said Eduardo. 'They're all rigged.'

He sounded calm but the knuckles were white where he clutched his gun.

'I've had enough,' said Ricardo. 'If they've got my mother, they're quite capable of doing things to her. I'm packing it in.'

'So am I,' said Carlos.

Bella felt a surge of hope that died almost immediately.

'No you're not,' said Eduardo, his voice suddenly full of ice. 'We came here to do a job, and we're going to do it. Later Juan will protect us.'

'Not if you're dead, he can't,' said Bella.

'Shut up, you bitch,' snarled Eduardo.

He waved his gun at Ricardo. 'Tie their legs up again,' he said.

Ricardo's hands were shaking so much it took him a long time to tie the knots.

'Now blindfold them.'

'No,' said Carlos, starting to argue.

'Go on – blindfold them,' said Eduardo.

401

And Bella knew it was the voice of the executioner.

Cold fear paralysed her; her throat was completely dry; she wanted to scream for help, to tell them not to kill her, but as the soft scarf was tied over her eyes, she was incapable of speech.

Someone turned her to face the wall.

She heard Eduardo order Pablo to cover the front door with the sub-machine gun, and Ricardo and Carlos to guard the two windows.

'They're going to kill us, aren't they?' whispered Chrissie beside her.

'I'm not sure,' said Bella.

'Will it hurt very much?'

'I don't think so. They say when the wound's mortal, it hurts very little.'

Ricardo was arguing again.

'Shut up,' said Eduardo. 'I'm going to do this. I'll take the complete blame.'

There was a long pause.

No, prayed Bella. Please God, no. She had a sudden vision of Lazlo, of his face softened, holding out his arms to her. Then it seemed to merge with her father with his laughing tawny eyes gathering her up in his arms and holding her, shrieking with delight, above his head. Then she remembered her first night in *Othello*, and the audience clapping and clapping, and the deafening way they'd clapped the night Lazlo had made her go on after the diamond was stolen. And suddenly the deafening applause seemed to turn into a volley of machine-gun fire, and the next moment she heard a groan and a scream as a body slumped at her side.

'Chrissie,' she screamed. 'You've killed her, bastards, bastards.'

She tensed herself waiting for another volley of shooting, but it never came. Suddenly the blindfold was removed from her eyes. She looked down at Chrissie lying at her feet, expecting her to be full of holes, and realized with sudden, incredulous joy, that she was still breathing.

Hardly daring to turn her head, she suddenly saw a trickle of blood coming down the floorboards towards her feet. It slowly impinged on her half-crazed mind that it was Eduardo lying dead, riddled with bullets.

And now Pablo was talking for the first time, in a young, hoarse voice, telling Ricardo to throw all the guns out of the window.

Cautiously Ricardo opened the window, ducking to avoid a spurt of machine-gun fire from the ground, and then threw two guns out. The firing started for a second, then died away. Ricardo picked up the remaining guns and threw them out.

Bella managed to bring Chrissie round, while Carlos was untying her ropes.

'What happened?' she gasped.

'You fainted,' said Bella. 'Pablo shot Eduardo. They're just throwing their guns out.'

Hope sparked in Chrissie's dull, bloodshot eyes.

But Pablo still held the machine gun. The next moment he shoved it into Bella's back, making a gesture towards the stairs with his head.

'Out you go,' he said.

She had to support Chrissie down the stairs; she seemed very frail; she must have lost pounds. Pablo came to the door with them, still clutching his gun.

Bella turned to them, 'It's a trick,' she said. 'You'll shoot me in the back.'

Pablo shook his head.

403

'Why did you shoot Eduardo?'

'To prevent him shooting you,' said Pablo. 'He had to, you see. He couldn't give in like the rest of us. It was a matter of honour. He's Juan's youngest brother.'

Then he opened the door and threw his smoking gun on to the grass.

'Thank you,' said Bella. 'I'll tell them you saved our lives.'

He gave a crooked smile, stood back, and with a curious mock salute, ushered her out on to the grass.

For a minute she was dazzled by the brilliant sunlight, and then the world came back to her in sharp focus. Fifty yards of parched grass stretched out before her. To her left the guns lay in a pile like spillikins. Beyond the grass, the trees and the sandbags began.

It was deadly quiet. There was no-one in sight. A dog barked on the left.

Bella walked slowly and hesitantly on, half carrying the stumbling, trembling Chrissie, tensing her backbone against a possible bullet.

She was only a few yards from the shadow of the trees now, and she realized once more the strength of the operation – the dog handlers, the armoured cars, the television cameras, the ambulances, the hordes of policemen. Next moment she had reached the sandbags and collapsed into the arms of a waiting policeman, feeling his silver buttons against her chest, and a hundred arms seemed to be pulling them both to safety behind the sandbags. Then there were people all round her, and photographers flashing and cameras whirring.

And suddenly there was Lazlo, and she hardly

recognized him. She had remembered him catlike, sunburnt, exotic-looking in that white suit. Now he was deathly pale, unshaven, his face seamed with exhaustion, his eyes bloodshot, his jaw quilted with muscles to stop himself breaking down.

'Oh Lazlo,' sobbed Chrissie, and collapsed, coughing and sobbing, into his arms.

'It's all right, baby,' he said shakily. 'It's all over. You're going to be all right. You're safe now.'

Over her shoulder, his eyes met Bella's.

'Everything's all right now,' he repeated mechanically.

The next moment, like a dog that's been deprived of its master's company for days, a figure threw himself on Chrissie, tugging her away from Lazlo, cradling her in his arms, kissing her face over and over again. 'Oh my darling, my only love.'

It was Rupert.

'You're all right? You're not hurt?' he went on, pausing and looking down at her.

Chrissie started to laugh and cry at the same time.

'I'm all right, but I'm so dirty and horrible and revolting.'

'You're not, you're not; you're mine and you're lovely.'

Bella turned her head away to stop herself breaking down. And then Lazlo was beside her, and she was overwhelmed with shyness. For a moment, as the crowd pushed him forward and he held her tight against him, she could feel his shirt drenched with sweat and the frantic thudding of his heart. Then she pulled away. There were so many people around and she was so filthy and stinking, and she was so ashamed of her terrible hair. She had rehearsed this reunion with him so long, and now she couldn't say anything because she was so terrified of saying too much.

'Chrissie,' she blurted out. 'She's ill. You must get her to a hospital.' She swayed. Lazlo caught hold of her. Then everyone was round her, offering congratulations. A senior policeman in a peaked hat fought his way through the crowd.

'Thank God you're safe,' he said. 'What's happening in there?'

'It's quite safe,' said Bella. 'They've thrown out all their guns.'

'Are they all alive?'

'Three of them. Eduardo's dead. Pablo killed him because he was going to shoot us.'

'Do you feel up to answering a few questions?' said the Inspector.

Bella nodded. 'But I don't think Chrissie ought to; she needs a doctor at once.'

'And how's my star attraction?' said a voice in her ear.

Bella swung round, and there beside her was the wonderfully familiar freckled face of Roger Field.

'Oh, Roger,' she said, her control snapping, and, sobbing, she flung her arms round his neck.

23

They had to fight their way out. Photographers were snapping frenziedly, journalists pressing forward, but a row of policemen made a gangway, and the next moment, she, Lazlo and Roger were bundled into a police car and driven off.

She clutched on to Roger all the way, shaking uncontrollably, still feeling hopelessly shy of Lazlo who was sitting beside her. Two other policemen in the car inhibited her even further.

Speechless, she gazed out of the window at the countryside she thought she would never see again – at the angelic greenness of the trees, the wild roses hanging in festoons from the banks, the buttercups golden in the fields. Every time a car passed them coming from either direction, she ducked down. She couldn't get used to the fact that no-one was pointing a gun at her any longer.

'How's everyone in the company?' she said to Roger.

'Worried stiff about you.'

'I was quite worried myself.' Her laugh wasn't quite steady enough. She half turned to Lazlo. 'Is Diego all right? He got through to you?'

Lazlo nodded.

'And his wife and little boy?' said Bella.

'They're being flown over here tomorrow or the next day. I've alerted all the right people at Great Ormond Street, they'll get the best attention.'

'Oh I am pleased.' She still couldn't look him straight in the eye. 'It wasn't too much of a problem? You didn't mind my saying you'd do that for him?'

'Christ no,' said Roger. 'It was the best hand you've ever played darling. You obviously knocked him for six. I said to Lazlo it's the old Parkinson sex appeal working again.'

She started to laugh, but it strangled in her throat and she started to cry. Roger squeezed her hand harder:

'It's all right, sweetheart. We all know what you've been through. Give her a slug from your hip flask, Lazlo.'

At the police station there were incredible mob scenes: people standing on each other's shoulders, hundreds of reporters and television cameras: 'Let me look at her,' 'That's the girl friend.' 'Look at her hair.' 'Good old Bella.' 'What was it like?' 'Did they hurt you?'

They were all trying to touch her, pulling at her clothing.

Four policemen hustled her inside, where she was allowed to have a cup of coffee and a wash before they started interrogating her. The room was absolutely jammed with cops firing questions from all sides. Roger sat beside her, holding her hand tightly, de-fusing the whole thing when it became over-emotional. Lazlo seemed temporarily to have disappeared.

When they got on to the shooting, she started trembling again.

'You're sure it was Pablo who shot Eduardo?' said the Superintendent.

'Yes, of course.'

'But you were blindfolded,' said an Inspector with a big moustache.

'I could tell from the direction the shots came from,' said Bella. 'And besides, he was the only one with a machine gun.'

'But at first you thought it was Eduardo who had shot Chrissie.'

'I know, but only because I was expecting it.'

'And two machine guns were thrown out of the window.'

'Well they were only using one at the time, and I *know* it was Pablo because he'd been so retiring up until then. Then suddenly he took charge.'

'But you didn't actually see him fire the shot?' persisted the Superintendent.

The possibility that they might not believe she was speaking the truth became too much for her. Suddenly they seemed indistinguishable from Ricardo and Eduardo slapping her face back and forth to get information out of her.

'It's worse out than in,' she said, and laying down her head on the table, she started to cry. 'I'm not up to it. I'm simply not up to it.'

Next moment Lazlo walked in. He had shaved and put on a clean shirt, and seemed to be his old forceful self once again.

'If you don't get off her back,' he said, walking over to the Superintendent, 'I'll make the most bloody awful scandal that'll destroy any public image you've built up over this case.

'It's all right, lovey,' he added, taking Bella's other hand. 'It won't take much longer,' and with infinite tact and gentleness, he took her over the morning's happenings.

'And that's enough,' he said, when she had finished. 'I've just seen my sister. She's not as ill as all that. She'll be perfectly able to give you her story later in the day if you're capable of showing a little consideration.'

The Superintendent shot Lazlo a look both of dislike and respect.

'All right, Mr Henriques,' he said.

'I'd like somewhere where Miss Parkinson and I can have two minutes alone, together,' Lazlo went on. 'Then you can take her straight to hospital.'

They were ushered into an ante-room with a table and two chairs, which smelt of furniture polish and chalk and fear. A potted plant was wilting on the window ledge.

Bella collapsed on to one of the chairs. 'I don't want to go to hospital,' she said in a shaking voice. 'I'm quite all right.'

'It's only for a check-up, so you can catch up on some sleep. Not for long, only for a day or two until I get back.'

She looked up in horror.

'Where are you going?'

He paused, his face inscrutable.

'Buenos Aires.'

'Oh no! So they were bluffing. Juan hasn't been pulled in yet.'

'Not yet. But I've got all the evidence I need to nail him – and the Argentinian police aren't going to let a chance like this slip through their fingers. So I'll get every co-operation.'

'What's happened to Steve?' she said, and felt herself going crimson.

'Inside,' said Lazlo flatly. 'He was picked up yesterday, trying to leave the country.'

'And he talked?'

Lazlo nodded. 'Straightaway, sang to the rooftops.'

Bella winced. Wretched Steve, not even the guts to protect his own crooked friends.

'He and Juan had been planning to snatch Chrissie for months,' Lazlo went on.

'So contacting me through the personal columns, and pretending to be still madly in love with me . . .'

'Was just a ruse,' said Lazlo. 'He read about you and Rupert in the papers, and went through all the personal column palaver, just to lull your suspicions. He realized how cliquey we are as a family, how we resist outsiders. You were the ideal way in.'

It came out more brutally than he had intended.

'Oh God,' said Bella, feeling suddenly defeated. 'So it was all my fault.'

'Of course it wasn't,' said Lazlo irritably.

There was a knock and a policeman's head came round the door. 'You're going to miss that plane Mr Henriques, unless you hurry.'

'Just coming,' said Lazlo. 'Give me a few seconds more.'

The head retreated. Bella was staring listlessly at her hands. For a moment it seemed even Lazlo was at a loss for words.

The tension between them was unbearable. She felt an appalling urge to collapse, sobbing in his arms, pleading with him not to go, but she just went on gazing at her bitten nails.

411

'Bella,' he said gently, 'please look at me.'

'I can't,' she said in a stifled voice. There was another agonizing pause. He sighed and stood up.

'All right, I suppose it's no good trying to sort anything out at the moment. You're all in. Roger'll look after you. Get as much rest as you can. I'll ring you from BA as soon as I've got anything to report.'

'You will be careful, won't you?' she said, still not looking up.

'I'll try,' he said wearily, and was gone. And Bella was overwhelmed with a terrible sense of anti-climax.

24

They released her after forty-eight hours in hospital. The doctors said she must have an extremely strong constitution. Apart from the fact that at night she was continually woken by nightmares about guns pointing at her, and by day she thought obsessively about Lazlo, she seemed to have made an excellent recovery. Roger steered her through a gruelling press conference when she came out.

The questions about the actual kidnapping and living with the gunmen were bad enough, but soon they moved on to her private life.

'You were engaged to Rupert Henriques,' said the gossip writer from the *Daily Mail*.

'Yes,' said Bella.

'But you broke it off,' he persisted.

'Yes.'

'Why?'

'Because we weren't suited.'

'Or because you were more suited to his cousin, Lazlo?'

'No!' said Bella, going scarlet.

'Lazlo tried to cut his cousin out with you, didn't he?'

'This is *not* a court of law,' said Roger Field, firmly. 'So will you stop pestering Bella with irrelevant questions.'

But throughout the press conference, journalist after journalist harked back to the question of her and Lazlo, until suddenly she lost her temper.

'Will you stop hounding me,' she screamed. 'There is absolutely nothing between Lazlo Henriques and me, and I'm not answering any more of your bloody questions.'

It took all Roger Field's tact to calm everyone down.

'In considerable distress,' wrote down the journalists in their shorthand notebooks, as a minute later Bella suddenly stood up, burst into tears and fled out of the room.

'I can't stand any more,' she sobbed to Roger.

'You won't have to,' said Roger.

Five minutes later she and Roger were smuggled out of a side door and into a waiting police car.

'Where are we going?' said Bella.

'To a bolt hole of Lazlo's in Maida Vale,' said Roger. 'He's been hiding out there since you and Chrissie were kidnapped. Too many people, including the Press, know the addreess of his own flat.'

They were welcomed at the flat by Roger's wife, Sabina. She was a tall, slim brunette and her beauty in the flesh and in the photograph on Roger's desk at the theatre had blighted the hopes of many a young actress who would otherwise have set her cap at Roger. She gathered Bella into a voluptuous scented hug.

'Welcome home, darling. This flat has to be seen to be believed. I'm sure it's where Lazlo keeps his first eleven mistresses, all that peach-coloured satin and mirrors in the bedroom.'

'Nonsense,' said Roger sharply. 'Lazlo bought it as a base for visiting clients. It merely happens to be empty at the moment because no-one's over here. The Arabs go wild about that bedroom.'

'Business must be disintegrating,' said Sabina. 'He hasn't been near the office for days. A huge pile of mail arrived this morning that hadn't been opened since before you were kidnapped. I've put it all in his bedroom. I've put you in there, too, Bella, so you can lie in bed all night and admire your reflection against peach-coloured satin, in the mirror on the ceiling,' she added, carrying Bella's suitcase into the room on the right. Several of Lazlo's sweaters lay on an armchair and on the dressing-table were jumbled together cuff-links, nail scissors, bottles of aftershave, ivory hair brushes, ties, cheque books, a wallet, several race cards, a fountain pen, a huge stack of mail and a pile of five pound notes.

Bella sniffed one of the bottles of aftershave – it had strong overtones of lavender and musk, and immediately conjured up the old smooth, opulent, mocking, self-assured Lazlo she knew before the kidnapping, not the pale, trembling, shattered man who'd greeted her on her escape.

It was almost as though Sabina read her thoughts.

'I don't know how Lazlo survived the last ten days,' she said. 'He never went to bed, working flat out trying to trace you – and not getting a lead from anyone. Just those damn telephone calls at twenty-four hour intervals, getting more and more threatening. Then those absurd tapes they sent to prove that you were still alive, that might have been made any time.'

She took off the fur counterpane from the bed and began folding it up.

'Then your hair arrived through the post. That was the last straw. He was convinced you were both dead. He completely broke down. It's always much worse when someone you never think will, does. Roger thought he was finished. Then, just as he was trying to cheer him up, the telephone rang and it was Diego. After that he was all right.'

Bella felt herself going scarlet. More than anything in the world she wanted to ask Sabina what Lazlo felt about her – but she was too frightened of getting a negative answer.

'I wish he'd ring,' she said for the hundredth time.

'Oh, he'll be all right,' said Sabina. 'He's a cat with ninety-nine lives. I'll leave you to get yourself sorted out. I'm going to cook supper. Come and have a drink when you're ready.'

After she'd gone, Bella looked at herself in the mirror. God, she hated her hair. She wondered if it would be worth getting a wig. She sniffed the aftershave again and felt a sudden spasm of lust and longing. Then, with a beating heart, she started to leaf through the unopened mail. Halfway down she found what she was dreading – a letter from France in a blue airmail envelope with the address written in violet ink in a flowing, expansive hand.

The name on the back was, of course, Angora's. Trust the silly bitch to use violet ink. Bella was itching to open it. It was dated nine days ago, so, probably, Angora didn't even know of the kid-

416

napping when she'd written it. Firmly, Bella put it at the bottom of the pile. Then she changed into a green and black dress. It was in the style of a cheongsam with a high neck – and a slit skirt.

'That's more like the old Bella,' said Roger appreciatively when she went into the drawing-room.

'I feel very un-Gaysha,' she said, 'and what the hell am I going to do about my bloody hair?'

'I rather like it,' said Roger. 'It brings out the latent fag in me. I've decided the next thing you're going to do is Viola.'

' "She never told her love, but let concealment, like a worm i' the bud, feed on her damask cheek",' quoted Bella. 'Sounds just like me.'

After dinner, at about ten o'clock when, for the first time that evening, Bella was not wondering when Lazlo was going to ring, the telephone rang. Roger answered. Suddenly his face relaxed into a smile.

'You're OK. Great, well done. Well, that's for the best under the circumstances. He won't bother anyone any more. Do you want to talk to Bella?' He handed her the receiver. 'It's Lazlo.'

Her heart was cracking her ribs, her throat was so dry she could hardly speak.

'Oh thank God, you're not hurt.'

'Not a scratch. Everything's sorted out this end.'

'Oh I'm so glad. What about Juan?'

'He's dead. He tried to shoot his way out and wounded a policeman, so they let him have it.'

'God, how horrible!'

'It wasn't very nice. But at least now he's dead a lot of people in Buenos Aires will have their first decent night's sleep in years.

417

'Look, I can't talk very long, I'm catching a plane in a few minutes.'

'What time do you get into Heathrow?'

'About ten-thirty tomorrow, flight B-725.'

'Shall I meet you?' (Oh God! She could have bitten her tongue off. He probably had half London meeting him, and there she was, forcing herself on him.)

But he merely said, 'Yes, please, and could you ask Roger to ring Diego and say I'm bringing his wife and the child with me, so they had better have an ambulance waiting at the airport.'

'Oh that's sensational,' cried Bella. 'He'll be so pleased. Have a quick word with Roger. I'll see you tomorrow.'

She handed the receiver back to Roger and went into the bedroom and sat down on the bed, burying her burning face in her hands. Oh I love him, I love him, she said to herself. I'll never be able to live through the next twelve hours. In a dream she started wondering what to wear to the airport. Perhaps Sabina would lend her a big hat, but then the brim would get in the way when Lazlo kissed her. Stop it, she said to herself, you're counting your chickens before they're even laid.

Roger came into the bedroom.

'Well, that's nice isn't it?' he said, grinning. 'Good old Lazlo. Rosie Hassell's in a play on ITV in a minute. Do you want to come and watch her?'

'I'm just going to wash my hair first,' said Bella.

After she'd washed it, she went back into the bedroom to comb it into some sort of shape. She was still walking on air. She looked at the mail on the dressing table again. Suddenly, she felt so relaxed, although she knew she shouldn't, she couldn't resist having a read of Angora's letter. With wet fingers she tore open the envelope, and skimmed through the contents. Pandora's Box! Suddenly she gave a gasp of horror and her hand went to her cheek as she read it again properly.

'My darling, darling Lazlo,' every word burnt into her soul. 'Christ, this movie is a bore . . . the director, the producer, the first assistant, have never stopped trying to bang me. The leading man, on the other hand, is trying to bang the first assistant – but that's movies for you. The director is also determined to have a scene in which I take off all my clothes, but so far I've resisted it, keeping myself on toast for you darling.

'I tried to get you on the telephone, but there was no answer, but filming should be finished by the 12th,' that's today, thought Bella numbly, 'and I plan to fly home on the 13th. I hope you've at last managed to extract Bella from Rupert. You should have no difficulty in getting her to transfer her affections to you but what a drag it must have been.

'Anyway, I'll make it up ten thousand times when we meet. All my love and anticipation, Angora.'

Bella started to cry very quietly. So that really was the truth, she said to herself. As she'd been frightened all along, Lazlo had only been paying her so much attention, deliberately to make her fall in love with him, turning the full searchlight beam of his notorious sex appeal on her, just to make sure she'd never go back to Rupert. Well, he'd won all round. She *had* fallen for him, she could never go back to Rupert. Anyway, Rupert had Chrissie now, as Lazlo had always intended. Now he'd achieved his object, he could go back to Angora, who was one of his own kind.

In agony she remembered the Henriques family motto with which Lazlo had taunted her the first time they'd met, 'Scratch a Henriques and you draw your own blood.'

Where could she go? Where could she escape to? Then suddenly she decided to go back to Nalesworth, the slum where she'd been born. Perhaps there she might find some kind of peace.

Roger and Sabina were well stuck into the play. She scribbled a quick note to Lazlo.

'Dear Lazlo, I'm afraid I snooped and opened this letter of Angora's. It's explanatory really. I'm sorry I've been such a bother to you all. I haven't got any money, so I've borrowed fifty pounds. I'll send it back to you when I've got it. Thank you for getting me out. With my love, Bella.'

Stuffing the fivers into her bag, she pinched a pair of dark glasses and tiptoed out of the flat.

Later, shivering with misery, cold and exhaustion, she crept into an empty carriage and cried without stopping until the train cranked its way into Leeds station.

25

The flowers on the graves were spattered with mud and bent in the harsh, bleak wind. Bella stood shaking, still in her green and black cheongsam, her teeth chattering, the rain trickling down her neck, and looked down at the lichened tombstone over her mother's grave.

'Bridget Figge, died 1969 – a saint and deeply loved,' said the inscription.

She was a right bitch, thought Bella, and not at all deeply loved by me. Still, she reflected, she might have been different if she hadn't married my poor feckless father. Then she started thinking about Lazlo. And she looked beyond the dark yews of the churchyard at the grey houses and the grey stone walls and the set grey faces of the passers by. This is home, she thought, and I don't like it one bit. I'm going back to London.

When she got on the train, she headed straight for the bar. The commercial travellers and the men in tweed suits around her, were trying to steer Brown Windsor soup into their mouths. It was only after her fourth double gin and tonic that she realized she hadn't eaten properly since last night. By then it seemed too late to start. She ordered another drink. It was funny to see her face on the front of everyone's newspaper, with short shaggy hair and frightened eyes.

'Ten Days of Terror Take Their Toll,' said one headline. 'Bella cracks up during Press conference and denies romance,' said another.

She shrunk further behind her dark glasses, took a slug of gin, and went back to brooding over Lazlo. His behaviour towards her had never been remotely lover-like. In fact, most of the time it had been quite abominable, and yet, and yet, her thoughts kept straying back to the first time he had pretended to be Steve and nearly raped her in the dark. He must have felt something to kiss her like that, and also the way he'd broken down when they sent him her hair.

Everything suddenly became quite simple. She would find Lazlo as soon as she got to London and have it out with him.

By the time she came off the train, she was very drunk indeed. She tottered down the platform, reeling round porters and oncoming luggage trucks. She had great difficulty in finding a telephone booth.

Someone picked up the telephone in Lazlo's Maida Vale flat on the first ring, but it wasn't Lazlo. It sounded like a policeman.

'He's at the office,' said a voice. 'But who's that calling?' Bella didn't answer. 'Who is that calling?' said the voice again with some urgency.

Bella put the receiver down and rang Lazlo's office where she was told Lazlo was in a meeting, but who should they say called. Again the same urgency. Bella rang off.

Suddenly, the fact that Lazlo was somewhere in

London was too much for her. I'm going to rout him out, she said to herself.

In the taxi she tried to tidy herself up a bit. Her dress was still soaking wet from the rain, her cheeks were flushed, her eyes glittering. She managed to put eye-shadow on one eye, then got bored and gave up, and emptied the remains of a bottle of scent over herself. She kept rehearsing what she was going to say to him.

Now look here . . . it began.

The taxi got lost three times, but finally drew up outside a vast, tall grey building. Over a sea of bowler hats, Bella read the letters: Henriques Bros.

'Eureka,' she shouted, falling out into the street, and belting through the front door into the building.

The beautiful red-headed receptionist looked at her in fascinated horror.

'Have you come to collect something?' she said slowly.

'Only Lazlo Henriques,' said Bella, tugging her rain sodden skirt down over her bottom.

'Have you got an appointment?'

'No, but it's terribly important I see him,' said Bella, trying to keep the mounting despair out of her voice.

The receptionist caught her first fumes of gin, her cold blue eyes flickered over Bella's stomach.

'Oh gosh, I'm not pregnant,' she gasped. 'Not a bit, in fact, if that's what you're thinking.'

A man in a commissionaire's uniform came out of the lift. The receptionist beckoned to him.

'This – er – person insists on seeing Mr Lazlo.'

The Commissionaire looked at Bella, then started.

'My Goodness, it's Miss Parkinson isn't it?'

'Yes, yes,' said Bella. 'I must see him, you can't throw me out.' Her voice was rising hysterically.

Suddenly a nearby door opened and a red-faced man came out.

'Can't you stop this damned row, Heywood?' he said.

'Sir, it's Miss Parkinson,' said the commission-aire.

Bella staggered towards the red-faced man. Suddenly, her self-control snapped. 'Please, oh please,' she sobbed, 'I must see Lazlo. You've got to help me.'

Then, over his shoulder, through the haze of cigarette smoke, she looked into a room and saw a long, polished table, and her eyes travelled down two rows of flushed distinguished looking faces, to the man lounging at the end, whose face was as white as theirs were pink. Her heart lurched into her mouth. It was Lazlo.

'Bella,' he roared, getting to his feet and striding down the room. 'Where the bloody hell have you been? I've got half London looking for you.'

'I went to Yorkshire, but it was raining, so I came back again.'

She was beginning to feel very peculiar. Lazlo caught her as she swayed.

'You're drunk,' he said accusingly.

'Horribly, horribly drunk, and horribly, horribly in love with you,' she mumbled and passed out cold in his arms.

26

The first thing that hit her eyes when she woke up was brilliant scarlet wallpaper. She winced, shut her eyes and opened them again quickly and took in the row of ivory hair brushes, the photographs of racehorses on the dressing-table and the rows and rows of suits in the wardrobe. No-one else in the world had as many suits as that. She was back in Lazlo's old flat.

She levered herself out of bed and stood on a fur rug, feeling sick. She was wearing a pair of black pyjamas that were far too large for her. She stumbled into the drawing-room. Lazlo was sitting in an armchair watching racing on television and drinking champagne. He looked up and smiled.

'I feel dreadful,' she said, cringing with embarrassment.

He got up and turned down the television sound and poured her a Fernet Branca.

'Ugh – I couldn't drink anything,' she said.

'Shut up and drink it.'

Grumbling she obeyed.

'I'm going to clean my teeth,' she muttered and shot into the bathroom.

As the pounding in her head began to subside,

she started to piece the events of the previous day together. She went back into the drawing-room.

'I'm sorry,' she said in a small voice.

'What about?'

'Barging into your office like that. Did I do anything awful?'

'You declared passionate love to me in front of my entire board of directors, and then passed out like a light.'

'Oh God! Were they very shocked?'

'Riveted I should think. There hasn't been anything half so exciting since decimalization.'

'W-what happened then?'

'Oh, I brought you back here.'

'What time is it?' she muttered.

'Nearly ten past three. I was just about to watch the three-fifteen.'

'I'm sorry about being in your bed . . . and things. What happened to my clothes? I mean did we . . .' she blushed scarlet. 'Er – did we?'

'No we didn't. You were dead to the world and I've never been keen on necrophilia.'

He was laughing at her now.

'I can't help it,' she said sulkily, scuffing the carpet with her feet. 'I didn't mean to behave badly or fall in love with you. It wasn't on the agenda at all. Particularly when you're probably aching to be rid of me, and rush off to Paris on some loathsome, dirty weekend with Angora. All my love and anticipation indeed – the foxy cow.'

Lazlo laughed. 'Bella, darling,' he said. 'You should learn not to open other people's letters. That was Angora's letter to me, not mine to her.'

Then he got to his feet, crossed the room and took her in his arms. Then he bent his head and kissed her very gently. His mouth tasted cool, and faintly of champagne, and halfway through, Bella joined in and kissed him back and the whole thing became extremely ungentle.

Then he said, 'Now, do you still think I'm aching to be in Paris with Angora?'

Bella said she didn't and he kissed her again.

Then he sat down on the sofa and pulled her on to his knee and said:

'Christ, I've been wanting to do that since the night we played murder.'

'Why didn't you, then?'

'I couldn't. I was in one hell of a position. I'd played you a rotten trick, quite deliberately setting out to seduce you by pretending I was Steve. I knew you loathed my guts, I couldn't just move in. One false move would have sent you scuttling back to Steve. But suddenly the biter was well and truly bit. I had to go on seeing you, not because I wanted to take you away from Rupert, but because I simply couldn't keep away.'

'But after Chrissie was kidnapped, you didn't come near me, didn't even ring me up.'

'That was different. Once Juan knew I was hooked on you, I was scared stiff he'd grab you too, as he did in the end. That's why I kept my distance, but I kept tabs on you. You were being followed all the time. Unfortunately, the night they picked you up, the man trailing you had nipped into a café to get some cigarettes. By the time he'd caught up, it was too late. All he saw was you being bundled into a car and driven off. He didn't even get the number plate.

'Jesus, darling, if you knew what I went through those five days when I didn't know where you were. I was so terrified they'd kill you before I had a chance to tell you I loved you. It became an absolute obsession to tell you. I was worried stiff about Chrissie, but the thought of losing you was what was really crucifying me.'

'I was the same,' said Bella. 'The whole time I was in there I thought about you. It was the only thing that kept me sane. I kept dreaming what would happen if I got out and by some miracle we ever did get together. I rehearsed coming out so often, and what I was going to say to you.'

Lazlo picked up her hand and held it against his cheek.

'Oh so did I, so did I,' he sighed. 'And then there was that terrible volley of shooting, and I thought you must be dead, then suddenly you and Chrissie came out. And I lost my nerve. I couldn't do it, I couldn't tell you I loved you in front of all those hordes of people. In case you weren't ready for it, in case you still hated me.'

'And what about rotten Angora and that letter she sent you?'

Lazlo grinned ruefully.

'I'll admit in the beginning I set out to seduce you because I didn't want you to marry Rupert (now I realize it was because I wanted you for myself) so I lined up Angora to get her off with Steve and promised to give her a weekend in Paris if you actually broke it off with Rupert. Well, I don't mind paying for her weekend, but she'll have to find another man to spend it with.'

Bella blushed.

'How's Chrissie?'

'Fine, coming out of hospital today. Rupert won't let her out of his sight.'

'So all your plans have materialized,' said Bella, unable to keep the slight edge out of her voice.

'Not quite,' said Lazlo, tipping her gently off his knee and going over and turning off the television.

'I think just this once I'll miss the three-fifteen.'

Bella nervously cast around for something to say.

'I'm sure Rupert and Chrissie will be very happy,' she said.

'And me? Do you think I'll make you happy?' said Lazlo, moving towards her deliberately and taking her in his arms.

'I know I look sexually experienced,' she mumbled, in panic, 'but I'm not really, not a bit.'

'You don't look as experienced as you might think,' he said softly. 'But we can have the first lesson right now.'

'Oh darling,' she said, burying her face in his shoulder. 'Don't joke about it.'

Careful, she thought, careful. Don't give in straightaway. Oh dear, I shouldn't succumb so easily, was her last coherent thought.

So here I am in bed, she said to herself a couple of hours later, and I should be in heaven. Why do I feel as though I want to cut my throat?

'What's the matter?' said Lazlo.

Bella gazed down at her hands.

'I was thinking that now you've had me, you won't want me any more,' she said in a small voice.

'Bella, you have the faith of a gnat,' he said.

'Oh please don't be angry,' she said. 'I want to believe you love me, but you've had such millions and millions of women.'

'I'm glad you put that in the past tense,' he said. He lit a cigarette, inhaled deeply and handed it to her.

Then he said, 'Look, let's get married.'

Bella choked on the cigarette. Then she lay motionless not daring to say anything. He was joking, he must be joking.

'Well you don't seem frightfully enthusiastic,' he said.

'I thought you weren't very keen on marriage.'

'I'm not, in the general run of things. I've never wanted to get married before; never thought it was quite me, going out to dinner every night with the same person. But about you, somehow I feel completely different. I'm scared stiff to let you out of my sight ever again.'

'What about Maria Rodriguez?'

'That was a boy-girl Romeo and Juliet thing. It would never have lasted. What screwed me up was her getting acid thrown in her face and doing herself in.

'I love you, you crazy child,' he went on, taking her face in his hands. 'I'm turned inside out by you. I haven't been so hooked on anyone since I fell in love with the cricket captain at Eton.'

Bella giggled and looked, and saw that although he smiled, the tarmac black eyes were filled with a tenderness that made her quite dizzy.

'Oh please,' she said. 'If you really mean what you said about marriage, I should like it very very much, and could we do it very soon?'

'I'll get a licence tomorrow,' said Lazlo. 'I'm a great believer in bolting the stable door once the horse is well and truly in. And I'm going to ask Roger to give you a sabbatical, so that after we get married, I can take you on a long, long honeymoon, so we can both stop having nightmares about Juan.'

'Oh God,' said Bella with a sob, flinging her arms round his neck. 'I must have done something amazingly good in a former existence to deserve this.'

'You did something amazingly good during the last couple of hours,' said Lazlo, and he kissed her again.

'Another nice thing,' he said, when he finally came up for air, 'is that Aunt Constance will be insane with rage.'

Bella giggled again, then she suddenly caught sight of herself in Lazlo's arms in the huge looking glass above the fire.

We do look beautiful together, she thought dreamily, but something is wrong.

'Would you mind terribly if I went back to being blonde again?' she said.

THE END

A LIST OF OTHER JILLY COOPER TITLES
AVAILABLE FROM CORGI BOOKS AND
BANTAM PRESS

14662 5	CLASS	£6.99
14663 3	THE COMMON YEARS	£5.99
14696 X	HARRIET & OCTAVIA	£6.99
14697 8	IMOGEN & PRUDENCE	£5.99
12041 3	LISA & CO	£5.99
14103 8	RIDERS	£6.99
13264 0	RIVALS	£6.99
13552 6	POLO	£6.99
13895 9	THE MAN WHO MADE HUSBANDS JEALOUS	£6.99
14323 5	APPASSIONATA	£6.99
14579 3	SCORE	£6.99
04404 5	HOW TO SURVIVE CHRISTMAS (Hardback)	£9.99
14367 7	THE MAN WHO MADE HUSBANDS JEALOUS–AUDIO	£12.99*

* Including VAT